Rhyannon Byrd is the national best~~...~~
thirty contemporary and paranormal ~~...~~
Dangerous Tides series, and her book~~...~~
languages. After years of enjoying the sunshine in ~~...~~
South and Southwest, Rhyannon now lives in the beautiful
(but often chilly) county of Warwickshire in England
with her family and their loveable Rottweiler.

For more information on Rhyannon's books and the latest
news, you can visit her website at www.rhyannonbyrd.com or find
her on Facebook at www.facebook.com/RhyannonByrd
or on Instagram @RhyannonByrd.

Praise for Rhyannon Byrd:

'*London Affair* is signature Rhyannon Byrd – exciting, sexy, and
romantic. Byrd brilliantly crafts a steamy love story with a
couple that dazzles, and I couldn't put it down!' Virna DePaul,
New York Times bestselling author

'From London to the English countryside, Jase and Emmy burn up
the sheets' P.T. Michelle, *New York Times* bestselling author

'Raw, addictive, and blisteringly hot . . . a sizzling success'
Romantic Times (Top Pick)

'No one writes lip-biting sexual tension and sizzling romance
like Rhyannon Byrd' Shayla Black, *New York Times*
bestselling author

'Rhyannon Byrd has a gift for beautiful, sensual storytelling'
Cheyenne McCray, *New York Times* bestselling author

'Filled with love, lust, loyalty, betrayal, sensuality, and heady
romance. Readers will find themselves reaching for a Kleenex
and fanning themselves all at the same time as they devour
this page-turner' *Night Owl Reviews*

'Combines passion and suspense with a touch of deadly danger
guaranteed to keep you reading until the very last page'
Joyfully Reviewed

'Hold on to your iceboxes, girls! This one is a scorcher!'
A Romance Review

By Rhyannon Byrd

London Affair

London Affair

THE COMPLETE NOVEL

RHYANNON BYRD

HEADLINE
ETERNAL

First published in 2017 as an ebook serialisation
as *The Weekend*, *The Chase* and *The Confession*

First published in paperback in Great Britain in 2019
by HEADLINE ETERNAL
An imprint of HEADLINE PUBLISHING GROUP

1

Cataloguing in Publication Data is available from the British Library

ISBN 978 1 4722 5123 7

Typeset in 11/14 pt Minion Pro by Jouve (UK), Milton Keynes

Printed and bound in Great Britain by CPI Group (UK) Ltd, Croydon, CR0 4YY

Headline's policy is to use papers that are natural, renewable and recyclable
products and made from wood grown in well-managed forests and other
controlled sources. The logging and manufacturing processes are expected to
conform to the environmental regulations of the country of origin.

HEADLINE PUBLISHING GROUP
An Hachette UK Company
Carmelite House
50 Victoria Embankment
London EC4Y 0DZ

www.headlineeternal.com
www.headline.co.uk
www.hachette.co.uk

For Cassandra

~

As Tyler would say, you are *the coolest of the cool*, sweetheart.
I'm so incredibly proud of you,
and I love you more than you could ever possibly know.

London
Affair

The Weekend

Chapter One

Thursday afternoon

EMMY

Why do we always have to be dazzled by the things we can't have? The things that could destroy us? Ruin us? Tear us into pieces and turn us into something that we no longer even recognize? Why does human nature have to be so goddamn destructive?

These are the thoughts that run through my head the second I set eyes on him. I don't know his name. He's just a gorgeous stranger dressed in an immaculate, high-priced gray suit, looking completely out of place in the same stuffy, stifling London Underground carriage I'm traveling in. An unknown male who's the embodiment of what my subconscious desires dream up in the heavy darkness of night, but never actually want in the light of day. I avoid his type for too many reasons to count, the least of which being that I have a low tolerance for egotism and the typical *I've got a big dick and money so I'm a god* bullshit that men like him pull so well.

But I can sure as hell look and enjoy.

I'm sitting in one of the grungy seats on the right of the carriage, while he stands no more than five feet away, one arm lifted as he holds on to the metal overhead bar. I know he's watching me, because I'm watching his reflection in the window, only pretending to be reading the steamy romance book on my e-reader. I imagine what he would look like stripped of all that expensive silk and feel my face heat, which is ridiculous. I'm not some shy virgin who's hung up about sex. Haven't been one since I slept with my boyfriend in my freshman year of college. But my sexual experiences have never been with a man like *him*. I steer clear of the mouthwatering alphas, no matter how handsome they are. I'm not their type anyway. With my shortish, curvy bod, honey-gold curls and dimples, I look neither like a fuck bunny nor a trophy wife. Which leaves me to spend my time with close friends and focus on my fledgling career in the art world.

But a bit of fantasy never killed a girl. And he would be prime material for a midnight session with my vibrator. So I use what brief time there is before my stop to watch him as carefully as I can.

The jacket that stretches across his broad shoulders no doubt cost more than a month's rent on my tiny apartment back in San Diego. It's dark charcoal with a light pinstripe, clearly tailored for his tall, muscular build. I can't see those muscles under the jacket, but from the way he fills it out, I know they're there. *Yum.* I like imagining Mr Hotshot Corporate Player in nothing but a scraggy pair of gym shorts, that tall body slick with sweat, muscles bunching and flexing beneath his dark skin as he works out. His complexion is more olive toned than most British, which probably means he has some beautiful Italian or Spanish countess somewhere in his ancestry – unless he's not a local at all, and is actually a foreigner like myself.

Wherever he's from, those sharp blue eyes look amazing

with his skin tone, and the gods were obviously feeling generous when they molded that bone structure. Bold, straight nose. Wide, firm mouth. Straight, dark brows and ink-black hair that has that naturally tousled look that's so outrageously sexy on the right kind of man. Oh yeah, this guy is definitely going to play front and center in my vibrator sessions for a while.

Feeling warm, I shift in my seat and grab my long hair, twisting it over one shoulder to get it off the back of my neck. He's still watching me, and it makes about as much sense as a guy like him traveling on the Tube in the first place. I'm usually good at reading people, and I don't get that 'creepy crawly' feeling from him. The one that makes me keep my distance from a man and make sure I have other people around me in case he turns out to be a nutcase. Living as a single woman in the city, you either hone that sense or run the risk of being in the wrong place at the wrong time. But Mr Hot and Gorgeous isn't freaking me out. At least, not in a bad way. I just don't like how my body is reacting to him – my pulse pounding and my skin glowing with a sheen that has nothing to do with the muggy summer heat – because I know it isn't going anywhere. I'm not his type.

I frown as that last thought echoes around in my head, wondering why I keep repeating myself. It isn't like me, and as much as I enjoy looking at this particular male, I'm ready to put some distance between us and get my equilibrium back.

A craggy voice comes through the speakers, telling us that the next stop is Canada Water, so we're not far from Canary Wharf. I'm getting off there to meet up with Lola, one of my local friends and a fellow art lover. Lola and I met during the semester I spent in London four years ago, through a study abroad program at my university. We were roommates, and hit it off right away. And thanks to FaceTime, we've been able to stay close over the years. She's even coming to San Diego next summer to visit me, and we're planning to drive up Pacific Coast Highway to spend a week in San Francisco.

Despite her art history degree, Lola works as a receptionist at one of the swanky high-rise office buildings on the wharf, and there's a Starbucks in the lobby, so that's where I'm meeting up with her for a coffee during her afternoon break.

We pull into the Canada Water station, and when the driver comes over the PA system again to tell us that we're going to be delayed for a second time, I pull my phone out of my bag and hook into the Wi-Fi so that I can text Lola to let her know I'm running late. But just as my phone connects, it starts belting out an ear-piercing sequence from QOTSA's 'Go With The Flow', and I quickly fumble for the volume control, embarrassed that I'd forgotten to turn it down.

'Hey,' I murmur, knowing from the quick peek I took at the screen that it's Lola. 'We've had a couple of delays on the line, so it's going to be about another fifteen minutes before I get there.'

I can feel the weight of Mr H & G's (Hot and Gorgeous is too much of a mouthful, even in my head) attention like a physical touch, and know he's listening to my every word. If he hadn't already figured out I'm an American – though I'm not sure how he could have just from looking at me – he knows now. You could take the girl out of Georgia, but you couldn't ever take Georgia out of the girl. I might have spent the last six years of my life attending school in California, but I still have that molasses-covered drawl that I grew up with.

'No worries,' Lola says. 'Someone called in sick, so I won't even be able to get away for another twenty minutes. Did you bring the notes you want me to look over?'

'Yeah, I've got all the notes. But the Harrison Trust refused my request again.' J.J. Harrison is a cantankerous, reclusive modern artist who has more twisted hang-ups about women than Venice has canals, which makes him a prime focus for the piece I'm writing on the role of the dominated female subject in modern art. 'So unless I hit gold somehow, this article is going to suck and the editor at *Luxe* is going to laugh her ass off at me.'

Thanks to one of my professors, I've been lucky enough to be asked to submit an article to one of the premier art magazines in the business – but if I don't uncover some groundbreaking material soon, they aren't going to look twice at me ever again. I usually visit England to catch up with the friends I have here, but this trip is for business instead of pleasure. I'm in the UK for a few weeks to research Harrison, who's British, and if I don't get an in-depth perspective on him now, I'm not ever going to get one. Others have tried before me and failed, but I'm counting on the fire in my gut to help me get what I want.

Lola pops a bubble in my ear, making me jump. 'Just come find me at the desk when you get here. We'll figure something out, sweet cheeks.'

I smile, because she's one of my most favorite people in the world, and say goodbye, then disconnect the call and slip the phone back in my bag, along with my e-reader. I can still feel Mr H & G watching me, but my worries over the article are doing their best to eclipse the lust this man inspires. I find myself choking back a husky chuckle as I wonder what ol' J.J. Harrison would make of him. As a rule, Harrison's male forms are as powerful and arrogant as his females are vulnerable and weak.

When the train finally pulls into the Canary Wharf station, I move to my feet, and the man shifts toward me, standing so close I can actually smell the mouthwatering tang of his expensive aftershave. Something thick and sexual sweeps through my veins, warming me from the inside out, and I know my face is flushed. When I flick a quick glance in his direction, I find him staring right at me, which only makes me burn hotter. I bite my lip, and I swear his eyes get heavy as he watches, that hooded gaze capable of rendering even the most cynical female into a drooling, breathless mess.

The Tube carriage pulls to a stop at the platform, doors swishing open, and I have the strangest feeling he's going to say something to me, but a group of young, rough-looking guys shoves between us, earning a low grunt from the suit. I pay them little attention as I disembark, too busy wondering if I'm disappointed or relieved that he's missed his chance to say whatever he wanted to say. For some reason, the idea of talking to him is unnerving, even though I'm not shy. He just isn't the type of man I usually interact with, and I don't like feeling uncertain. He's thrown me off balance, probably because I know my personality doesn't mesh well with that of a cocky, money-driven suit. I'm too outspoken and suck at simpering. Am I being judgmental? Perhaps. But I've been around my father's family enough times to know *exactly* how much I don't like that kind of man, no matter how incredible-looking he is.

The sexy Brit might be the epitome of my deepest, darkest fantasies in the flesh, but like I'd been thinking when I first saw him, he could leave me broken in ways I didn't need if I let him get too close. Ways I've spent years working hard to protect myself against. He would know all the right things to say. All the right moves to make. And it's an unarguable fact that I have flawed DNA in my bloodline when it comes to resistance. Which is why I'm going to put him out of my mind and keep him there.

Walking as fast as I can in the swarm of people exiting the carriage, I don't pay attention to what's happening around me until I'm yanked into one of the narrow passages that connect the platforms. I'm wondering what the hell is going on, when my head suddenly smacks into the brick wall on my left. *Fuck, that hurt!*

'Don't be stupid and try to fight,' a man grunts in my ear, his accent East End. 'Just give us the purse, bitch.'

My purse? I have a hobo bag looped diagonally across my body and can feel a hand tugging aggressively at the strap. I can't believe this is happening in the middle of the day, surrounded by crowds of people. What are these idiots thinking? But as I flash a quick look left and right, I realize they must have done this before. A guy stands guard at each end of the small passageway, blocking the view of those rushing by, the masses too focused on getting where they're going as quickly as possible to notice what's happening.

'Get the fuck away from me!' I scream, but the noise of an approaching carriage on the northbound platform drowns out the sound. The guy holding me snarls something and grips a fistful of my hair, slamming the side of my head into the wall again, and I think *Oh, shit, this is bad*. Blinding pain shoots through my skull, and I can feel my thoughts splintering. As my eyes roll back in my head, I dimly hear a low growl just before what sounds like a powerful fist crunching bone. The brutal grip on my arm and hair loosens, leaving me to crash to the floor, my head hitting the ground so hard I'd probably be seeing stars if my eyes were still working, and a deep voice curses so viciously I'm sure someone's going to die. I just hope it isn't me!

I listen to more punches being thrown through a fog of pain and confusion, pissed at myself for not getting in at least one groin shot on these jerks. And then, the next thing I know, I'm being carefully lifted from the floor, in a pair of solid, silk-covered arms that smell so good I moan in a way that has nothing at all to do with the pain in my head.

There's something divinely familiar about this particular scent that I know I need to place.

But I lose consciousness before I can figure out what it is.

*   *   *

With a startled gasp, I blink my eyes open, trying to figure out why my head feels like someone's used it for boxing practice. I make a rough, strangled sound of confusion when I realize I'm lying on a sofa, my hands digging into the butter-soft leather beneath me as a kind face slowly comes into focus.

'Hello, miss. I'm Martin, Mr Beckett's personal assistant,' the man says with a crisp British accent. He's sitting in an antique chair that's been drawn up to face the sofa, wearing a suit over his thin frame, and looks like the highly competent sort who could balance the national budget with one hand while cooking a gourmet meal with the other. Sunlight from the windows glints against his silver hair. 'Try not to move too quickly. From what Jase has told me, you took quite a few knocks to your head.'

Jase? Who the hell is Jase? 'Where am I?' I ask, surprised by the throaty rasp of my voice.

'In Jase's – that is Mr Beckett's – private office.'

Licking my lips, I replay the last things I can remember through my aching head, but still can't come up with an explanation for my current situation. 'How did I get here? I remember a group of jerks trying to mug me at the station . . . but that's it.'

I have a feeling the pink tinge blooming in Martin's cheeks means I'm not going to like his answer. 'Er, well, he carried you here.'

Ohmygod, I mutter to myself, so mortified I could die. I suddenly know exactly who this man means by *he*, my poor brain finally figuring out who that intoxicating scent had belonged to when I'd been lifted from the floor. And he'd carried me all the way here? *Just . . . no*, I think, shuddering with embarrassment. It's too much. I mean, I was probably drooling all over his priceless suit!

Oh . . . and Jesus, I hope I didn't say anything. I've been told by my friends that I talk in my sleep, but who knows if that extends to blacking out. With my luck, I could have spent the whole trip up to his breathtaking office mumbling about how gorgeous he is. Or how I planned on using him for inspiration during my next date with my vibrator!

Honestly, if there were a hole in the floor right now I would freaking crawl right into it.

Martin clears his throat, drawing my attention back to his friendly face. 'Do you mind if I ask your name, miss?'

'Emmy. Emmy Reed,' I murmur, managing to get myself up into a sitting position and swing my legs down to the floor without Martin's assistance, even though his hands are lifted, as if he expects me to tumble back over at any moment. I can only imagine how wrecked I look. My skirt is twisted around my knees and my slouchy cream shirt is hanging off one shoulder, showing the strap of my camisole.

'Emmy's a lovely name,' he says with a smile, once he seems confident I can sit up without toppling. He leans back in his chair with his elbows braced on the armrests, his hands clasped before him. 'If you'll just stay put, we'll have you better in no time, Miss Reed. The doctor is already on his way.'

'*What doctor?*' I wince as my sharp words ring through my head.

'The Beckett family's personal physician, Dr Riley.'

Panic starts to sweep through me in a slow, dizzying surge, killing the embarrassment. 'Why do I need a doctor?'

A faint crease appears on his brow. 'You're lucky no skin was broken, but I'm afraid you might have a concussion. Before you move around, it's best to have the doctor take a look at you.'

'Shit,' I blurt, then immediately wince again. Martin doesn't look as if he's ever cussed a day in his life. He probably thinks

I'm an uncouth, potty-mouthed American redneck. 'Uh, sorry,' I murmur, biting my lip.

Another gentle smile tugs at his mouth. 'No apology necessary. I'm afraid you could curse until you were blue in the face and it wouldn't even put a dent in the mountain of foul language I've heard during my years with Mr Beckett.' He leans toward me and lowers his voice. 'I might have actually picked up a few of his more colorful phrases over the years, but don't tell anyone.'

I laugh, and his eyes twinkle. It's a relief that ol' Martin isn't as stiff-upper-lipped as I'd suspected. And speaking of Mr Beckett, I'm about to ask where he is, hoping I can get out of there before he returns, when a movement across the room catches my eye. He stands on the other side of the expansive office, his deep voice clipped as he says something into a cell phone that I can't make out. But I hear enough to confirm that he's definitely British – and he sounds irritated.

Oh, dear. My rescue has probably kept him from something important, like trashing some poor country's economy, I think snidely, and I'm more than a little surprised by my vehemence. I guess there's just something about this guy – and all the obvious signs of his extreme wealth that are currently surrounding me – that's really setting me on edge.

'Are you in a relationship, Miss Reed?'

I start, swinging my gaze back to Martin. 'Why on earth do you need to know *that*?'

'I don't.' He grins a bit shyly. 'But I know Jase – that is, Mr Beckett – is wondering, so I thought I'd help the boy out.'

I give a soft snort. 'He's hardly a boy. And I can assure you that I'm the *last* woman he'd be interested in.'

As if to validate the fact that I have the worst luck in the world, Beckett chooses that precise moment to end his call and head our way. He's removed his jacket and rolled up the sleeves of his crisp white dress shirt, and he casually pushes his hands into the front pockets of his trousers as he walks toward us. When he finally comes to a stop, I have to tilt my head back to keep looking at his face. He's tall, and seriously gorgeous, but he does *not* look happy. 'Why would you say that?' he asks in a deliciously masculine voice, standing no more than a few feet from where I'm sitting on the sofa.

'Uh, say what?' I sound like an idiot, but his husky voice is so incredible it's left me a little stunned. Tyler, my best friend back in San Diego, would be freaking drooling right about now. But then Tyler is all about the testosterone-oozing, rough-voiced alphas.

Beckett comes even closer, the tips of his polished dress shoes touching the toes of my ballet flats as he towers over me. 'That I wouldn't be interested in you.'

Laughing off my unease, I scoot a bit down the sofa so that I'll be able to move to my feet without brushing against him when I finally feel stable enough to stand. The guy apparently has some kind of problem with personal space, since he's invading mine. And here I thought the British upper class were supposed to be all stuffy and reserved. Beckett could give any hard-core, hot-blooded American male a run for his money. The sexy-as-hell accent is just overkill. He probably has women at his beck and call, triple booked and ready to preen and dance to whatever tune he chooses – which makes me really want to know what he's messing with *me* for.

'Sir, this is Miss Emmy Reed,' Martin interjects, clearly trying to relieve the tension that's arcing in the air between his employer and me.

'You know damn well that any man would have to be blind not to be interested,' Beckett says in a quieter tone, as if his assistant hasn't even spoken.

'Oh, sure,' I scoff, not liking the way this ass is screwing with my head. 'And I bet this is the part where I'm meant to melt all over you, making a fool of myself. You put that smoldering vibe in a woman's face and she normally just drops her panties. Am I right?'

Martin's trying not to laugh, but failing miserably, while Beckett gives me a slightly crooked, impossibly wicked grin . . . and slowly drops his gaze to my lap. 'Apparently not, seeing as how you're still wearing yours.'

I give another feminine snort, a little relieved to realize he's every bit as arrogant as I'd assumed he would be. 'Trust me, I don't count. But I can definitely see how you must affect the women in your crowd.'

'My crowd?' His brows nearly lift to his hairline, his eyes turning dark with some indecipherable emotion.

'Oh, you know. All the "*divine*" and "*dahling*" and "*kiss kiss*" on the cheeks kind of girls. I bet you have them all panting for it, don't you?'

With a low, dry laugh, he sticks a big, masculine hand toward me and says, 'I'm going to ignore that for the moment and just introduce myself. Jasper Beckett, but my friends call me Jase.'

'Emmy Reed,' I practically croak, my throat working with a hard swallow the moment his large hand envelops mine. How can I be so attracted to someone who's the antithesis of everything I know I should want in a man? My more devout Women's Studies friends would be shaking their heads at me in disgust, but there's no hiding from the hormone frenzy going on inside my overwhelmed body.

'And your friends call you?'

I pull my hand back out of sheer self-preservation. 'That's none of your business.'

He shakes his head a little as he holds my gaze, probably at a loss for how to handle a woman who isn't fawning all over him. A heavy silence settles between the two of us – three of us, actually, since poor Martin's still sitting there all proper-looking in his chair – until I finally relent. 'My friends call me Em, and you don't look at all like a Jasper.'

'Yeah, I get that a lot.' His beautiful mouth twitches as he slides his strong hand back into his pocket. 'The only thing I can think is that my mother must have hated me.'

'Must have?'

'She died when I was six.'

'Oh.' Now I feel like a bitch moron who's just stuck her foot in her mouth. 'I'm sorry.'

'Don't be,' he murmurs. 'It was obviously a long time ago.'

There's something there, in the things he isn't saying, that tells me his mother's death is anything but a blasé, forgotten part of his past.

Changing the subject, he asks, 'How are you feeling?' A hard, sharp-edged glint flashes through his sinful blue gaze. 'I could have dismembered those little shits for touching you.'

'I'm fine, except for a slight headache. It could have been so much worse if you hadn't helped me, so thank you.'

'In the future, you need to keep an eye out for men like that when you're on your own,' he lectures.

I clench my jaw, since I can't very well tell him that I normally would have been doing exactly that, but I'd been too busy thinking about *him* to pay any attention to what the thugs were doing. But the smirk sneaking on to his lips says that he's already guessed where my attention had been focused. I roll my eyes, mouthing the word 'ass' at him, which for some reason makes his smirk slip into a full-fledged grin. Seriously, what is up with this guy?

'The doctor will be here soon,' Martin says, sounding a bit

worried now. He is no doubt at a loss over what to make of Beckett and me.

I catch my lip in my teeth, hating the idea of an unknown doctor coming here to check on me. 'I really don't think—'

'Don't bother arguing,' Beckett cuts in, 'because you *are* seeing him.'

I bristle, but don't kick up a stink. Instead, I just glare at him and ask, 'Where's my bag?'

He jerks his chin toward the far side of the room, where his massive desk sprawls before the wall of windows, the summer sky becoming a gray blur of rainclouds beyond the tinted glass. My bag is sitting on a corner of the desk, looking completely out of place. Make that my recently opened bag, since my phone is lying beside it.

As I swing my gaze back to Beckett, I'm wondering where he gets off thinking he can just go through my personal things like that. Then I find myself wondering what his cock looks like, and color floods my face. What in the world is wrong with me? Yeah, I have as many hormones as the next girl, but I don't let them rule me. Not when it comes to men. That's what I have my vibrator for, damn it.

'Have dinner with me tonight.'

I blink, positive I've heard him wrong. 'Excuse me?'

'Have dinner with me,' he says again. 'It's going to take a few hours for your new bank cards to arrive. In the meantime, you don't have any money to go anywhere. What will it hurt to spend that time with me?'

'What are you talking about? What happened to my cards?'

'Everything's being taken care of.' He stares down at me with an inscrutable expression that's impossible to read, but the palpable force of his intensity makes my chest tight, my breath quickening. 'So there's no reason we can't enjoy a meal together.'

I fist my hands as I realize what's happened. 'Are you telling me those jackasses stole my cards?' I'd brought two debit cards and a credit card with me when I'd left San Diego, which I'd meant to keep in separate places, in the event anything like this happened while I was traveling. But like an idiot, I hadn't gotten around to separating them yet. They'd been in a card holder in the inside pocket of my bag.

'One of the men pulled some cards from your purse while I was dealing with the bastard who hurt you,' Beckett explains, rubbing a hand across the dark five o'clock shadow on his jaw.

'Son of a bitch!' Now I'm pissed.

He narrows his eyes, as if he doesn't like seeing me lose my temper. Not that I give a damn. 'Don't worry about the cards. I've called your bank and they're already issuing new ones. Plus, they've safeguarded your accounts.'

'They let you do that?'

He shrugs. 'I had to pull a few strings.'

I want to shout that my bank accounts are none of his fucking business, but choke it back, seeing as how I would have probably had to wait a few days for the bank to move at its usual leisurely pace. 'Are the cards being delivered here? I'm meant to travel to Surrey tonight and stay in a B&B.'

Instead of answering my question, he asks, 'Where are your things?'

'What things?'

He merely raises his brows at me. 'Surely you planned to take your clothes with you to Surrey.'

'Oh. I left my suitcase with a friend,' I mutter, this emotional rollercoaster making my head hurt even worse. I lift my fingertips to my temples and rub. 'I'm meant to pick it up before leaving town.'

'Give me the address and I'll send someone for the case.

Then, this evening, you and I can have dinner and I'll get a room for the night.'

I slowly lower my hands to the sofa, digging them into the plush leather. This man might have helped me out, but I'm not going to use that as an excuse to spread my legs for him. 'You think I'm just going to spend the night with you? I don't even know you.' And I'm not his type! Which makes this whole situation seem like a farce. Is he playing some kind of game with me?

His head tilts a bit to the side in response to my strained, *get-a-clue* tone. 'All I'm asking for is dinner. My family owns a hotel in Chelsea. The room will be yours alone, Emmy.'

Oh. Now I kinda feel like a fool.

Mentally running through my options, I realize I don't actually have any. Lola lives with her boyfriend, who I can't stand. And Ben, the friend whose flat my suitcase is currently stored at, has his mother visiting him for a few days, which means he'll be sleeping on the sofa I usually crash on when I'm in London. I met Ben at the same time as Lola, when he was living in the university flat just below ours, and we bonded over our love of the Foo Fighters and Thai takeaway.

Beckett is still waiting on a response, so I clear my throat a bit and say, 'Then, um, thanks. But I'll pay you back for the room and the meal as soon as I have my cards and find a cash machine. Then you can be on your way and I'll be out of your hair.'

He laughs, and this time I'm the one who narrows their eyes. 'What's so funny?'

'Not funny. Just –' he seems to be searching for the right word – 'refreshing.'

My voice is almost painfully tight. 'Because?'

Another shrug lifts his broad shoulders. 'You're not interested in my money. And you honestly don't want to spend time with me. It's not what I'm used to.'

'Wow,' I laugh, shaking my head. 'Ego much?'

He grins, showing his straight, white teeth. 'Not ego, sweet-heart. It's just the way it is. But I like this – that you're not like the other women I know. Which is why I want to make you an offer. One you're going to find impossible to refuse.' The heat in his blue eyes has me full-on blushing, my heart beating so hard I know he can see my pulse pounding at the base of my throat. 'I'll see to it that you have complete access to J.J. Harrison's pri-vate collection of his work and, if we're lucky, an interview with the man himself,' he says in a low, deceptively casual tone. 'And in exchange, you'll agree to be my date at a family wedding this weekend in Kent.'

I jolt to my feet, forced to place a steadying hand on Mar-tin's chair. Date? Family wedding? An offer I can't refuse? 'What the hell are you talking about?'

Beckett had started to reach for me when I wobbled, and only lowers his arms when he sees that I'm not going to fall. 'You want information about Harrison, and I don't want to spend an entire weekend listening to another woman prattle on about shopping or her nails and making catty comments about everyone she sees.'

My eyes are wide. 'How do you know about my research?'

'Your phone call,' he answers simply.

I think back, remembering that he'd overheard my conver-sation with Lola on the Tube. 'Oh.' I try to get my thoughts straight, but my head is still pounding. 'Um, I need to—'

As though he's reading my mind, he says, 'Don't worry about your friend. I used your phone to call her. She knows you're all right.'

I screw my face up, wanting so badly to tell him that he didn't have any right to go snooping through my phone – not to mention using my thumbprint to unlock it when I'd been unconscious – but stop myself at the last second. The man *did* save me, so I'm going to sound like a raging bitch if I call him out for contacting Lola for me. But it still rankles.

'So about this weekend?' he prompts, and there's the slightest edge of command in his deep voice that makes me bristle, as if he's fighting his natural instinct to *tell* me what's going to happen between us, instead of waiting for my response.

Taking a shaky breath, I say, 'Aside from the obvious fact that I would have to be crazy to go somewhere with someone I don't even know, you mentioned that you didn't want to spend time with a woman who makes catty comments.'

He lifts his chin in that way that men do. 'That's right.'

'And how do you know I wouldn't?' I ask with a baffled note of exasperation, my attention so focused on the gorgeous male staring me down that I'm only vaguely aware of Martin sliding to his feet and escaping the office. Not that I blame him. Things are getting pretty weird in here.

Another grin suddenly curls Beckett's mouth, and I can see the shift of powerful muscle beneath his white shirt as he shoves his hands back into his pockets. 'Something tells me that smart-arse mouth of yours would only be cutting *me*. Not anyone else.'

Huh? Is this guy for real? 'And that sounds like fun to you?'

His low laugh melts down my spine, settling with liquid warmth between my thighs. 'Don't ask me to explain it.'

I cross my arms over my chest, giving him a steely stare. 'And how exactly do you plan on getting me in to see Harrison's private collection?' I ask, not even bothering to mention the interview, since I know that will *never* happen. 'Because you had better not be bullshitting me. I'm not lying when I say that I have zero interest in being your go-to-girl for a weekend surrounded by a bunch of posh snobs.'

'I'm not bullshitting you.' I can tell from his tone that he doesn't like what I've said. He's obviously the kind of man who's used to women jumping to do what he wants as quickly as possible. *Too* used to it. And I'm so not the subservient type.

'Then how?' I press, more than a little surprised by how bitchy I sound. To hear me at this moment, you would never guess that I'm considered a really nice person who easily makes friends. I might not be great at relationships, but it usually takes a lot to rile me. There's something about Beckett, though, that just sets me on edge.

I can sense he's about to blast me with something stunning as he steps closer, tipping his head down so that he can hold my stare, his blue eyes gleaming and hot. 'I'm going to give you a clue,' he murmurs, the husky notes of his voice sliding through me like a physical touch, making my body feel heavy and damp. 'My full name is Jasper John Beckett, and my mother's maiden name was Prescott.'

'Ohmygod,' I whisper, my thoughts spinning as I finally put it all together. I have to reach out and grab the back of Martin's chair again. J.J. Harrison's full name is Jasper John Harrison Prescott!

'I was named after the artist, because that's the way it's done in my family,' he adds, and his wide smile is the cockiest damn thing I've ever seen. 'The misogynistic old bastard you're so interested in is my maternal grandfather.'

Chapter Two

Friday morning

JASE

For the first time in my thirty-two years of life, I've met a woman I can't figure out. It sounds shitty and arrogant, but it's true. At least from my perspective. I mean, sure, I've probably been wrong about a lot of the women I've known, but my experiences with them have always played out with no surprises. This one though ... Yeah, this one has me spinning so hard I barely know my own name.

For the past half-hour, I've been driving the new love of my life – a custom-designed matte black Range Rover – down the motorway, while Emmy Reed sits in the passenger seat, doing her best to ignore me. She's wearing a lightweight yellow cardigan and a long, strapless sundress in a darker shade of yellow, along with a pair of leather sandals that lace up her calves. The whole outfit should make her look like she's heading for some bohemian music festival, but it suits her in a way that's impossible for a woman to buy, no matter how much money she spends. Emmy could wear the willowy hippy dress to a bloody black tie event, and still turn heads. And she smells like something that belongs in my mouth. Like something I want to bury my face in and never come up for air.

Without even trying, she's making me have to fight not to go as hard as a goddamn rock while I'm driving, and my head feels like . . . Jesus, I can't even describe what I'm feeling. Too much, for one. A smart man might have cut his losses while he still could and got the hell away from her, but maybe I'm not as smart as I've always thought I was. After all, the only reason she's sitting beside me is because of my shit of a grandfather.

But I don't give a damn.

It would probably sound weird to most people, given the attitude she was throwing my way in my office yesterday, but she's honestly too refreshing to let her just slip away. I need to at least spend the weekend with her, and enjoy the experience of her, before I walk. And I will. I always do. According to the gossip rags in London, my longest relationship was three weeks, and that's only because Melissa ended up in hospital with severe appendicitis after our first week together, and it wasn't like I could end things while she was ill.

Most of my exes might consider me a dick, but even I'm not a big enough prick to dump a woman while her arse is poking out of a hospital gown and she's having fluids pumped into her through an IV.

'So who is she?' the little American asks, and for a second I'm thrown, wondering how she knew I was thinking about an ex.

'Who is who?' I hedge, not about to confess to anything I don't have to.

'The pretty redhead,' she says without looking at me. I'm stealing glances at her from the corner of my eye whenever I can, and she's been staring out the side window for so long now she's probably got a crick in her neck. 'You know, the one who delivered all the new clothes to my hotel room last night.'

Ah. It's embarrassing to admit, but I'm relieved as hell that she hadn't been reading my mind.

'I have no idea who she is. I just called Harrods and asked for a personal shopper to pick out some dresses and shoes for you, along with something that would work for a wedding.'

Her head turns my way, and I can feel her dark gaze moving over my profile. '*You* called them?'

'Yes. Why the tone?'

'It just seems a bit . . . *menial* for someone like you. I would have thought you had Martin do it.'

'No. I'd prefer for Martin not to think about you in thongs and see-through bras.'

It makes me smile when she snorts. 'Yeah, the lingerie was a nice, if not perverted, touch.'

'You already think I'm a lech. Might as well live up to the part.'

I can actually feel her rolling her eyes at me, and it keeps the grin on my face. I can't recall a woman ever giving me this much attitude before, and I know I'm going to miss it when she's gone. Not that I'll do anything about it. She might be different from the others, and so damn hot it's driving me mad, but I'm not looking for anything more than a distraction. Something to ease the monotony of routine, and Emmy is definitely that. I want to touch her soft, golden skin more than I've wanted to touch anything in a hell of a long time. Want to break through that armor she wears and make the woman beneath claw at me like an animal. Want to hear her scream with pleasure and feel those short nails digging into my back as I fuck her hard enough to break the bloody bed.

But that armor of hers is fierce. So fierce, she actually ditched me for dinner last night, claiming her head was still hurting too badly to leave her room.

My fingers tighten around the steering wheel as I think

about the bastards who mugged her, and I wish I could go back in time and pound the little shits all over again. Or better yet, ignore the call from my chief financial officer that had held me back those crucial seconds, and stop them from ever getting their hands on her in the first place.

Just after I'd dropped the grandfather bomb on her in my office, Dr Riley had arrived. I could tell Emmy didn't want the doc looking her over, but she didn't argue with me about it. Luckily, thanks to that thick, beautiful hair of hers, the knocks to her head hadn't broken the skin, but she had two lumps that Riley had poked and prodded until I'd thought she might kick him. His prognosis had been a slight concussion and regular doses of over-the-counter painkillers for a few days. I'd planned to drive her to the hotel myself when he was done, but an emergency came up with one of my overseas projects that I had to deal with, so Martin had driven her to my family's hotel, checked her into a suite, and had the medicine delivered. Then he'd gone to collect her suitcase for her, and since I doubted she'd brought the kind of clothes she'd need for a weekend spent in the countryside at a posh wedding on a research trip, I'd called Harrods and had them send over some things.

When I'd shown up at her door just after seven, planning to take her up to the rooftop restaurant for dinner, she hadn't even let me into the suite. Wearing one of the hotel's fluffy white robes, she'd cracked the door open and told me she wasn't up for going out, or having company, which I took to mean get lost. Not wanting to come across as a total dick, I'd given her the new cards that'd been delivered to my office, then told her to rest and that I'd be back to pick her up at eight a.m. Which brings us to where we are now, speeding down the M20, every mile bringing us closer to my childhood home . . . and the last fucking place in the world that I want to be.

After our brief exchange about the redhead, we slip back into another heavy silence, and I have to bite my tongue to keep from hounding her with questions, worried I'll scare her off. There's time for patience, because I've got all weekend with her. Until Monday evening, actually, since Caroline, my step-mother, has insured my cousin Oliver's wedding is the most ostentatious event of the year. I'm surprised she hasn't invited any of the royals, though I think there might be an earl or two there, along with several members of Parliament. Caroline judges every social affair by the size of the guests' bank accounts and the prestige of their positions in society, and this wedding won't be any different.

Needing something to do, I turn the radio on, hoping Emmy isn't a pop fanatic. The corner of my mouth twitches when she starts to quietly sing along to the Arctic Monkeys song that's playing, and I wonder if she'd be surprised to know that I've seen them in concert a few times. Given the things she says, she probably thinks I only attend the symphony and ballet – and I have to admit that I'm looking forward to prov-ing her wrong. To showing her that I'm a hell of a lot more laid-back than she's given me credit for.

Yes, I might have money. But I've worked my arse off for every penny of it, never expecting the world to give me any-thing. Alistair, my father, was proof enough of how shit things could go when you lived your life on what was handed to you, rather than what you'd earned, and I knew early on that the last thing I wanted to be was like him.

For a moment, I wonder if I should warn Emmy just how screwed up my family is, then decide to keep quiet. She'll learn for herself soon enough, and I'd rather spend this time just enjoying having her all to myself.

'You know, my boyfriend back in San Diego really isn't

going to like this,' she suddenly throws out, still staring out the window.

This time, I'm the one who snorts. 'Nice try,' I say, turning the radio down, 'but you don't have one.'

Even though my eyes are on the road, I can feel her turn her head to stare at me. 'How do you—'

'Lola,' I cut in with a grin. 'I asked her when I had her on the phone yesterday.'

She doesn't respond, and I have a feeling I've just landed her friend in a ton of shit. Thinking I owe it to Lola to get the focus off her indiscretion, I say, 'I thought it was cute how Martin tried to get it out of you, though.'

She gives a quiet laugh, and I have to fight back another smile when she shifts a bit in her seat to face me, her right leg curled up under her. 'Speaking of Martin, how did you land him?'

'Land him?'

'Yeah. He's like an Alfred, but you're definitely no Batman. So what's the story?'

'Why can't I be Batman?' I sound like an idiot, but I honestly want to know why this beautiful blonde thinks I'm so far off the mark.

'If you were Batman,' she says all matter-of-factly, 'you'd have caught me yesterday before I cracked my head against the floor.'

I slant her a quick look to see if she's serious, and I'm relieved that she's smirking at me.

'Fair point,' I murmur, wanting to kiss that sexy, crooked smile off her lips so badly I can taste it. Can literally fucking taste the need that's twisting inside me, and I shake my head a little as I force my attention back on the road.

'So what's it like having J.J. Harrison for a grandfather?' she asks, obviously in the mood to talk now, which is fine by me. I just wish she didn't want to talk about Harrison. But I'll take what I can get.

'To be honest,' I tell her, 'I wouldn't really know.'

'What do you mean? He *is* your grandfather. I spent an hour last night looking you up online, and eventually found some family photos that had been posted of you with him. They looked like they might have been from some awards ceremony he'd been forced to go to.'

'Yes, he's my biological grandfather, but he's never acted like it,' I explain, unable to remember when a photo of me and Harrison would have been taken. I've done my best to stay out of his way for years now. 'He's more like this cantankerous old bastard I run into from time to time.'

'Oh. That sucks. I almost feel like I should say I'm sorry.'

'Almost?' I ask with a husky laugh.

'Well, I mean, it's not like you're hurting for family. From what I read, you've got enough relatives to populate a small town.'

Christ, if she only knew how badly I wish it were otherwise. But I'm not getting into it now. I've only got a few days with this girl, and I'm sure as hell not going to waste them complaining about the dysfunctional Becketts.

We spend the next fifty miles talking about anything and everything. I ask her about the degree she's just finished, and why she chose this new career of hers. I'm fascinated by her answer – *I love writing and I love art. The mystery and beauty of them. The emotion, the secrets, the spaces in between what we see and what we think. So it seemed natural to put them together.*

Yeah, this girl doesn't think like anyone else I know, and I wonder if that's because she's so perfectly unique, or if I just keep really shallow company.

When she asks me to explain what I do for a living, I can tell she's surprised that I don't just sit behind my big desk and look at stock values twenty-four seven. That I actually spend a lot of my time overseeing the building of megastructures around the world that not only push the cutting edge in design technology, but are environmentally progressive, as well as a boost to the local economies. I think she's even beginning to warm to me a little, though she's still wary. But I can sense there's a tiny part of her that's starting to see me as more than just some prick in a high-priced suit. It's clear that at some point in her life, someone with money has treated her like shit, and it makes me want to pound the bastard's face in. Strange, when I usually prefer to keep my temper under tight control these days, since it tended to get the better of me when I was younger.

But I want Emmy to give me names and addresses, and I want to track down every tosser who's ever hurt her and make them pay. And these aren't just meaningless thoughts. I actually *want* to do it.

Bloody hell, I think, rubbing my hand along my rigid jaw. This girl is twisting me up and down and every way in between, and I haven't even touched her yet, other than that brief, innocent handshake in my office. And God knows that wasn't nearly enough.

As we pull off the motorway and start winding through the British countryside, her attention is pulled to what's outside the window again. This time, though, she seems content to keep the conversation going while she enjoys the view. 'It's so beautiful here,' she says, and I can hear the smile in her voice as she takes in the rolling green hills, ancient trees, and quaint thatch-roofed cottages.

'You enjoy visiting the UK?' I ask her, slowing my speed as we pass through another village.

'Of course I do,' she says, turning her head to look my way. 'Why is that surprising?'

It's a little unnerving, how good she is at reading my emotions. 'From our conversation yesterday, I guess I just figured you had us all pegged as pretentious, power-hungry snobs.'

'God no,' she says with conviction. 'Some of the most amazing people I know are British.'

'Ah. So then it's just me and my crowd who you think are the snobs?'

I glance over just in time to catch her pink, soft-looking lips curve into another smirk. 'Naw,' she drawls, exaggerating her southern accent. 'I know quite a few of you in America too.'

I laugh as I shake my head. This girl. I have a feeling she's starting to get a kick out of giving me a hard time. And yet, I also sense that there's definitely a story there. One I'm determined to hear before the end of our weekend. For now, though, I simply ask, 'What were you planning on doing in Surrey? As far as I know, none of Harrison's paintings are there.'

'I'll tell you if you tell me who you were talking to on the phone when I woke up on your office sofa yesterday.'

Confused, I say, 'Why on earth would you care about that?'

She lifts her feminine shoulders in a little shrug. 'You sounded . . . angry. I just wondered why.'

A gritty laugh jerks from my chest. 'Because my cousin Cameron is a dickhead. That's who I was talking to.'

'Does the "dickhead" piss you off often?'

I shoot her a tight smile. 'Every time he opens his pompous mouth.' Looking back at the road, I add, 'When you meet him today, you'll understand why.'

'Can't wait,' she murmurs drily, before answering my question. 'I was heading down to Surrey because I discovered that one of your grandfather's former employees lives there. A woman named Margaret Dunnet.'

I raise my eyebrows in surprise. 'Margie? I didn't know she'd retired there.'

'You know her?'

She does the whole leg thing again as she faces me, and I swear the little glimpse I get of smooth, golden thigh before she sorts out her dress makes my cock give a dangerous twitch. I honestly haven't had this much trouble controlling myself since I was a hormone-ridden teenager, and I have to cough to clear the lump of lust in my throat before I can say, 'She used to bake me cookies when I was a kid.' A smile kicks up a corner of my mouth at the memory. 'Margie basically ran the old man's household until she retired when I was twelve and Anna, whom you'll also meet this weekend, took over.' Realizing that I still have no idea what she wants to talk to Harrison about, I ask, 'What's the angle of your piece, anyway?'

'Are you really interested?' she asks skeptically.

'I wouldn't ask if I wasn't.'

'I'm writing an article on the role of the dominated female subject in modern art.'

'Then it's no wonder you want to talk to good ol' Granddad,' I drawl, thinking she's definitely got him pegged.

I can hear the wry smile in her voice as she says, 'Yeah, well, I'm hoping to get some insight into what drives him. I mean, why does he portray women as such spineless, sexually desperate creatures, and men as these dominating, god-like figures of power? Is it to shock and provoke? Is he just a chauvinistic, misogynistic asshole? Or is there a deeper meaning beneath the brushstrokes?'

'Knowing Harrison, it might be all three,' I tell her. 'But it was a clever idea, going to Margie. I don't think she would have divulged any of his secrets, but she would have been happy to give you her opinion about his work. I remember her being pretty vocal about what a chauvinist he is, though at the time I had no idea what she was talking about, because I was seven and didn't know what a chauvinist was.'

She laughs, and I swear I nearly drive off the road when I look over and catch the way she's looking at me. 'Wow, look at that. A genuine smile.'

'Shut up,' she mutters, though she's still grinning.

'You should do that more often. You're beautiful even when you're pissed off – but when you smile like that, you're fucking breathtaking.'

She blushes so bright she looks sunburned, and I fight the urge to tease her about it. There isn't time, anyway, because I'm turning on to the long drive that leads to my childhood home, thinking that any progress I've made with her during the drive is no doubt about to be ruined. I have a bad feeling that the sheer ostentatiousness of Beckett House, and most of the people inside it, aren't going to help me convince Emmy that wealthy doesn't automatically mean arsehole. And since we're about to go head-to-head with the enemy, there are some important things that I still need to talk to her about, so I get on with it.

Less than fifteen minutes later, two members of staff are already taking our bags up to my private room, and Emmy and I are heading up the front steps of the mansion. My father's long-time butler, Angus, opens the ornate front doors before I even have a chance to use the knocker, and I exchange a few words with him, asking after his family, as Emmy and I walk inside.

Unfortunately, we're not in the expansive foyer for more than two seconds before Caroline, my stepmother, comes walking towards us from the central hallway. *Fuck*. At least my father's nowhere to be seen. Alistair Beckett tends to stay as close to his well-stocked bar as he can, so we probably won't see him until we venture into the back of the house.

I hear the quiet gasp on Emmy's lips as Caroline draws near, and wish I'd warned her that there's a viper lying beneath her beauty. She looks like one of the old Hollywood starlets, tall and statuesque, with porcelain-smooth skin, platinum-blond hair and ruby-red lips. I know, aesthetically speaking, that she's a stunning woman – but it's difficult to still see her attractiveness once you know just how vile she is on the inside.

'Emmy,' I say, loving the way it feels as I grab her soft, feminine hand and tug her body closer to mine, 'this is my stepmother, Caroline. Caroline, I'm beyond thrilled to introduce my girlfriend, Emmy Reed.'

As I'd driven up the long drive and parked the Rover, we'd hammered out the details of our weekend arrangement, and I have to admit that she's a shrewd negotiator. I agreed to almost everything she wanted, with the proviso that I could do my best to persuade her to change her mind about going to bed with me. And given how thick the sexual tension is between us, I'm confident that we'll have had our fill of each other before we're back in London on Monday night. But the one point I refused to budge on was how I portrayed our relationship to my family, and that was because I wanted her protected. I'm hoping they'll be better behaved if they think I'm serious about this girl – and, yeah, I'm definitely going to enjoy being able to hold her close, like I'm doing now, without having to worry that she's going to stomp on my foot or knee me in the balls.

'It's nice to meet you,' Emmy says, giving Caro – whose eyes start to go wide at the sound of my girl's American accent – an uncomfortable smile. 'You have a, um, lovely home.'

Caroline blinks and runs her comically shocked gaze over Emmy from head to toe, before turning to me and saying,

'You've brought an American redneck hippy to your cousin's wedding? Honestly, Jase. What on earth were you thinking?'

I tense, so furious my nostrils flare as I suck in a sharp breath, and my voice turns guttural. 'Right now I'm thinking that you're a rude, classless bitch, Caroline. But then that's nothing new, now is it?'

Christ, so much for hoping she might act decent for once.

'Just make sure you keep her away from the silver,' she snaps, and I let go of Emmy's hand to get right in the viper's face.

'You utter one more rude word about Emmy,' I warn in a low, seething rasp, 'or so much as look at her the wrong way, and you're going to discover that your dirty little secrets aren't so secret after all, Caro.'

She stiffens as she stares up into my enraged face. 'What are you talking about?'

I give her a slow, mean smile as I quietly say, 'You think I don't know about all your toy boys in London? Hasn't anyone ever told you that there are no secrets in the city?'

Her pale blue gaze turns icy and sharp. 'You're lying.'

'Yeah?' I let a low laugh fall from my lips. 'You really willing to take that chance?'

Something on her face changes with my words, like an imperceptible crack in a porcelain vase. I can't see it, but I *know* it's there, breaking under that unnaturally smooth surface. Feeling that I've made my point, I start to turn back to my girl, when Caroline grabs my right hand, glaring at my knuckles that are battered from punching the bastards who'd mugged Emmy. 'Do I even want to know? I thought you'd outgrown your temper issues, Jase.'

I pull my hand back, resisting the urge to wipe it on my jeans. Ever since I was a child, Caroline's touch has creeped me out. I open my mouth, ready to tell her to keep her fucking hands to herself, when Emmy surprises me by saying, 'He saved my life yesterday. So if you ask me, your stepson is a hero and you should be showing a little goddamn respect.'

'Don't bother, sweetheart,' I murmur, taking her hand again. 'My stepmother and I don't get along.'

She stiffens a bit at the sweetheart remark, but doesn't snap at me in front of the enemy. And she doesn't pull her hand away from mine as I start heading towards the massive staircase that curves up the right side of the foyer.

'Oh, and by the way,' Caroline drawls, the satisfaction oozing from her voice warning me that I'm not going to like whatever she's about to say, 'at least five of your exes are on the guest list for this weekend. So try not to cause any scenes.'

'Bitch,' I mutter under my breath, knowing she invited them here on purpose.

Gripping Emmy's hand a bit tighter, I force my mind off my stepmother and her twisted games, and focus instead on the beautiful, intriguing woman at my side. My heart is still pounding from the way she stood up for me, and I want nothing more than to pull her into my arms and kiss her until she can taste me in every part of her. Until she's melting and panting . . . and begging me to give her what we both need.

But I gave her my word that I won't touch her unless she asks me to – so until she's ready, I'll be keeping my hands and my mouth to myself. It sucks, but hey, it's not like it'll kill me.

Then it hits me that we're heading up to my private bedroom, where we'll be alone together with a big, fuck-off bed, and my heart starts pounding even harder.

Bloody hell, I take it back.

This just might kill me after all.

Chapter Three

EMMY

As I lean back in a ridiculously comfortable chair that sits upon a gleaming hardwood floor, I run my gaze over the masculine, exquisitely decorated room in a state of shock. I honestly can't believe that I'm doing this – that I'm here. I must have lost my freaking mind!

The day before, I was riding on the Tube, doing a bit of reading, and the next thing I know I'm sitting in a spacious bedroom in a sprawling mansion in the English countryside, while Jase-Fucking-Beckett takes a phone call out on the balcony.

Huh. Maybe I hit my head harder than I'd realized when those ass-hats knocked me unconscious.

But, no, this is definitely real. Even in my wildest dreams, I could never come up with something this bizarre.

On the wall above the high sleigh bed is one of J.J. Harrison's earlier works that I've read about but never seen. It's of a young woman whose face is covered by her pale, windblown hair, her nude body wrapped in flowers and sea foam as she stands in the waves, the sky a storm-dark horizon at her back, as if something dark and menacing is looming in the distance. There's a story on the canvas, but one that pre-dates the misogynistic themes of his later work. My eyes burn as I stare at it, and I feel like some twisted strain of kismet has led me here. How else to explain it?

I still can't believe that I didn't immediately make the connection between Harrison and Jasper 'Jase' Beckett, given how intensely I've been studying the artist. I'd felt like an idiot for a few moments after he'd told me the reclusive artist is his grandfather, and then I'd quickly pinballed between a confusing mix of emotions. Excitement. Shock. Disbelief. Hope. Desire.

And we can't forget irritation, considering Jase used his connection to Harrison to bribe me into participating in this farce. The stepmom alone is something worthy of a nightmare, and I know I need to toughen up a bit if I'm going to survive the weekend unscathed. I was either incredibly lucky to have been rescued by one of the few men in the country who could get me access to J.J. Harrison, or I had the shittiest luck in the world. I think it all depends on whether you're looking at the situation from a professional standpoint or a personal one.

Professionally, this could be the feather in my cap that I need to open doors in the world I plan to work in.

Personally, it's like my own customized version of some sick reality show, where I'm forced to socialize with people who make me uncomfortable, and who are no doubt going to like me even less. Case in point: Beckett's stepmother from hell.

Then there's the problem of temptation. He's promised not to lay a finger on me unless I ask him to, and I'd be lying through my teeth if I said I wasn't thinking about it. About having Beckett's fingers and mouth and every other gorgeous, mouthwatering part of him on me and in me and everywhere in between. I have never, in my entire life, felt such an intense level of attraction to a man. And as much as I try to convince myself that he comes from the same exact world as my father, I'm beginning to see that there could be far more differences than similarities between the two powerful men.

Or . . . am I just trying to justify being so attracted to him? God, I don't know. The only certainty right now is that I've never felt more off balance than I do at this moment.

He's been standing out on the balcony, taking a call from Hong Kong, but comes back in through one of the room's two sets of French doors, his phone in his hand.

When I'd opened the hotel room door that morning after he'd knocked, it'd taken everything I have not to hyperventilate at the sight of him in a well-worn pair of Levi's, white polo shirt, and brown leather boots. The guy killed it in a suit, but these casual clothes, in combination with the dark scruff on his rugged jaw, make him damn near lethal.

'What's wrong?' he asks when he sees that I'm rubbing my temples, his gaze instantly darkening with concern. 'Is your head hurting?'

I give him a little nod. 'It's nothing that paracetamol can't fix. I just took some while you were outside.'

He studies my face for a moment, then seems to accept my answer and walks over to his leather bag, taking a phone charger out and plugging it in by the beautiful dressing table that sits against the room's back wall. 'There's only one bed in here,' he offers casually, his attention on his phone as he connects it to the charger.

'Yeah, I kinda noticed that.'

He shoots me a smoldering look over one of those broad, muscular shoulders that I can't stop thinking about sinking my teeth into. 'Are you going to let me sleep with you tonight, or am I roughing it on our tiny sofa?'

The room's sofa sits against the portion of wall between the two sets of French doors, and I almost laugh at the idea of him squeezing that tall, god-like body on to it.

'Is that what you want to do?' I ask. 'Sleep?'

There's a sexy curve to his lips as he turns around and rests his fine ass against the dressing table, his hands curling around the front edge on either side of his hips. 'Actually, I just want to spend the entire night buried balls deep inside your breathtaking body, fucking your brains out. But I was trying to sound restrained.'

'Don't restrain yourself on my account,' I say drily, smirking at him. 'I mean, why start now?'

'Oh, Em. You have no idea.'

'Maybe not, but I knew you were going to be trouble.' The grin on my face is completely real, and I honestly can't help it. As much as I want to remain unaffected by this man, it's impossible. Yeah, he's arrogant as hell, but he's also incredibly fun to be around. Maybe not easy or comfortable, considering the level of sexual attraction making my body buzz in his presence – but he's not a dick.

Proving that point, he immediately launches into an apology. 'I'm sorry about what happened downstairs. My stepmother is a vile bitch on the best of days, but with so many younger women in the house, I think she's feeling threatened.'

'Speaking of all the women,' I murmur, 'was she telling the truth about your ex-girlfriends?'

He laughs and shakes his head. 'What is it you Americans say? I'd like to plead the fifth on that?'

He's trying to make a joke of it, but I can tell that having a slew of his exes here isn't something he's looking forward to. I wonder what went wrong with the relationships. Were they as short-lived and casual as the online gossip rags claimed all his 'relationships' are? Or did he actually feel something for these women, and now they're going to be shoved in his face all weekend?

I realize that even considering the possibility that Beckett could have been emotionally involved with a woman means I no longer have him locked quite so firmly in that 'rich asshole' box. I should probably be worried about that, seeing as how my opinion of him is changing so rapidly, and it's not even ten a.m. yet. If I'm not careful, he's going to have the box smashed into tiny pieces, and then . . . No, I don't even want to think about what could happen then. That box is my protection. My chastity belt. The thing that keeps me from traveling down the same miserable road as my mom, and while I know it's not fair, it's something that I've come to rely on around certain types of guys.

But with Beckett . . . It's not what I want, but I'm starting to see that he isn't the type of man that could *ever* be boxed or labeled.

'I need to run downstairs and touch base with the groom quickly,' he says, drawing my gaze back to his handsome face. 'Do you want to come with me?'

I know, from our talk during the drive, that it's one of his younger cousins who's getting married on Sunday in the gardens of the estate.

'Would you mind if I stay here and freshen up instead? I feel like I need to glitz up a bit if I'm going to try to fit in around here.' I'd been expecting a mansion, but Beckett House . . . Yeah, it's like a friggin' palace.

'You don't need to do a thing, Emmy. You're perfect exactly the way you are.'

I give him a *Yeah right* look. 'If that's true, then why the new mini wardrobe?'

'Honestly? I just wanted you to have options. I know you

feel ... forced into this, so whatever choices I can give you while we're here, I'm going to see to it that you have them. But you could wear cut-offs all weekend, and I'd still think you were the most beautiful thing I'd ever seen.'

God, that was ... Yeah, that was pretty perfect.

I swipe my tongue over my lower lip and can't help but smile. 'I'm afraid I left all my cut-offs back at home.'

Heat slides though his gaze, making the blue burn like a summer sky. 'Are they short?'

'The shortest,' I tease in a whisper, leaning forward like I'm sharing a secret. 'I only wear them over my bathing suit.'

'I think the thought of that might give me a heart attack.' He puts his hand over his heart and falls back against the mirror like he's been wounded, making me laugh. Needing to put some distance between us before I find myself doing a hell of a lot more than flirting, I stand up, grab my toiletries bag from my suitcase, and head for the bathroom. As I'm standing in front of the marble countertop, trying not to gawk at how gorgeous it is, I hear the bedroom door close behind him, and a breath of relief slips past my lips.

I really do want a shower – my neck and head are still sore, and the idea of standing under some hot water right now sounds awesome – but the truth is that no matter how I was feeling, I'd still be planning on taking as long in here as I can, in no rush to start socializing with his family. Oddly, though, I end up moving things along a lot more quickly than expected, and I have a bad feeling that I know why. Despite this being the most luxurious bathroom I've ever been in, I'm looking forward to seeing Beckett again, and I shake my head at myself as I step out of the rainfall shower, knowing I'm in trouble.

In addition to the sexy lingerie I'd teased Beckett about, the redhead from Harrods delivered six different dresses, all with matching heels, in a slight range of sizes, since he'd obviously had to make a calculated guess when he'd phoned in the order. As I carefully unpack them all from the bags they'd been delivered in, my body wrapped up in a fluffy white towel and my damp hair draped over one shoulder, my inner fashion addict can't help but swoon. The designer outfits range from sexy casual to sexy evening wear, along with a dress I was told is specifically for the wedding itself, and they're all jaw-droppingly beautiful. They also most likely cost a small fortune, and while I know I'll be nervous while wearing them, I also don't want to embarrass Beckett by not looking the part. After all, I'm standing in a room that has a freaking J.J. Harrison original hanging over the bed. He really is the artist's grandson, and I believe him when he says that I'll have a chance to study Harrison's private collection of paintings. So the least I can do is play the doting girlfriend and dress up in the fancy duds.

I shift from foot to foot, wishing Lola was here to help me decide what I should pick out for today. I would video call her, but she teaches back-to-back Pilates classes on Friday mornings, so I know she's busy. I change my mind about ten different times, and then finally decide on a fifties'-inspired halter top dress with a flared skirt in a deep blue satin, thinking it'll look awesome with Beckett's eyes. I pick out a lacy pair of panties that match, and am just about to drop the towel when I hear the bedroom door start to open. I freeze in shock and embarrassment, and a second later Beckett walks back into the room, his lips twitching with a deliciously wicked smile the instant he spots me beside the bed.

'Jesus Christ, you could knock,' I snap, glaring at him as he closes the door and locks it again.

'I could,' he agrees in a husky drawl, 'but where the fuck would be the fun in that?'

'Don't be an ass,' I say, crossing my arms over my chest. 'You knew I might not be dressed yet.'

He slowly arches one dark eyebrow. 'But we *are* sharing this room, so you had to know that I might come walking back in.'

I scowl because he has a point, but before I can apologize for biting his head off, he shoves his battered hand back through his thick hair and drops into the chair that I'd been sitting in earlier. 'I thought I'd be able to stomach it down there without you,' he mutters, 'but I had to get away from them. They're already driving me crazy.'

That I can understand, so I cut him some slack. It seems as little as twenty minutes with the Beckett family is a lot for someone to take, even if you're one of them.

Thinking I'll just put on the lingerie and dress in the privacy of the bathroom, I gather them up in my arms and turn, but freeze again when I hear him suck in a sharp breath.

'What's the ink mean?' he asks, his deep voice little more than a throaty rasp.

I smile as I look at him over my shoulder, surprised by his terminology. 'Maybe it doesn't mean anything. Maybe I just thought it was pretty.'

He studies the array of small, black birds flying from one side of my upper back to the other for a moment, then slowly lifts his smoldering gaze back to mine. 'Any others?'

I shiver from that rough, sexy-as-hell tone of voice he just used, but manage to keep from blushing as I say, 'None that you're seeing, mister.'

His teeth flash in a wide grin as he sprawls back even further in the chair, his long fingers curling over the end of its padded arms. 'Dangerous move, Em. That's like waving a red flag at a bull.'

Not about to be outdone, I say, 'Or throwing blood in shark-infested waters?'

'Or dangling a juicy little bunny over a pit of vipers.'

'Ohmygod, that's awful!' I laugh. 'I give. You win.'

'I usually do,' he says silkily. 'But I have a feeling you're going to make me fight for it.'

I blink, thrown by how powerfully his voice and expression are affecting me. He's so damn sexy I'm practically panting, and he isn't even trying. I mean, I honestly think this is just him being him. Which means I'm so freaking far out of my league with this man. Suddenly *I* feel like the little baby bunny, and he's the beautiful predator getting ready to eat me alive.

When I realize that I was actually just thinking about him *eating* me, I feel my face go hot, and know it's going to be oh-so-obvious to him that he's getting under my skin.

Taking a deep breath, I use everything I've got to sound calm as I say, 'Uh, no. You can trust me when I say that I'm not that kind of girl, Beckett. I don't fight for, or with, guys.'

He gives a masculine snort and smirks. 'Only because you've never needed to.'

'Actually, I'm more of a beta girl. You're *way* too alpha for me.'

He leans forward in the chair, bracing his elbows on his spread knees as he says, 'Bullshit.'

'You have no idea what you're talking about,' I argue, giving him the stink eye. 'You don't know me.'

'I'm learning more every moment I spend with you, Emmy. And I know you sure as hell aren't attracted to wimps.'

'Betas aren't wimps. They just aren't juiced up on testosterone like you alpha beasts are.'

'A little testosterone never hurts, when it comes to certain things,' he states with the cockiest, sexiest freaking smile I've ever seen. I know exactly what 'things' he's referring to, and I decide that retreat is the safest option. Especially seeing as how there's a sharper edge to him at the moment – a kind of contained, volatile tension – and I can't help but wonder what happened when he went downstairs.

'I'm, um, just going to get dressed in the bathroom,' I blurt, already moving toward the door. But his next words stop me in my tracks.

'Or you could stay right where you are and do it in here.'

I peer over at him again, my breath catching at the raw intensity that's burning in those sky-blue eyes as he stares at my bare legs. At the carnal look of hunger on his hard, beautiful face. 'What?' I ask, and I swear my voice has never been so breathless.

His heavy gaze slowly lifts back to my face, locking tight with my startled one. 'I won't touch you. Not yet. So your rules won't be broken. But I want you to drop the towel and show me your body.'

My throat vibrates with emotion, but I don't say anything. I just stand there and stare at him.

'Don't be scared,' he murmurs, stretching out his long legs as he sprawls back in the chair again. 'Just do it.'

His words jolt me out of my freeze and my chin jerks up. 'I'm not scared,' I shoot back, trying to ignore how mouthwatering he looks sitting there like that, with his powerful thighs spread apart and his big, masculine hands locked together behind his dark head, his bulging biceps straining the sleeves of his shirt. And I *know* that if I lower my gaze to his groin, I'll see a hard, thick ridge straining against the denim of his jeans. So I take another deep breath and use every ounce of willpower I possess to stop myself from looking.

'If you're not scared, then let me watch.' His voice is still soft, but it's becoming grittier with every word. 'Rub how fucking lovely you are in my face. We both know damn well that you'll enjoy making me suffer.'

My brows draw together with a frown. 'Now you're just being a dick.'

'Emmy, sweetheart, I'm beginning to think you wouldn't know a dick if it was swinging in your face.'

I know he's just trying to goad me into action, but it's working, because now I'm pissed. Pissed enough to *want* him to suffer a bit, the same as I am. So I walk back to the bed, set down everything in my arms, and drop the towel. He curses something guttural under his breath, but I pretend like I can't feel the searing intensity of his stare burning against my naked body as I start to dress. Pretend I can't hear the way his breaths deepen and become rougher, or the second gritty curse on his lips that sounds like he's desperate. For *me*.

I can't control the way I'm shivering, my own breaths quietly panting past my trembling lips, but I somehow manage to slip on the blue panties without stumbling, then step into the dress, my nipples hard, tight buds as I lift the bodice over my chest and fasten the clasp behind my neck. Then I grab my make-up bag and head back into the bathroom, my mind dazed, body working on autopilot as I apply some light make-up and dry my hair until it's falling in thick waves over my bare shoulders. The whole process doesn't take more than ten minutes, and unless I want to hide in here all day, it's time to walk out and face the music. So I do.

No longer sitting in the chair, Beckett's standing by the dressing table now, taking his phone off the charger, and I see not only from my viewpoint, but also from his reflection in the mirror, that he's changed into a pair of dark, expensive-looking jeans and a gray button-down shirt that's open at the neck, the sleeves rolled up on his masculine, hair-dusted forearms. He's so insanely gorgeous that I start to forget why I should be freaking out – but then he turns around and I lift my gaze to his face, and suddenly it all comes rushing back at me. That handsome face is still tight with lust, his blue eyes dark and hooded, and I swear I can actually *feel* the physical hunger pulsing off every inch of his hard, athletic body.

But all he says is 'Come on,' sounding like he has a throat full of gravel as he watches me slip into an outrageously sexy pair of heels that are weirdly comfortable. 'We're expected downstairs.'

I slip my lip-gloss into the little clutch that matches the dress, then follow him into the hallway, watching as he pulls a key from his pocket and locks the door behind us.

'Why do you have a key to your bedroom?' I ask, thinking it's kind of strange. I mean, it's not like this is a hotel. It's his family home.

His voice is still rough when he says, 'Before I moved out at eighteen, I didn't like leaving my room unlocked.'

I don't say anything in response, but I'm working his words over in my mind as he takes my hand and we make our way down the wide staircase, wondering about his reasons. I'm tempted to just ask him, but we run into a group of people in the foyer, and the next thing I know, Beckett is introducing me to Lottie, the bride, and his cousin Oliver, the groom.

Lottie is lovely and sweet, reminding me of a young Michelle Williams. Her blond hair is short, with stylish bangs that sweep over her forehead, and she's just an inch or so taller than I am, but with a slender figure I would have killed for.

Oliver, on the other hand, has Beckett's same thick, dark hair, only with paler skin and dark brown eyes. He's a few inches shorter than Beckett, and built more like a swimmer, and while I can admit that he's a good-looking guy – in a polished, pampered kind of way – I have no idea what Lottie sees in him, because his personality is so obnoxious I'm forced to bite my tongue to keep from calling him a rude jackass.

I often wonder why it's always the woman who's expected to give up so much for a relationship. Her name. Her independence. Her goddamn soul. It sounds dramatic, I know. But, God, I've seen it happen. And watching Lottie and Oliver, it's like I'm seeing it play out in real time. She starts to tell me about her master's thesis, and he quiets her with a look. When I ask her what her plans are after she graduates from university, he tells her he needs a refill on his gin and tonic, and off she goes. The only thing that keeps me from thinking I've slipped into some twisted fifties' sitcom is that Beckett seems to like his cousin even less than I do.

'Shit,' I hear him suddenly mutter under his breath, and I follow his line of sight to see a tall, brown-haired man with flushed cheeks and glazed eyes walking toward us from the back of the house, a glass in his hand, and a cold, bitter look in his eyes. That look turns colder when he spots us, and I stiffen, an uncomfortable feeling crawling up the back of my neck just as Beckett says, 'Brace yourself, Em. My father looks like he's already wrecked.'

Unlike his wife, Alistair at least has the decency to shake my hand as his son introduces us, though the way he drunkenly leers at my breasts is not only rude, but creepy. Thankfully he doesn't stay for long, but he takes Beckett with him when he goes, saying they need to have a word. They disappear through a door that's just down the wide central hallway leading toward the back of the house, and I find myself left alone with Lottie and Oliver, who is bragging about the new yacht he's bought for himself as a wedding gift. He's just pulled out his phone to show me some photos, when I hear it.

At first, I'm not even sure what the sound is. But then I place the voice, and I realize it's Caroline Beckett screeching like a harpy, and the object of her fury appears to be my weekend date. I know the three of us can all hear her, but Lottie's eyes just get big, and Oliver starts talking a little louder, not wanting to be outdone. The screeching turns into full-fledged scream- ing, and I start to feel ill at the thought of Jase as a beautiful little boy getting yelled at by this bitch.

Unable to fight the impulse, I murmur a quick 'Sorry, but I need to go' to Lottie and a bewildered-looking Oliver, as if he can't believe a woman would actually walk away from him when he's speaking, and hurry toward the hallway. It's easy to find the right door, given how loudly Caroline is shouting, and I don't waste any time opening it and striding into what appears to be a music room. Caroline's eyes nearly bug out of her skull when she sees me, while Alistair frowns before taking another swig of his drink. And Jase . . .

My God. Jase gives me the most tender, breathtaking smile I've ever seen, his sexy-as-hell accent sounding even thicker as he says, 'Emmy, love, have you come to save me?'

Chapter Four

EMMY

'Always,' I reply a bit breathlessly, walking to Jase's side, and as he takes my hand we share a look. One that . . . *Whoa*. In all honesty, it's a look that scares the ever-loving hell out of me.

Before Caroline can get another word out, Jase wraps his arm around my waist and leads me back out into the hallway, shutting the door behind us. I desperately want to ask him what has her so irate, but we're immediately surrounded by a slew of wedding guests who've just arrived. We end up having pastries and coffee with them out on the back terrace that runs the entire length of the house, overlooking stunning gardens that spread out for what seems like acres. I try to remember the names as Jase introduces me to everyone, but it's impossible. All I know is that there are several politicians among the group, an earl and a countess, and then a number of men and women who either seem to be relatives, friends of the family, or people Alistair does business with. But while their professions may vary, it's clear that they're all as rich as Croesus . . . and every single one of them seems to have a tremendous amount of respect for the man standing beside me.

A man who seems proud to introduce me as his 'girlfriend', who includes me in each of his conversations, always paying close attention to what I say, and who can't seem to keep his eyes off me. All of which has me shocked, flustered, and feeling like I'm slipping into dangerous emotional territory, seeing as how we're not actually a couple at all. We're just an aspiring art journalist in need of information, and a wealthy playboy who didn't want a catty date for the weekend.

But, even knowing these things, I'm still falling deeper into lust with the gorgeous Brit with each second that passes by.

Our weird little power play in the bedroom earlier is forgotten, and we spend the rest of the day participating in everything from a hayride and picnic lunch by a beautiful lake, to a hilarious croquet tournament – and what I had thought would be one of the longest days of my life speeds by so quickly I can barely keep up. The final game of croquet goes on for so long that we don't even have time to go up and change before dinner. And while I say game, it was more laughter and goofing around than anything else, with Jase spending more time smacking my ball out of bounds than trying for the hoops, and me quoting lines from *Alice in Wonderland*. When I shouted, 'Off with his head!' it made him laugh and say, 'Baby, you're too hot to be the crazy queen.' At my surprised expression, he admitted to watching the movie a lot when he was a boy, and my freaking heart broke a little as I remembered him mentioning that his mother had died when he was six. If his father had married Caroline while Jase was still only a child, I bet he'd wanted to escape down a rabbit hole just like Alice and get the hell away from this place. I know that's what I'd wanted when I was a little girl, which is one of the reasons I've always loved the movie.

As Jase escorts me into what looks like an actual ballroom, I'm glad that I chose such a pretty dress that morning, seeing as how everyone is done up to the nines. The high-ceilinged room is filled with linen-draped tables and chairs, the golden light twinkling down from the ornate chandeliers making everything, and everyone, look like something from a fairy tale. A quick glance at the seating chart that's displayed near the door gives us our table number, and as we start to weave our way among the seated guests, our good moods linger on. People have continued to arrive throughout the day, and though the room is huge, it's a tight fit with everyone gathered in the same place. By the time we've made it halfway across the room, we're both laughing from the number of times we've had to say 'Excuse me' and 'Pardon me' . . . and even a few instances of 'I'm so sorry for stepping on your foot.'

'We're almost there,' Jase says to me over his shoulder. But when he looks forward again, he stops dead in his tracks and I nearly plow right into his back.

'What's wrong?' I ask, leaning around his side to get a better look at whatever's caused his reaction.

'That crazy bitch,' he curses under his breath.

I study the stunningly beautiful women glaring at us from a nearby table that has two empty seats – obviously ours – and try to figure out who he's talking about. 'Which one?'

'Caroline,' he mutters, now scanning the room. I have no idea what he's looking for, but I'm finally figuring out the problem.

'Let me guess,' I say, giving him a comforting pat on his shoulder. 'She's tried to *Four Weddings and a Funeral* you, hasn't she?'

He turns his head, smiling down at me, those blue eyes so

gorgeous I get a little light headed staring up at them. 'You've lost me,' he says with another soft, rugged laugh.

'You know, the old Hugh Grant movie, where he shows up at wedding number two and finds his table filled with ex-girlfriends.'

'I don't think I've ever seen it –' he takes my arm and starts walking us away from the table, toward the far side of the room – 'but the nightmare sounds right.'

'Let's just find somewhere else to sit,' I suggest, unwilling to let Caroline ruin our night by being such a vicious twat. At least that's what Lola would call her, and I think it definitely fits. Unfortunately, the room *is* packed, and we can't see any other available seats. But Jase has gone out of his way to make sure I had a good time today, and no way in hell am I going to let it end like this. I take a moment to study the room, then get an idea and say, 'Hold tight. I'll be right back.'

'Emmy, wait!' he calls out after me, but I'm already slipping through one of the side doors that the staff are using. It only takes me a moment to find two waiters who are willing to help me, and a minute later they're carrying a small table and two chairs from the terrace into a corner of the ballroom.

'Wanna share a cozy table for two with me?' I ask Jase with a cheeky grin as he comes over, and he takes my hand, lifting it to his smiling mouth.

'I'd like nothing more,' he says against my palm, and I swear the heat of his lips as he presses a kiss to the sensitive flesh shoots straight to my core. It's a wave of heat that has me melting with need, and I let out a shaky breath, hoping the riot in my body isn't blasting across my face like a neon sign.

We take our seats and pretend we're oblivious to the fact that nearly everyone in the teeming ballroom is staring at us. Signaling one of the wait staff, Jase asks me, 'What would you like to drink?'

'Oh, I'm not sure. What are you having?'

'A cola.' My thoughts must show on my face, because he gives a wry laugh. 'You've met Alistair, Em. It can't be that much of a shock that I don't drink much.'

Oh. Wow. I'm surprised . . . but then, I guess I shouldn't be. With each hour that's passed by today, I've learned that this man sitting across from me has deeper layers than I would have ever believed was possible. He might look the part, but he's no one-dimensional, money-hungry player, and I'm ashamed that I tried to peg him as one without knowing a single thing about him. Thinking that I have some issues I clearly need to work through, I tell him, 'Actually, a soda sounds great to me too.'

His brows knit together for a moment, and then he sighs and leans back in his chair. 'Emmy, I'm a grown man. You don't need to worry about me. At least not about this.' A slow, sin-laced grin begins to kick up the corner of his mouth. 'Save me from as many snarling exes and evil stepmothers as you can, but don't worry about drinking if you want to, because you're a grown woman who can make her own choices. If you want a drink, then let me get you one.'

'Oh. Um, sorry,' I whisper, fiddling with my napkin as I feel my face start to heat. Somehow, I feel like I might have insulted him, when I was only trying to be nice.

'Nothing to be sorry for,' he murmurs, the warm tone of his voice helping me to relax. 'Now, what would you really like?'

'A white wine please.'

'You got it,' he says, and as he gives our order to the waiter who comes over, I force myself to take a deep breath and chill. And Jase makes it easy to do as we start talking about casual things, like whether we should have the beef or the chicken, and placing bets on what the wedding song will be. I go with

Ed Sheeran's 'Thinking Out Loud'. It's not one of my favorites of his, but I've heard it's popular at weddings. Jase chooses Pearl Jam's 'Just Breathe', and I'm frustrated I didn't go with that one, since it *is* one of my favorites. But as much as I like Lottie, I feel the lyrics would be wasted on Oliver, and I really hope that Jase is wrong.

'There's something I've been wanting to ask you all day,' I say quietly, as our dessert plates are being carried away. 'What's the story with Lottie and Oliver?'

'What do you mean?' The question is innocent enough, but the guarded look in his dark eyes tells me he knows *exactly* what I'm talking about.

'Come on, Jase. Have you paid any attention to them today? They don't exactly act like two people who are thrilled about tying the knot together.'

'They're smiling,' he points out, tilting his head toward the table where they're sitting with Alistair, Caroline, Oliver's mother and brother, and Lottie's elderly aunt and uncle.

I snort as I shake my head. 'True. But if you think those smiles are genuine – especially Lottie's – then I've got some prime real estate in Florida to sell you. It's, like, totally choice and an awesome investment.'

His head goes back as he laughs out loud, his tanned, corded throat drawing my eye. It's a husky, infectious sound – one that's as sexy as everything else about him – and it attracts a fresh wave of attention to our little corner table for two, the table of exes casting venomous glares our way. I want to warn the poor girls that scowling like that will give them premature wrinkles, but resist the urge, since it would mean having to talk to them. And I plan to avoid that lot the way a vegan avoids a juicy ribeye.

With the meal over, everyone heads outside for drinks on

the terrace, while a string quartet plays down in the garden, the warm night lit by thousands of fairy lights. Caroline Beckett might be a raging bitch, but whoever she hired to plan and decorate for the wedding has done an amazing job.

Stopping at only one glass of wine, I'm about to take my first sip of a steaming caramel cappuccino when a man I haven't seen until now heads our way. After he and Jase exchange what can only be described as a bro-hug, clapping each other hard on the back, Jase introduces the handsome American as Callan Hathaway. I learn that they went to university together at Oxford, and I imagine they had their choice of the girls there, seeing as how they're both drop-dead gorgeous. But whereas Jase is all rugged sophistication, Callan, who lives in New York, looks like he'd be better suited on the back of a Harley, with the wind blowing through his bronze, shaggy hair that has a bit of a curl to it. He wears a thick beard and must be nearly six-five, so about an inch or two taller than Jase, and he's built like a Viking warrior. I should probably be intimidated by the sheer size of him, but his brown eyes are warm and friendly, and he's got a killer smile, as well as a great sense of humor, so it's fun to hang out with him and Jase as they catch up together.

It's a lovely summer night, and the three of us eventually take our drinks to a table in the garden, some of the other guests doing the same, and I can't help but notice that Callan can't keep his eyes off Lottie, who is sitting at a nearby table with her aunt and uncle (they're the only guests here who seem to be hers, other than a few of the bridesmaids). Callan's stare is hot and hungry, as if he'd like nothing more than to strip the soon-to-be bride's slim body of the little black dress she's wearing and get personally acquainted with every inch of her fair skin. But there's also a touch of concern in the way he looks at her, and I wonder if he thinks she's making as big of a mistake as I do. And Jase as well, I suspect, though he still hasn't admitted it.

Just as the wind starts to blow a bit too cool for my liking, Jase and Callan get caught up with some MP his father has brought over to our table, so I excuse myself and head inside. Using one of the downstairs powder rooms, I freshen up my lipstick, make sure my mascara isn't running, and then head back out into the spacious hallway. The door to the room across the way is open, and I can see what looks like walls of books, so I peek inside and find a breathtaking library. It's the kind of place where I could get lost for hours, and I'm wondering how soon I can get Jase to give me a tour when I turn and walk smack into Cameron Beckett.

Ugh. I'd honestly thought Oliver was bad, until I met his older brother. Cameron hadn't arrived until late that afternoon, and as Jase introduced us, I could tell that the tall, well-built, good-looking Brit was jealous as hell of his younger cousin. I know Jase just turned thirty-two a month ago, but Cameron looks closer to forty. It should have lent him some maturity, but he has the cocky swagger of an adolescent. And the way he's smirking down at me has the fine hairs on my skin standing on end.

'Jase normally tires of new pussy within a few hours, but you've lasted a whole day,' he murmurs, standing so close that I can smell the heavy scent of his aftershave and the vodka on his breath. 'That's impressive.'

'Aw, aren't you sweet,' I say, refusing to let this jerk intimidate me.

The corner of his mouth kicks up even higher. 'You're something else, aren't you?'

'And what are *you*, Cameron?'

He gives a gritty laugh, but there's no humor in it. 'What have you heard?'

The ego pulsing off him is insane, but ego I know how to handle. What makes me wary is the darkness lingering behind his sharp smile. This guy has so many secrets inside him, you can see them hiding in his eyes, and I try to sidestep around him, but he latches on to my arms, stopping me in my tracks. His grip is tight enough that I have to fight to keep from letting the discomfort show on my face.

'What in the hell—' I start to snarl, but he cuts me off by hauling me up against him and smashing his mouth over mine. I react on instinct, slamming my knee up into his balls so hard I'm pretty sure he's going to be walking funny for at least a week.

'You stupid little bitch,' he hisses, lowering one hand to cradle his testicles. I have no idea where he's going with this, or why he's doing it, until I see the smile that curls his lips when he slowly turns his head and looks over his shoulder.

'You know,' he drawls, seeming to inflate with victory even as I'm shoving against his shoulders, 'if you were better at pleasing your women, cousin, then they wouldn't have to come begging me for it.'

Oh, *shit*. I instantly understand exactly what this is: an asshole's stupid power play, and he's trying to use me as the pawn!

'Get your goddamn hands off her,' Jase says in a low, menacing voice, and I stomp on Cameron's stupid loafer as I shove against his chest and wrench to my right, peering around him. Jase stands no more than ten feet away, his big hands fisted at his sides, looking like he could easily tear a man apart with them, and I've never been so happy to see anyone in my entire life. His dark eyes burn with a hot, angry glow, his words clipped as he says, 'Don't make me tell you twice, Cam.'

Cameron's chest shakes with another gritty laugh as he releases me, and I take an instinctive step back from him, wanting to get as far away as I can. Then Caroline suddenly comes through one of the doors at Jase's right, her red lips curling in a malicious smile as she takes in the scene. 'What's going on? Is the little American tramp causing problems?'

Jase completely ignores her, his blue eyes locked hard on mine. 'Emmy, come here.'

He doesn't have to tell me twice, either. As I quickly move around Cameron, the idiot says, 'I'm serious, man. She's the one who came on to *me*.'

I reach Jase, and he immediately lifts his hands to my face, studying me, his thumbs gently brushing across my cheeks. Once he's sure that I'm all right, he scowls at his cousin. 'If you'd bothered to talk to her, then you'd know just how fucking stupid this was. You're the last kind of man Emmy would want anything to do with.' His voice is rough with anger, and he cuts a disgusted look from his cousin to Caroline, who he clearly thinks was in on it.

'Since when do women not like rich men?' she asks with a brittle laugh.

Given what he knows about me, I think Jase would probably have a good laugh at that as well, if he weren't so pissed off. But he is. I can feel the fury blasting from his big, powerful body in blistering waves. 'Come near her again,' he warns, 'and you'll both wish to God that you hadn't.'

Then he grabs my hand and tugs me along with him as he heads toward the front of the house.

'Are you really okay?' he asks, the second we're out of the back hallway. 'He didn't hurt you, did he?'

The concern in his deep voice makes me sigh with relief, but I still don't want him having the wrong idea. 'Jase, that was—'

'Not your idea,' he cuts in, sounding pissed again. 'Trust me, Em, I know. The idiot tried to set us up, but he wasn't smart enough to do his research first.'

'He grabbed me before I could get around him.'

He pops his jaw a few times, and I can tell that he's trying hard to retain control of his temper. 'Did he hurt you?' he asks again, sounding like he's having to force the words through his gritted teeth.

I shake my head, stumbling a bit to keep up with him. 'No, I'm fine. Really. But can you slow down a little?'

'Shit, I'm sorry.' He slows his pace, his chest rising and falling with a harsh breath. 'I'm just trying to put some distance between us and him. It's taking everything I've got not to go back there and beat his damn face in, family wedding or not.'

'He isn't worth it,' I tell him, curling my free hand around the tense one he's using to hold mine. 'Just forget him.'

He blows out another jagged breath, then slants me a tight smile. 'You nailed him in the balls so hard he was still green when I got there.'

I raise my brows. 'Maybe you should remember that the next time you tick me off,' I tease, hoping to make him laugh. When his chest shakes with a quiet rumble of amusement, I smile, letting him pull me up the wide staircase to the first floor, the sounds of the wedding guests fading to a distant murmur.

When we reach his bedroom, Jase locks the door behind us and heads straight to an antique bureau that houses a mini-bar. As he pours a drink, I wonder if he's so angry he's decided he needs to knock one back, but he turns and holds the tumbler out to me.

'What is this?' I ask, frowning down at the amber-colored, strong-smelling alcohol as I take the glass.

'Whiskey.'

My lips quirk as I lift my gaze back to his. 'Jase, I'm really not much of a drinker. Something this strong will probably kill me.'

'You're shivering,' he grates, his expression tight as he crosses his arms over his chest and jerks his chin at the glass. 'It'll help.'

I don't realize until he says it that I am literally shaking in my heels, my limbs vibrating with a fine tremor.

'I'm not upset,' I tell him. 'It's just leftover adrenaline.' But I still do as he says and down the whiskey in one quick swallow. I manage to take a deep breath without coughing it all back up, though it burns like a bastard. As I set the glass on the small table that sits beside the chair, I feel the warmth hit my system, and it's nice – but my body and thoughts are caught up in a maelstrom of conflicting emotions, and the next thing I know, I'm saying, 'He kissed me. That's when I kneed him in the nuts.'

'That son of a bitch,' he growls, curling his battered right hand into a hard fist. 'I should've smashed his fucking teeth in.'

'No.' I grab his hand with both of mine and pull it to my mouth. 'Your hand has already had enough abuse because of me.' And then I kiss his bruised knuckles, and his breath sucks in with a sharp hiss that sounds like a cannon in the quiet stillness of the room.

Oh, God. *What am I doing?* Slowly, I lift my head, looking up at him, and his dark eyes are volcanic blue in that breathtaking face, scorching and hot. 'Jase,' I whisper, and we each lunge for the other, grabbing and tugging, our bodies slamming together as he fists his hand in my hair and yanks my head back. He leans down, and then that beautiful, delicious mouth of his is on mine, kissing me like he needs to draw sustenance from my body – like I'm the next freaking breath in his lungs – and I love it. He only just started giving me what he's giving me, and I'm already helplessly hooked on it. Already craving it like a junkie with her fix.

His free hand slides down my back, curving around my ass

and pulling me tight against his rigid length as his tongue slides along mine, the taste and feel of him so damn addictive that I realize my nails are digging into his shoulders, trying to keep him right where he is. Then he moves both hands down to my thighs, hoisting me up as I wrap my legs around his lean hips, and I shove my hands into his silky hair as he carries me to the side of the bed, our mouths never once separating. Leaning over, he lays me down on the cashmere-covered duvet, my thighs automatically spreading even wider for him as he comes down between them, covering me with that rugged, powerful body.

My dress is bunched up around my waist, crinkling between us, and I couldn't care less. All that matters is keeping his mouth on mine, but he pulls away as he braces himself over me on his muscular forearms, and he's breathing hard as he stares down at me with that hooded, blistering gaze. Between my legs, his cock is diamond-hard and thick, and his hips give a deliberate roll that rubs him against my slick, lace-covered pussy, making us both moan like we're in pain. But it's just a raw, dark pleasure, and I put my hands behind his neck and pull him back down to me, turning my head so that I can press my lips against the rasp of dark stubble on his jaw, nipping it with my teeth.

He makes a purely savage sound in the back of his throat, and then his hungry mouth is back on mine as he thrusts against me, and I'm so desperate for him that I mewl. I freaking mewl! Who in the hell mewls?

Any woman who finds herself lucky enough to be under Jasper Beckett, a voice drawls in my head, and I almost laugh. If that's my inner wild woman, she sure as hell took her sweet time making an appearance. I mean, I'm twenty-four, for crying out loud. Or maybe she's been hibernating beneath a layer of ice all these years, and it's taken this incredible man lying on top of me to thaw her out.

Through the roar of my pulse in my ears and our ragged, panting breaths, I swear I hear a sound at the door, and then someone calls out Caroline's name, and I wonder if that crazy bitch is out there in the hallway listening to us. I turn my head to break our kiss, thinking I need to say something about it, but Jase dips his head, nipping at one of my tight nipples through the bodice of my dress at the same time he pulses his hips again, grinding his rock-hard cock against that perfect spot, and I detonate. My sweet little old grandma from Georgia could be out there in the hallway listening, and I still wouldn't be able to control the sharp, keening cry that breaks from my lips as I come for him. He growls as he feels me shatter, grinding against my clit even harder, his open mouth buried against the side of my neck, his hot breaths pelting across my sensitive skin while I writhe and moan, half-thrilled and half-terrified by what I *know* is going to come next.

Me. Him. And his massive cock buried so deep inside me I'll probably be able to feel him pounding against my heart. Only, my heart's hammering so hard right now I think it might burst from my chest.

I'm all harsh gasps and urgent hunger at the thought of how amazing it's going to be – but I'm also shaking apart inside, because I have no idea how it's going to affect me emotionally. Still, what's happened up to this point has been more breathtaking than anything I could have ever imagined, and as Jase reaches down, twists the side of my panties around his fingers, and starts to slowly pull them over my hips, I know I'm not going to call a halt.

But then he lifts his head, sees the look on my face, and *stops*.

One second bleeds into two . . . three . . . four, and when he just keeps staring down at me with that heavy, smoldering gaze, I start to get the feeling that he isn't ever going to start again, and all I can manage to force past my trembling lips is 'W-why?'

'You.'

That's all he says, and I'm so confused I feel like I've got another concussion. 'Me? What about me?'

'I want you so bad it's killing me,' he scrapes out, and I swear I feel those husky words all the way down in my soul. 'But you're not ready, Em. You're not ready for *this*.'

I open my mouth, prepared to argue, because what I definitely don't need is him making decisions for me. Heck, at this point, I might even beg a little. But . . . damn it, he's right. I'm *not* ready. Not completely. Not yet.

His mouth curves with one of those sexy, crooked smiles that never fail to melt me down, only this one has an unmistakable edge of sadness to it that nearly tears me apart – and without another word, he pushes back to his feet, reaches down to rearrange the thick erection that's trapped inside his jeans, and walks out the door.

He leaves!

Suddenly I'm alone in the room, sprawled in the middle of the bed with an expensive dress crushed around my midriff, in a lacy pair of panties that are drenched with my cum, listening to him locking the door behind him.

I'm fucking alone, with nothing but need and regret for company.

God, I've only known this man for a day, and already I'm a wreck. Is that why I had such a visceral reaction – of attraction as well as fear – when I saw him on the Tube? Did I know, on some instinctual level, that Jasper Beckett would get so deep under my skin it would throw my life into chaos? That he would hold so much power over me? *Enthrall* me?

Rolling over, I look up and see my phone sitting on the bedside table, and I quickly reach for it, needing something to do. *Anything* to get my head in a different place than the one it's in now, because I'm freaking out here.

But instead of a distraction, I find myself texting Tyler the kind of message that I've never imagined I would send.

I've met a guy, and he's . . .

I pause, thumbs poised over the keypad, trying to think of a fitting adjective. *Gorgeous. Funny. Smart. Cocky.* Or one of Tyler's personal favorites: *So fit you could bounce a quarter off his mouthwatering abs.*

But the one word I really want to be able to write, but can't, because it will never, ever be true, is *Mine.*

Chapter Five

Saturday morning

JASE

I'm just coming in from my morning run when I see it: Oliver and one of Lottie's bridesmaids sucking each other's faces off in the doorway of what must be the girl's room. It's obvious that he's spent the night with her, which makes her the second woman I've found him with this weekend, and neither one of them is the one he's marrying tomorrow.

When I went downstairs yesterday to touch base with the dickhead after Emmy and I arrived, I found him banging the eighteen-year-old daughter of one of Alistair's business associates in the library, of all places. And just like yesterday, Olly smirks when he turns his head and spots me, not at all embarrassed to be caught out, and I lose it. Before he even knows it's coming, I have my hand fisted in the front of his wrinkled shirt and I smack him against the hallway wall. The girl shrieks and quickly slams the door to her room, obviously not wanting to get involved. Or maybe the scowl I'm wearing has made her think twice about standing up for him.

I get right in the prick's face, which is a mistake since his breath smells like stale whiskey, cigarettes and God only knows what else. 'What the hell are you doing?' I growl. 'You're meant to be getting married tomorrow.'

He looks at me as if I've lost my mind. 'So? If Lottie thinks I'm not dipping my wick in hot pussy whenever I get the chance, then she's dumber than she looks.'

What the ever-loving fuck? I'm seething, and it takes every bit of self-control I have to release him and take a step back, my hands curling into heavy fists at my sides. 'If that's how it is, then why are you marrying her?'

'Why?' A bitter laugh jerks from his chest. 'Because my mother's a cunt.'

'Jesus,' I breathe, embarrassed that I'm related to this idiot.

'She's threatened to cut me off if I don't tie the knot. So I needed a wife, and Lottie needed . . . Hell, who knows? I've got a prenup that keeps her from getting jack if she tries to divorce me, so I have no idea why she's going through with it.'

'Did you ever think that she's in love with you?'

His laugh is so obnoxious it makes me grit my teeth. 'She's stupid, but not *that* stupid,' he says, and then a smarmy smile curves his lips. 'Between you and me, I think she just likes my dick.'

'She's a sweet girl,' I mutter with disgust. 'She doesn't deserve this.'

'Christ, Jase. Since when did you become such a bloody boy scout?'

I turn my back on him, any tension I'd managed to burn off during my twelve-mile run now back tenfold. Striding into the gym, where I left my kit bag before heading out, I jerk my chin at Callan, who's bench-pressing what looks like nearly two hundred and fifty pounds. The guy's a beast, and I wonder if he's lifting to burn off his own mountain of tension. 'Bad morning?' he asks, reaching back and racking the weights.

I work my jaw a few times before saying, 'My cousin's a knobhead.'

Callan sits up and grabs his towel, wiping it over his sweaty face. 'Which one?'

'Both,' I admit with a humorless laugh, thinking we Becketts are a real winning family. 'But Oliver is the one I was just dealing with.'

'Yeah,' he snorts, looking as though he thinks about as highly of ol' Olly as I do. 'He's a dickless little shit.'

I grunt my agreement, dropping down on to a nearby bench that's pressed against the wall. 'How did you get roped into this gig anyway? Weddings don't really seem your style.'

'My mom. She can't make the flight anymore, but was determined that the Hathaway family got represented. Don't know why she cares about that kind of thing, but I couldn't tell her no.'

'Yeah,' I murmur, though I really have no idea how to relate. Callan's got six brothers and sisters, and they're all not only tight with each other, but with their mother as well. It's the kind of family I was always jealous of as a kid, then grew up and doubted they even really existed. That is, until my father started doing business with Hathaway International, right around the time I met Callan at Oxford.

'So the girl you're with,' he just drops out there, lifting his brows as if he's waiting for me to answer some unspoken question.

'What about her?' I'm trying to play it cool, but I must ask the question a little too aggressively, because the shit starts grinning at me.

'I'm just saying that she's something else, man. Gorgeous, smart, funny. And *real*. Definitely not your usual type.'

What the fuck? 'I don't have a *type*,' I argue, sharply aware of the fact that I don't like the way my friend is singing Emmy's praises. I know she's all of those things, damn it. I just don't like other men noticing. And definitely not ones who look like Callan.

'Sure you do. Every chick you dated at school, and since, was beautiful, but . . . cold. I've never known you to be with someone so warm and genuine.'

I narrow my eyes at him. 'What the hell do you know about how warm she is?'

He looks like he's trying hard not to laugh. 'I'm talking about her personality, dickhead.'

'Jesus,' I mutter, getting more irritated – and more uneasy – by the second. 'You sound like a daytime talk show.'

He laughs as he moves to his feet, tossing the towel over his tattooed shoulder. 'Just take some friendly advice and try to hold on to this one. She's not the kind of girl guys like us usually get a shot with. So show some bloody gratitude, as you Brits say, and don't screw it up.'

With those unexpectedly philosophical words, Callan turns and heads for the showers. When he comes out minutes later, I'm still sitting there on my arse, stewing in my sweat, and he just shakes his head at me and laughs again. Fucking idiot. He knows damn well that he's messed with my head, and with a rough sound of frustration crawling up the back of my throat, I force myself up and make my way into the showers.

I'm so damn tempted to go back up to my room and shower there, but know that if I get within ten feet of Emmy, I'm going to be all over her. And since she's not going to be any readier for that this morning than she was last night, I suck it up and make the water as cold as possible.

After I'd spent a good hour last night just walking the grounds of the estate, focused on getting my control back, I'd finally gone back up to the room. She'd been sound asleep, all that golden hair spread out over her pillow, and I hadn't been able to resist. Stripping down to my boxers, I'd climbed into bed beside her and pulled her into my arms, holding her close. She'd stirred, but didn't wake up, snuggling even tighter against me, and I'd buried my nose in her silken hair, trying to quiet the chaos in my head while ignoring the need in my body, until I'd eventually drifted off to sleep.

Surprisingly, it'd turned out to be one of the best nights of sleep that I've had in years. But I'd woken at six with my arms still holding her plastered against me . . . and a hard-on that could have hammered a nail through a wall, and knew I had to get out of there.

Gritting my teeth against the icy blast of the shower, I try not to think about how sweet her mouth is, or how perfect her soft body felt beneath mine, even with our clothes still on. Hell, even the memory of goofing off with her in the garden yesterday has my pulse surging. Every time the wind had blown the thick waves of her hair to the side and I'd seen those beautiful birds in flight across her shoulders, I'd been a bit stunned by how hot I found it. I wanted the time to study them at my leisure. Wanted to explore the intricate design I'd seen inked into her right hip when she'd let her towel drop to the floor, damn near bringing me to my knees. Wanted to taste those swirling stars and moons with my tongue – and then get personally acquainted with every other sensual, mouthwatering inch of her.

Emmy Reed could twist me around her little finger so fucking easily, and I'd probably have a smile on my face the entire time. Christ, she even makes being in this house, which I've hated since the day I found my mother's body swinging from the ceiling fan in my playroom, tolerable. Even just knowing she's here, cuddled up in that big bed in my room, looking like a wet dream, is enough to make me happier than I've been in a hell of a long time. But the feeling immediately slips when I walk out of the gym ten minutes later, dressed in the clean set of clothes I'd had in my bag, and see my father and Cameron talking at the end of the hallway. Their heads are close together, and God only knows what they're discussing. Cameron works at my father's investment firm, so it could be work related. But I'm more inclined to think they're planning on how to tag team one or more of the bridesmaids.

My old man's been about as faithful to Caroline as she's been to him, and I've heard rumors that he and Cameron like to hit the more popular gentlemen's clubs in the city together. It probably makes Alistair feel younger to have Cameron by his side, and Cam no doubt enjoys the way people kiss his arse when he's with someone whose pockets are as deep as my father's. Even though my Aunt Simone, Oliver and Cameron's mother, inherited a good portion of the Beckett fortune when Alistair's younger brother died, it's nowhere close to the wealth that my old man inherited as the oldest son. And there's no one more motivated by money than my cousin.

I might like to keep my emotions close to my chest, but there are times when I could swear Cam doesn't even have any. He's the coldest bastard I've ever known, and as I hoist my kit bag higher on to my shoulder, I can't help but think about what Callan had said – because he was right. Despite her sometimes prickly attitude, I've honestly never known anyone as real and as warm as Emmy, and right now I just want to crawl back into bed with her, wrap myself around her, and hold on as tight as I can, until some of that heat melts into me.

Damn it. I *can't* stay away.

Lengthening my strides, I jerk my chin at my father and Cam without uttering a word, and keep heading toward the front of the house. With my thoughts focused hard on Emmy, I'm not really paying attention to my surroundings as I turn into the front foyer, until I nearly run smack into the last person that I want to see: *Fucking Stepmother Dearest*. And from the sinister gleam in her eye, I can tell just how much she's looking forward to playing the part.

Shit, I think, realizing that I really am a stupid idiot. Because a smart man wouldn't be in this situation.

No, a smart man would've started the day off right . . . lying in bed with a bright-eyed, Southern-sounding, beautiful little American.

And he'd have done whatever it took to stay there.

Chapter Six

EMMY

I wake up alone in the luxurious bed, and I groan, still feeling the sting from last night's . . . God, I don't even know what to call it. My body is on edge, skin all tingly and warm. I feel like I'm vibing with energy, and my thoughts are flying a thousand miles a minute, wondering where Jase is and what he's doing.

Not to mention where he slept last night.

I shower quickly, dry my hair, and then spend a good ten minutes staring into the wardrobe. From talking to Lottie, I know there are some formal activities today, like the ceremony rehearsal and a luncheon in the wedding marquee that's being set up in the gardens, so I choose a white, sleeveless swing dress with a floral design at the neckline and hem, since it's both classic and comfortable. I keep my make-up summery, with a slick of nude gloss, and pull my hair up in a high, hopefully stylish messy bun. Hair has never been my strongpoint, but Lola's been trying to teach me some new styles, and given that it's meant to be another warm day, it'll feel good to have my hair off my shoulders.

I can unlock the bedroom door from the inside, but I search both top drawers in the bedside tables and luckily find a spare key, enabling me to lock it behind me. Taking a deep breath, since there's no telling what or whom I'm going to encounter when I head downstairs, I start off with a purposeful stride. But I'm not even to the bottom of the sweeping staircase yet when I hear Caroline yelling Jase's name, and I nearly stumble in shock. She sounds enraged, and given how much ass she was kissing yesterday among the guests, I'm surprised that she would create such an audible scene when so many people are here now.

They're in the front sitting room, but even with the door closed, I can clearly make out her words as she rants about everything from my embarrassing presence (yeah, this lady is definitely a bitch), to how she was mortified to learn just last night that Jase is personally funding the construction of several shelters for homeless teens across London. As I'm nearing the door, intent on getting him out of there, I hear Jase tell her that when it comes to class, I could 'wipe the bloody floor with her', and warmth unfurls in my chest like a sun, making me smile. Then it quickly freezes when she shouts, 'You're as unstable and selfish as your psycho mother was, throwing your time and money away on trash!'

What. The. Hell? Snarling like a mama bear, I start to reach for the door, when someone comes up behind me, and I instantly recognize the voice as they say, 'He'll eat you up and spit out the pieces. You do know that, right?'

'Cameron, I'm going to be as nice as possible here and simply say *Get lost.*'

'Excuse me?'

I look at him over my shoulder. 'I think you heard me pretty clearly. Go the fuck away.'

He doesn't move – just gives me this strange, chilling smile that makes me want to put some distance between us. And, yeah, I really want Jase out of that freaking room, so I reach for the door handle.

'Ohmygod!' Caroline gasps as I open the door and step inside. 'Were you eavesdropping again?'

Seriously? *That* from the woman who was probably listening to Jase give me an orgasm last night. 'Caroline,' I sigh, fighting the urge to roll my eyes, 'I can't help it if you screech so loudly the entire house can hear you. And for the record, it sounds like what Jase is doing for those kids is awesome. So why don't you stick your shitty attitude back up your ass and leave him alone?'

She glares at me while turning an interesting shade of red, and I have a feeling she might actually come at me. But then Jase puts his arm around my waist and pulls me into his side – which, I must admit, is an incredible place to be – and Alistair, who I hadn't even realized was in the room with them, grabs Caroline's arm, holding her back as Jase and I make our escape.

Whew, I think. *Way to start the day off with a bang.*

Jase shuts the door behind us, then sets down the gym bag he's carrying, and I'm relieved that his cousin is nowhere to be seen in the foyer. As I tilt my head back to look up at him, I find that his blue gaze is taking me in from head to toe, and my pulse starts pounding. 'Thanks for rescuing me again,' he husks, locking those molten blue eyes with mine as I try not to visibly melt.

'No thanks necessary,' I say a little too breathlessly – but it can't be helped, because holy freaking hell am I breathless. The guy's looking at me like he wants to eat me alive, and the last time I saw him I'd been coming so hard I'd nearly blacked out. 'I'm just sorry I didn't get here sooner. That, uh, didn't exactly sound like a lot of fun in there.'

A wry smile lifts the edge of his mouth, and he lowers his head a bit, rubbing at the back of his neck, which is probably knotted with tension. 'Yeah, it's always a good time around here.'

'So, are you really building a bunch of shelters for homeless teens?'

'Something like that,' he hedges, clearly not wanting to talk about it. I have a feeling that could be because of me, and the fact that he knows how I feel about guys with a shitload of money. I'm ashamed for making so many early assumptions about him, and I know this is something I need to think about and try to change. Because that's not the kind of person I want to be.

Wetting my lips, I give him an earnest look. 'I meant what I said in there, Jase. I think it's amazing that you're able to do what you're doing for those kids.'

'Yeah?' he asks, looking a bit skeptical. 'I thought you hated that I have money.'

I can't help but wince. 'I know I'm messed up when it comes to wealth – but you're honestly not anything like what I thought. So I'm sorry, and it was wrong of me to judge you because you're . . . you know, loaded.'

'What I have, I worked my arse off for. I didn't fuck anyone over to get it, and I try to do what I can for those who aren't as fortunate as I've been,' he tells me in a low voice, shifting a little closer to me, his blue eyes dark and burning. 'But don't let the "good guy" act fool you, Em. I've been trying to get you on your back, so I've done my charming routine. But at the end of the day, I'm probably just as much of a prick as my dad and Cameron and every other rich bastard you've ever known.'

I want to ask him if he's trying to scare me off, and if so, why. Has he let Caroline's comment about his mom get to him? Or is it last night, and the fact that we had to basically make-out like a couple of teens because he promised me he'd keep his dick in his pants? 'I can't say I find you particularly charming,' I end up murmuring, keeping my questions to myself, 'but I do know that you are nothing like your father or Cameron.'

Another wry smile tugs at the corner of his mouth. 'Not charming?'

'More like a bulldozer,' I joke. 'You plow right through everything in your path.'

His dark eyes start to gleam. 'I wouldn't mind plow—'

I cover his mouth with my fingers, already laughing. 'Don't you dare say it!'

His brows lift, and he tickles my fingers with his tongue. I gasp as I jump back, my fingers curling into my palm, and he gives a deliciously low, sexy laugh. 'You afraid of my tongue, Emmy?'

'Uh, no,' I reply, rubbing my hands over my upper arms as lust coils thick and deep in my belly. 'Fear is definitely *not* the emotion I feel when I think of your, um, tongue.'

His gaze sharpens, and I can tell that I've surprised him again. 'You always say exactly what you're thinking, don't you?'

'My worst flaw,' I admit with a shrug. And a lie, since I've managed to keep from spouting off about the raging level of lust he inspires in me. Well, for the most part.

'I can't agree, Em. I think it's incredible.'

I'm wearing what is undoubtedly a dazed expression as I stare up into that gorgeous face of his. 'You know, Mr Beckett, you're not at all what I expected.'

'Miss Reed,' he murmurs huskily, 'I didn't even know a woman like you could exist.'

I blush so hard it makes him laugh, and my freaking knees nearly give out when he leans down and brushes the softest kiss I've ever had over my left cheek. My throat is thrumming with emotion, and before I can manage to say anything, we're joined by Lottie and a group of guests who are coming through the front door from a trip to the local historic village. Jase quickly runs his gym bag up to his room, and then we join them all for coffee and breakfast out on the terrace, and the rest of the day is spent rushing from one pre-wedding event to the other. It's hectic and tiring, but Jase stays by my side, making sure that I'm having fun. I think there's an element of protection to his presence as well, since he keeps me away from Caroline and Cameron. But I also get the sense that he simply enjoys my company, and it's making me feel all kinds of warm and fuzzy inside.

God, I'm being such a girl! Not that I'm not always, you know, a girl. But he's making me act girlie in a way that I never have before, probably because I've never had this kind of crush on another human being. Never even close. Even the guy I gave my virginity to was more of a good friend than anything else. And now look at me! I'm practically a drooling, hormonal mess, and I know that if Tyler were here, he'd be teasing me so hard right now. Well, when he wasn't busy flirting his ass off with Callan and Jase.

Jase . . . Wow. I'm not sure when I started thinking of him by his first name, rather than as Beckett. Probably around the time I was lying underneath him, my nipple in his mouth and his cock grinding against my pussy, while I came for him so hard I screamed.

No . . . it was before that. I keep thinking back, and realize it was after the first time I 'rescued' him from Caroline's ranting, which I guess makes sense. I mean, that scene was unpleasant, but it opened my eyes to the fact that his life, while blessed, is hardly perfect.

As a good portion of the guests gather on the terrace in the early evening for pre-dinner drinks, I get caught up helping

Lottie look over some possible *thank you* gifts on her phone, so Jase gives us a moment and goes over to talk to Callan and another man, who are standing by the back entrance to the house. I enjoy getting a chance to chat with Lottie, and when she says something that makes me laugh, I happen to glance over in Jase's direction, and find him looking right at me. He's not even trying to hide the fact that his attention is focused completely on *me*, and if the men are giving him a hard time about the way he's ignoring them, he doesn't let it show. He just keeps watching me, the hunger in his eyes so freaking hot I have to take a long swallow of my iced water. Then he lifts his hand and rubs it across his mouth, like he's struggling for control, and I can feel the panties I'd slipped on that morning getting seriously wet.

Needing something to do before I make an idiot of myself and run over there, throwing myself in his arms and begging him to fuck me, I tell Lottie that I'll grab us a pitcher of Pimm's and stand up, weaving through the tables that are filled with other guests. I smile and nod at a few people whom Jase has introduced me to, and am just about to reach the refreshments table, where dozens of pitchers have been set out, when I feel something icy and cold hit my back. I gasp, spinning, trying to find the source, and come face-to-face with one of Jase's exes. The woman gives me big, innocent eyes, and whispers 'Oops' like it was an accident that she just dumped her entire glass of Pimm's down my back, but I know it's bullshit. I can see the truth in the twitch of her lips, her friends who are still sitting at her table all snickering under their breath, and it takes everything I have to keep from slapping this bitch into next Tuesday.

Gritting my teeth, I peer around her and catch Lottie's eye. She looks horrified and is already on her feet, but I shake my head, silently telling her to stay out of it. Then I turn my back on Jase's catty ex and start heading for the smaller entrance that's located at the far end of the terrace. Just as I step inside the house, Jase catches up to me, and I throw him a warning glare over my shoulder when he suddenly gives a sharp crack of laughter.

'You think this is funny?' I snap, hoping like hell that I'm not about to walk into anything since I'm still trying to put some distance between me and that ... that ... *twat*! 'Whoever that was, she did this on purpose!'

'I'm sorry, Em. She's vile and horrible and I'm ashamed that I ever got within ten feet of her.' I look forward again, fighting the urge to turn around and kick him, since the jerk is still laughing. 'But I can see straight through your dress now, and I'm digging the *Star Wars* knickers.'

'Ohmygod!' I sputter, jerking to a stop in the middle of the hallway as I reach back to plaster my hands over my wet bottom, which makes Jase laugh even harder.

'So,' he says, when he's finally able to get control of himself, 'I take it you're a *Star Wars* fan, yeah?'

His deep-grooved grin is impossibly beautiful, his humor infectious, and despite my embarrassment, my lips start to twitch. 'I am,' I tell him. 'But the panties were a gag gift from Tyler.'

The change in his expression is so swift it makes me blink. 'Who the hell is Tyler?'

I start walking again before I answer his question. 'He's my best friend. And you don't need to pretend to be jealous, even though he's outrageously hot, because he's even more into men than I am. The more alpha they are, the more he loves them.'

'Ah. He, uh, sounds like an excellent judge of character then.'

'He's awesome,' I murmur, and it's easy to smile as I say the words because they're true. Tyler is the freaking bomb.

'And who says I'm pretending to be jealous?' he asks, walking beside me as we enter the foyer. 'The idea of you with another man makes me insane.'

Since I have no idea what to say to *that*, I keep my mouth shut as we make our way up the stairs. There's another formal dinner in an hour, and I can't wait to hop into a warm shower before I get dressed in something appropriate for tonight.

As he shuts and locks the bedroom door behind us, my gaze lands on the Harrison painting hanging over the bed, and I'm stunned to realize I haven't thought about my article in hours. I know Jase will uphold his end of our bargain, but I'm anxious to see the collection. I have a feeling, though, that he's going to keep me waiting, worried I might say 'Enough' to this madness and get the hell out once I've gotten what I came for.

Yeah, after what just happened out on the terrace, I wouldn't be at all surprised if that's what he's thinking.

'I'm going to jump in a quick shower,' I say, heading for the bathroom without even looking at him. I'm feeling drained and just need a few moments of quiet to get my head sorted out again. Plus, I really want out of this damn wet dress.

Fifteen minutes later, I come out wrapped in one of the extra-large towels, basically looking like I'm wearing a blanket. Jase gives me a crooked grin, then heads into the bathroom for a shower himself, so I use the time to quickly slip into one of the new silk-and-lace lingerie sets from Harrods, along with a little matching black silk robe, not wanting to put on the dress I've chosen for tonight until I've done my make-up.

I'm just finishing another messy top bun, using the mirror over the dressing table to make sure I've got it right, when Jase comes out in nothing but a small white towel that's wrapped around his lean waist, beads of water still clinging to his sculpted chest and abs, and I feel like the floor has just been ripped right out from under me. I even have to brace a freaking hand against the table!

As he strides toward the wardrobe, I watch the fascinating shift of powerful muscle beneath his sleek, olive-toned skin, his body even more mouthwatering than I'd imagined. I also notice that his cock is creating an interesting bulge under the towel, and I can't help but stare. I mean, it's a *big* freaking bulge, so staring kinda seems appropriate. Then he turns, opens one of the wardrobe's doors, and whips the towel right off – and instead of playing it cool, I let out an audible gasp at the sight of his tight, muscular ass, completely giving away the fact that I'm ogling him.

Mortified, I force myself to turn around and focus on finishing my mascara, though my hand is shaking so badly I nearly blind myself. My heart is pounding, thoughts scattering like a few brain cells might have just been fried, and I find myself blurting out the first question that comes to mind. 'Where did you sleep last night?' I ask in a hoarse, breathless rush.

'Why? Jealous?'

'Yes,' I admit a little shakily, setting the mascara down before I turn around.

Dressed in a pair of dark gray trousers, a blue shirt the color of his eyes hanging open over his chest, he turns to face me, and all traces of humor on his gorgeous face have vanished. He looks . . . *starved*, and I realize too late that my admission was like waving that proverbial red flag. My eyes go wide, the sexual tension between us so intense I feel it like a physical thing brushing and crackling against my skin – and I watch as he pulls in a deep breath, then slowly exhales, as if he's trying to find a measure of control. But it doesn't work, and before I can so much as blink, he starts coming toward me, all those hard, rugged muscles moving under his skin, and he's so beautiful it's unreal. So ripped and raw and masculine, I feel like I might orgasm just looking at him.

When he reaches me, his eyes crinkle sexily at the corners as he stares down into my face, and he smiles just a little. Just enough that it makes me want to let him do whatever the hell he wants to me.

'Kiss me,' he husks, not even touching me, and I'm suddenly terrified because I *know* that this man could get under my skin in a way that can't be undone. In a way that will follow me forever, no matter how many miles of ocean and land lie between us.

'I . . . I can't.' *If I do, I'll be lost.*

Another hard, deep breath lifts his chest. 'Christ, Em. Just kiss me, sweetheart.'

'Jase,' I whisper, and I wonder if he can read everything going on inside my head right now on my face, because the way he looks at me . . . God, no man has ever looked at me like that before. Like he *knows* me – body, heart, and soul. It's something that I never would have expected from such a hardcore alpha, and I want so desperately to give in, but the last thing I want to be here is a tease. 'We . . . we can't keep messing around. It isn't fair to you if it isn't going any further than . . . you know. Than what we did last night.'

The laugh that falls from his lips is so freaking sexy it makes me feel a little light headed. 'When it comes to my dick, why don't you let me decide what's fair and what's not?'

I swallow, shaking, knowing damn well that I'm in over my head here. And then he says, 'Last night, I walked around the gardens for about an hour, came back, crawled into bed with you, and held you till morning.'

At those quietly spoken words, I can't *not* throw myself at him. So I do, and he catches me like it's what he was born for. As my legs and arms wrap around him, Jase moves one hand down to my ass, the other curling around the back of my neck, and he tugs me toward him as he lowers his head, our mouths coming together in a hot, open-mouthed kiss that bypasses gentle and shoots straight into raw and explicit. I'm so lost in the pleasure of it that I don't even realize he's carried me across the room until he lays me down on the edge of the bed. Then the breathtaking kiss ends as he braces himself over me on a straight arm, his shirt hanging open to reveal his incredible torso, and I reach up to grab each side of the fabric, buttons digging into my left hand as I arch my back and gasp – because Jase has just shoved his other hand straight down the front of my black lace panties.

Ohmygod!

With his blistering gaze locked tight on my face, he doesn't waste any time, his thumb rolling across my sensitive clit as he shoves two big fingers up into my body. I'm already hot and wet for him, but it's still an almost painfully snug fit, and my breath hisses through my teeth as he starts working my clit and thrusting his fingers inside me so hard and deep that I'm gasping, speeding toward another mind-blowing orgasm.

'Damn, you're tight,' he growls, lowering his gaze to my breasts, the swaying, lace-covered mounds barely covered now by my gaping robe, and then lower, to where he's pumping his talented fingers in and out of my pussy. 'So fucking tight and wet. Can't wait to get my mouth on you, baby.'

'Be careful,' I gasp, writhing as he does this thing with his fingers that makes my inner muscles clamp down so hard he can barely move inside them. 'I . . . I don't want you to hurt your hand. It's already been through enough.'

He smiles in a way that makes my sex clench even tighter, and another husky laugh rumbles up from his chest. 'My hand's in heaven right now, Em. Fucking heaven.'

I want to return that gorgeous smile, but I make the mistake of running my greedy gaze back down his ripped torso, and this time I go lower too, taking in the impressive sight of his big, hard cock tenting the front of his trousers. I blink in pure female appreciation, and hear Jase make a rough, guttural sound in the back of his throat. I know he's caught me staring wide eyed at his dick, trying hard to imagine what it looks like in the flesh, and it all comes crashing over me – his deliciously wicked touch . . . our ragged breaths . . . the wet, slick sound of his fingers working me into a frenzy – and I shatter. A breathless cry breaks from my lips, and I hold on to his shirt for dear life as my pussy clenches and melts, drenching his fingers . . . and no doubt his hand, my vision nothing but a dark, star-studded blur.

'That's it,' he groans, leaning down and licking the inner curve of my breast. 'Let me feel this perfect little cunt coming all over me, Em.'

The orgasm goes on and on in a bliss-soaked forever, until I finally sink into the feather-filled duvet in exhaustion, my body boneless and my throat raw from my cries of pleasure. Still softly panting, I finally manage to blink my eyes open just in time to watch Jase pull his glistening fingers from my body and slip them inside his mouth. His molten gaze locks hard with mine as he growls and sucks them clean, his nostrils flaring, and I have never in my life seen anything so wildly erotic.

He doesn't need to say anything as he pulls his fingers from between his lips, because I can tell from the way he's looking at me that he likes the way I taste. Okay . . . maybe *more* than likes it. I know I need to thank him or something, because that was freaking awesome, but I can't get a single word out before his mouth is back on mine. I hold on to his broad, muscular shoulders and kiss him back like my life depends on it, and I can taste myself on his tongue, salty and sweet – which, let's face it, is just *hot*. The kiss deepens, getting steamier and wetter, until a loud burst of laughter and voices comes from out in the hallway, and I gasp as he pulls away.

'We'd better finish getting ready,' he scrapes out, looking like that's actually the *last* thing in the world he wants to be doing as he straightens to his full height and offers me the same hand that's just been inside me, helping me up.

'Um, yeah,' I whisper, and I'm grateful that my legs are able to support me as I somehow make my way over to the wardrobe, grab my dress, snatch my make-up bag off the dressing table, and slip into the bathroom.

When I stare into the mirror over the sink, I realize I no longer look like the awkward student trying to hide from the world. Instead, there's a flushed, bright-eyed woman gazing back at me. She appears a little dazed, and a whole lot satisfied. And, if I'm going for the honesty thing again, she seems . . . *happy*. But she's also torn, because I caught the way Jase was looking at me – in the mirror over the dressing table – when I turned to walk away from him, and it was clear that the guy's in a world of discomfort. So even though he told me not to worry about his dick, it's impossible not to. Especially after he's been so freaking generous with me, making me come harder than I'd even thought was possible.

He does a double take when I exit the bathroom wearing another classic throwback to the fifties, only this dress is in pink satin with a black lace overlay and a scooped neckline, and I can feel the physical heat of his stare as I slip on the amazing black Jimmy Choo heels that were delivered with it.

'Jesus, Em. You look beautiful.'

'Thanks.' I smile and say, 'You do too.' He's slipped on a tie in a slightly darker shade of blue than the shirt I'd nearly destroyed, along with a dark gray waistcoat and jacket, and the effect is striking. He could easily grace the cover of a magazine, and I'm glad that I took a few extra minutes to redo my hair and freshen my make-up. I even spritzed on some of my favorite perfume, which I rarely do, since it's pricey and I live on a fairly tight budget.

We're both quiet as we make our way downstairs, a little lost in our heads, but it isn't uncomfortable. If anything, the sexual tension is thicker than ever between us – but there's an easiness there as well, as if we've somehow started to become friends.

Tonight, we're at a table with Callan and a few married couples whom Jase seems to know through his business dealings, without an ex in sight. Caroline was either so appalled by the way we made our own seating arrangements last night to bother being a bitch, or Jase found a way to ensure that she didn't screw with us again. Whatever the reason, I'm grateful for the ease with which we get through the meal, as Callan keeps everyone entertained with hilarious stories about his family back in New York, though for the most part it all goes by in a blur. I'm not even sure I could tell you what exactly we had to eat, because there's a roar in my ears like the ocean surf, and I'm flushed, my skin so sensitive even the brush of Jase's arm against mine has me shivering, like I've been switched on to my highest setting.

When the dessert plates are cleared away, and everyone at our table is either hitting the dance floor set up in an adjoining room or gathering around the open bar, Jase leans over and murmurs something in my ear, and I blink as I run my tongue over my lower lip, sure that I've misheard him. 'I'm sorry, I didn't catch that.'

Instead of repeating what he said, he eyes my mouth like he wants to own it, and then slowly lifts his hooded gaze back to mine. 'It's fucking hot as hell when you lick your lip like that.'

I try to cover how flustered I am with a smirk. 'You think *everything* is hot.'

'When it comes to you,' he rasps, 'it would seem so.'

I'm saved from having to come up with a response because Callan returns to the table with a soda for Jase, a bottle of beer for himself, and a glass of white wine for me – and he and Jase start talking about some new type of motorcycle that Callan plans on buying when he gets home. Since motorcycles terrify me, I spend the time sipping my wine and watching Lottie, worried for her. Oliver is nowhere in sight again, and for the hundredth time since meeting those two, I'm wondering what the hell she's doing here.

When the melodic notes of a new song begin, Jase suddenly pushes back from the table and moves to his feet. Holding out his hand, he repeats what I thought I'd heard him say before. 'Dance with me.'

'I . . . I don't know how.' I mean, sure, I can dance in a club. But this is slow dancing to lovely music being performed by what sounds like a small orchestra.

'I'll do all the work,' he assures me, taking my hand and pulling me to my feet. 'All you'll have to do is hold on.'

As I follow him into the other room, I want to tell him that I'll hold on all night long – *even when he's fucking my brains out* – but the words are locked in my throat, some last piece of emotional armor keeping them hostage.

Seconds later I'm in his arms, and true to his word, all I have to do is follow his lead. He holds me so close I swear I can feel the pounding of his heart against mine, and as he stares down into my upturned face, his eyes are so heavy that the blue is just a sliver of stormy sky, and I can't look away. I'm falling into those sky-colored depths like a body sinking into the ocean, slipping deeper beneath the waves, and I don't try nearly as hard as I should to swim for the surface – because I'm no longer sure it's where I want to be. I'm all chaos and nerves and churning confusion, my own heart hammering so hard that it hurts.

Any minute now, we're going to walk off this dance floor, go back upstairs, and I honestly don't know which side will win in the battle between my body and my mind. I guess it all depends whose side my heart decides to take, and just as I'm frantically trying to reach the right decision, I'm saved by the bell.

Well, by a gorgeous beast of a man from New York City.

Callan's face is grim as he steps up to us right in the middle of the crowded dance floor. 'Jase,' he says quietly, 'we've got a problem.'

'What's going on?' Jase asks, as soon as we've made our way through the other dancing couples and reached the side of the room.

Callan shakes his head. 'Not here, man. But we need to hurry.'

'I'll be fine,' I say, when Jase gives me a concerned look. 'Go with Callan. I'll head right up to the room.'

His dark brows are pulling into a deep frown. 'You'll be okay?'

'I'll be fine,' I say again, sensing Callan's urgency.

Jase cuts a sharp look over at Cameron, who's just walked into the room, then back at his friend. 'I'm walking her up. Meet me at the bottom of the stairs. This'll only take a minute.'

Instead of wasting more time by arguing, I simply hold his hand as we quickly exit the room, drawing a few stares, but those watching us probably think we're just desperate to get into each other's pants, given how closely we'd been dancing.

'What do you think's happened?' I ask as we practically run up the staircase.

'I have no clue. But I'm guessing it has something to do with

Oliver. He disappeared right after dinner,' he mutters, making it clear that I hadn't been the only one to notice his cousin's absence.

Jase swiftly opens the door to his bedroom, and he doesn't even shut it behind us once we've gone in. 'Don't open the door for anyone. And try to get some sleep. I can let myself in when I come back up.'

'Okay. Just . . . whatever the problem is, be careful.'

'Always.' His expression is still tense, but there's a ghost of a smile on his beautiful lips now, and I know it's because he's just repeated my response from yesterday morning back to me. He pulls me into his arms and runs the damp heat of his mouth along my jaw, then nips my sensitive earlobe with his teeth. 'If you're going to dream tonight,' he whispers in my ear, 'it better be about me.'

Then he walks out, locks the door behind him, and I just stand there in the middle of the quiet room . . . wondering what the hell is going on.

Chapter Seven

Sunday morning

JASE

I wake when Emmy stirs beside me, and even though I've only had a few hours of sleep, I'm instantly charged by the fact that she's here with me.

'Why is he on top of the covers?' she quietly asks herself, thinking I'm still asleep.

'Because I didn't trust myself to get under them with you,' I reply gruffly, cracking my eyes open. My body instantly tightens, and I blink, unable to believe how gorgeous she looks in the morning.

'Jase, you must be freezing.'

'You cold? Come here,' I rumble, tugging her closer with a wicked smile. 'I'll warm you right up.'

'I tried to wait up for you,' she tells me in a soft voice, stroking her thumb under my eye, where there's undoubtedly a shadow. 'But I must have fallen asleep.'

'It took forever to get things sorted.'

'What happened?' she asks, that feminine hand now moving into my hair, the gentle touch feeling so good I have to bite back a moan. It suddenly occurs to me that I've never shared a moment like this with a woman – but then, I've never wanted to. Never wanted to hold any of the women I've known in my arms on a sleepy Sunday morning and just look at her, breathing her in, for the sheer pleasure of having her company. Being close to her. Being *with* her.

It's taken only three fucking days for this girl to turn my life on its head, and now I'm reeling. She has her walls and guards, and I'm starting to understand that I have mine too. That I've lived my life the way I've lived it, surrounding myself with a certain type of people, because I wanted to remain apart. Keep anyone from getting too close.

Emmy and I are so alike, and I wonder if she even realizes it. If she sees it. If she sees *me*, or if she still thinks I'm just a jerk and is only waiting for the scoop on Harrison.

No, she isn't like that, I tell myself. But I decide, right then, to stop putting off the visit to Elm Manor that I've promised her, and to take her there this morning.

I still haven't answered her question about last night, and she gives me a worried look. 'I get that you don't want to talk about it, but was it bad?'

'Yeah, it was.' *It fucking sucked.*

Her gaze darkens with concern. 'Are you okay?'

'I am now,' I say, reaching up and curling my hand around hers, intending to draw it to my mouth for a kiss. But her eyes go wide the instant she sees my knuckles.

'Ohmygod, you're not okay!' she says in a rush, sitting up and pulling my hand toward her for a closer inspection. 'Your knuckles are all busted up again. What happened?'

Propping myself up on the pillows, I say, 'Cameron needs to learn to control his damn mouth.'

Keeping hold of my hand, she turns so that she's facing me as she sits cross-legged beneath the fluffy duvet. 'Why is he like that?' she asks, while I try to keep my gaze on her face, and not on her beautiful breasts which are currently covered by nothing more than a thin cotton top. 'I mean, why does he hate you so badly?'

'Honestly? I have no idea. He's been this way for as long as I can remember.' I have a few vague memories of playing with Cameron shortly after my mother died, when he came to stay with us, like he did most summers, because his own mother was always traveling around the world with her friends. But then something changed, and we never got along again.

'And Caroline?' she asks, the morning sunlight streaming through the French doors glinting against the honey-colored waves of her hair.

'I'll tell you,' I say, turning over the hand she's been holding and giving her fingers a gentle squeeze, 'if you tell me why you hate doctors.'

She raises her brows. 'What makes you think I hate doctors?'

I give her a *Come on* look. 'Em, I saw you with Dr Riley. You couldn't have been more creeped out if I'd told you to stick your hand inside a box of snakes.'

Frowning, she says, 'I was that obvious?'

'Yeah, sweetheart. You were.'

'I . . . When I was eight, I got ill with a severe case of pneumonia. I had to be in the hospital for two weeks, and my dad insisted that my mom go on a business trip with him.' She pauses, pulls her hand from mine to reach up and grab her hair, twisting it as she pulls it over one shoulder, and I realize it's a nervous gesture as she quietly goes on. 'There was this doctor who would spend a lot of time in my room. He never . . . he never tried anything with me, but he would ask me these disturbing questions, and watch me in a way that made me so uncomfortable I felt like my skin was crawling with bugs.'

'Did you tell your parents?' I ask, forcing the words through my gritted teeth.

She nods her head. 'Every time they called. Mom was freaked out, but Dad said I was just trying to get attention and to give it up.' A bitter smile kicks up the corner of her soft, pink lips. 'He wasn't about to let me screw up one of his biggest deals of the year.'

'That bloody bastard,' I rasp, thinking it's no wonder Emmy has issues about guys with money. From the sound of it, she grew up with a money-hungry dickhead who cared more about his bank balance than his baby girl, and it makes me want to track the tosser down and show him exactly what I think of him.

Then a thought occurs to me, and I pull my battered hand down my face as I mutter, 'Shit.'

'What?'

I force myself to look her in the eye. 'It kills me that you went through that as a little girl. Fucking kills me, Emmy. And I feel like such a prick for insisting that Riley look you over on Thursday.'

'Hey, you didn't know,' she says softly, giving me a tender look. 'And I'm a grown woman, Jase. I knew I wasn't in any danger with Riley – and if I had been, I could have handled it.'

I don't doubt that for a second, given how brilliantly she'd kneed Cam in the balls.

'So about Caroline,' she prompts, taking us back to her earlier question, now that she's answered mine.

This time *I'm* the one with the bitter smile. 'That's easy. My earliest memory of Caro is her telling me I looked too much like my "dead bitch of a mother" and to stay out of her way. I was seven at the time.'

'Jase,' she whispers, her face going pale.

'Yeah,' I sigh, scrubbing my hand over my jaw. 'She was a classy act from the start.'

Suddenly Emmy's leaning forward, one hand braced against the top of the headboard, the other against my shoulder, and her soft lips are brushing over mine. It's the sweetest, most caring kiss I've ever been given, and it ignites something inside me. Some inner fire that I never even knew was there, burning deeper than sexual need or appetite. It's more brutal than lust, and a thousand times more powerful, and it makes me groan. Makes me fucking shake as I wrap my arms around her and jerk her closer, the damn bedding tangled between us.

For long, blistering moments, I claim every part of her hot, sweet mouth that I can, raking it with my tongue, until it's too much and I know I have to stop. I pull my head back, breaking the kiss, my hands fisted in her hair, and run my greedy gaze over every inch of her beautiful body. She's golden from head to toe, like a drop of pure sunshine, and I can't wait to feel her burn me alive.

And then there are those thick-lashed, cinnamon-colored eyes, with that dark rim of black around the outer edge. Gorgeous. Mesmerizing. I guess I'm staring into them a little too intently, because her cheeks start to go pink and her breaths are quickening. I'm so damn tempted just to pull her beneath me and keep kissing the hell out of her, but every instinct I possess tells me that's not the way this should play out, so I leave her kneeling there in the middle of the bed as I roll up to my feet, saying, 'Come on, babe. We need to hurry if we're going to make this happen.'

'Make what happen?' She's staring at me standing there in my tented boxers like I'm crazy, and I can tell that I've shocked her. That she fully expected to get seduced right out of her little pink top and pajama shorts . . . and have my cock buried a mile inside her before we ever left this room again. But as badly as I wish that were happening right now – that I was taking her so hard and deep it burned away the memory of every other guy she's so much as even kissed – I know I've made the right choice. That it's the only choice I can live with when it comes to this girl.

If we have sex, and I'm hoping to God that we do, she needs to decide that it's what she wants *before* we're already in bed together.

She needs to come to me with her eyes wide open – and then I'm going to fuck her so damn hard that we knock Harrison's bloody painting off the wall.

Leaning over, I pick her up and set her on her feet, then point her towards the bathroom. 'You need to hurry and get ready for the wedding, because we're going to head over to Harrison's place to view his private collection this morning and we might not make it back in time to change before the ceremony starts.' The wedding is scheduled for eleven thirty, with an afternoon reception to follow.

She looks at me over her shoulder, and I laugh at the huge smile my words have put on her face. I'm betting she thought I'd eke my part of our deal out to the very end, worried that she'd bail once I gave her what she came for. But the truth is that after spending these last couple of days together, I trust her to see this through.

We take turns showering, and while I'm forcing myself to look at some emails, desperate for a distraction from the lust that's crackling in the air like static, she carries her things into the bathroom to get dressed. She comes out twenty minutes later with her hair falling in shimmering waves over her shoulders, a silk black rose pinning up one side behind her ear, and whoever picked out the dress she's wearing deserves one hell of a bonus. They've all been great, but this one ... This one is breathtaking. It's made of a pale, creamy lace, with a short, flared skirt and a band of thick black satin wrapped around her waist, with an under-layer of black lace around the hem. And the way the tight, sleeveless bodice fits over her breasts is probably going to have every guy here tripping over his feet, it's that incredible.

Yeah, Emmy's body in this little dress is something that I know, with every fiber of my being, I will never forget. On my deathbed, when I think back on the beautiful things that I've seen in this world – Paris, Venice, Cairo – the sight of Emmy Reed wrapped up in cream lace and black satin is going to be at the top of the list.

'What?' she asks, when I just keep staring. 'Is it too short?'

'No. God, no. Sorry,' I mutter as I move to my feet. 'You just ... You're stunning.'

She blushes at the compliment. 'Thanks.'

'I mean it, Em. You damn near knocked the breath out of me.'

She laughs, the feminine sound soft and husky, and her eyes are shining with pleasure. She's honestly the most gorgeous thing I've ever seen – and so much more. I have a feeling I've only scratched the surface of Emmy Reed, and I know that when this weekend is over and we head our separate ways, I won't be ready to see her go. Not by a long shot, and that's going to suck.

But I still think that following her on to the Tube was the smartest fucking thing I've ever done. So I'm not going to regret this weekend with her. Instead, I'm determined to enjoy the hell out of the time we have left together.

We make our way downstairs, have a quick breakfast of coffee and pastries, then head down the terrace steps, since it's easier to reach Elm Manor by walking along the garden pathways that connect the two estates.

I'm relieved we make it out of the house without running into either my father or Caroline. He's drinking so heavily, I'm surprised he hasn't pickled himself, and Caro . . . Yeah, she's acting even more bat-shit crazy than usual, having a meltdown every two seconds and giving me the third degree yesterday about where Emmy lives in California. She must have overheard Em talking to one of the other guests, but God knows why the crazy bitch would care about where Em's from. As far as she and Alistair are concerned, Emmy and I are a couple and she's currently staying with me in London.

The walk over to Elm Manor takes only about ten minutes. Anna, my grandfather's housekeeper, lets us in with a friendly smile and tells us that he's already at work in his studio.

'I'm going to give Emmy a tour of his private collection, but please let him know that I'm here,' I say, after kissing her on the cheek, 'and that there's someone I'd like him to meet.'

She gives me a startled look, knowing the odds are low that Harrison would acknowledge my presence even if I were alone, and practically nonexistent when I've brought a stranger to meet him, no matter how beautiful that stranger is. My grandfather avoids people the way the rest of us avoid nettles, and a meeting with him usually leaves a person with the same kind of wounds. But I've given my word to Emmy that I'd at least try to get her that interview, and I'm not about to back down now. If he doesn't come out of his studio after Anna delivers my message, I'll go and try to badger him into it. It won't be pleasant, but it's the least I can do after the way she's faced down Caroline for me.

It doesn't take long to reach the gallery, which is located on the first floor of the house. Before I open the door, I look at Emmy and give her a playful wink. 'You're about to get up close and personal with a shitload of disturbing but erotic art. So if you feel the need to ravage me or anything, I just want you to know that I'm okay with that.'

She shakes her head as she snuffles a soft burst of laughter under her breath. 'There you go again, being all funny.'

'What can I say? I like cracking you up.' I open the door to the gallery for her, and she's smiling as she walks past me, until I lean down and whisper in her ear, 'Almost as much as I like making you come.'

She flushes and hurries away from me, and my quiet rumble of laughter follows her into the long, high-ceilinged room.

I stay over to one side, content to ignore the paintings in favor of watching the woman. I hear her gasp as she turns in a circle, taking it all in. This is where Harrison keeps his most famous paintings, only allowing them to be shown in museums when the mood strikes him, and I can tell how much it means to Emmy to be here. Hell, some of these paintings have never even been shown to the public, so she should have some great material for her article.

She takes her phone out of the small bag that's attached to her wrist, using the voice recording function as she begins to dictate her notes, and I love to watch her at work. Love the way her head tilts to one side as she studies each painting, and how she'll sometimes catch her lower lip in her teeth when she's deep in thought. She's fucking perfection, and I'm so addicted it's not even funny.

I notice that there are security cameras mounted in each corner of the room, and I wonder if the old man is watching us. Watching *her*. It makes me want to walk to her and pull her into my arms, laying my claim on her in the most primitive, animal-istic way I can, so that the old bastard knows she's mine.

Mine.

Huh, that's a word that's sure as hell never been in my

vocabulary before. At least not when talking about a woman. But there's no denying that, when it comes to Emmy, I like the way it feels in my mouth. Like it's right where it belongs.

I don't know what's going on between us. Don't understand half of the crap I'm thinking and feeling. But I do know one thing with absolute, undying certainty, and it's this: I haven't had my fill of her yet. Not even close.

And I'm scared shitless that I never will.

EMMY

I feel . . . different, as I look at these raw depictions of sex and violence, of love and hate, that adorn the walls. I'm not studying them with the same eyes as I did before. The same judgments. The same emotions. And I know why.

The reason is wearing a sexy-as-hell suit as he props his broad shoulders against the wall over by the door, arms crossed over his hard chest, watching me in that tender, intense, impossibly hungry way of his that makes me so wet it's crazy. So needy I just want to tackle him to the polished floor, rip his clothes off, and lick every inch of his gorgeous, muscular, mouthwatering body.

Every. Single. Inch.

And, God, does he have a lot of them.

But I know, now, that there's a hell of a lot more to Jase Beckett than just his huge cock and his fat bank account. He's teaching me, with every moment I spend with him, that there's another kind of powerful *alpha male* in the world. Teaching me that the term is so much bigger and wider than I'd let myself see.

And, yeah, there's definitely so much more that I want before this weekend is over, and it has nothing to do with artwork. But I'm still terrified of making a mistake. Of walking away with so much regret that it drowns me. Ruins me.

'Some of these used to hang in Beckett House,' he tells me, as I finish my first circuit of the gallery. 'But after my mum died, he took them all back, except for the one that hangs in my room.'

'Really?'

'Yeah.' He smirks as he laughs. 'The old man can't stand Alistair and Caroline any more than I can.'

'I can't say that I blame him,' I murmur, thinking that's at least one thing that Harrison and I agree on.

'I don't bloody believe it,' Jase suddenly mutters under his breath, jerking away from the wall, and I look over my shoulder to see J.J. Harrison, in the flesh, walking into the gallery from a doorway at the far end of the room. He's shorter than Jase, but carries himself like a giant, his dark jeans and black T-shirt spattered with brilliant streaks of paint, as if he's been working for hours in the midst of a color storm.

'What a surprise,' Harrison says in a deep, scratchy voice, sounding like he's smoked three packs of cigarettes a day for the past fifty years.

'Bullshit,' Jase says with a snort. 'Anna told you we were here. And I know you've been watching us.'

Harrison's lips twist in a semblance of a smile, though there's no warmth in it. 'My house, my right. What I do here, it isn't any business of yours, Jasper.'

I'm clueless as to what they're talking about, until I notice the cameras in each corner of the room. I wonder what's prompted the artist to grant us with his presence, because it sure as hell isn't out of any familial desire to visit with his grandson. The dislike between the two men is impossible to miss, and it's heartbreaking that I've yet to meet a relative of Jase's who holds any actual affection for him. Feeling the need to show him my support, I cross the short distance between us and stand by his side.

'Is that why you haven't fucked her against the wall yet?' Harrison asks, stopping with his hands in his pockets just a few yards from where we stand. 'Because you didn't want an audience?'

'Careful,' Jase cautions in a low voice, and I wait with bated breath to see how this cantankerous artist who's lived his life by no one's rules but his own will react. He takes a moment to study his grandson's expression, searching for something known only to him, then lifts his shoulders in a careless shrug.

'I see you've brought a friend,' is all he ends up saying, as he takes a pack of cigarettes from his back pocket, pulls one out, and lights up. *So that explains the voice*, I think, taking him in. His body is strong and robust, his hair still salt-and-pepper rather than completely gray. But while his physique could belong to a much younger man, Harrison wears his age on his face. And in his dark eyes. They look ancient, as if he's lived a thousand lives, each one more painful than the last.

Before Jase can introduce us, I lift my chin and say, 'My name is Emmy Reed, Mr Harrison. I'm writing an article about your work, and Jase was kind enough to offer me a private viewing.'

'You're an American?' he asks as he blows out a heavy stream of smoke, the lift of his brows the first sign of actual emotion that he's shown us.

'Yes.'

'And a writer?' His gaze begins to narrow as he takes another long drag on the cigarette. 'About art?'

'Yes.'

The corner of his mouth twitches so slightly that I almost miss it. 'Are you any good?'

My own lips part as I'm about to respond, when he waves

my answer off with a *whatever* gesture of his hand and looks at his grandson. 'I've decided that I'll talk with Miss Reed. You can wait for her back at Beckett House. I'll have Anna drive her over when we're done.'

'Like hell,' Jase clips, glaring at his grandfather.

'I might feel like talking to a pretty girl,' Harrison drawls, blowing out another cloud of smoke. 'Doesn't mean I want to talk to *you*.'

'Christ,' Jase mutters, before turning his head and locking his shadowed gaze with mine. I know he's reading the look in my eyes, trying to determine if I'll be okay without him. I try to convey that I'll be fine, but that I'm sorry his grandfather is such an ass-hat. I have no idea if I pull the message off, and maybe I just look a bit crazy, because I can see a flash of humor spark in Jase's dark eyes. He leans down and presses a soft kiss against the center of my forehead that makes me go all swoony inside, then puts his lips right at my ear and whispers, 'Give him hell.'

Without even throwing another glance at Harrison, Jase exits the room, and I turn to face the rude old bastard with my game face on, thinking he's the biggest bully that I've ever met. And considering I know my father, that's really saying something.

Noticing the phone in my hand, he takes another long drag and says, 'You can record this if you want.'

'Thanks,' I murmur, wishing my freaking hands weren't shaking as I deal with the phone.

'If I were to guess, I'd say your first question is going to be why. Why this? Why that?' He turns and begins walking around the perimeter of the room, gesturing to the array of his paintings that cover the walls, and I follow after him. 'So let me just start by saying that the reason is actually quite simple.' He pauses, but it's not for dramatic effect. He's simply taking another drag, and I'm shocked when he tosses the partially smoked cigarette on the lovely wooden floor and grinds it out with his shoe. But then, he's been dropping his ashes on the floor this entire time, so the man clearly has no regard for material objects. Or for his housekeeper, for the matter.

'And your reason?' I prompt him, when he starts to light another cigarette.

He turns his head, slanting me a sharp smile. 'I just like to fuck with people's minds.'

'Is that why you depict women in such a derogatory manner?'

His brows lift, disappearing under the shaggy fall of his hair. 'Is that what I do?'

'What would you call it?'

'I paint the world the way I see it,' he answers, gesturing with the hand holding his cigarette toward one of his more controversial works in which a faceless, hulking beast of a man is leading a beautiful, crying blonde, who's on her hands and knees, around like a dog, his hand fisted in her long hair, using it like a leash. He's pulling so hard that blood drips down the sides of her face, and they're both sinking into what looks like rotting food and excrement.

As I stare up at the painting, I say, 'Then I believe you see the world through a cloud of pain.'

His laugh is low and gritty. 'You're not the first to think that.'

'And I won't be the last, I'm sure,' I murmur, bringing my gaze back to his. 'I just want to know why.'

'Why? What business is it of the world's?'

'Because they write about you like you're a monster. And to be honest, that's what I thought I would find. But you're not.'

Even though I get the sense that my words have surprised him as much as they've surprised me, he only says, 'Looks can be deceiving.'

'I'm not basing my opinion on your looks, Mr Harrison. I'm basing it on the way I feel.'

'The way you feel,' he husks, rolling the phrase over his tongue.

'I've been around my share of men who hate women. The air in this room doesn't feel the same. I think you hate *one* woman.'

His head tilts the barest fraction to the side. 'Do you now?'

I do, I think, and she wasn't his wife, Janine. From the photos I've seen, Janine was a striking brunette. But J.J. Harrison paints the story of a petite, sensual blonde. Her features might always be blurred, but I'd bet every penny I own that it's the same woman.

But to Harrison, I simply say, 'Or maybe you hate yourself.'

'Women are vindictive, money-hungry creatures. Just look at Jase's stepmother.'

'There are rich bitches and there are rich bastards,' I point out. 'But that coin can be flipped just as easily.'

'So you don't judge? You didn't take one look at Jase in his expensive suit with his pretty face and decide you knew exactly what kind of man he was?'

I stifle my wince, but the old man can read me like a book, and his chest shakes with another gritty slice of laughter.

'We *all* see through a lens of pain, Miss Reed. It's what makes us human.'

Understanding that the only way I might get something more out of him is if I offer up my own pound of flesh, I say, 'But who forged that lens for you? My father made mine. I gave him that power, and it's not something I'm proud of. It's something I wish I could change.'

'Your father hurt you?' he asks through another cloud of smoke.

'I'm past letting him hurt me now.' Tension gathers across my shoulders, and in the pit of my stomach, as I add, 'But he hurts my mother.'

For the first time since he entered the room, there's a hint of softness in his ancient gaze. 'And you love your mother.'

'More than anything.'

'But you resent her too,' he says with a mocking smile, all hints of tenderness gone. 'Because she's still living in the shit, letting your father treat her like an extension of his ego.'

I frown, hating how much this man sees. God, no wonder he's so good at twisting humanity's emotions.

'You despise that weakness in her,' he goes on, turning to face me fully, 'because of what it does to her. But also because if it lives in her, then it lives in *you*.' He smiles again, knowing he's right, and my throat works as I take a hard swallow.

Screw this. I want to tell him to go to hell and storm out, and I'm two seconds away from doing it, when I realize that it's exactly what he expects. So I suck in a deep breath and force myself to get back on track. 'I think a woman made yours – your lens of pain.'

Studying the cigarette in his hand, as if he's mesmerized by the swirling column of its smoke, he says, 'I was married to Jasper's grandmother for thirty years without a single argument, except for when she forced our daughter, Sarah, to marry that peacock next door.'

'So you didn't approve of Sarah and Alistair's marriage?'

He looks at me with the most condescending smirk I've ever seen. 'The list of things women have done that I don't approve of is endless, Miss Reed.'

'You're difficult to please,' I murmur, wondering why a man like him ever decided to marry in the first place.

'Did you know my Sarah hanged herself from the ceiling fan in Jasper's playroom?' he tosses out so casually, you'd think he was asking me if I thought it might rain. 'That he's the one who found her body?'

His tone might be casual, but my reaction is anything but. I flinch as if he's just dealt me a physical blow, and can feel the blood draining from my face. *My God*. Tears burn at the backs of my eyes as I imagine how horrific that must have been for Jase. He'd only been six years old!

Harrison quietly laughs, but it's a bitter, hollow sound. 'And you wonder why I see women as spineless, vindictive creatures.'

'She must not have been thinking clearly,' I force from my tight throat, trying to comprehend how a mother could do that to her child. I swallow again, then pull in another deep breath and lock my burning gaze with his. 'And you know as well as I do that that's not Sarah on those canvases.'

'No, it's not,' he agrees, resuming his walk around the room.

'It's not your wife, either.'

He arches an eyebrow at me from over his shoulder. 'You've done your homework, Miss Reed.'

'Enough to know that Sarah and Janine were both brunettes. And from what I've read, your wife was a mild-mannered woman who weathered your moods with a grace you didn't deserve.'

'That's one way of putting it,' he mutters under his breath.

'So then it was someone you knew before you married Janine.'

'Who says I didn't have an affair?' he drawls, stopping for a moment to drop his second only partially smoked cigarette on to the floor, which is bizarre on so many levels. Once he's ground it out, he continues his odd stroll around the room as I follow behind him, his attention focused on his paintings as he goes on. 'Who says I didn't have endless affairs? Who says I wasn't fucking a younger woman in my studio when Janine set the precedent for the women in this family and downed an entire bottle of sleeping pills upstairs in her bedroom?'

I'd read that Harrison's wife and daughter both died in tragic accidents, but never was it mentioned that both women had taken their own lives. Swallowing against the lump of shock in my throat, I reach deep for my courage and say, 'Maybe you were. Maybe you cheated with hundreds of women. But they didn't mean anything to you, the same as your wife. Because no one has meant anything to you in years, by your own design.'

He stops, but doesn't look my way. 'You're not short of opinions, are you, Miss Reed?'

'When an artist puts their inner demons on a canvas and shows it to the world, they're inviting us to peel back the layers and look inside. That's even truer when the artist gives the world such a disturbing view of those demons. You want us to look at the canvas and *feel, hurt, bleed.* But when something makes us bleed, we can't help but wonder how the weapon was forged.'

He lights yet another cigarette, then turns to face me, his dark eyes drilling hard into mine. 'An artist makes a creation and gives it to the world. Some may like it, some may hate it. And the world is welcome to their opinions. To their praise and their rants. They're welcome to be cruel or kind, and they will be both, often at the same time. But no matter their response, my work is done when the paint has dried. I owe them no explanations. Art is an engine, art is a mirror, art is a journey,' he states in a low voice, lifting the cigarette to his lips. 'But if you see art as a doorway into my soul, then consider that door slammed. Your eyes and curiosity have no claim to the meat and core of me.'

'The world will continue to write a truth for you built on a mountain of conjecture.'

'Let them,' he sighs through a cloud of smoke. 'What do I care about the world?'

I can tell that we're done here, but I can't walk away without saying, 'Whoever she was, does she deserve this? Does she deserve your hate and your rage? Or does she deserve to live the rest of her life in peace, without your monsters breathing down her neck?'

He can't quite hide the scowl that twitches between his brows, and I know I've struck a nerve. And in that moment, I see the true driving force of this man's work as clearly as if he's spoken the word himself: *regret*. He's drowning in it, battered by it, like a cancer inside his body that's consuming him from the inside out. Somewhere along the way, one or two or countless times, this man made choices that led to where he is now. Alone. Unloved. So bitter it haloes him like a toxic cloud.

In the end, loss is something that affects us all, rich or poor, loved or unloved. We can't change it, can't stop it. All we can do is control the circumstances of its birth. At the end of our days, will we regret that we've experienced loss because we made the wrong decisions . . . or because we made the right ones? Will we have taken chances and enjoyed the good in our world while we had it . . . or will we have painted it black before the color ever even had a chance to touch us?

I almost stumble, I'm so overwhelmed by everything burning through me, blazing and bright, breaking and shattering pieces in every corner of my being. I'm seeing so clearly now it hurts. Seeing that I've used my past to breed a wall of prejudice that I thought would protect me, but instead, just keeps pushing me farther and farther away from the real world. From the good things that come into my life, whether they'll be there forever . . . or only for a matter of days.

When I'm back in San Diego, wouldn't I rather regret the loss of something beautiful than the emptiness of something that never even was? That I was too cowardly to grab on to and enjoy while I had the chance?

I've been given a stolen moment in time with a man who truly *gets* me . . . and I don't want to waste that. Yeah, I might want to keep Jasper Beckett forever, but just because I *can't* doesn't mean I have to pretend that we haven't been given this time together *now*. When I'm old and gray and taking my last breaths, I want to look back and remember beautiful losses that were vivid and full of color – not an empty wasteland of nothing.

Needing to get to Jase, I head for the door and open it, but stop just before I leave the room. Looking back, I say, 'To thank you for your time, Mr Harrison, I'm going to clue you in on something you've obviously been too blind to see.'

'And what's that?' he asks, the way he arches one eyebrow reminding me so much of his grandson.

'Jase – you're wrong about him.'

'Am I?'

'He's not like them. He's not like anyone I've ever known.'

'He's Alistair's. Like father, like—'

'Bullshit,' I say with a harsh laugh, cutting him off. 'He's *nothing* like his father. But you don't have a clue, do you? Because you've never crawled out of your misery long enough to learn one goddamn thing about him.'

'And you think that you do? That you know him?'

I lift my chin, hoping my conviction is written over every inch of my face. 'I know there's a goodness in him that judgmental idiots like us don't deserve. But unlike you, I'm not going to waste what little time I've got left with him.'

As I walk out of the gallery, I realize that I mean those last words more than I've ever meant anything I've said in my entire life. They play on a continual loop in my head as Anna drives me the short distance back to Beckett House, and my pulse is racing as I thank her and quickly start up the stairs.

The front door opens as soon as I reach the top step, and Jase grabs my hand, tugging me inside. We're alone in the foyer, and as I stare up into his handsome face, I can't for the life of me focus on anything other than what I want from him. What I *need*.

'Jase,' I whisper, pressing my free hand against the center of his chest, over the thundering beat of his heart. 'Take me back to your room and keep me there until we have to leave.'

He sucks in a sharp breath, and the look he gives me is so fucking hot I feel burned.

Scorched.

God, I don't know how I'm not melting into a puddle of molten, liquid lust on the floor.

Without a single word, his hold on my hand tightens – but we've taken only one step toward the staircase when Caroline enters the foyer on her stiletto heels, her expression pinched with rage.

'Why in the hell aren't you in the garden?' she snaps. 'The wedding's about to begin.'

Chapter Eight

EMMY

I've never known a wedding to be such a long, uneasy affair. Honestly, it takes forever to get through the ceremony and the elaborate photographs, and I'm torn the entire time between wanting to drag Jase upstairs, where I can rip that delicious suit off his mouthwatering body, and pushing poor Lottie toward the door, shouting, 'Run! Get the hell out of here!'

Unfortunately, I can't do either. Jase and I are both aware of the fact that we can't disappear until the bride and groom do, and Lottie is a grown woman, capable of making her own decisions. It's not my place to tell her that she's making the biggest mistake of her life. But I can tell that more than a few of the guests here are thinking it – including Callan – and it fills a part of me with sadness, while the rest is consumed by need. A burning, pulsing need that threatens to make me say something outrageous, like *Jase, take me upstairs and fuck me until I can't even remember what city I live in.*

If I say it, I know he'll do it. And we still have the freaking luncheon and toasts to get through!

I only take a few sips of my champagne, wanting to be completely clearheaded when he takes me apart. I don't want a single second of the memory to be blurred when I'm back at home in San Diego, missing the hell out of him.

We're standing off to the side of the crowd while everyone's trying to find their seats in the reception marquee, far enough away that we can't be overheard, and I seriously need something to help me focus. So I say, 'Are you ever going to tell me what happened last night?'

He sighs and works his jaw in that way that men do when they're tense. 'My family is fucked up, Em.'

'Jase, whatever happened, I'm not going to judge you for it. I know you're nothing like them.'

He exhales a rough breath of air, his narrowed gaze focused on the head table, where his cousin sits with Lottie. 'A nineteen-year-old girl showed up at the front door last night in tears,' he tells me in a low voice. 'She's six months pregnant.'

'Oh, God,' I whisper.

'Yeah. Seems she works as a maid in a building in Edinburgh where Oliver keeps a flat. He spends a lot of time up there when he's pretending to work, but really he's been spending all his time with her. The girl, Grace, thought he was going to marry her, until her mother caught sight of his and Lottie's wedding announcement in the paper. Grace showed up last night in hysterics, demanding an explanation.'

'Is she all right?'

'She will be,' he says with another heavy sigh. 'Callan had seen Oliver take her into the library, and we got there just in time to hear the little prick tell her that men like him don't marry "the help". When she pointed out that she'd heard Lottie is a waitress, he told her that was only so Lottie can pay for her degree, and that she hadn't stooped to scrubbing his piss out of a toilet. I started to tell him to shut his mouth, but Grace picked up one of those heavy-arse tumblers that Alistair's always leaving around the house and threw it at his head. Thing hit him so hard it knocked him clear off his feet, and when he got up he had blood running down the side of his face.'

I normally don't condone violence, but I find myself sending Grace a mental high-five. 'Is that why he looks so nauseous today? I thought he was just hungover.'

'It's probably both,' he mutters. 'I wouldn't be surprised if the fucker's got one hell of a concussion.'

I shift my attention from a queasy-looking Oliver to his new wife. 'Lottie knows, doesn't she?' I ask, noticing the way she keeps shifting away from him whenever he leans too close.

'By the time Callan and I got to the library, Oliver and Grace had been screaming loud enough that it'd drawn a crowd out in the hallway. I'm sure most of them could figure out what was going on, and one of them was Lottie's maid of honor, so I'm guessing she knows. She just must not have cared enough to call things off.'

I shake my head in disbelief. 'That's . . . crazy.'

'I know,' he murmurs, nodding at an older gentleman who's walking by.

'What happened to Grace?'

'Callan and I were worried about her, so we drove her to the local A&E. We waited while they checked on the baby, and when she was given the all-clear but told to lie down and relax, we took her to a hotel by the station and got her a room for the night, along with a first-class train ticket to Edinburgh this morning. She should be home in a few hours, and if she's smart, she'll file a paternity suit against Oliver, get some money for her and her kid, and never see his pathetic arse again.'

'Do you think she'll do it?'

'I don't know,' he admits with a grim twist of his lips. 'Right now, the poor girl believes that her *heart* is broken, so she's not thinking clearly. But she finally saw Oliver's true colors last night, so hopefully that's helped get her head out of the clouds.'

From his words, I get the feeling that Jase doesn't put a lot of stock in deeper emotions, like romantic love – not that I can blame him. I find it a difficult concept to understand myself, having never felt it before. But while I do believe in its existence, I'm not so sure that he does. And if I'd been surrounded by his crazy-ass family all my life, I might feel the same way. Hell, my own family is nearly as twisted as his. But I have friends, both in London and back at home, who are in true, committed relationships where love is the driving force, and it's undoubtedly a beautiful thing.

It's also something I find it difficult not to feel envious of, even though it's the last thing I'm looking for at this point in my life. My time with Jase this weekend has made it clear that I need to work harder at tearing down my protective walls and opening myself up a bit more to the world around me, but I imagine it's going to be a long process and isn't something that will just change for me overnight.

As he lifts the glass in his hand to take a drink of his iced water, I glance at his bruised knuckles. His older cousin is sporting a nasty-looking shiner today that he's tried to conceal with make-up, but it hasn't worked. When Jase notices I'm staring at his hand, he says, 'Right after Grace clocked Oliver with the tumbler, Cameron showed up and started laying into her. I tried to get him to leave, but he took a swing at me, so I knocked the bastard out.'

I lift my gaze to his, but he keeps talking before I can say anything. 'Not my finest moment, I know.'

'Oh, I don't know about that. Call me bloodthirsty, but it

sounds like the jackass got exactly what he deserved,' I drawl, lifting my glass of champagne to my lips. 'And, hey, just think, only one more day of this crazy wedding, and then I'll be gone and you'll be able to get back to your normal life where you don't have to rescue Americans from muggers or deal with your obnoxious cousins.'

I'd hoped he would laugh, but that's not the reaction I get. Instead, he takes my free hand and holds it tight in his, as if he's trying to keep me right where I am. Or at least that's what I'm fantasizing it means when he leads me over to our table. We're sitting with almost the exact same group from last night, and even though I know the food must be incredible, judging by everyone's reactions, I don't taste anything that passes my lips. Jase and I are in a focused little bubble, counting down each second, simply going through the motions until we can finally be alone.

When the last toast is made, and the bride and groom take to the dance floor, I feel the hunger building in Jase's body kick into overdrive. The music starts, and I can barely keep my breathing normal as I say, 'I was right about the song. So what do I win?'

He leans over and puts his warm lips against my ear. 'My mouth between your legs, Emmy, for as long as you can take it.'

My breath hitches as I blush, and the last of Jase's restraint snaps. There's still the cutting of the cake to get through, but we won't be here for it. Taking hold of my hand, he pulls me to my feet and out of the marquee, pushing me against the wall the second we enter the house through the terrace entrance.

This part of the mansion is empty and still, and with the first touch of his tongue against mine, my senses surge back to life, his taste so devastating it makes me cry out. I want to swallow him whole. Want to take every part of him into my mouth and make him shudder with pleasure. Make his beautiful head shoot back, the tendons in his strong throat straining, as I suck his thick cock so hard and deep it destroys him.

'Damn,' he curses against my mouth, as if he's just tasted every one of my filthy, provocative thoughts on my lips. 'We need privacy for this, Em.'

The next thing I know, he's tugging me down the central hallway, and I'm practically running in my heels to keep up with him. Then we're upstairs, and he shoves the bedroom door closed behind us, locks it, and turns to look at me. I just stand there in the middle of the room, panting, flushed, unable to take my greedy eyes off him. Both sets of French doors have been left open, letting in the humid summer breeze, the band's bluesy rendition of Muse's 'Starlight' filling the air. I can feel the throb of the bass in my body, my pulse pumping a hard, heavy beat in my veins, my skin so sensitive I swear I can feel the heat of his heavy-lidded stare like a physical touch.

'Lose the fucking dress,' he growls, his jacket and waistcoat already dropped on the floor, his big hands working at his tie. 'I want you in nothing but skin.'

I fumble with the tiny side zipper on my dress, so excited I can barely concentrate, my attention fully focused on watching Jase toss the tie aside, then undoing the buttons down the front of his shirt. The dress finally slips down my body just as he's ripping off his socks, and even though he's still in his trousers and I'm wearing my panties and heels, he says, 'Get on the bed.'

He's so hot and intense, I can't stand it. Can't fight it. I'm already wet between my legs, my panties soaked, and I shiver as I walk to the side of the bed. I turn and sit down, then start scooting back, my heels digging into the cashmere duvet, and I don't even care. I keep my gaze locked tight with Jase's hooded one as he comes toward me, all those powerful muscles flexing and coiling beneath his dark skin, and I don't care about anything but the way he's looking at me . . . *watching* me. It's the most carnal, possessive look I've ever seen, and I love it. Fucking *love* it.

When he reaches the side of the bed, the sexy slant of his smile as he stares down at me makes me gasp, my body so ready for him I'm literally drenched. I've never been this wet before, and there's no hiding from how badly I want *this*. *Us*. *Him*. But it's okay, because for once I'm not worrying about how I act with a man. How much I reveal. I'm just ready to enjoy the hell out of him.

He slips off my shoes, then leans over and grabs the sides of my panties, pulling them down my legs. His heavy, smoldering gaze has been moving over every inch of my naked skin since my dress fell to the floor – but the second I start to open my legs for him, he focuses in hard and tight on the glistening pink folds of my sex.

'Spread your legs as wide as you can,' he tells me in a low voice, devouring me with that blistering stare as he climbs on to the bed. 'Wider,' he rasps, my own gaze taking in how hot his broad, muscular shoulders look between my legs, his biceps bulging in his arms as he grips my thighs and shoves them back to tilt my hips up.

I tremble and close my eyes, ready to come from nothing more than the heady sound of his voice and his dominant touch. Then I feel his hot, wet tongue flick across my swollen clit, and my eyes shoot wide in surprise, my hands fisting in the bedding as he pushes my thighs back even more.

He goes wild on me then, and *my God*, it's freaking insane how incredible it is. He doesn't just lick. He rubs and thrusts . . . and *sucks*. He literally closes his mouth around my slick entrance and sucks at my juices, the low, aggressive sounds rumbling in his chest making it clear that he's getting off on doing it every bit as much as I'm getting off on having it done to me. It's so raw and savage and explicit that I'm just this bundle of nerves lying there shaking and panting, falling apart – and there's honestly nothing in my life that has ever come anywhere close to being this blindingly awesome.

I orgasm with a sharp, tight cry, a surreal wave of pleasure crashing over me that has me burning and shivering all at once. I can feel my sex tightening, pulsing around his tongue as he fucks me with it, and his strong hands grip my thighs in a hold that I'm sure will leave marks. But I'm not complaining, because I want to hold on to him just as tightly.

'Give me another one,' he growls, shoving two big fingers into my pulsing slit as he flicks that molten gaze up to my face. 'I need to get you wet enough that you'll be able to take me.'

'I am . . . I'm ready!' I insist, my breathy voice cracking with emotion.

He forces a third finger inside me, then smiles like a devil. 'Nowhere even close, baby.'

'God, Jase, I need you now!' I practically wail, grabbing on to his hair.

'Not done with you,' he mutters in a guttural slide of words, and then he pulls his fingers out and his wicked mouth is on me again. He's ruthless and deliciously rough, eating at my sensitive flesh in a way that's completely unapologetic, taking exactly what he wants, and I'm no longer arguing.

No, I'm too busy writhing and pulling his hair – trying to keep him right where he is – to say anything other than *More*, *Please*, and *God . . . Oh, God*, as my pussy convulses around his thrusting tongue, gushing for him.

The orgasm is so intense, I think I might black out a little at the end, because the next thing I know I'm blinking my eyes open and Jase is bracing himself over me on his powerful forearms. He lowers his head, his mouth working over mine, and I love how I can taste myself on his clever tongue. Love how he controls the kiss, taking my mouth like it was made for him. Like he knows exactly how to touch and taste me to make me crazy, and I can't wait any longer to explore him just as thoroughly as he's explored me.

'Let me,' I say against his lips, as I reach down and rub my hand over his hard, heavy erection. He lets out a long, serrated groan and pushes up, holding himself over me on his straight arms. His dark, hooded gaze is focused on my naked breasts, my pink nipples drawing tighter beneath his hungry stare as I work to undo his belt, then hurry to open his trousers. It isn't easy to do, with his massive cock pressing against the material, but I finally manage to get them open, shoving his trousers and boxers over his hips with one hand, a kind of husky, fascinated moan falling from my lips when my other hand latches on to his beautiful penis.

And, yeah, it might sound weird, calling this brutal part of him *beautiful*, but it's true. Jase's cock is freaking mouthwatering, the dark shaft long and thick, with a fat, swollen crown that's already slick with pre-cum at the tip. I use my thumb to spread the moisture around the taut skin on that broad, flushed head, thinking he looks succulent and ripe. He's so big I can't even wrap my fingers around him fully, but I grip him as firmly as I can, and the heavy knotwork of veins that run the length of his textured shaft pulse against my palm. The skin is sleek and silky, in such sharp contrast to the rigid hardness beneath, and if he's half as good at fucking as he is at everything else we've done, I realize it's no wonder all his exes have turned into such catty bitches. They're all probably going through withdrawals, starving for something they're never going to get again.

His corded throat works with a hard swallow as I squeeze and pull on him, his chest rising and falling as his breathing gets choppy, and I feel high on the joy of knowing he's enjoying my touch. It makes me want to give him more . . . and to take more for myself, and I mean every word when I look up into his scorching gaze and say, 'I want to taste you too.'

JASE

'Hell no,' I grunt, knowing if she gets her mouth on me this will all be over far too soon. So I catch Emmy's soft, feminine hands in mine, pull them over her head, and say, 'Keep them there.'

I stand up, take off my trousers and boxers, and head over to my bag for the condoms that are always stashed in a side pocket. I rip one packet open with my teeth, sliding the latex over my throbbing shaft as I walk across the room, and the way she's watching me . . . *Christ.* I want to bury myself so deep inside this girl, she can't ever get me out.

Tossing the rest of the condoms in my hand on to the bedside table, I climb back on to the bed with Emmy, bracing a hand against the mattress at her side, and push two fingers back inside her, stretching her tight opening. Even though she's melting for me, her cunt creamy and hot, I know my cock's going to be a painful fit. I wish to God I could take more time to get her ready, but I feel like I've waited a lifetime already, and my control is shredded.

Leaning down, I press my open mouth against the tattoo on her hip, tasting the silky heat of her skin with my tongue, then work my way higher, licking and softly biting, until I'm taking one of those impossibly sweet, candy-pink nipples between my lips. I suck and lick as she digs her short nails into my shoulders and pumps her hips up against me, taking my fingers even deeper. I switch to the other breast, unable to wait another second as I pull my fingers free, grab my dick, and notch the engorged head against her tender entrance. And even though I know that I need to be easy, I lose it and shove myself inside her with one hammering thrust, and it feels so bloody good that my head tilts back and I roar, the primitive sound blending with her sharp cry.

'I'm sorry,' I groan, tipping my head back down. 'So fucking sorry.'

'S'okay,' she gasps, her kiss-swollen lips trembling into a breathtaking smile as she blinks up at me, and I'm destroyed. Any control I've got left is fracturing into pieces, shattered by the overwhelming reality of her, and I can't help but drive forward that final bit, burying my cock inside her until she's taken me completely to the root, where I'm the thickest. Her nails bite into my biceps in reaction, her eyes shocked wide by the pain, and with my pulse thundering in my ears, I stir myself inside her tight, wet clinch, grinding my body against the moist cushion of her sex, trying to give her a moment to get used to me. She pulls in a couple of deep, choppy breaths and lifts her head, watching the way my abs move as I pulse against her, my balls so heavy and aching it feels like they're about to unload – and the last remaining fragment of my control is annihilated when she swipes her pink little tongue across her lower lip.

I lose it for good this time, my hips hammering against her as I start fucking her so hard and deep that I'm hitting the end of her. We're all steely, rutting cock and soft, snug core, our heat-slick bodies steaming and sliding, and it's mind-blowing. The room fills with the wet, primal sound of my cock pounding the hell out of her as the bed slams repeatedly against the wall, her provocative moans and the tight, juicy clasp of her cunt driving me mad.

'You're so damn beautiful,' I growl, fully aware that I've never lost myself like this with a woman. We're sweat and heat and carnal hunger, animalistic in our need, going at it like our lives depend on how hard I can give it to her and how deep she can take me.

The pressure in my dick is extreme, but I grit my teeth and fight to hold it back, because I want this to last. I don't ever want it to end. I want to spend an eternity inside this woman and never leave. Want to keep fucking her until I'm too bloody old to do it right, and even then I'll die trying.

She's breaking me down so goddamn easily, her intoxicating sexuality just a natural part of her. She's acting on pure instinct, starving for this primal connection as fiercely as I am, and when she uses her cushiony inner muscles to squeeze down on me, I swear my eyes nearly roll back in my head. I make a raw, visceral sound deep in my chest, and as I reach between us and set the pad of my thumb against her clit, pressing and rolling it, I groan, 'God, Em. You're killing me, baby.'

She climaxes with a breathless cry, her open mouth pressed against my bulging biceps, her nails digging into my shoulders, pussy pulsing and clenching as she writhes beneath me. I move harder, deeper, so fast I'm like a piston hammering into the tight, wet suction of her cunt, and I growl like an animal as it slams into me. My head goes back again, a bellow surging up from my chest as I erupt into the condom so violently it's a bloody miracle the thing doesn't break. I shudder as I drop my head forward, still thrusting as my body tries to turn itself inside out for her, and *Jesus*, it feels good. I don't think I've ever felt this good in my entire life.

Curling one hand around the back of her neck, I lean down and kiss her, hoping she can still taste the salty sweetness of her cum on my lips. It's a taste I'm eager to have on my tongue again and again, as addictive as the feel of being packed up deep inside her gorgeous body, and I know that should send me running. But I don't. I *can't*. I just want to keep holding this girl, kissing her soft lips and fucking her plush cunt, for as long as I can. Over . . . and over . . . and over.

'Don't move an inch,' I tell her, when I'm finally forced to pull out to deal with the condom. I move to my feet and head to the bathroom, quickly splashing some water on my face, and then hurry back to the bed, hating to be away from her. It probably makes me sound whipped, but I don't give a shit. I've never come anywhere close to feeling this level of satisfaction – and yet, I'm still as hard as a rock.

She's sprawled across the bed, exactly where I left her, and I keep my heavy-lidded gaze locked tight with her smoky one as I grab another condom and slip it on. Then I crawl back between her soft thighs, notch the head of my dick against her slick, swollen entrance, and ask, 'Are you sore?'

'Yeah,' she says, the corner of her mouth twitching with a smile as she curls her hands around my hips and tries to tug me deeper. 'But I don't care.'

'I'll be careful,' I breathe against her lips.

'Don't you dare,' she shoots back, making me shake with a rough laugh as I start to push back inside her. She feels so damn good around me, I have to clench my jaw to keep from spouting a bunch of emotional shit I'd undoubtedly end up regretting later. But when I'm once again buried to the root inside her, and she's clinging to me, so tight and hot and perfect, I hear myself say, 'I followed you on to the Tube on Thursday.'

She blinks up at me, looking confused. 'What?'

'I was in my car and I saw you walking down the street. The sun was shining on your skin and the wind was blowing through your hair, and I thought you were the most beautiful thing I'd ever seen. I knew I couldn't just watch you walk away, so I made my driver stop, got out of my car, and I followed you.'

Her tongue sweeps across her lower lip again, and she says, 'There was a moment, right before we got off, where I thought you were going to talk to me.'

I slowly withdraw, then thrust back in just as slowly, until she's taken every inch of me. Running my right hand down the side of her body, I grind against her, loving the way her lips part for a gasp, and there's a crooked smile on my own lips when I admit, 'I was trying to think of something – *anything* – I could say that wouldn't make me sound like a stalker.'

She laughs, stroking her hands down my back, then lower, over my arse, and I know if she keeps that up this is going to be over way too fast. So I grab her hands in mine and lift them over her head again, trapping her beneath me. She's flushed from her cheeks down to her mouthwatering breasts, her big eyes dark with pleasure, and I'm doing everything I can to be gentle with her.

But then she goes and says, 'If we're going for complete honesty here, I thought you were the most beautiful thing I'd ever seen as well.'

And with those husky words, gentle goes out the bloody window.

Bracing myself on my left arm, I lick my thumb and press it against her clit again, while I watch my cock pumping in and out of her pink, tender slit, the silky folds of her cunt stretched around me like a hot little mouth. Her pussy squeezes me like a fist, and I know she's close when I feel that first tiny pulse against my shaft.

My control is slipping, each thrust more powerful than the last, and I dig a knee into the bedding for leverage, my balls slapping against her arse as I start driving into her so fast and deep it makes her cry out. *Damn*, but I love that sound. The way her voice gets all raspy and soft. It's the sexiest thing I've ever heard, and I groan when she cries out, 'Harder, Jase. Oh, God. Fuck me harder!'

I give her exactly what she's demanding, and within seconds we crash over that explosive, bone-melting edge together, our sweat-slick bodies grinding against each other as we curse and gasp and hold on to one another so tightly I couldn't for the life of me say where I end and she begins.

Somehow, I find the strength to lift my head, and instead of easing off, my pulse keeps roaring in my ears. She's staring up at me, the tears not caught in her long lashes spilling over her smooth cheeks, and I know – *I fucking know* – that what we just experienced hit her as hard as it hit me. I feel like someone has just slammed a mallet into my chest, knocking the air from my lungs, and I want nothing more than to collapse on top of her, but know I'll be too heavy. So I wrap my arms around her instead and roll us to our sides. Unwilling to leave her, I pull out of her as carefully as I can, reach down and slip off the condom, then toss it on the floor. I'll have to clean up the mess later, but right now I just don't give a shit, because I've got Emmy Reed right where I want her: *boneless, satisfied, and in my arms.*

'You never did tell me how it went with the old man,' I murmur, stroking my hand down the silky line of her spine.

'It was . . . interesting. And you're right. He's an old grump.'

My chest shakes with a quiet laugh, and she snuggles up closer against me. 'I don't ever want to move from this spot,' she says softly, with a little catch in her voice.

The next words out of my mouth catch me by surprise. 'You could stay.'

She tenses in my arms. 'What?'

'You could stay in London, Em. With me,' I say, trying not to panic and just going with my gut.

She sits up, holding one of the decorative pillows against her chest, and her glistening eyes are wide with shock. 'Are you serious?'

I sit up too, scrubbing a hand over my jaw. 'I wouldn't have said it if I wasn't.'

'Why?'

'Why?' I repeat, wondering what in the hell she's looking for as she searches my expression.

EMMY

Emotion washes over me like a storm, and my heart nearly pounds its way past my ribs as I wait for Jase's response. At first I don't recognize the strange feeling that's churning around in my chest, and then I manage to put a name to it: *hope*. I'm so freaking hopeful that what just happened between us was the same for him. Because for me . . . God, what we just shared, it *changed* me.

Yesterday, if you'd asked me to explain what it feels like to have sex with someone you have an intense, emotional connection with, my response would have been vague and ill formed, as if I were trying to describe the details of a face that I'd only seen through a fog.

But now . . . I think I *finally* get it.

Being with him tonight was amazing and mind-blowing and every other adjective you can throw at it. Jase might be from this privileged world of money and prestige, but he sure as hell doesn't act like a gentleman when he's between a woman's thighs. He'd been rough and wild, his body working like a god as he pounded into me, the feel of him moving inside me so perfect it was unreal. We'd fucked like our lives depended on it, and I honestly wouldn't have given a damn if the entire wedding party had been crowded outside our door.

When Jase kept those beautiful blue eyes locked tight with mine as he pushed inside my body, I'd known. Known it was going to be different. That when it was over, *I* would be different. And I am.

But he still hasn't answered my question, and some of that mounting hope begins to fizzle. 'Jase? I . . . I need to know why.'

He holds my gaze with his hooded one, and for a moment I think he's actually going to open up to me. But then a frown weaves its way between his dark brows, and he says, 'We haven't had nearly enough of each other yet.'

Disappointment hits me so hard and fast, it takes everything I have not to flinch. I lift up on my knees in the middle of the bed, still holding the pillow against my body like a shield. 'That's not a reason.' I sound baffled even to my own ears, and the last bits of hope in my chest turn to ash. 'Being good together in bed isn't a reason for me to . . . What? Stay with you for a week or two? Maybe three?'

'Good? Christ, Em, that was the best I've ever had. It was fucking mind-blowing.' He moves out of the bed, grabs his tight, black boxers off the floor, and slips them on. Then he turns toward me, crosses his arms over his broad chest, and says, 'I'm asking you to not go back to whoever's sofa you've been sleeping on, and to not get on a plane. Stay with me and write your article. Spend more time with Lola and your other friends here. Give us a chance to get our fill.'

'And then what?'

'We don't have to plan out every detail,' he says with frustration. 'That's not how life works.'

The confusion in my head and my heart is killing me. Is this really how he sees the world when it comes to relationships? Fuck until he's gotten his fill, and that's that. It makes me hurt for him, because I know he's capable of so much more. I just don't think that Jase knows it. I think this right here is his wall, his *shield*. The way he protects himself from emotional pain.

I'm not expecting him to proclaim undying love for me or anything, but . . . God, he's got to at least give me *something*. Some kind of sign that he's feeling that same shocking, completely unexpected connection that I am. Because even as guarded as I am, I damn well know that there's something special going on here. Something that deserves more than a 'we haven't had our fill yet' label.

'I can't,' I force from my tight throat, knowing it's the right choice, even if it's not the one I *want* to make. But I have to cut my losses now, no matter how much it hurts. If I don't, my beautiful memory of this time with him *will* become something dark and wrenching, and I could so easily find myself looking back on it with something similar to the twisted regret that burdens Harrison. And that's not what I want. Not even close. So I say, 'I won't be that girl, Jase. The one who puts herself out there for a guy who will just use me up and move on before I even know what's happening.'

He braces his hands on the footboard of the sleigh bed, gripping the dark wood so hard that his knuckles are turning white as he leans toward me, and a muscle starts to pulse in the rigid line of his jaw. 'You really think I would do that?'

'I don't know what to think. You're not giving me a whole hell of a lot to go on here other than that we're good at screwing each other and you want more of it.'

He curses and shoves both hands back through his hair, uncaring that he's standing there in little more than muscle and skin. It'd be difficult not to drool at the mouthwatering sight, if my freaking heart wasn't in the process of cracking apart.

'So you're just going to run back to San Diego?' he scrapes out.

I clutch the pillow a bit tighter. 'I'm not running. I'm going home. But if you want . . .'

'If I want what?' he presses, when my voice trails off.

I shake my head and laugh, unable to believe I was about to ask him to visit me. 'Nothing. Never mind. I'm not thinking straight.'

He grips the footboard again, and his nostrils flare as he pulls in a sharp breath. 'I won't beg you,' he grates, his deep voice low and rough. 'If that's what you're looking for, it's never going to happen.'

Quietly, I say, 'I would never expect that.'

'Then stop,' he bites out. 'Stop acting like a bitch just because I'm not coming to heel.'

It would be so easy to let anger filter through my hurt, over-taking it, but I fight to hold it back.

And, hey, at least he's not lying to me. No, he's being bru-tally honest, and so that's what I give him in return. 'I hope you have a wonderful life, Jase. Because you deserve it.'

He flinches, and I can see him work his jaw a few times, before he says, 'The deal was you stay till the end, and then we go back to London together.'

'I know the terms of our deal.'

His breath leaves his lungs in a harsh, angry burst, and he straightens, scrubbing both hands over his face. Then he turns his head toward the open French doors, staring out into the soft evening light, and I'm thrown when he says, 'I'm going to grab a shower.'

'Uh, okay.'

He brings that dark, glittering gaze back to mine. 'We'll finish talking when I'm out.'

I don't say anything to those gritty words, but it's like he can read my thoughts on my face, because he growls, 'You owe me that much, Emmy. You've got your fucking article. The least you can do is stay and talk this over with me.'

I'm silent as I watch him walk into the bathroom and slam the door closed behind him, because I already know that isn't going to happen. The part of me that wants to stay with him, no matter the emotional consequences, is too powerful to test it, and I understand that if I don't go now I might not go at all. That I might stay, waiting it out with him until the bitter end, when he decides he's had enough and is done.

No, I think, scurrying out of the bed and heading for the wardrobe. *No way in hell.*

Less than a minute later, I'm dressed and heading downstairs with my hastily packed suitcase, making a run for it.

I have a horrible feeling as I head toward the back of the house, trying to find Angus or someone who can maybe give me a ride to the nearest train station, that I'm leaving Jase to the wolves in this place. But it's a pack he survived in before, and one he'll conquer in the end. He's too damn strong to ever let them crush him.

The reception is in full swing outside, but this part of the house is quiet. I remember Jase saying that the kitchens and staff quarters are located in the rear east wing, and as I turn into the back hallway, I nearly run straight into one of the last people in this place I want to see: the evil queen herself.

Caroline starts to scowl at me as if she's actually caught me stealing the silver, until she notices the suitcase I'm lugging behind me, the flash of hatred in her blue eyes instantly turning to a look of cold calculation. 'Do you need something, Miss Reed?'

'A ride,' I force through my gritted teeth. 'To the train station.'

She lifts her brows. 'You're leaving?'

'Yes,' I mutter, hating how much satisfaction that's going to give her. 'And as quickly as possible.'

Her eyes gleam, red lips curling in a catlike smile that's slow and gloating and mean, and I so badly want to tell this bitch to go to hell. Somehow, though, I manage to hold it back, because I know she's going to help me. Not out of any kindness or female solidarity, but because she's never wanted me here in the first place.

'Wait here,' she says, already turning away, her next words tossed over her shoulder. 'I'll have someone come to collect you in just a moment.'

I bite my lip so hard it hurts, fighting not to burst into tears, my emotions in chaos. My body wants nothing more than to turn around and run back upstairs, so I can throw myself into Jase's strong arms and hold on to him so tightly he can't ever slip away, which is madness. Pure, fucking insanity! No matter how emotionally stunning our sexual chemistry might be, he's made it clear he isn't looking for a relationship, and I can't risk falling in any deeper with him than I already have.

Even an inch or two more, and I may not be able to keep my head above water.

Caroline isn't gone two seconds when I hear someone come up behind me, and the worry that it's Jase makes it feel like my heart is trying to crawl into my throat. I'm so terrified I won't have the willpower to walk away from him twice that I make a small sound of relief when I turn and see that it's not Jase at all, but Callan. He starts to smile at me in that friendly, easy-going way of his, until he notices the rolling suitcase I'm still holding by the extended handle.

'What's going on?' he asks, his dark eyes locking hard on mine.

'Oh, um, I . . . I have to go,' I ramble, sounding like an idiot. And I have no doubt that I look like an emotional wreck.

Callan's brows lift with surprise. 'Now? It's the middle of the reception.'

'Yeah, um, something's come up.' As far as excuses go, it's freaking lame. But I'm too shattered to be clever.

'Is Jase pulling his car around front?' he asks, holding out one of those big, brawny hands. 'Let me have the case. I'll carry it out for you.'

'Oh . . . um, no,' I stammer, taking a little step back, my grip on the handle tightening. 'Jase is, uh, taking a shower.'

The look on Callan's face would've been priceless, if I were in any frame of mind to appreciate it. But I'm not. I'm shaking with nerves, and it's taking everything I've got not to start sobbing like a child.

He spends a few seconds studying my expression, and then, in a quiet voice, he asks, 'Emmy, are you doing a runner?'

'What? No!' I lie, wishing Caroline would just hurry the hell up. 'Of course not.'

Doubt begins to roughen every word that comes out of Callan's mouth. 'Something just came up while Jase was showering, and you had to run down here to ask Caroline for help?' At my sharp look, he says, 'I saw you talking to her, and now you're just waiting here, and Jase is still upstairs. It doesn't take a genius to figure out that she's getting you a ride.'

I lift my free hand to my forehead and begin rubbing, the headache building there even worse than the one I'd had on Thursday.

Callan pushes his big hands into his trouser pockets and

exhales a heavy sigh. 'At least wait and let Jase take you to the train station.'

I'm shaking my head before the low words have even finished coming out of his mouth. 'No. I . . . I can't.'

That V between his brows gets deeper. 'If we were talking about any other guy, Emmy, I'd probably start thinking something bad had happened. But I know Jase, which means I *know* that's not the case. So what's going on?'

I bite my lip, instinctively taking another step back from him, my composure as shaky as an active fault line. I'm thinking that I need to turn and just walk away, putting an end to this uncomfortable conversation, when I hear myself quietly say, 'He wants me to stay.'

Callan looks more confused than ever. 'And your answer is to leave? You won't even give your relationship a shot?'

'Um . . . there is no relationship. That's not what he's offering. He just wants . . .' My voice trails off, and I'm mortified that I almost babbled about how Jase just wants us to get our fill of each other in the sack. Hell, I'm mortified that I've told Callan Hathaway *any* of this stuff, but it's like I can't contain it. The words are churning and twisting inside me, desperate to break free.

'Fuck.' It's a blunt, raspy curse, and I can tell by his frown that Callan's put the pathetic pieces of this night together. 'I don't know whether I should argue for him, or go upstairs and kick his ass for being such an idiot.'

'Callan, stay out of it, please,' I say imploringly, a strange mix of relief and pain pulsing through my system when I hear heavy footsteps behind me, as well as the sharp click of Caroline's heels. 'There's honestly nothing you can do. It is what it is.'

'Come here,' he mutters, pulling me into his arms and giving me a hard, quick hug. It's what I need right now, and it gives me the strength to sniff back my tears and pull in a deep breath.

'Tell him I'm sorry,' I whisper huskily, not wanting Caroline and whoever she's found to drive me to the station to overhear my words. 'Tell him . . . Tell him I won't ever forget him.'

Callan steps to the side, shocking the hell out of me when he says, 'Jase is one of the smartest men I've ever known, Emmy. Once he's pulled his head out of his ass, he'll come after you.'

'No. He won't.'

But, God, how I wish he was right.

A gentle smile kicks up the corner of Callan's wide mouth. 'Just know that the next time I see you, honey, I'm going to enjoy saying "I told you so".'

I give him a sad smile before I turn away to face Caroline and Angus, who have just reached us. I don't bother looking at the evil bitch, keeping my gaze on Angus's friendly, concerned expression, and without a word he takes the case from me. Caroline manages to bite back any catty remarks she's probably dying to make, and as awkward as the conversation was with Callan, I'm grateful he found me, because his presence is no doubt what's keeping her silent.

Leaving Caroline and Callan behind, I walk beside Angus as we head toward the front of the house, and he tells me he's already pulled his car around.

'Thank you,' I murmur, unable to say any more without crying, Callan's last words playing over and over through my head.

I may have never been a dreamer, but now I want it. I want it so badly I can taste it.

It's pointless and stupid and is probably going to cause me a lot of misery in the months to come, because it's never going to happen. But there's no sense in lying to myself about it, because it's a bright, burning truth at the center of my being, screaming through every part of me.

I want Jase.

I want a future with him.

I want him to come running after me, telling me he was wrong. That he felt something more than just a physical attraction he wanted to work out of his system.

God, I've become the biggest cliché of them all, because there's no denying the truth.

I, Emmy Reed, one of the most cynical girls in the world, want the dream. The spark. The magic.

Somehow, some way, I want the fucking fairy tale.

The
Chase

Chapter One

Sunday evening

JASE

With my hands braced in front of me, pressed against the mar-bled shower wall, I hold my head under the hot spray as I work my jaw back and forth. Despite the two mind-blowing fucks that Emmy and I have just had, I'm so tense I could crack, and my heart won't stop pounding like a bloody jackhammer.

I came in here because I needed a few minutes alone to get my head together, and it's not like I had a lot of other options. Lottie and Oliver's wedding reception is in full swing down in the gardens, which meant my usual way of dealing with shit that puts me on edge – going on a hard, grueling run – was out of the question. So here I am, washing Emmy's mouthwatering scent off my skin, when that's the last damn thing that I want, just so I can take a moment to figure out what the hell I need to say to her.

Christ, this is so fucked. When I'd asked her to stay with me in London, I never expected her to come right out and put me on the spot, demanding a reason. Never imagined she'd want me to open up and spill my guts to her, when I don't have a clue what to say. Half the time I don't even know how to admit what I'm feeling about her to myself, so how in God's name am I meant to explain any of it to her? That's not the way I'm wired, and the frustration pumping through my system has me fisting my hands against the tiles. I fight the urge to punch them, which would not only be juvenile, but probably break my hand. And I'm already breaking apart enough as it is.

I've only known the girl for three days, but she's already got under my skin in a way that no one else ever has. And while I instinctively want to hate it, and rage against it, the truth is that being with a woman has never felt so fucking right or good or *real*.

It's literally the best I've ever had – from the sex to the conversation to just holding her hand in mine – and I'm acting like an idiot by hiding out in here. I have no idea how much time has passed, but my skin is starting to prune. I turn off the water and send droplets flying as I shake my head, still no clue what I'm going to say to her. No idea what it will take to make her change her mind. I'm not going to lie to her, and a part of me just wants to keep arguing with her until she finally grows the hell up and sees that this isn't how adults handle their relationships.

But deep down inside, I can't shake off the uncomfortable feeling that just because this is *my* way, that doesn't necessarily mean it's the *correct* one. That I'm the one acting like a petulant child here, instead of her. That in the real world, men face up to what they're feeling and go with it, rather than sticking their damn heads in the sand, thinking that the *If I ignore it, it can't hurt me* game is going to somehow protect them, when all it really does is prevent people from ever getting close to you.

That tactic might have always worked for me in the past, because I've honestly never met anyone I could see myself going the distance with. Never met anyone who made me even want to try. But I'm strongly suspecting that fact has changed, and that's . . . Yeah, that's what's scaring the ever-loving hell out of me.

I force myself out of the shower, grab a towel, run it over my face, and wrap it around my waist. Deliberately avoiding my reflection in the mirror, since the last thing I want to see is that scared little kid I used to be haunting my eyes, I suck in a sharp breath and rip the door open, deciding that the best course of action is simply to tell her that I need more time. That I see her point, but am on a learning curve here, and can't just give her what she's looking for without the opportunity to think it through.

It's lame as fuck, but it's all I've got.

It's also completely goddamn pointless, because when I step into the bedroom, Emmy isn't there waiting for me in the bed.

'Shit!' I shove the word through my clenched teeth, scanning every corner of the room for any sign of her. But aside from the dress she wore to the wedding that's still lying in the middle of the floor, and the killer heels I'd pulled off her slender feet, it's like she was never even here. I stalk over to the antique wardrobe, ripping it open, and my heart drops when I see that it's been emptied of all her things, except for the clothes and shoes I'd bought for her. Her suitcase is gone as well, which means she hasn't just left the room, but the entire estate. She's doing a fucking runner, and with my blood rushing through my head, I let out a guttural bellow and lurch for the door.

Hoping I might still catch her, I run out of the room with nothing but this sodding towel wrapped around my waist, and nearly do a header when my bare feet slip on the top step of the sweeping staircase. Gripping on the banister with one hand, the other holding the loosening towel closed at my hip, I fly down the stairs. I'm so angry I'm amazed I don't have steam pouring from my ears, my vision shaded by a red haze, and I've never felt the acidic burn of hatred like I do the instant I spot my stepmother, Caroline, standing by the front door, her red lips curved in a malicious, gloating smile that says more than any words ever could.

'What the hell?' is all I can manage to growl at her, just as my cousin Cameron steps through a nearby doorway to stand by her side. For as long as I can remember, the two of them have been close, which is probably one of the reasons I can't stand the tosser. Anyone who chooses to be friends with Caroline isn't someone I want in my life. And he's an even bigger dick than his younger brother, Oliver, which is really saying something.

'You're too late,' she drawls, and I physically cringe from the way she's looking me over, the burn of hunger in her blue eyes making me sick. 'Angus is already driving her to the station.'

I run my tongue over the edge of my teeth, fighting to keep control of my temper, so angry I could literally roar. Not only has Emmy left me, but she let this bitch help her, and I'm so fucking furious that I realize I am finally *done*. Done dealing with this family's twisted shit. Done putting up with them for the sake of public appearances. Done not saying to hell with it all and finally cutting myself free.

With my chest heaving, I step towards Caroline. 'You are the sickest bitch I have ever known.'

Something in her eyes lights up in a way that tells me she's getting off on my anger. 'Jase, we're *family*.'

'You're not my family. You're nothing but a bloody nightmare and I'm done with you.' I cut a seething look at Cam. 'With the whole lot of you.'

I turn to leave before either of them can respond, already tuning them out, and catch sight of my friend Callan coming down the hall. He doesn't look surprised to see me standing in the foyer with nothing but a towel covering my bare arse, which means he either saw Emmy leave or thinks we're all bat-shit crazy in this house.

'I thought she'd probably want to make a scene,' he tells me, jerking his chin at Caroline, 'so I've put someone on the back door. They'll keep the wedding guests from coming inside until I give the word that it's clear.'

'Was she okay?' I scrape out, my voice so gritty it doesn't even sound like me.

'I was coming inside to use the john and found her with her suitcase in the back hall,' he explains, barely stifling a wince. 'I tried to get her to wait for you, but she was pretty upset.'

I grind my teeth together so hard I think I hear a crack. 'Upset how?'

Callan frowns. 'She was trying to keep it together, but she was crying.'

'*Fuck*.'

He steps closer and lowers his voice. 'I wouldn't have let her leave with anyone but Angus. You know he'll look after her. And he can tell you where her train is headed when he gets back.'

I nod, too angry at myself to speak. I never should have left her alone, and while I know Callan's probably thinking I'm going to head after her, he's wrong. I'm too damn raw inside, in a way I haven't felt since . . . *No!* No way. I don't even want to think about it.

But even though I'm not willing to go chasing after Emmy Reed like some pathetic, lovesick idiot, begging her to come back after she just ran out on me, I'm not staying. I'm never spending a night in this fucked-up house again.

'I'm getting the hell out of here.'

'I'll bring your car around while you get packed,' Callan says, reminding me why I've always liked him. He's as stand-up as they come, so long as you're not a woman trying to date him, since he's got his own demons riding hard on his back. 'I'll follow you up to get the keys.'

'Thanks,' I grunt, my throat so tight I have to force the word out as I head for the stairs.

'Jase! Where are you going?' Caroline snaps behind me. 'I haven't finished talking to you.'

I don't even bother turning around as I say, 'Why don't you just fuck off and leave me alone?'

'You can't leave this house, Jasper Beckett! We're in the middle of a reception!'

A bitter laugh burns up from my chest. 'Jesus, Caroline. Like I give a damn.'

'Let him go,' Cameron mutters under his breath. 'Why do you even care what he does? I thought you hated his guts.'

The guy sounds upset, which is weird. I mean, what's going on between these two anyway? And I can hear them both following Callan and me up the stairs. Or Caroline is following us, while Cameron follows after her like a puppy.

She ignores my cousin and keeps hounding me. 'Honestly, Jase, this is for the best. Can't you see that? Your father and I could never accept you being in a serious relationship with someone like her. What would our friends say? She's so . . . *common*.'

I nearly lose the towel as I stop and turn on the top step, throwing off the hand she's just placed on my arm. 'For the love of God, woman, enough!' I shout, my hard voice vibrating with fury. 'I don't know what the hell is wrong with you, but I am done dealing with your shit. I do not want to see or hear from you again!'

She pales and steps back, bumping into Cameron who is just behind her.

'Jase,' I hear my father murmur, and a quick glance down the stairs shows him standing at the bottom, staring up at us with bloodshot eyes.

'Don't even bother,' I bite out, and I have no doubt that my disgust for him is written all over my face.

Without another word, I turn and head straight for my bedroom, and thankfully the only one who follows me this time is Callan. He's quiet as he waits near the door while I fish my keys off one of the bedside tables. As I walk over and hand them to him, I can tell that he wants to say something, but I shake my head, and he leaves without a word.

When the door closes behind him, I stalk to the wardrobe again, yank open the doors, and another low curse rips out of me as I realize how many of the designer dresses Emmy has left behind. For some irrational reason, it makes me even angrier that she didn't take them with her. Like it was a final 'piss off', making it clear that she wants nothing to do with me. No reminders that will last beyond the echoes in her body of how hard and deep I fucked her.

I'm so bloody tempted to go chasing after her, but what's the point? She's made her answer as clear as she could, and I said everything I have to say. Emmy's demand for me to break myself open for her was as naive as it was hopeless – especially when she was unwilling to do the same. And I'm not going to spout a bunch of romantic, emotional bullshit just to placate her. *Fuck that.*

But, *Christ*, I hate that she's gone. I wasn't ready to lose her, and it's killing me that I didn't get to hold her one last time. Didn't get to kiss her. *Fuck* her. I'd planned to explore every beautiful inch of her, soaking each detail into my system, inking them into my brain, so that I could replay the memories again and again once she was gone. Had planned to gorge myself on her, taking as much as I could get, before we went our separate ways, whether that was tomorrow or weeks from now.

And now that opportunity is gone. Lost. Killed. And all because she wanted me to peel back my skin and give her things that I've never given anyone. Things I wouldn't even know *how* to give, even if I wanted to. But I don't. Damn it, I . . . *can't*. The idea of baring myself like that is one of the most terrifying things I can imagine.

Even if it's for the sweetest, strongest, most fascinating woman I've ever known.

The woman who fucked me, and then bailed, leaving me in this twisted house with my twisted fucking family.

I honestly don't know why I haven't said 'Sod off' to this place and the people who live here long before now. Was I holding on to some childish hope that one day they might start to give a damn about me? That Alistair might crawl out of his gin bottle, and Caroline . . . No, I've always known she was a lost cause. But this house is the last link I have to my mother, and while my memories of her are fuzzy, I can remember her telling me that she loved me. She's the only person in the world I can recall ever saying those words to me, and while Sarah might not have lived up to them, at least there'd been a time when she'd cared enough about me to say them. Is that why I've kept coming back to this nightmare, putting up with their shit, year after year?

If so, I'm breaking the chain right now. Because my mother is gone, and the only people left in this place are as toxic as they come.

It's an epiphany that's long overdue – and one that I have Emmy to thank for.

Emmy . . . Jesus, just the thought of her makes me flinch, and I kick my head back and let out another guttural bellow, before locking my hands behind my neck and dropping my head forward. I start to pace from one side of the room to the other, seething with frustration and an undeniable sense of loss, while the wedding band plays the Thirty Seconds to Mars cover of 'Bad Romance' out in the garden. I love this version, but right now it's making me grit my teeth, the lyrics scraping across my raw nerve-endings like a rusty nail.

When someone suddenly knocks on my bedroom door, I throw the towel on the sex-wrecked bed and grab a pair of jeans, yanking them on. Assuming it's going to be Callan, I open the door without asking who it is, and tense when I find myself staring into my grandfather's dark, ancient eyes.

'What the hell do you want?' I grate, too pissed off to pretend that we're anything but reluctant acquaintances.

He lifts his brows, still wearing the same dark jeans and paint-spattered shirt I'd seen him in that morning, when he gave Emmy her interview. 'May I come in?' he rasps in his deep smoker's voice.

I sound like a total bastard as I laugh and shake my head. 'Sure, why not?' I mutter, thinking *God, what a day.* I lose Emmy and gain a visit from dear ol' Grandad. Talk about shitty karma. And what in the name of ever-loving hell is he doing here? As far as I know, Harrison hasn't set foot in this house since my mother killed herself. Not even when I was a kid, stuck in this place with a drunk father and a psychotic stepmother.

I leave the door open for him and walk over to the far side of the room, kicking the condom I'd dropped on the floor earlier under the bed before he can catch sight of it. But when I look over at him, I find that he's not at all curious about the room. No, he's shut the door behind him, made it to the middle of the hardwood floor, and just stopped, his attention completely focused on the painting that hangs over the bed. Even though it's one of his own creations, he stares at it like it's something new to him, and there's an emotion burning in his eyes that I've never seen before. It's too desolate to be anger, and too vibrant to be indifference, which are the sentiments I'm used to seeing on Harrison's face.

Shoving my hands back through my damp hair, I say, 'Look, I'm not trying to be a dick, but this isn't a great time for me. So maybe you should just get to the point of why you're here.'

He pushes his hands into his front pockets as he slides that dark, enigmatic gaze over to me. 'Yes, I heard.'

'Heard what?' I clip, daring the old man to say something that'll piss me off even more than I already am.

His lips twitch, as if he's fighting back a smile. 'I heard you basically tell Caroline to go and fuck herself. Emmy will be proud of you.'

'Emmy's not here,' I force through my gritted teeth, needing him to get to the point of his visit. And then I need him to get the hell out.

'Yes.' He sighs as he finally looks around him, taking in the room. 'I gathered that she's left.'

'So what couldn't wait that you had to come over here and see me now?'

'Your American said some things this morning that got me thinking.'

I lift my brows, and even though I want to tell the prick to get lost, I'm intrigued. 'Yeah? Like what?'

His shoulders go back, and he exhales so loudly I can hear it. 'She said I was wrong about you and that you're nothing like your father.' He glances back up at the painting, and then over to me again, his dark eyes burning with regret. 'After what I'm guessing has happened today, I have a feeling she'd say you're like *me*.'

'Shit,' I mutter, scrubbing a hand over my jaw. 'All these years, you've thought I was like Alistair?'

He cocks his head, saying, 'I'm beginning to see that I was wrong.'

I snort like an arse, but there's no help for it. I was angry going into this conversation, and his assumptions aren't making my mood any better. 'You'd have figured it out sooner if you ever took the time to focus on anything other than your damn paintings.'

He laughs low and deep, and I pop my jaw, wondering what the hell he thinks is so funny. 'Yes, that's true. But I'm here now, and it seems that we're long overdue for a talk.'

I lift my brows again, thinking this must be the most surreal moment of my entire life. 'What exactly do you want to talk about?'

Instead of answering my question, he stalls with an observation. 'I didn't realize you and Caroline don't get along.'

'Why would you? It's not like we know each other.'

'True,' he murmurs with a slow nod. 'I suppose I just assumed. Alistair . . . Well, he likes to brag. I try to avoid him, but there are times when it's impossible.'

'Alistair is a drunk and a fuckwit. Only an idiot would believe anything that comes out of his mouth.'

He cocks his head again, and there's a gleaming spark in his dark gaze that wasn't there a moment ago, as if something long dormant inside him is finally coming back to life. 'Hmm, I'm beginning to see Emmy's point. You're not like Alistair at all. You really do sound like me.'

I narrow my gaze. 'Is that supposed to make me *happy*?'

'God, no.'

This time, I'm the one who quietly laughs, though the sound is hollow. Fitting, since I feel like I've been scraped out inside.

Like I'm just meat and muscle wrapped around bone, with nothing at the heart of me.

Maybe that's why Emmy left. Maybe that's what she could see. What I couldn't hide from her.

'So what happened?' the old man asks.

'With what?' I say, being deliberately obtuse.

He gives me a look that says a thousand words, and my breath leaves my lungs in a sharp huff. I work my jaw a few times, then find myself muttering, 'I fucked up.'

'Not surprising,' he drawls drily. 'Most of us do.'

'I asked her to stay, but she . . .' My voice trails off, the unspoken words sitting on my tongue like ashes, sour and cold.

'I know I haven't given you much advice in your life. Hell, I haven't given you any. But I'm going to do so now, and if you're smart, you'll take it.'

He pauses for my response, but I just cross my arms over my chest and jerk my chin at him.

'Don't make the same mistakes that I've made, Jase. If she means what I think she means to you, then go after her.'

My brows pull into a deep scowl. 'What mistakes?'

'Your girl, she's perceptive. She knows why I paint the way I do.' He walks over to the chair, settling into it in clothes that still have wet paint on them, completely uncaring that he's probably ruining a piece of furniture that cost thousands of pounds. Not that I give a shit. When I leave here tonight, the only things I'm taking are my clothes . . . and the painting.

For some reason, I know it would drive me crazy if I left it. That I wouldn't be able to stop thinking about it, though I'm not sure why. Why it's resonating with me so powerfully now, when it never has before.

Harrison sprawls back in the chair like a king on his throne, as if he owns it. I realize that he's always been like this, the master of all he surveys, alone at the top of his kingdom, and I wonder what made him that way. What drove him to a life of solitude and savage art, where his only companions were his paints, nicotine and eviscerating bitterness.

'I need to tell you a story,' he husks, reaching into his pocket and pulling out a battered pack of cigarettes, along with his lighter. 'And you, young man, are going to listen.'

* * *

An hour later, my car is packed with my things and I'm driving hell-bent for London, my grandfather's words still ringing through my head.

Tonight, I learned things about the old man that I never knew. About the young woman he lost because of his pride. And his fear. So much sodding fear that it'd locked him down. Closed him off.

Jesus, we really are alike.

But after listening to him, and seeing what he's become because of the choices he made, I'm determined that our story isn't going to be the same.

Once he finished telling me all about the beautiful blonde in the painting that hung above my bed, I'd scrubbed my hands down my face, growling, '*Fuck!* I've been an idiot.'

'Not too late to fix it.'

'You don't know this girl. She's not like—'

'Trust me,' he'd said, cutting me off. 'I learned a hell of a lot about her from the way she spoke about you. Talk to her, Jase. Give yourself the chance to explain.'

'I don't even know what I would say.'

'The right words will come when they need to.'

'They didn't before,' I'd muttered with frustration.

'Because you were walking around with your head up your

arse. Nothing that's said at a time like that is going to be anything other than bullshit. This time, she'll know the difference.'

I'd had to laugh, thinking he has as colorful a way with
words as he does with a paintbrush.

He'd left then, and as I started shoving all my shit into my
bag, as well as grabbing the things that Emmy had left behind,
I kept stealing glances at the painting over the bed. The old
man was right: the blonde standing in the ocean really does
bear a striking resemblance to *my* girl. And even now, as it sits
in the backseat of the Range Rover, I feel like it's mocking me
for being such a stupid fool – and I promise myself that whatever it takes to make it happen, I'll one day be fucking Emmy
again in a bed with that painting hanging over it.

When Callan had knocked on my bedroom door just after
Harrison left, he must have been able to read the determination
carved into my face, because the first words he said to me were,
'You're going after her.'

Not a question, but a statement of fact, and I'd smiled. 'As
fast as I fucking can.'

An answering grin had spread across his mouth, and he
helped me carry everything down.

Unfortunately, we hadn't been able to make a clean getaway.
Caroline and Alistair had been arguing in the foyer, and the
instant she saw me, she said, 'Harrison took a lot of pleasure in
telling us that you're going after her before he left. Why, Jase? If
you do this, you'll ruin everything!'

I have no idea what she was talking about, but a strong sus-
picion that she's been hitting the gin as heavily as Alistair
today. She's fixated on Emmy in an unhealthy way, and I'm
beginning to think that Caroline's having a middle-aged crisis.
Or maybe she just can't stand the thought of someone in this
family actually being happy for a change.

Without a word, I'd moved past them, heading straight for the door. I'd already said everything I have to say, and honestly don't give a shit what they think of my relationship with Emmy. At this point, I'm just praying that I have one. That she'll forgive me and give me another chance, once I find her.

I'm pushing the car to its top speed as I race to reach London in time to catch her at the train station. I've been calling her mobile repeatedly with the Range Rover's hands-free system, but she won't answer. Desperate, I call one of my IT guys at home and have him track down her friend Lola's contact numbers. I call Lola's mobile, as well as her home line, and then her mobile again. She finally answers on the fourth ring, and I suck in a sharp breath, struggling to sound calm so she won't think I'm falling apart. Even though I am. I'm panicking in a way I never have before, as if my entire future hinges on reaching Emmy as quickly as possible.

'Lola, this is Jase. Jase Beckett. Have you heard from Emmy today?'

'I sure have,' she replies, and I can tell from her tone that she thinks I'm a prick. And she's not shy about sharing her opinion, either. 'You really fucked up, didn't you? I mean, do you have any idea how awesome Emmy is? Not even a guy like you is going to find someone like her twice in a lifetime.'

Even though she's giving me shit, I like this girl and am glad that Emmy has such a loyal friend. 'Lola, I need to talk to her.'

'Yeah?' she says. 'About what?'

'It's personal and you know it. Where is she?'

'Are you on your way back to London?' she asks, popping a bubble in my ear so loudly I wince.

'Yes.'

'I'd head straight to Heathrow, if I were you, then. That's the only shot in hell you have of catching her.'

Fuck! I hadn't expected her to bail out of the entire country so quickly. Had assumed she would stay with her London friends for at least a few days before taking off, and my panic takes on a new dimension. Even though it's a Sunday night, there's no telling what traffic might be like near the airport. 'Do you know when her flight leaves?'

'She had her ticket changed. She'll be taking off in a little over an hour.'

Bloody hell. If I'm lucky, I might make it, but it's going to be close. Too close. 'Lola, will you call her for me?'

'And say what?'

'Tell her that I need to talk to her.'

'Have you tried calling her?'

'About a thousand times,' I grunt, 'but she's not picking up.'

'Well, then. I guess she doesn't really want to hear whatever else you have to say.'

What the hell? Did I actually think I liked this woman? 'Damn it, Lola, I need your help!'

'Look, if you were smart, you wouldn't be in this mess. So I guess you're just going to have to hope that you're lucky.'

The connection goes dead, and it takes everything I have not to pick my phone up from the center console and hurl it out the window. I fight the urge, in case I decide to call Lola back. But, Christ, it's not like I can say anything to get her to change her mind about helping me, because I still haven't even figured out what I'm going to say to Emmy if I reach her in time. The talk with my grandfather has made me realize that pretending I can keep my emotions in check – that locking them up is the smartest move – is nothing but a load of bullshit, if I ever want a shot at happiness. But I have no idea what I'm feeling, so how in the fuck will I explain it to Emmy? It's like I'm experiencing every emotion there is all at once, and it's terrifying. Especially when the woman I need to talk it out with, to work through it with me, is dead set on getting away from me.

But here's what I do know.

I know that I don't want Harrison's story, because it sucks.

And I know that Emmy is the only woman I want in my life.

But where does our story go from there?

I'm hoping like hell that it ends with us being together. But there's going to be a lot of shit to get through before we reach that point, and we can't start until I reach *her* and get down on my knees to beg her for another chance.

I make good time to Epsom, but then everything goes to hell because I get caught up in traffic from a massive accident that's clogged up the M25. I keep trying to call Emmy's phone, and start leaving rambling messages that probably just make me sound like an idiot, but she never calls me back. And finally, when I'm still about twenty minutes from the airport, I realize that her flight has already left and I've failed.

Amazingly, that's when the fear finally calms and I'm left with nothing but real, raw insight, and I *know*. I know, without any doubt, exactly what I want my story to be. What I need to say to her when I finally track her down.

I want the beautiful, stubborn, frustrating, fascinating, addictive Emmy Reed in my life and in my bed and in my fucking heart.

And I don't just want her there for a day. Or a month. Or a year.

If I have to chase her halfway around the bloody world, then that's exactly what I'll do. Because I want this woman to be a permanent part of my life.

I want her to be *mine*.

Chapter Two

Thursday morning

EMMY

One week ago today, I met Jase Beckett.

And now it's two hours shy of being exactly four days since I last saw him. It's probably pathetic that I know that, but hey, at least I'm not counting the minutes.

For the most part, they've been a shitty four days. But while my heart has been aching, my brain's been in overdrive. Since I woke up from sleeping for twelve hours straight after my emotional flight home, I've poured everything I have into my article on J.J. Harrison, and I honestly feel that it's the best writing I've ever done.

An hour ago, I submitted the piece to the editor at *Luxe*, so now it's just a waiting game until I hear back from the magazine. Since it could take anywhere from an hour to several weeks before they get back to me, I called my best friend, Tyler, about two seconds after I'd hit send on the email and asked him if he wanted to meet me for a coffee down at our favorite local hangout, Maggie's Java and Books. It's a great little bookstore and coffeehouse, and I'm in desperate need of some 'talk time' with the guy who knows me better than anyone in the world. Tyler is an awesome listener, without being one of those annoying people who feel the need to tell you that they would have done everything differently. He's candid, without being a dick about it. And right now I just need to unload on the poor guy some more, because the weight on my chest is crushing, and it's only getting worse.

I keep telling myself, over and over again, that coming home was the right decision. Jase is from one world, and I'm from another, and our brief weekend together wasn't the start of some star-crossed Shakespearean romance.

But that doesn't mean that getting over him is going to be any easier.

Every time I close my eyes, I remember. Remember every sharp, piercing, electric detail. And not just the sexual stuff – though a lot of that is playing front and center in my mind, because the way he made me feel isn't something a woman can just forget. In fact, I swear there are still echoes of pleasure swirling through my body from the hot, explicit way that he fucked me. And I can't forget how his big, magnificent body had moved. The way his powerful muscles had coiled and flexed as he rode me, nailing me to the bed with so much mastery and hunger, I know I'll never be the same.

God, I miss his scent. The tenor of his voice. The way he looked at me, as if I always had his complete and total focus. In my entire life, no one has ever looked at me the way that Jase did, or listened to me as carefully, and I can't forget it.

I can't forget *him*.

If anything, the ache has only grown deeper with each day that's passed since Angus drove me away from Beckett House, and I'm drowning in it. And knowing that Jase tried to reach out to me only makes it so much worse.

I'd been such a wreck when I was on the train, after I managed to call Lola and have her help me change my flight, that I spilled the cup of coffee I'd bought from the food cart on my phone and the damn thing stopped working. I still haven't taken the time to get it fixed or buy a new one, because I've been so buried in my article – and let's face it, after paying the exorbitant fee to change my ticket, I'm strapped for cash – so I have no idea if Jase has called and left me any messages. But I'd phoned Lola again, when I finally got home, sounding like a zombie, and she told me that Jase had called her on Sunday night, desperate to find me.

I'm trying not to read too much into the fact that he'd called one of my closest friends, since for all I know he just wanted to throw the same argument in my face – that the sex was too incredible to give up, until we burned out on it – and I can't go through that. Whatever courage I'd built up before going to bed with him was shattered when I realized just how far I'd already fallen for him. What I thought was a friendly case of intense lust and genuine affection ran so much deeper, and I know that I can't risk flying back there. If I do, I'll stay and do it. Fuck him for fun – and then what would be left of me, and of my heart, in the end?

No. I have to cut myself off *now*, while I'm still able to function.

Grabbing my keys, I take one last look at myself in the mirror, checking my eyes to make sure the concealer I used under them is doing its job. I haven't slept for shit since collapsing with exhaustion when I got home, and it's starting to show. But since there's nothing I can do about it, I turn away from the unforgiving mirror and head out.

As I open my front door, flinching when the bright California sunshine hits my eyes for the first time in days, my initial thought is that I must be hallucinating. Through the glare of golden light, I think I see a tall, muscular guy dressed in jeans and a T-shirt, leaning back against a sleek, black sports car. He's got familiar broad shoulders and dark hair, with an air of alpha arrogance about him that's so freaking sexy, and I press my hand against the center of my chest as a bolt of pain slams into me.

I shake my head a little as I get closer, a nearby jacaranda tree blocking the sun enough that I'm able to see him clearly, and shock slams into me so hard I nearly fall back on my ass.

It's Jase! Jase-Freaking-Beckett is parked in front of my apartment! And he looks . . . God, he looks delicious, but exhausted, like he hasn't slept in days. My lips part, but it takes me two tries before I'm able to croak, 'Wh-what are you doing here?'

He straightens and steps away from the car, which brings him close enough that I can see the frustration burning in those dark-lashed, beautiful blue eyes. 'I expected a proper goodbye, Emmy.'

I gape at him, which probably makes me look like a fish. But I can't help it. This is just too bizarre. 'Jase, what *the hell* are you doing here?'

He works his jaw for a moment, while his dark gaze moves over me, taking me in. And then he just grates, 'We need to talk.'

'And say what? I already told you I can't accept your offer of some super fun fuck time in the UK,' I snap, sounding so bitter that I cringe. I'm also talking way too loudly, and I give a fervent prayer that my nosy grump of a neighbor, Mr Jennings, is already out for the day.

Jase lifts one of his big, masculine hands, his biceps looking freaking mouthwatering as he shoves his fingers back through his hair. The thick, silky locks are already tousled, either by the wind or his hands, and if I had to guess, I'd pick the latter.

Completely ignoring what I've said, he tells me, 'I would have been here sooner, but I had to get some things settled in London before I could take off.'

'Oh,' I murmur, too freaking confused to figure out what's going on. Is he here for business? For me? For sex? 'How long are you here for?' I ask, thinking his answer might clarify things a bit.

'That's what I had to get settled. I'm staying at the Hotel Del out on Coronado, and I plan to stay there for as long as it takes.'

His response just confuses me even more. 'As long as *what* takes?'

'For us to make this solid.' His smoldering blue gaze is locked so hard on mine, I couldn't have looked away to save my life. 'If that's what you want.'

'I . . . I'm . . . God, Jase. Is that what *you* want?'

'It is. I want you, Em. I don't know how to say it any clearer than that,' he husks, and the flush of color on his cheekbones tells me his emotions are running just as high as mine. 'I fucking want you, and I don't want to lose you. Not again. I'll do whatever it takes to keep that from happening.'

'Holy shit,' I breathe, feeling light headed. 'Is this for real?'

A frown starts to knit its way between his dark brows. 'Of course it is.'

'And I'm . . . I'm just meant to believe you?'

'I'm here, aren't I?'

In that moment, I'm nothing but chaos, and I cling to my anger in a desperate bid for focus and balance. 'But you said that—'

He cuts me off, growling, 'I said a lot of shitty things, I know. And you're the one who threw me away. But I chased after you anyway, because I fucking care about you.'

Those words on his lips, spoken in his deep, gravelly, accented voice, are nearly my undoing. But I'm too pissed to back down, and God only knows what my neighbors must be thinking, because I shout, 'You can't throw away something you never had!'

'You never even *tried* to have me,' he bites out. 'We had one argument, and then you *ran*.'

'You didn't give me any reason to stay! Because like I said before, "we're good at screwing each other" doesn't count!'

'Why the fuck do you think I'm here now?' he roars, and before I can respond, I'm flying through the air. The Neanderthal actually tosses me over his shoulder like a fireman, his long legs eating up the yards of cracked concrete that make up the walkway as he heads right for my front door.

'What the hell are you doing?' I seethe, banging my fists against his back.

'I'm not doing this on the street.'

'Then don't do it at all,' I snap, wriggling when I feel him reach into the back pocket of my shorts for my keys. He'd obviously seen me slip them in there, and the bastard gets lucky when he tries the right one first. As he opens my front door, I snarl, 'Just get back in your fancy rental car and drive back to the goddamn airport!'

'You don't mean that,' he grunts, kicking the door shut behind us. He carries me over to my small sofa, drops me on it from so high that I bounce, shoves the coffee table out of his way, and then leans over and cages me in with his hands braced against the sofa's back and side. 'That's not what you want,' he says low, his blue eyes like fire as he stares down at me, his chest working hard with his heavy breaths. 'Not even close.'

'You have no idea what I want!'

'Of course I do, Em. You want *me*. You want me just as badly as I want you. Because if you didn't, you wouldn't be so damn angry. And now you're going to shut up for two seconds and listen to what I have to say.'

I cross my arms over my chest and glare up at him.

'I was too terrified to give you a reason to stay with me in England.' His deep voice is rougher than I've ever heard it. 'But I'm ready to explain my reasons for coming after you.'

I can tell from the way he's looking at me, from the raw emotion burning in those incredible eyes, that he's going to say something that breaks me, and I scream at him to stop it from happening. 'It's too late, Jase. It's too fucking late!'

'Why?' he demands, giving me a look that's as tender as it is fierce. 'Did you fall for someone else?'

I roll my eyes, since it's obvious that I haven't.

Quietly, he says, 'Emmy, has there been anyone else?'

'What?' I scoff. 'You think I was so upset over you, I had to go and find some new dick to fool around with the instant I was stateside?'

'Jesus, woman. Just answer the bloody question.'

I want to shout at him again, but my voice comes out soft with pain. 'And what if there was, Jase? What then?'

'I'd hate it,' he says with a hard breath, staring at me so intensely it feels like a physical touch. 'And I'd want to kill the bastard with my bare hands. But we didn't have any promises between us, so I'd get the hell over it.'

'What about you? What have *you* been doing since I left?'

'I've barely slept, barely eaten. I haven't been fit to be near, as I'm sure Martin would be happy to tell you. I swear he was about ready to quit on me before I flew out. But I haven't been with anyone, obviously.'

I arch one eyebrow as I snort with derision. 'Hardly obvious, Jase.'

'When I just chased a beautiful, cranky American halfway around the world?' he asks with a husky laugh.

'I'm not cranky!'

'You're scared,' he says, his tone so gentle and caring it nearly destroys me. 'I know, baby. But you don't need to be.'

I can't stop the stupid tears that are suddenly burning at the backs of my eyes, but I'm too stubborn to give in.

'And just to be clear,' he adds, bringing his gorgeous face even closer to mine, 'I don't want any other man laying his hands on you. Not even a finger.'

'And what about you and all your other women?'

He cocks his head, lips twitching with a sexy smile. 'There are no other women, Em. I don't want anyone else. The only woman I want is *you*.'

'Why?'

'Fucked if I know,' he drawls, that delicious accent of his nearly my undoing.

I glare again and it makes him laugh.

'You drive me crazy. Run from me. Insult me. But hell if I can stay away from you, sweetheart.'

'It's the challenge,' I snap, clutching at arguments. 'If you had me, you'd be bored. Lose interest.'

His dark brows lift, and he gives me a knowing look. 'I've already had you. *Twice*. And you know what? There wasn't a single boring thing about it. And all I can think about is having you again . . . and again . . . and again.'

I look away and shove my hair back from my face, squeezing my eyes shut. My shoulders lift as I take in a couple of deep, shaky breaths, and without looking at him, I start to say, 'Jase, we—'

But he cuts me off before I can get another word out.

'I mean it, Em.' He grips my chin, pulling my face forward again, and I open my eyes to find him so close our noses are nearly touching, his warm breaths pelting across my trembling lips. 'It was the fucking best I've ever had, and now I'm hooked, woman. Addicted. *Obsessed*. I want to bury myself inside you and stay there forever.' His thumb strokes my skin, and his hot, heavy-lidded gaze has me melting like taffy that's been left out in the sun. 'But I also want to just hold you and talk to you. Hear you laugh. Watch you smile. And so I left my business in as good of shape as I could, got my arse on a plane, and now I'm here. And I'm not going anywhere.'

I don't know if it's his words, or the way we're looking at each other, but something happens. Suddenly we can't seem to fight the pull a second longer, because I manage to take one quick, shivery breath, and then we're smashing together like the sea and the shore, and the instant we touch, we go wild on each other. There's no better way to describe it. He pulls me down longways on the sofa as I rip his shirt up over his head and run my hands over his hard, muscular shoulders. My clothes fly as he brushes his mouth over my jaw, my throat, until he's bared me completely. Then he twists and turns me, tasting me everywhere, his clever tongue stroking over my tattoos like he's tasting their meaning on my skin.

We're all greed and hunger and lust, and I'm so wet for him I'm literally dripping down the insides of my thighs. He drops down on his knees in front of the sofa, shoves my thighs as wide as they'll go, and starts licking up the trails of moisture, working closer and closer to that pulsing, swelling part of me.

'Your taste makes me so damn hard it hurts,' he growls against my inner thigh, nipping it with his teeth.

'I need you,' I gasp, fisting my hands in his dark hair as his tongue flicks over my slick opening, then shoves inside, and I'm arching from the breathtaking sensation when I feel the tip of his thumb press against the tiny hole buried between my ass cheeks. It makes me cry out, because I've never had anyone touch me there. But I'm not surprised, because I knew, from the first time he kissed me, that Jase would be filthy in the sack. And even out of it, considering we're still in my tiny living room, getting ready to fuck on my sofa.

He licks and laps at me, sucking on my clit, and then running the flat of his tongue nearly all the way down to where his thumb is still stroking that tight, sensitive ring. I come hard and fast, gushing against his open mouth as he swallows and growls, drinking me down. Then he jerks up, ripping his jeans open as he takes a condom out of his back pocket, and I know in about five seconds he's going to be shoving that massive cock inside me. But there's something I need first, and I cry, 'Wait! Just wait. It's my turn.'

He stills, staring at me in confusion. 'What?'

'I thought I would never get the chance to get my mouth on you,' I pant, swiftly moving to my knees, 'and it killed me. So get up here. *Now.*'

'Fuck,' he grunts, as I push him into a corner of the sofa and tug his jeans and boxers over his hips, my hungry gaze glued to the beautiful sight of his heavy cock as it springs out, bouncing against his ridged abs. Veins bulge over the dark, silky shaft, the bruise-colored head shiny and slick, and as I lick my lips, he curses something gritty and raw under his breath.

'Shh,' I murmur, already lowering my head as I kneel beside him. 'Just relax and let me have some fun.'

'I'm not gonna last two seconds,' he groans, sounding more excited than I've ever heard him, and there's a smile on my lips as I feel him pull my hair to the side so he can watch. The skin on the crown of his cock is taut and wet with salty drops of pre-cum, and as I swipe at them with my tongue, I love the guttural sound that rumbles up from his chest. But I'm in no mood to tease, so I open my mouth and push down, determined to take as much of his big, thick dick as I can, desperate to make it as good for him as he's done for me. I suck hard as I stroke him with my wet mouth, and I gag a little as the fat head hits the back of my throat, but force myself to breathe through it, loving how wild it's making him. He's sweating and cursing and his muscles are so firm it's like he's been chiseled from a block of granite. He's all thick veins and stiff lines of sinew, his abs so cut he could grace the cover of any romance book and have readers all over the world drooling over him.

But he's *mine*. Every hot, thick, delicious inch of him, and I've never imagined that I could enjoy making a guy lose control the way I'm enjoying it now.

And he's definitely losing it. His head goes back, eyes squeezed shut, both hands fisted in my hair, and I watch him greedily from under my lashes. Watch the way his corded throat works as he gives a hard swallow. The way his broad chest rises and falls with his choppy breaths.

'Emmy,' he growls, and I look up again to find his heavy-lidded gaze locked in on me, sharp and tight. The blue is raging and violent, like a storm-tossed sea, telling me everything I need to know. His jaw goes rigid, his nostrils flare, and his grip on my hair tightens, holding me still as he starts jacking himself into my open mouth. He goes deep, gagging me again, but I work through it, sucking on him with everything I've got, and he starts to shudder.

'*No more*,' he snarls, suddenly pulling my head back, his thick shaft slipping from my mouth.

'What? Why?' I gasp, knowing he was close. That I'd almost taken him over the edge. And while this has never been my thing in the past, I'd be lying if I said I didn't freaking *love* the feel of Jase Beckett throbbing between my lips, while his mouthwatering scent filled my head.

'I haven't had you in days,' he bites out, grabbing the

condom packet he'd tossed on to the arm of the sofa when I made it clear that I wanted to go down on him. He rips the packet open with his teeth, and his hands are shaking as he smooths it over his dark, bulging shaft. 'When I come,' he says, 'I'm coming inside you, Emmy. As deep inside you as I can get.'

The next thing I know, he's pulled me beneath him, my back to the sofa, legs spread wide, and his gorgeous body is coming down over me, his weight braced on one hand by my shoulder, while he fists his cock with the other.

And with our faces so close together our noses are nearly touching again, he looks me right in the eye and husks, 'You'd better hold on, love. This is gonna be rough.'

JASE

Her eyes go wide at my words, and I thrust inside her so hard and deep that she screams, her tight cunt so wet that she's able to take me all the way to the root, even though I'm stretching her narrow sheath as wide as it'll go. I withdraw almost to the tip and then drive back in even harder, until I'm hitting the end of her, and I know damn well that I'm too desperate for her to make this anything but a raw, aggressive fucking.

I move inside her with a rhythm that turns our bodies warm and slick, my cock nearly steaming from the snug, slippery heat of her cunt. I ride her like my goddamn life depends on how deep I can take her. Ride her so hard that something actually falls off her apartment wall, crashing against the hardwood floor. Then there's a loud knocking, like someone banging their fist on the other side of the wall, and a muffled voice shouts, 'For the love of God, give it a rest in there!'

We laugh as we kiss, not even slowing down. Our mouths

are wet and eager, and even though we're smiling, we're still fucking so hard we're like animals, her nails digging into my shoulders and my free hand curling around the back of her neck, holding her still as I take her sweet mouth just as thoroughly as I'm taking her sweet little pussy.

I want it to last forever, but all too soon the end is bearing down on me, and my head goes back, a harsh shout on my lips as I start to unload. The pleasure's so intense I feel like I'm being turned inside out, and I shudder with relief when I feel her cunt tighten on me like a cushiony vise, and then convulse, her soft cry joining my own carnal sounds as she comes for me. Her orgasm is so intense that she keeps milking the cum right out of me, my seed spilling until I'm worried I'll overflow the condom.

Reaching down, I hold the condom in place as I carefully pull out of her snug clasp, my forehead pressed against hers as I pant for breath. 'Christ, Em. I think you broke me.'

She's shaking with a breathless burst of laughter as I wrap my arms around her, lift up, then turn and fall back into a corner of the sofa, her body sprawled across my chest, legs on either side of my hips, my dick trapped between us. We shiver as the sweat starts to dry on our skin, our breaths slowly evening out, and I can't stop touching her. I stroke the feminine line of her spine, then her golden curls, the flare of her hips. She's so damn soft and plush, and I can't get enough of how she feels under my hands and against my body.

'I need to call Tyler,' she says eventually, her hands spreading over my chest as she sits up on my thighs and locks her cinnamon-brown gaze with mine. 'He's expecting me for coffee. That's where I was headed when I walked outside.'

'Can't you just text him?'

She shakes her head. 'My phone broke when I was still in England.'

I lift my brows and ask, 'On Sunday night?'

She nods as a wry smile kicks up the corner of her pink, kiss-swollen lips. 'I spilled coffee all over it on the train.'

'So you really didn't get any of my messages?'

She tilts her head a bit, her gaze curious. 'Not a single one. What did they say?'

With my hands sliding up and down her ribs, my thumbs stroking the sides of her beautiful breasts, I snort and give a gritty laugh. 'About fifty of them were nothing but frustrated rantings, and the other fifty were just me begging you not to leave.'

'When I didn't respond, I'm sure you could have gotten my home number or my email. That is, if you don't already have them.'

'I could've,' I admit. And then, with a sheepish grin, I say, 'But once I'd calmed down, I started planning to come after you, and I didn't want to give you the opportunity to tell me not to.'

She laughs at that, which is a relief. But her gaze slides to the side as she catches her bottom lip in her teeth, and then she looks at me again and asks, 'What happened after I left?'

'I had it out with Caroline,' I answer with a heavy breath. 'And I finally realized that I'm done with them, Em. I'm not going back there.'

'I don't blame you, Jase. They don't deserve you.'

I close my eyes at those soft, sweet words, then open them and say, 'J.J. came to see me before I left.'

Her eyes go wide as she searches my expression for clues. 'What did he say?'

My chest shakes with a quiet laugh, and I settle my hands on her hips. 'He wanted to tell me a story.'

'A story?' Her golden brows pinch with confusion. 'I don't understand.'

'He said that you'd got him thinking, and at first, I think he just wanted to talk to me. To see if what you'd told him was true. That I'm not like Alistair.'

'He believed me?' she asks with surprise.

With a small shrug, I say, 'I don't know if he did at first. But your words definitely got him thinking. And he overheard me having it out with Caroline.'

'Well, it's about damn time that he knew the truth. And he has no one to blame but himself for treating you like he has all these years.' She tilts her head again as she says, 'But what was this story he wanted to tell you?'

'His initial reason for coming over was just to see for himself if you were right. But after he learned that you'd left me, I guess it . . .' Another laugh rumbles up from my chest and I shake my head. 'To be honest, Em, I'm not really sure *what* made him do it, but he told me about the blonde in his paintings. He said that her name is Gianna, and that he . . . That he *worshipped* her. Those were his exact words. That he fucking worshipped her, and she felt the same way about him.'

'Then what went wrong?'

'His feelings for her were so strong that they scared the hell out of him. He was so terrified they would make him weak that he married Janine instead, who he considered a safe choice, and offered to keep Gianna on the side as his mistress. Figured that way she wouldn't ever have too much control over his emotions.'

'Oh, God,' she whispers. 'That's so tragic.'

'Yeah, it didn't go well. From what I could gather, Gianna basically told him to piss off. He said that he knew, instantly, that he'd made a mistake. One that he was going to regret for the rest of his life. But he'd been too proud to beg her forgiveness.' I tighten my grip on her hips, and my next words come out as little more than a throaty rasp. 'He told me that you reminded him of her.'

She blinks with a soft look of shock. 'Really?'

'Yeah.' I swallow to clear the lump of emotion in my throat, and go on. 'I have a feeling that's probably the biggest compliment he could give a person.'

'Why doesn't he just find her and admit that he made a mistake?'

With a grim smile, I tell her, 'Because she's happily married with a huge family, Em. She got on with her life.'

'But all these years, she might have still been in love with him.'

'I know,' I say with a hard sigh. 'It sucks.'

'And so you talked to him, and decided . . . What?' she asks, giving me another one of those deep, searching looks. 'What made you come here?'

'I took a long, hard look at myself and was finally honest about what I feel. And what I want.' I sit up, cupping the side of her face in my hand as I say, 'I don't want his story, Em. I don't want to grow into the old fool who let the only woman he ever truly cared about slip through his fingers because he was too much of a coward to let her in.'

'Jase.'

'So you need to know that you've fucking got me. By the balls,' I tell her, brushing a soft kiss across her trembling lips, 'and every other part of me too. You just need to decide if you want to keep me.'

She reaches up and curls both hands around my forearm, the tightness of her grip making me want to shout with triumph. 'I won't lie and say that I'm not terrified, because I am. But, yeah, you gorgeous, frustrating alpha, I want to keep you.'

Her words make me smile, and I can't help pressing my advantage. 'For how long, baby?'

'For as long as I can, Jase.' Her beautiful brown eyes gleam with emotion. 'For as long as you'll let me.'

'God,' I groan, every part of me shaking as I wrap my arms

around her, pulling her close. 'Hold on to me,' I tell her. 'Whatever happens, Em, don't let me go.'

She stares into my eyes like she can see all the way down into my soul, and I know that she gets what I'm saying. That I don't just mean now, but for forever.

'Promise me,' I growl.

She leans forward, pressing her sweet mouth to mine, and whispers, *'I promise.'*

* * *

After our conversation about Harrison and why I'm here, the morning goes by in a soft, hazy blur that's sharpened only by pleasure and need. I pull up my jeans and go out to my car, grabbing the small bag that I'd tossed in the backseat. It's got a change of clothes, as well as the rest of the condoms from the box that I'd bought at the hotel.

When I get back inside, I pick Emmy up again and carry her to her bedroom. The room is just what I would have imagined for her, with a wrought-iron bed covered in white cotton, a quirky chest of drawers painted a deep, dark purple, a few packed bookshelves, a desk, and framed posters of famous paintings all over the walls.

I lay her down on the bed, hurry to ditch my clothes and shoes, and then I've got another condom on and I'm over her. *In* her. I've never stayed this hard for a woman in my entire life, and as mind-blowing as our connection is, I have a feeling it has something to do with how we're connecting on other levels as well. We keep smiling as we kiss, as if we can't believe we're together, and I know that getting on that plane was the smartest decision I've ever made.

I can't get enough of holding her down and driving into her perfect little cunt as hard and as deep as I can, determined to wipe out the memory of every other man she's ever known. Because God only knows she's blown every other woman from mine. It's *that* incredible. That fucking intense, literally.

I lose count of how many times I take her, but as the clock on her bedside table ticks up to eleven, I'm lying on my back with my head on a pillow, and she's cuddled up against my side, one leg over mine, her arm thrown over my abdomen as she rests her head on my biceps.

I want to roll over and pull her under me again, right now, but she's drowsy from all the orgasms, and so I settle for tugging her up closer against me, neither of us saying a word as she snuggles against my chest and I stroke her hair. She slips into a heavy sleep, despite it being so early in the day, and I wish I could do the same. But as exhausted as I am, I can't close my eyes yet. It's like I'm terrified she'll slip away, and I'll wake up to find her gone. So I spend the minutes while she dozes just watching her, holding her, my mind going a mile a minute as I try to formulate a plan for where we go from here.

Christ, there are so many questions that I still don't know the answers to.

But the one thing I *do* know, and with absolute certainty, is that I've done the right thing by coming here. I've fallen for this beautiful girl so hard, and that isn't going to change. I have no doubt that what I'm feeling is going to keep on growing wider and deeper, and while that would have scared the hell out of me before, I'm holding J.J.'s story tight to my chest.

I'm not a particularly religious or spiritual kind of guy, but there's no ignoring the hand of fate that's at work here.

The way I rescued Emmy.

Her article on J.J.

Her effect on the old man, and how it prompted him to come and talk to me.

Jesus, it's all so fucking unlikely, but so goddamn perfect. And maybe this is how good things happen. In a burst of *what the ever-loving hell is going on*. Some random, magnificent roll of the dice, where two people crash together in one vibrant, blinding moment of potential.

I grabbed at the opportunity when I had her in my office last Thursday. And then again, when I chased after her all the way to America.

Now that I'm here, and I'm holding her, the way Emmy fits against me is so fucking perfect it's like she was made for me, and I know that I'm not letting go. Only an idiot would let this woman slip through his fingers a second time, and I won't make that mistake.

Somewhere out on the street, a dog starts barking, and I can hear what I think must be a skateboard on the road. Cool air is blowing down on us from the vents up near the ceiling, and I press a soft kiss to the top of her head, then finally close my eyes, unable to keep them open.

But there's one last thing I need to do before I let the exhaustion take me under.

And that's to send up a silent 'thank you' to whoever's up there that might be listening.

Chapter Three

JASE

We wake in the early afternoon, and we're both starving. But we're hungrier for each other.

I'm sitting with my back propped up against her headboard, and Emmy's straddling me, sitting in my lap as I finger her snug, juicy cunt. I tell her to arch her back, then lower my head, sucking and nipping at her pink, tender nipples, unable to get enough of how they feel on my tongue, or the sharp cries I'm pulling up out of her throat. Her cream covers my fingers, spilling over my hand, the feel and scent of her making my mouth water.

Undone by the way she responds to me, I slide on to my back as I lift her up, then bring her down on my face, eating her out like it's my bloody job in life to make her come all over me. I can't stop swallowing her down, loving how warm and sweet she is, her pink, swollen pussy so soft it's like silk.

She comes for me again with a husky, sexy cry, and my hands are busy sliding another condom on as I lick up every drop she's giving me, her taste the most incredible thing I've ever had on my lips. She's still pulsing with little aftershocks when I pull her under me and lift her arms up high over her head, stretching her out. Threading our fingers together, I stare into her eyes as I shove inside her tight cunt, going so deep it makes her flinch. I grind my teeth as I pull back, loving the way her body tries to hold me inside, then thrust back in, fighting not to lose control. She's so small that I could easily fuck her so hard it hurts her, and while I know she likes a bit of bite with her pleasure, I'd damn well die before taking her past that point where all she wants is to kick her head back, dig her heels into my arse, and demand that I give her exactly what she needs.

'One of these days, Em, I'm going to fill you up,' I growl on a downstroke, grinding against her sensitive clit before I pull back again. 'I want you to be full of my cum. Want you drenched in it.'

She arches and moans, the little pulse in her cunt telling me that her body likes the idea of me taking her without anything between us. Bracing myself on one arm, I reach down and stroke my fingers over her clit, giving it a few hard flicks that make her arch like she's been zapped with a current. Then I reach lower, stroking the edges of the slick, slippery opening I'm currently claiming with my cock, loving how stretched she is around me, the silky flesh barely able to take me.

Words are crowding into my throat, shoved there by my building emotions, but I don't know how to get them past my lips. All I can do is keep fucking her, claiming her, and when I come, she's right there with me, her nails digging into my back and her teeth in my shoulder. I love the way she gets so lost in the pleasure that it makes her wild. Makes her greedy.

We're still trying to catch our breaths when someone knocks on her front door, and her heavy-lidded eyes go comically wide. 'Shoot, I forgot to call Tyler!'

As if he's heard her whisper, the guy I know is her best friend shouts, 'Hey, Em, are you in there?'

She scurries off the bed, hurriedly throwing on her shorts and shirt, minus any underwear, and yells, 'I'm here!'

She quickly runs out into the hallway, and I grab my jeans, tugging them on as I follow behind her. I'm just entering the living room when she cracks the front door open and whispers, 'I'm sorry I didn't call you, but I'm with Jase. He, um, flew all the way here to see me. And to, uh, talk.'

The guy gives a quiet laugh and drawls, 'Talk, huh? Is that what you call going at it so hard I could hear your headboard slamming into the wall the moment I climbed out of my car?'

'Ohmygod!' she gasps, and I know her cheeks have probably gone bright pink. And then her voice gets lower. 'I'm warning you now, Ty. If you say one embarrassing thing in front of him, I'm kicking you in the balls.'

He laughs again, then clucks his tongue. 'So I suppose his presence explains the shiny black Ferrari parked behind me, yeah?'

'Um, yeah.'

'You gonna let me in so I can meet him?'

'Of course. Just, um, give me a second.'

She shuts the door, immediately looking over at me, and I can tell that she's completely panicked, which is pretty freaking cute. I'm just not sure what has her the most worried: that I'll be a dick to surfer boy, or that he'll be a dick to me.

'Um, Ty's here,' she says, and sure enough, her little face looks like she's been sunburned.

'I gathered that, baby.'

'Okay,' she says, taking a deep breath and smoothing her hands over her tousled curls, 'I'm going to let him in now.'

I just smile in response, since I have a feeling she was talking more to herself there than to me.

She opens the door then, and the guy walks inside, sliding her a smirk as she shuts the door behind him.

I know, from talking to Emmy during our weekend in Kent, that Tyler is a dedicated surfer by day who works as a bartender by night to pay the bills. She told me he was tall, built and blond, as well as good looking, but I hadn't expected him to be one of the best-looking guys I've ever seen. Jesus, he fucking looks like he could play Thor in a movie, and I take a moment to thank that higher power again that this bloke is gay, or I know his friendship with Emmy would make me jealous as hell.

And, yeah, I'm already fighting a battle with the green-eyed monster when I watch the way she suddenly throws herself into his arms, hugging him like she hasn't seen him in years, when it's only been a few weeks.

'Should I put on some coffee?' I ask, thinking it might be a good idea to give them a moment alone. Especially since the way he's holding her is making me want to beat my chest like a bloody caveman.

'Thanks, but I can't stay that long,' Tyler says, looking over at me. He takes his time, checking me out from my bare feet up to my own sex-wrecked hair, and there's another smirk on his lips when he says, 'Wow, Em. I figured the day would come when you finally decided to give my type a try. Way to go, baby girl.'

She shoots him a sharp look, then takes another deep breath and says, 'Tyler, this is Jase Beckett. Jase, this is my best friend and a sometimes complete pain in the ass, Tyler Landon.'

Tyler and I are both laughing as I shake the hand he's offering me. 'It's good to meet you,' I say, thinking this meeting might go better than I'd expected.

But then the guy pulls his hand back, crosses his muscular arms over his chest, and snorts under his breath. 'I wish I could say the same.'

'Ty,' Em snaps, but he's not listening to her. No, he's too busy giving me a steely look that tells me she's told him everything. That I fucked her, and then made my stupid offer to stay with me in London until we'd had our fill of each other.

Shit, when I think about it, I guess I don't blame the guy for looking at me like he wants to take me out for a special hunting trip. One where he comes back, but I don't.

He opens his mouth again, no doubt about to lay into me, but I cut him off at the pass. 'I'm not going to hurt her.'

He gives another snort as he jerks his chin at me. 'Too late, man. You already have.'

'And I've flown over five thousand miles to say that I made a mistake. I've left behind my business. My life. *Everything*. Because I realized she's more important.'

Emmy gives a soft gasp, my words obviously taking her by surprise, but Tyler just arches one of his golden brows. 'And now you're here and the two of you have had what I can tell was the motherfucking bomb of reunions, seeing as how my girl looks like she can barely walk straight. So what's next, Jase?'

'Ty, don't,' she says low, glaring at him.

'Sorry, Em, but I love you,' he mutters, scraping a palm over his bearded jaw, 'and I can't help worrying about the pieces I'm gonna have to put back together when Brit boy here gets his fill of you and scampers back home.'

'Ty!'

'I'm not going to hurt her,' I say again, my narrowed gaze locked in hard on his green one. 'And I know damn well that I'm never getting my fill. Not today. Not tomorrow. Not years from now. She's *mine*.'

'So you're moving here?' he laughs, giving me a knowing smile. 'Should I start planning a citizenship party for you?'

Tension slides up my spine. 'We haven't got that far yet.'

'Well, when you do, Jase, make sure I'm the first to know.'

He steps towards me, and we're nearly nose to nose. 'Because I'm watching you, big guy.'

I brace, thinking he might actually take a swing at me, but it never comes. Instead, he just grins and gives me a wink, before turning and walking back over to Emmy. He grabs her up in his arms, squishing her tight as he leans down and whispers something in her ear that I can't hear. But it makes her blush, and then he presses a kiss to her cheek that I know is for my benefit, making sure I get just how close they are.

'Fuck,' I mutter to myself as he heads out and Emmy shuts the door behind him, knowing I've made a shitty first impression. Still, I can't help but like and admire the guy. And I can see why Emmy cares about him, because it's clear that Tyler Landon would take a fucking bullet for her. To be honest, I'm a little in awe of him, because he doesn't have a single guard or shield or wall in sight. He isn't afraid to show whatever motherfucking thing he's feeling, and I feel like there's a hell of a lot I could learn from him.

'So, um, yeah,' she says with a sharp sigh, as she locks the door and turns to face me. 'That was Tyler.'

EMMY

I don't think I've ever actually been relieved to see Tyler leave before, but *damn*. That was *so* uncomfortable, and I know my face must be beet red from the heat pulsing in it.

He's always been protective, but I had no idea he'd go so mama bear on Jase. I love him for it, but that . . . That was so embarrassing!

I get where Ty is coming from though. This was the first I've seen him since flying home, but we've talked every day on the phone, and he knows how wrecked I've been. I'm taking a huge leap of faith by accepting Jase with open arms, and I haven't been able to explain any of it yet to Ty.

Am I scared? Of course I am. But after the incredible morning I've just shared with Jase . . . Let's just say that the fear is completely worth it.

I loved the intimacy of sleeping in his arms today – something I've never done before with a man, except for when Jase and I were together in England. Loved the warmth and weight of him beside me, his hair all spiky and the beard on his jaw even darker than it'd been when I found him leaning against the beautiful car that's currently parked out on the street. But it's the way I keep catching him looking at me, and the things he's said, that have thrown me. Changed me. Completely *undone* me.

Still standing in the middle of my living room, Jase pushes his hands into his front pockets, and I'm sliding an appreciative gaze over the hard muscles in his chest and abdomen when I hear him say, 'I like him.'

My jaw immediately drops as I jerk my wide-eyed gaze back up to his. 'You do? Because I'm pretty sure he was acting like a total ass to you.'

'Only because he's looking out for you, sweetheart. And I'm sure as hell not going to fault the guy for that.'

'Huh,' is all I can manage as I walk past him, and I'm thinking that maybe I need some serious levels of caffeine before any of this starts making sense.

'By the way,' Jase drawls with a crooked smile that I catch in the mirror hanging over my dresser, as he follows me into my bedroom, 'in case you missed it, Tyler totally thinks I'm hot.'

'You are so freaking cocky,' I say, rolling my eyes. 'Not to mention conceited!'

His laugh is deliciously low. 'And you're the only woman in the world who would dare insult me.'

I snort as I grab my hairbrush. 'That's just because they're all so busy kissing your ass,' I tell him, trying not to cringe as I finally take a good look at myself in the mirror. God, I'm surprised Tyler didn't fall down with laughter when he saw me, because I definitely look like I've been ridden hard and put away wet.

Before I even realize what Jase is doing, he comes up behind me and drops down on his knees. With his hands on my hips, he lowers his head and nuzzles his mouth up under the frayed hem of my shorts, pressing his lips to the under-curve of my right butt cheek. 'That's what's so different about you,' he murmurs, flicking his tongue against me. 'Because here I am, kissing *yours* instead.'

'Only because you're getting what you want.'

'We *both* are,' he says roughly, running his hands up my sides as he moves back to his feet.

'Are you so sure you're what I want?' I tease, meeting his heavy-lidded gaze in the mirror.

'I have to be, Em. If I don't believe it, I might start bawling my eyes out.'

I shiver at those telling words, and he just leans down, kissing my shoulder before he walks back out to the living room, where the T-shirt he was wearing this morning is still lying on the floor.

We finish getting dressed and head into my ridiculously tiny kitchen, where he helps me make some sandwiches for lunch. We eat them with chips and some sodas, sitting at the small table that's pressed up against the wall in my living room, and I use the time to ask about his flight over. He tells me that they were late getting in yesterday, and he didn't land until after midnight, which is why he waited till this morning to come over. I curl my feet around the bottom rungs of the chair and spend more time just staring at him than I do eating, unable to believe he's really sitting here at my table. That he left a multi-million-pound company in the hands of his most trusted employee, and dropped everything just to come after me.

It's the most amazing, stunning thing that anyone has ever done for me, and my senses are buzzing, my skin tingling like I'm touching a live wire. It's like he's woken me up from a deep and heavy sleep, and now I'm turned on and fully charged, ready to drag him back into my bedroom and feast on him until I'm gorged.

When we're done, we load the dishes into my slimline dish-washer, and before I carry out my bedroom plan, he drags me into my bathroom, strips my clothes off along with his own, and pulls me into the shower with him. Then he pushes me up against the tiled back wall, and goes down on his knees again.

Only this time, it's not my ass Jase is kissing, but my drenched pussy. And he's taking it like he owns it. Like he's the only man I want between my legs, not just today, but for . . . always.

For forever.

Oh, God. I shove that thought out of my head, unable to deal with it, and focus instead on the sensations. On the lush, exquisite pleasure.

'I can't get enough of you,' he growls, licking me like a cat with cream, the slow, intimate strokes of his tongue making me tremble and pant.

I've read about guys who like going down on women so much that they did it all the time, but never imagined they really existed. Much less that I would have one in my life . . . and in my shower.

'Are you always like this?' I gasp, trying to catch my breath.

'Like what?' he asks, flicking that molten gaze up to my face, and I can't help but notice that his lips are wet with my juices.

'So . . . intent on giving oral sex.'

His dark brows knit together, and his gaze turns sharp. 'Don't do that, Em.'

I blink down at him. 'Do what?'

'Start getting scared.' His deep voice is rough and low. 'You're trying to piss me off so you can put some distance back between us.'

'I . . . wasn't,' I lie, knowing damn well that he's right. That I'd started freaking out, because of that particular F-word that just threw me for such a loop. 'I was just . . . curious.'

He doesn't believe me, but he goes with it anyway. 'Have I eaten pussy before? Yeah. Have I done it with every woman I've fucked? Hell no. And I've never . . . I mean, I don't . . .'

'Don't what?' I ask, when his voice trails off.

'You're *different*,' he says in a gritty tone. 'Don't ask me to explain, because I can't. I just know that I'm addicted to the taste of your hot little cunt, so instead of trying to start a fight, why don't you just open your legs wider and let me eat you out until I get what I want?'

'Which is *what*, exactly?'

Instead of answering, he just gives one of those low, wicked laughs that always make me melt, and I hear him rasp, 'You'll know when it happens,' as he lowers his head again, and keeps licking me until I come so hard that I'm actually shouting and begging him not to stop. And *that's* when I understand what he was going for. My complete and total surrender.

I can barely stand by the time he moves back to his feet, and we thankfully have enough hot water to soap up and wash our hair. My legs are still wobbly when we finish, but I manage to stumble out of the shower and grab two towels for us, handing the bigger one to Jase. I try not to drool as I watch him run the white cotton over his gorgeous physique, and I swear he looks even more ripped than he did last weekend, as if he's spent some grueling sessions in the gym since I last saw him.

I've just wrapped my towel around my body and knotted it in front, when I hear a soft chime come from my bedroom.

'What was that?' he asks, tying his own towel around his lean hips.

I look up, catching my reflection in the mirror. My eyes are wide, and though my face is pale, there are twin bright splotches of pink on my cheekbones as I say, 'That was the email notification on my laptop.'

Jase frowns. 'Why do you look so scared?'

'Because it might be from the editor at *Luxe*!' I hurry down the hallway, and can hear him following me. 'But that would be crazy. I only just sent her the article this morning.'

'You've already finished it?'

'Yeah,' I say excitedly, rushing over to the little desk that's set in front of the window and sliding into my chair. 'I worked on it nonstop since getting home, and finished it not long before you got here.'

I pull up my email and start reading, unable to keep my legs from bouncing with nerves.

'Emmy, I'm trying to be mature here by not reading over your shoulder, but it's killing me,' he grumbles. 'Is it from the editor? What the fuck did she say?'

I can't keep the smile off my lips when I turn my head, looking at him over my shoulder. 'She says she loved it!'

He gives me a blinding smile, and I swear I can see his happiness for me shining right there in those beautiful blue eyes.

Twisting around in the chair to face him, I can't stop grinning as I tell him the rest. 'She wants to set up a time to talk on the phone next week, and says that she'd love for me to write another piece for them. They want me to put together some ideas, and then they'll choose which one they like best.'

'Emmy, baby, that's awesome.'

I blush as I surge to my feet and throw my arms around him, giving him a tight hug. 'I wouldn't have been able to do it if it weren't for you,' I tell him, which is the truth.

But he just shakes his head at me. 'Like hell you wouldn't.'

'Jase, you know—'

He cuts me off. 'I mean it, Em. You would have found a way to get the information you needed on Harrison.' He gives me another sexy smile as he lifts me up and spins me around, adding, 'And tonight, I'm taking you out to celebrate.'

'You don't have to do that,' I say a little breathlessly, knowing he must still be tired from his flight.

'But I want to.' A cocky smirk kicks up the corner of his mouth as he says, 'And you deserve it, for being brilliant and brave. I mean, you faced down the fire-breathing dragon himself.'

I smirk right back at him. 'Now, Jase. You're not *that* bad.'

'I was talking about J.J., you little smart-arse,' he says with a playful growl, and I laugh so hard I almost cry as he starts tickling me like crazy, while still holding me off the ground. 'Are you going to let me read it?' he asks, when he finally sets me back on my feet.

I blink up at him as I try to catch my breath. 'You really want to?'

His gaze is warm. 'Of course.'

'If you give me your email address, I'll send you a copy.'

He gives me the address, and I go back over to my computer and send him the file. Then his phone rings, and he says that he needs to take it when he sees that it's Martin who's calling him.

I need to dry my hair before I end up having to wet it down, so I use the time while he's talking to Martin to go back into the bathroom and get it done. I moisturize next, focusing on each individual task, since I'm too afraid to pay too much attention to the chaos in my head. My emotions are all over the place, zinging between elation and disbelief, hope and fear.

When I walk back into my bedroom, I see that Jase is no longer on his call. Instead, he's dressed in jeans and a T-shirt, sitting on my double bed with his back propped up against the headboard, flipping through one of the sketchbooks that sit on the nearby bookshelf.

'What are you doing?' My face instantly goes warm, and I have to fight the urge to go over and rip the thing out of his hands. 'You're such a snoop!'

He looks up at me. 'Yep,' he says with a smile that's totally unapologetic, and yet somehow completely charming. 'Once I started looking at your sketches, I couldn't stop.'

I bite my lip while the heat in my face starts to burn.

He sets the sketchbook aside, then throws his long legs over the side of the bed and braces his elbows on his spread knees. 'Why don't you do something with your art?' he asks me, and I love the little growl that he makes in the back of his throat when I drop my towel.

As I pull on a pair of panties and a bra, I tilt my head at his question. 'You mean like as a career?'

'That's exactly what I mean. You're more than talented enough.'

'But then it's work,' I say, scrunching up my nose as I slide on my favorite pair of jeans. 'I can work for a passion – which is why I want to write about something I love – but people also need to have something that they hold close that's just for . . . For *joy*, I guess. Because it simply makes them feel good.'

His thick eyelashes make it difficult to read the look in his eyes from where I'm standing, but he's staring at me like he's trying to read *me*. Read my thoughts, my dreams.

'What?' I ask softly, before pulling on a T-shirt. 'You probably think that's stupid, or childish, right?'

'No,' he husks. 'I think it's fucking hot, Em.'

'You think *everything* is hot,' I tease, though I'm secretly pleased that he's not mocking what I've just shared with him.

'When it comes to you, I certainly do.' He knifes up off the bed and grabs his phone, sliding it into his pocket. 'All my clothes are back at the hotel, so I need to run over and change. But it shouldn't take me more than an hour, even with traffic.'

'Can you make it three?'

'Why?' he asks, and I get the feeling he's worried I'm trying to get rid of him.

'I just need to run out for a few things,' I explain. 'But I'll be ready to go when you get here.'

I walk him to the door, where he gives me a deep, breathtaking kiss goodbye, and I'm grinning like a fool as I lock the door behind him. Then I hurry over to my phone to call Tyler, hoping he can go shopping with me. Because I want an outfit for tonight that'll knock Jase back on his gorgeous ass, and I know Ty will be willing to help me do some damage to my credit card. He's been harping on me to upgrade my wardrobe for years now, and even though he's wary of Jase's intentions, there's no way he won't jump at the opportunity to help me pick out something that's edgy and sexy, and perfect for the occasion.

Because while my date tonight might not be with a 'perfect' man, I have a strong feeling that Jase Beckett is perfect *for me*.

And that's all that fucking matters.

Chapter Four

JASE

As I make my way up to Emmy's front door, I blow out a rough breath, trying to get rid of the tension that's been riding my back ever since Martin's call earlier. There have been some strange rumblings from a few of the investors in my current Thailand build, and he's trying to uncover the source, but so far hasn't found any leads. It's early days though, and this shit happens when rivals get pissy over your success, so I know I have to be patient. But that's never been my strongpoint. I'm much more of a man of action, and underhanded crap like this drives me crazy. If someone's got a problem, I want them to come right out and say it to my face. Not scuttle around behind my back, being a pain in the arse.

As soon as I lift my hand to knock, a bright-eyed Emmy opens the door, and I suck in a sharp breath when I see her.

She's . . . *Christ*, she's fucking gorgeous, and I immediately forget all the shit that's happening in London, my complete focus on the breathtaking woman standing before me.

She's wearing a cream, flowy skirt that swings around her

knees, a tight little black top and leather jacket, along with a pair of leopard-printed high heels. She's done something to her hair that's made it straight and choppy at the ends, the edgy style a perfect complement to the sexy-as-hell ensemble.

'Damn,' I scrape out, unable to clear the lust from my throat. 'You look mouthwatering, baby.'

'So do you,' she says with a beautiful smile, sweeping an appreciative gaze over me that starts at my black shoes, moves up my dark jeans, then over my white shirt that's opened at the collar and my tailored blazer, until she's finally looking me right in the eye. She steps aside then, to let me in, and as I slide past her, careful to keep my right hand behind my back, she asks, 'What's behind your back, you sneak?'

'My fine arse,' I murmur, smirking at her.

She gives a soft snort as she laughs. 'Like I said before, so cocky.'

Bringing my arm around, I hand her the bag. 'I grabbed this for you on my way back over from the hotel.'

She holds the white bag with its iconic logo with a shaky hand, looking floored. 'Ohmygod, Jase.' Then she looks inside and gasps. 'This is the newest model! I can't bel—'

I cut her off right there, tilting her face back up with my fingers curled under her chin. 'You needed a new phone, right?'

'Yes, but that wasn't your responsibility,' she says, and I swear her big brown eyes are glassy with emotion. 'And these cost a fortune. I can't . . . I can't possibly take this.'

'Of course you can.'

'Jase—'

'Please, Em. Just let me do this. I *want* to do this.' As I wrap my arms around her, she clutches the bag against her chest as she stares up at me, and I give her a little smile. 'You're going to hurt my feelings if you don't take it. And then I'll just keep buying them, over and over, until you finally accept the inevitable.'

She laughs, but I know she can see that I'm serious, and she ends up shaking her head at me. 'Okay. All right,' she whispers, leaning up to press a sweet kiss against my lips. 'I'll keep it, even though it's *far* too generous.'

'Good.'

I get another kiss, and this time she nips my bottom lip, before pulling back and saying, 'Thank you, Jase.'

Knowing that if I don't get her out of here right now, we're going to be in her bed again – and I'll be buried about a mile inside her before she can even take her next breath – I ask her if she has everything she needs, take the bag from her and set it on the coffee table, and then rush her gorgeous arse out the door. She gives me a heavy-lidded look, as if she knows just how close we were to ending back up in bed together. And while I want to be there with her more than anything, I also want to take her out to have some fun and celebrate the first of what I know is going to be her many career accomplishments.

She's adorable when we get out to the car, *oohing* and *ahhing* over it. As we drive towards downtown, she fills me in on some local history, and it's easy to see how much she loves living in this beautiful city.

'By the way,' I say, after changing lanes to avoid a pothole that would be hell on the Ferrari's chassis, 'I read your article.'

'And?' she asks, unable to keep the nerves out of her voice.

'Thanks for sending it to me.'

From the corner of my eye, I see her shoulders slump. 'Oh, um, you're welcome.'

I laugh, knowing I'm being a shit. 'God, Em. I was just winding you up. I've already read the thing three times because I loved it.'

'Really?'

'Yeah, really. You shouldn't sound so surprised. I already knew you were amazing, but I had no idea you're such a talented writer.' I glance over to see that she's blushing, and say, 'I can see why you do it. You're too good at it not to.'

She gives a few playful hits to my arm for teasing her, and as soon as we hit the next red light, I curl my hand around the back of her neck and pull her over to me for a deep, apologetic kiss. And I know I'm forgiven, because the beautiful girl kisses me back with so much passion, I have to reach down and rearrange my dick in my jeans.

We hit some traffic as we get closer to downtown, and Emmy helps by guiding us through a couple of shortcuts. When I spoke to the concierge at the hotel this afternoon, he told me about this hip new restaurant downtown that's been getting a lot of buzz, and when I looked it up online, it seemed like the perfect choice for tonight. I didn't want to take her to a place that was too casual, and since this is meant to be a fun celebration, I didn't want stuffy and pretentious either. And when I saw that they have a dance floor where couples can slow dance, I was sold, so I called and booked us the best table in the house.

Though Emmy had been somewhat shy about dancing with me last weekend, I'd loved holding her in my arms as we moved to the music. Our dance that night had been cut short by Oliver's drama, but I figured we could rectify that tonight.

We find the restaurant easily, and I know every male in the place is watching her as we follow the hostess to our table. We're laughing and looking over the menu when our waiter approaches, and as Emmy tilts her head up to listen to his spiel about the specials, she immediately makes a sharp sound of surprise. 'Kevin!'

Kevin? What the hell? She obviously knows the guy, and

from the awkward look on Emmy's face, I'm guessing that they must have dated.

'Wow, Emmy! I . . . I haven't seen you in forever,' he says, and it's clear that he's not only a little thrown to see her here, but that he more than likes what he's seeing. There are a thousand questions sitting on my tongue at the moment, starting with how long ago she went out with him. And was it serious? Jesus, was she in love with him?

'Kevin, this is Jase Beckett. He's—'

I have a feeling she's about to say 'a friend of mine', so I cut in with, 'Her boyfriend. Nice to meet you, chap.'

Emmy blinks, looking a bit shocked, but I don't know if it's because I've called myself her boyfriend, or if she can't believe I've done it in front of one of her exes.

The guy's frowning now, glaring down at me from behind his horn-rimmed glasses, and I have to bite back a sharp smile.

'Um, if we could just have a few more minutes to look over the menu,' Emmy says to him, 'that would be great.'

'Sure, no problem,' he mumbles, and as I watch him skulk back to the kitchen, I shake my head, remembering her telling me last weekend that betas were more her type. And, really, this twenty-something American couldn't be more unlike me if he tried. He's of medium height, blond, and on the thin side, with a face that's prettier than it is handsome. Shit, he's even got fucking peach fuzz on his chin!

'Well that was fun,' she murmurs drily.

I slide her a wry grimace. 'He's going to spit in my food, isn't he?'

She covers her mouth as she tries not to laugh, but I can see the humor shining in her eyes.

'That's okay,' I sigh, really playing it up. 'I'll just eat when we get back to your place.'

With a wince, she reaches over and sets her soft hand on top of mine. 'Would it be awful if we just went back to my place now? It was so lovely of you to bring me here, but this is just too awkward.'

'We can do whatever you want, Em. But before we go, you have to dance with me.'

'Are you serious?' she groans, making me laugh.

'Come on, whiner,' I tease, taking her hand as I move to my feet. 'I know you can do it, because you danced with me in England. So no stalling.'

I take her into my arms the moment we're on the dance floor, and an acoustic version of Noel Gallagher's High Flying Birds' 'Broken Arrow' begins to play. We move together like we've danced this way hundreds of times before, and I hope like hell that we get that chance. That it's in the cards for us.

'I'm sorry for intruding,' says the stylishly dressed older woman who's dancing with an elderly gentleman beside us, 'but I just wanted to tell you both that it's lovely to see a young couple who look so in love.'

Emmy turns the color of a cherry, and I have no idea what my expression is saying. The old man winks at me, as if he knows just how big the bomb is that his wife just dropped on us, and I cough to clear my throat, trying to think of something to say. 'I, um—'

'Dad?' Emmy suddenly breathes, leaning to the right to look around me. 'Ohmygod, Jase. My dad is here!'

Wishing I'd picked any other bloody restaurant than this one, I look over my shoulder and see a tall, silver-haired man heading straight towards us, his brown gaze moving from Emmy to me, and then back to Emmy again. He's left a table of suited-up businessmen behind him, and with a glance I can see that they're all drinking and talking loudly, clearly out for a good time tonight.

'Hi, Dad,' she says, after we walk over to meet him at the edge of the dance floor. 'Uh, what are you doing here? I didn't even know you were in San Diego.'

'Business trip,' he drawls in a much deeper southern accent than Emmy has, making me think he must have lived in Georgia his entire life.

'Dad, this is Jase Beckett. Jase, this my father, Phillip Reed.'

'Nice to meet you,' he says, shaking my hand with a firm grip, and I murmur a polite, 'Likewise.' But I don't mean it. Not after what Emmy has told me about him.

'Um, where's Mom?' she asks with a soft note of confusion.

Looking at his daughter again, he pushes his hands into his pockets as he casually says, 'She had to have emergency surgery on Monday to get her ruptured appendix out, so she couldn't make the trip.'

Emmy instantly stiffens beside me, and I fight the urge to scowl at this dickhead. He's left his recuperating wife on the other side of the country to come here for business, and hasn't even bothered to let Emmy know he's in town or that her mother had surgery? What a fucking tosser.

'Are you . . . She had . . .' Emmy pulls in a deep breath, obviously struggling to control her temper, and her top lip curls as she steps up to him and growls, 'Why the hell didn't you call me?'

The man actually frowns, as if he doesn't get what has her so upset. 'I'm on a tight schedule, Emmy. I don't have time to—'

'Not about your visit,' she snaps, looking ready to stomp her foot in frustration. 'About Mom!'

'There's no need to make a scene. I'm here with clients,' he says tightly, his image obviously more important to him than his daughter's justifiable anger. 'And it's not like I left her on her own. I hired in a nurse to stay with her.'

'I don't care about the damn nurse. Did you ever think that

I'd want to know that my mother was ill? That she was having surgery?'

He blinks at her, as if she's confounded him.

Emmy shakes her head as she gives a derisive little snort. 'No, of course that never occurred to you, because it doesn't have anything to do with *you*, does it?'

Christ, I've met so many men like her father. Ones who think the bloody world revolves around them. Who can never appreciate what they have, because they're always consumed with wanting *more*. That's Phillip Reed to a T, and I can see the exact moment that my name finally clicks for him, because there's a new, calculating gleam in his eye as he completely ignores his daughter and leans toward me a little, saying, 'You wouldn't happen to be the same Beckett from that spectacular Dubai project last year, would you, son?'

'*Don't*,' Emmy snaps at him before I can even get a word out, and I have to bite back a smile. Jesus, this girl is sharp. She saw right through the bastard in two seconds flat.

He gives her an affronted look down his narrow nose. 'Excuse me?'

'Don't even think about it,' she says with a soft, thick note of disgust. 'Stay away from him. And stay away from me.'

He stiffens, and I can see the anger building in his eyes, so I decide it's time to get her the hell out of there. Because if the idiot tears into her, I'm going to lose my shit, and that's not how I planned for this night to go.

'I'm sorry about that,' she says, after we've grabbed our things from the table, told the hostess we won't be staying, and are on our way out to the car. 'I didn't mean to speak for you, but I know what he's like. He'd try to weasel in on your deals and expect special treatment because you know me. God, he's *awful*.'

'Hey, there's nothing to be sorry for,' I tell her, pulling her closer to my side as I hold her hand in mine. 'You want to just head home?'

'Yeah,' she says with another soft note of apology. 'I hate to call an early end to our night, but I need to get in touch with my mom and make sure she's okay.'

I tell her we can go out for dinner anytime she wants, and to stop feeling bad about it. She's quiet on the drive back to her apartment, and the minute we're through the front door, she slips off the killer leopard-print heels and grabs her cordless house phone. I take a seat on the sofa and watch her as she paces back and forth across the small living room.

'Hey,' she says a moment later. 'I tried to call you on Monday, to let you know that I'm back from England, but all I got was your voicemail. When I didn't hear back from you, I assumed you were busy while traveling with Dad, but I just ran into him and he told me what happened. I can't believe you didn't call me.'

She frowns as she listens, her grip tightening on the phone. And then she says, 'Mom, that's ridiculous. You can't keep things like this from me just because you don't want me to worry. I'm *supposed* to worry about you when you're ill. I can't believe he didn't call me when you went in for surgery.'

There's more listening, as well as pacing, and then she blurts, 'Stop! Just . . . stop. Don't defend him to me. I don't want to argue with you, but you know how I feel about him, so don't try to make it sound like he was acting in anyone's best interest but his own.'

Her shoulders stiffen as she listens to whatever her mother is saying in response, and then, in a softer tone, Emmy says, 'I love you, too. And I'm glad the nurse is taking good care of you. But please, just call me if you need anything, okay?'

Her chest lifts with a shaky breath as she disconnects the

call, then walks over to the end table at the side of the sofa and sets the phone back in its cradle.

'Come here, sweetheart,' I murmur, reaching over and grabbing her hand. I tug her into my lap, loving how it feels when she curls into me, seeking comfort, her cheek pressed against my chest. I wrap my arms around her and lower my head, pressing a kiss to the top of her honey-gold hair. 'You okay?'

'Yeah,' she sighs. 'It's just . . . God, he makes me so angry. She's just this . . . this beautiful, loyal, mistreated afterthought to him.'

'I'm sorry, baby, but your dad's a total knobhead.'

She starts to shake with quiet laughter. 'You're right. Knobhead is the *perfect* word for him.' She tilts her head back, and there's a soft, worried look in her eyes as she says, 'I'm so sorry for ruining our night out.'

'You didn't ruin anything. I'm just sorry you didn't get to relax and enjoy yourself. After writing such a brilliant article, that's what you deserved.'

A smile starts to twitch on her pink lips. 'What would you say to doing dinner and dancing another night, and for now just ordering some of the best, most mouthwatering pizza I swear you'll ever have and maybe watching something on Netflix?'

'I'd say that sounds like heaven, Em.'

After we look over the online menu and choose our toppings, Emmy calls in the order, and then we both change into shorts and T-shirts. It's not easy to keep my hands off her when she slips out of the sexy skirt and top, but I somehow manage to behave, knowing damn well that I need to feed her before I start fucking her again. But I catch the way she keeps stealing glances at me from the corner of her eye, and it's gratifying to know that she's finding it just as difficult to keep her hands to herself.

Just as we set our ice-cold drinks on her coffee table, the

pizza is delivered. It smells delicious, and she's right, my mouth is already watering as we pile up our plates and settle in to watch the first episode of *Stranger Things*, since I've never seen it and she says it's one of her favorites.

And when she casually mentions that the next season will be starting in October, and that we'll be able to watch it together, I get this burst of warmth in my chest that feels so good I start grinning like a sap. I don't even let the logistics of our situation concern me – I just give myself the chance to enjoy the moment, soaking it in as deeply as I can.

I end up loving the show, and after we finish the second episode, I hound her with questions about the plotline that she laughingly refuses to answer as we clear up our dishes. I haven't asked if it's okay that I sleep here, but when she pours two glasses of water for us and carries them into her bedroom, I'm relieved that she's going on the assumption that I plan to stay. Because I do. I want to spend every moment of every day with her, and that goes for the nighttime hours as well.

She washes her make-up off in the bathroom, and then I take my turn in there. As I walk back into her bedroom, she's already cuddled under the covers, and after the night she's had, I tell my dick to behave himself. Instead of crawling on top of her, I strip down to my boxers, lie down beside her, and simply take her into my arms to hold her.

She rests her cheek against my biceps, her fingertips swirling over the ridges of my abs, and I've never been so grateful as I am in that moment for the grueling hours I've spent in the gym.

I'm wondering what she's thinking, when she says, 'When my cards were stolen last week and you called the bank, how did you know that all my accounts were safe? How did you know I didn't have another account at a bank other than the one my checkbook came from?'

I shake my head as I laugh, because that's the last thing I was expecting her to say. And even though there's a chance my answer might piss her off, I still give her the truth, because that's all I'm *ever* going to give her. I learned my lesson with speaking in half-truths back in England, when I refused to tell her the real reason why I wanted her to stay with me.

'I had my finance team run a quick credit report on you.'

She lifts her head. 'Seriously?'

I shrug as I say, 'It was the only way I could make sure those dickheads weren't going to screw you over.'

'Wow,' she murmurs, snuffling a soft laugh under her breath as she lays her head back down. And then she tilts it back and smirks at me. 'I guess now you know all my secrets, huh?'

'To be honest, babe, I didn't read it that closely, since I was just looking for your account information.' Arching one of my eyebrows, I ask, 'So what salacious details did I miss?'

'Well, there's my scandalous coffee addiction.'

I widen my eyes in mock outrage. 'No! I'm shocked.'

'You should be,' she laughs, stroking her fingertips along the edge of my jaw. 'I spend *way* too much money at Maggie's every month.'

'What's Maggie's?'

'My and Ty's favorite coffeehouse. I'll have to take you there in the morning. You'll love it.'

'I'm looking forward to it,' I tell her, loving how silky her skin feels as I slip my hand up under the little tank top she's wearing and run it down her back. Then lower, over her gorgeous, panty-covered arse. 'Any other questions?'

'No, no questions,' she says, and there's a smile on her lips as she shoves hard at my shoulders. With a smile of my own, I roll on to my back, thinking she wants to get on top. My dick jerks with excitement, because the idea of watching Emmy bounce up and down on it, her pink-tipped breasts swaying and jiggling, is hot as fuck. But instead of climbing on, she presses her soft lips to the center of my chest, and starts working her way lower, sprinkling kisses all over me, and my heart starts pounding so hard I think the bloody thing might burst through my ribs.

This isn't just raw, deliciously aggressive sex, like we usually have. She's giving it a note of playful tenderness that I've never experienced, and it's undoing me. Breaking me down. But not in a bad way. Hell no.

Because I have a feeling that when Emmy is done with me tonight, I'm going to somehow be better than I was before.

This beautiful, amazing girl . . . She isn't with me for my money or what I can give her. All she wants is *me*. To make me laugh and smile and moan with pleasure, and *that* . . . Christ, it's the best damn feeling in the world.

By the time she's tugged off my boxers and is taking the slick, wet head of my dick between her lips, I'm shaking, my pulse roaring in my ears. I'm so turned on, I'm leaking pre-cum on to her tongue with every tight pull of her greedy mouth, and I know I'm not going to last two seconds if she keeps this up. And I need to feel her coming with me when I crash over that blinding edge. Need to forge as many connections with her as I can, each one making this thing between us tighter. Stronger.

Given how crazy our goddamn families are – especially mine – it needs to be fucking titanium, so that we can survive whatever they, and the rest of the world, decide to throw at us.

Grabbing hold of her, I pull her up and ravage her mouth as I strip her, licking the taste of me from her soft tongue, and I don't stop as I blindly reach over to the bedside table for a condom. I snag one, rip it open, and cover my cock. Then I roll us over, get up on my knees, her hips in my hands as I pull her snug, cushiony cunt over my diamond-hard shaft, and start pounding the hell out of her.

Her legs are spread, her upper back and head the only parts of her touching the bed, and from this position I can see everything. Every lush, exquisite detail of her. I stare so hard my eyes start to burn, watching the way my broad cock stretches her pink little hole, her juices covering me. I can't believe I'm this bloody hard for her again after already coming so many times today, but this girl . . . God, I have a feeling I'll always be hard for her.

'You want more?' I growl, lifting my heavy gaze to her glittering one, her cheeks flushed as she swipes her tongue over her lower lip and nods.

I scoop her up and shuffle forward on my knees until I've got her trapped between the headboard and my pounding body, taking her so hard that she's gasping with every inward thrust into her tight, sweet clasp. 'Fuck, Em. If we keep this up, you're gonna get so swollen I won't even be able to get inside you.'

'Just don't stop,' she moans against the side of my throat, her arms wrapped tight around my shoulders as I hold her thighs spread wide. 'Oh, God, Jase. Don't stop!'

'Never,' I husk, reaching between us and pressing my thumb to her clit. I press and rub the little nub of flesh, and she tightens around me even more, her body shaking as it builds, rising up, and then that blistering wave of pleasure crashes through her like a storm, dragging me along for the panting, pulsing, mind-blowing ride, our hoarse shouts no doubt waking up the entire neighborhood. But, hey, at least no one's banging on the wall and shouting at us.

I keep a tight hold on her as I collapse back on the bed, so worn out I feel like I've just run a marathon. Somehow, I find the strength to deal with the condom and get us the right way around, with our heads on the pillows, then reach over and turn off the lamp that sits on her bedside table. The room is cast into darkness, the closed curtains preventing even the moonlight from seeping in, and I wrap my arms back around her, holding her close, determined that I'll be able to hold her, just like this, for so many nights to come.

Hell, I want this woman for a lifetime. For *all* the nights I have left in this world, and I make a silent vow to myself to do whatever it takes to make that happen.

'Don't leave me,' she murmurs so softly I almost miss it, and it takes me a second to realize that she's talking in her sleep. 'Don't . . . Don't go . . .'

I hold her tighter against my pounding heart and press my lips to the top of her head, her words utterly destroying me.

Emmy's happy that I'm here; I know she is.

But I also know, from the way that I've caught her looking at me a few times now, that she's still not quite sure this is for real. I've made the big gesture by chasing her beautiful arse halfway around the world – but it's going to take more than that to get completely under that guard she can't quite let down, so that I can work my way into her heart.

And that's exactly what I'm going to do.

I don't care how long it takes. How hard I have to fight for it. Bleed for it. This girl is worth it all, because she's the one thing in this entire world that *I* hold close for joy.

And now that I've got her in my arms again, where she belongs, I'm never letting go.

Chapter Five

Friday morning

EMMY

As I open my eyes to the morning sunlight sneaking around the edges of the bedroom curtains, I feel my breath catch as I find myself face-to-face with the gorgeous sex god that is Jase Beckett. I swallow a little dreamy sigh as I soak him in, loving the way he scratches lazily at his chest, then rubs the dark stubble on his jaw, his hair sticking up all over the place. This is Jase at his most comfortable and relaxed, and he's mouthwatering.

He arches his brow at me, as if he wants to know what I'm thinking, but I just smile, not about to feed his ego any more than I already have. But the sexy wink that he shoots me, as he throws back the covers and climbs out of bed, says he's all too aware of what he does to me. His nude body is like a work of art, all golden skin and rippling muscle, and I can't help but stare at his perfect ass as he walks into the hallway, heading for the bathroom.

After we've both brushed our teeth, we get dressed in shorts and T-shirts, and hold hands as we make the short walk down to Maggie's. We splurge on her maple-and-bacon donuts, sipping on delicious coffees as the Foo Fighters' 'Stranger Things Have Happened' plays softly from the overhead speakers, and Jase helps me set up my new phone. Before we leave, I shoot Ty a quick text to let him know that I've got a new number, and he shoots back a heart and a kiss emoji, which has Jase shaking his head, like he thinks the guy is trying to mess with him. But Tyler's always been like this with me, from the moment we first became friends, and I know that he and Jase will get along well if they just give each other a chance.

When we get back to my apartment, Jase makes himself comfortable on my small sofa and I go straight to my house phone to check my messages, in case my mom has called. But there are no missed calls, and nothing new on my voicemail. Just as I turn to set the phone back down, there's a knock on my front door, and I give Jase an *I have no idea who it is* look as I walk over, then peek through the peephole.

'What the hell?' I mutter, unable to believe what I'm seeing.

'Who is it?' Jase asks, moving to his feet.

'My father,' I huff, yanking the door open. I can't believe the jackass's audacity in coming here, but I have no intention of letting him inside. I say nothing as I stare up into brown eyes that are almost the exact same shade as mine, waiting to hear what he'll say.

Puffing up his chest, he glares down at me and goes with an absolute doozy. 'I think you owe me an apology, young lady. Your behavior last night was beyond rude.'

'Seriously, Dad? *That's* what you open with?'

'What did you expect?' he snaps, and I can't miss the gleam in his eye when he looks over my shoulder and sees Jase standing behind me in the living room. He coughs to clear his throat, and in the good-ol'-boy tone I've heard him use during countless business calls, he says, 'Now move aside and let me in. I'd like a chance to speak with this young man you're dating.'

I tighten my grip on the door, and there's an even tighter smile on my lips as I say, 'You know what, Dad? When you're ready to act like a decent human being, then maybe I'll make Jase suffer your company. But until then, don't pull this crap again. Because it's not happening.'

Before he can even respond, I shut the door in his livid face and twist the lock, and find Jase smiling at me as I turn toward him, as if he's proud of what I've done. And while some people might think I just acted like a bitch, I can't help but feel a little proud as well.

'Let's get out of here for a while,' I say, returning Jase's smile. 'This is your first time in San Diego and you need to do some sightseeing.'

'I'm seeing one hell of a sight right now,' he drawls, walking over to me and wrapping his arms around my lower back, tugging me close.

I tilt my head back as I hold on to his biceps. 'Keep looking at me like that, and I really *won't* be able to walk straight anymore.'

He gets this wicked gleam in his dark eyes as he laughs, and I swear it's so freaking sexy that it makes me wet. 'And you saying things like that just makes me harder, sweetheart.'

I start to tell him that I can *feel* just how true those words are, but my phone rings. 'I'd better get that in case it's my mom,' I say, pulling out of his arms. I check the caller ID and it says private. 'Hello?'

'Emmy, it's Kevin.'

I find myself doing that thing that I've only seen in movies and on TV, where I pull the phone away from my ear for a moment to stare at it in bafflement, then slowly put it back to my ear again.

'Um, hey, Kevin' I say, and I hear Jase quietly laugh under his breath. Looking over to where he's lounging back on my sofa again, smirking at me, I cough to clear my throat a little. 'This, uh, isn't really a good time for me.'

'I'm sure you've got your new boyfriend there,' Kevin says sourly, sounding childish and immature, and I'm having a hard time remembering why I'd dated him for a few months the year before last. We'd taken a lot of the same classes, and enjoyed similar tastes in movies and music, and thinking back, I'd probably said yes because I'd known he was a safe choice. A nice guy who I could go out with, without worrying I'd develop an emotional attachment to him. And I'd thought he felt the same.

'Actually, yes, Jase is here.'

'I just wanted to tell you that it was good seeing you last night. You ran out before I got the chance to say that, and that . . . that I miss you.'

'Kevin,' I sigh, 'I've been single for over a year now, and suddenly you decide that you miss me?'

'It was easier not to think about you because we haven't hung out since things fizzled out between us. But seeing you last night, I realize that I've been waiting to run into you again.'

I frown, thinking that if he'd really missed me, he would have made more of an effort. Not that I would've been interested, but still. How's he ever going to get anywhere in life if he just waits for what he wants to come to him?

'Kev, you're a great guy, and I know there's someone out there who's perfect for you. But that person isn't me, okay? And don't sit around waiting for her to just pop into your life. Get out there and make more of an effort.'

'Maybe you're right,' he says after a brief pause. 'But it doesn't mean that getting over you is going to be any easier.'

'I'm sorry. I . . . I didn't mean to hurt you.'

'Yeah, I know,' he murmurs. 'You were always upfront about what you were looking for.'

'I need to go, okay?'

'Take care, Em.'

He hangs up then, and I let out a huge sigh of relief, wondering what kind of weird, cosmic shit-storm must be brewing over my head. First my dad, and then Kevin? It's like the awesomeness of having Jase here has thrown my universe out of whack, and now all this craziness is happening.

'I take it the boy isn't as over you as you thought,' Jase says, rubbing a hand over his stubble-covered jaw.

I set the phone back in its cradle. 'Um, something like that.'

'You know, I have a feeling you've left a lot more broken hearts in your wake than you realize, Em.'

Pushing my hair back from my face, I can hear the frustration in my voice as I say, 'Honestly, Jase, we weren't serious enough for him to get his heart broken.'

'Maybe not on your end, but on his . . .'

I shake my head. 'It wasn't like that. We were more friends than anything else.'

'And I think you don't see how powerfully you affect people, beautiful. You've had that armor of yours wrapped around you so tight, you thought it was going to keep people from getting too close. And it probably worked until you met me. But that doesn't mean they didn't see you, and fall for you, and hope like hell that they'd be the one who'd get to crawl inside that armor *with* you.'

'Is that what you've done?' I ask, my chest warm and my heart pounding. 'Crawled inside with me?'

'It's what I'm hoping for,' he says softly, his blue gaze heavy and molten as he moves to his feet and starts coming toward me. 'And then, once I've earned your trust, I'm hoping I can pull you right out of it, because you'll know you don't need it anymore. You'll trust me to be good to you, and for you.'

I melt, my lips trembling. 'Jase, th-that's—'

'Shh,' he whispers, pulling me into his arms and pressing a tender kiss to the center of my forehead. 'You don't have to say anything, Em. Just know that I'm happy as hell that I get to be the man standing here, holding you in my arms. And I will *never* fucking take it for granted.'

I wrap my arms around his waist and give him a tight hug, his words making my heart beat so hard it feels like it's trying to win a race.

Sensing that I need him to lighten the mood, he lifts me off the floor and spins me around a few times, until I'm laughing and squealing for him to stop. When he does, I'm grinning so wide that it hurts my cheeks as I kick my head back and gaze up into his smiling face. 'You ready to hit the road?' I ask him. 'God only know who's going to show up or call next. I say we should make a run for it.'

'Whatever you want, Em.'

We grab what we'll need, hop into the luxurious sports car, and head out to the Cabrillo National Monument in Point Loma. It's a state park that has breathtaking views of the city and the Pacific, with trails you can walk along at the top of the cliffs.

Once we're done looking around, and actually snap a few selfies with my new phone, we tour the Old Point Loma Lighthouse that's nearby, and then drive over to Pacific Beach. We park right by the sand, leave our shoes in the car, and head out to walk along the shore. It's a gorgeous day, with the sun shining bright off the roiling Pacific, the surfers out in huge numbers as they battle for the best spots on the waves.

'Hey, what's wrong?' I ask, when I notice that Jase has grown quiet, his brows pulled into a little V over his nose.

JASE

'Nothing's wrong. Nothing at all,' I say. 'I'm just taking it all in, Em.'

And I am, because the view stretching out in front of me is stunning, all ocean blue and golden sunshine. But that's not what's on my mind. I'm thinking about the life that Emmy has here, and how rich it is. Not with money, because it's clear from her tiny apartment and her crappy car that she lives on a tight budget.

No, I'm talking about the family she's made for herself. Tyler and her friends. All of them close by, living in this beautiful place where the sun shines nearly every day. How can I ask her to leave all this and come back to London with me? And is that what I want? Not the 'her coming with me' part, but the one where I go back to London too. Am I ready to leave the life I have there behind and move here permanently?

I don't really have any answers, except for one, and that's that no matter where I am, I need her to be there with me. By my side. We've skipped straight past casual dating and fallen headfirst into the heavy-duty emotional shit, and that means I want her living with me. Or hell, me living with her. I don't give a fuck how it's phrased; the important thing is that we're together.

I just hope she feels the same way.

'Are you hungry for lunch yet?' she asks, pushing her sunglasses up on her head as she looks up at me.

I give her a wolfish smile. 'Starving.'

'Good, because I'm going to take you to my and Ty's favorite place.'

We head into the beach town, making our way past the colorful shop windows, until we reach a little Mexican restaurant that looks like something out of a movie. It's got sand on the floor and a palm-covered front patio, with mariachi music playing loudly over the speakers. The waiters and waitresses smile and wave at Emmy, making it obvious that she's a regular. A few of those smiles are sly ones as they nod their heads at me, and she's blushing again as we slip into a corner table out on the patio. We put in our order, and they immediately bring out the two ice-cold drinks we asked for, along with a basket of hot, salty tortilla chips and the most amazing salsa I've ever tasted. We get stuck in, and by the time our main orders arrive, every single table in the place is filled and the order-to-go section is rammed.

I've never eaten much Mexican food, so I've let Emmy order for me. She gets me an enchilada platter that tastes so good I actually moan when I take my first bite, which has her giving me a cocky *I told you so* look.

Emmy's ordered a plate that's loaded with what she tells me are flautas. They're filled flour tortillas that have been fried to a crisp, then topped with guacamole, salsa and sour cream. They smell delicious, and my own meal is awesome, but all too soon our food is the last thing on my mind, and I'm sucking in a couple of deep breaths, trying to calm the hell down.

'Hey, what's wrong?' she asks me for the second time that hour. But unlike before, when I'd been getting lost in my head, this time it's my other damn head that's the problem. 'Is it too spicy?'

'No, the food's incredible.' I give her a wry grin. 'It's just that watching you put those things between your lips as you take a bite is making me hard.'

Her eyes go wide, and then she bursts out laughing. 'Are you telling me my flautas are making you think of me giving you head?'

I shrug a little as I take a drink of my cola, because what can I say? I'm a guy. If something is long and thick and going in a woman's mouth, odds are our minds are going to head straight for the gutter. And given how much I fucking love being in *this* girl's mouth – the only one I want to be in ever again – it's a hell of a job getting my brain to focus on anything but how good it feels when she's sucking me off.

With a soft snort, she jiggles her last flauta a little bit over her plate. 'I don't get it, because this thing is *way* smaller than you. I mean, there really isn't any comparison.'

'Jesus,' I mutter, closing my eyes as I suck in another deep breath. 'You talking about how big my dick is is *not* helping me get control, Em.'

'Sorry,' she says with a quiet laugh, and I feel the gentle touch of her hand against the side of my face. 'But you're just too adorable. You're even blushing.'

'I'm not blushing; I'm burning up,' I scrape out, giving her a heavy-lidded look as I grab her hand and bring it to my mouth, pressing a hot kiss against her palm that makes her shiver. 'Christ, a thirty-two-year-old man should have more control than this.'

She arches one of her golden brows and grins at me. 'Want me to take you home and show you how much I love it when a particular thirty-two-year-old man I know loses every ounce of his precious control and nails me to the wall?'

'That's it,' I growl, letting go of her hand to signal the waiter for our bill. Looking back at Emmy, I say, 'Give me your sweater.'

'Why?' she asks, picking up the lightweight cardigan that she'd brought along in case it was too breezy by the water. 'Because I don't think it'll fit you.'

A husky laugh rumbles up from my chest. 'I'm not going to

wear it, Em. I'm going to hold it over my arm so it covers my dick while we walk back to the car.'

'Oh!' She starts to laugh again, her brown eyes shining with humor, and I can't resist reaching over, curling my hand around the back of her neck, and tugging her towards me. And then, even though we're surrounded by people, I lean forward and take her mouth with every bit of hunger and craving that I have for her. I take it like I need the feel and taste of her mouth to satisfy some raging fire inside me. Like I need it to soothe me. To make me whole.

I kiss her like that because it's true. Every goddamn part.

By the time we make it back to the car, I've got myself under control, and we drive along the coast for a bit before heading back to Mission Beach, where she lives. As we travel down a palm-lined street not far from her place, she tells me that the Spanish-tiled little bungalow we've just passed is where Tyler lives, and I'm not surprised that he's so close by, given how much time they normally spend together.

Emmy's building is a two-story block of four apartments, with a small parking lot in the back for the residents, so I'm able to park the Ferrari right out front on the street. The sleek sports car is more extravagant than I need for a rental, but I'd wanted to have something fun for us to drive around in, and just seeing how much she enjoys it is worth the hefty fee the company is charging me.

We head inside, and I'm already calculating how quickly I can get her out of her little shorts and blouse, feeling like I haven't had her in months, when we must have fucked at least five or more times yesterday. I'm not too proud to admit that I'm completely addicted to her, and in a way that I know, in my gut, isn't ever going to fade. It doesn't matter how many times I touch her or taste her, I still get that heady jolt of adrenaline, and the unfamiliar feeling that I'm *right* where I'm meant to be, doing *exactly* what I'm meant to be doing, every single time.

I toss my keys on to one of the end tables, then turn, and just as I start to make my way over to where she's standing in the center of the room, watching me with a gaze that's just as heavy and hungry as mine, someone knocks on her door.

I halt my steps, fighting back a frustrated growl, and can't stop my lips from twitching when I see that she's scowling at the door, as if she can't believe our shitty luck.

'I'll get it,' I murmur, since I have something special I'd like to say to her father if it turns out to be him again. But as I flip the lock and pull open the door, I don't find myself staring into Phillip Reed's light brown eyes. No, I'm looking at what feels like a mirror image, only twenty or thirty years older. The man standing on Emmy's doorstep has my same olive-toned skin, height and muscular build. Same dark hair. Same blue eyes.

What the ever-loving fuck?

'Jasper Beckett?'

'Yeah,' I mutter, getting a bad feeling in my gut. 'Who the hell are you?'

'My name is Douglas Hart. I . . . I knew your mother. I was hoping we could talk for a moment.'

'How did you even know you could find me here?'

He lifts his right hand, showing me a printed photograph of me and Emmy dancing together last night. 'The restaurant you were at last night took this photograph and posted it on their social media sites. They probably saw the car you were driving, heard your accent, and looked you up, thinking you might be famous.'

'I'm not fucking famous,' I growl, at the end of my patience.

'But you *are* a wealthy, good-looking Brit who's dated some famous women,' he murmurs, 'and that was enough for one of the local gossip blogs to pick it up. It just so happens that my assistant follows this particular blog, and she brought this photo into my office this morning to show me, because she thought the resemblance between us was uncanny.' He folds the photograph in half and slides it into the back pocket of his designer jeans. 'When I looked the article up and saw your name, I knew I had to find you. I tried the Hotel Del first, but they said you weren't in your room. So I thought to try Miss Reed's address.'

'And how the hell did you get it?' I growl, confusion and anger building so quickly I'm getting a mother of a headache, my skull feeling like someone's taking a hammer to it.

He gives me a tight smile. 'Let's just say that I have a neighbor who's connected with the government, and who owes me a few favors.'

A gritty laugh of disbelief rips up from my chest. 'So you've invaded our privacy, breaking God knows how many laws, just so you can tell me that you knew my mother?'

'Actually,' he says, rubbing a hand over his jaw in the same way that I do, 'I came to tell you something a little more important than that. May I come in?'

'Just spit it out, Hart.'

His dark gaze bores into mine. 'All right. Alistair Beckett isn't your father.'

I hear Emmy gasp, but don't show any outward reaction of my own. It's like I'm locked down, frozen to this spot, my breath trapped in my lungs, while my mind is in bloody overdrive.

The man clears his throat a bit, looking uncomfortable as hell as he grunts, 'I am.'

'If this is your way of trying to get money,' I snarl, 'it won't work.'

With a small shake of his head, he says, 'I don't need your money, Jase. I have my own.'

'Then what the fuck *do* you want?'

Hart jerks his chin toward the inside of Emmy's apartment. 'I want you to let me in.' And then, for the second time in a week, I hear the words, 'Because I need to tell you a story.'

* * *

Thirty minutes later, I'm shutting the door behind Douglas Hart. As I turn around, I find Emmy studying me with a worried gaze, clearly trying to determine if I'm all right.

'We should've just stayed at the restaurant,' I mutter, trying to crack a joke. 'Because sporting wood in front of the world *has* to be better than this shit.'

A breathless rush of laughter bursts from her lips, before it quickly fades, replaced by a soft look of concern. Coming over to me, she says, 'God, Jase. Are you okay?'

I shake my head a little. 'I . . . I don't know.'

'Here, sit down,' she says, taking my hand and leading me over to the sofa. 'I'm going to make you a cup of tea, and then we can talk about what happened.'

I watch her walk out of the room, wanting to chase after her, and grimace. Christ, I'm like a puppy. But I've been floored, and Emmy is the fucking rock I need right now. The thing I need to cling to, because she's the only thing in this entire world that I completely trust. That I know is *real*.

My phone starts buzzing in my pocket, so I reach down and take it out. I have an urgent message from Martin, and as I read what he's written, I feel my blood run cold. Not only is someone screwing with my Thailand deal, but it seems that Caroline has called several of the county councilors that are involved in my plans to build homeless shelters for teens across London and told them that I've left the country for personal reasons that are causing my family grave concern. Martin has already contacted the councilors and assured them that I'm simply taking a vacation, and all the plans are still a go, but the damage she's done isn't going to be so easily fixed.

The psychotic bitch has gone too far this time, and I have to fight the urge to throw my bloody phone at the wall in a burst of rage. But I hold it back, because I'm not going to act like a destructive, belligerent dickhead in front of Emmy, which is exactly what Caroline wants. Me losing my cool and being an arse, then rushing back home to fix the mess she's created. Fuck that. I'm going to stay right here and keep my shit together, continuing to build what Emmy and I have.

I move to my feet when she comes back into the room, setting our cups of tea on the coffee table. Then I step close to her, and wrap my arms around her.

'This has been a crazy freaking day, hasn't it?' she says with a heavy sigh, hugging me back. 'I mean, I'm almost afraid who might knock on the door next.'

'No shit,' I agree, dropping my forehead against hers. And then, quietly, I say, 'I've got an idea.'

'Yeah?'

'Why don't you pack up a bunch of stuff and we'll head over to the hotel? Hide out there for a few days, where no one can find us.'

She blinks up at me as I lift my head, and I can tell that she wants to ask, 'And then what?' But she doesn't do it. Instead, her lips twitch into a little smile, and she says, 'I'd love that. But I'll need to bring my laptop. I have to get started on the ideas for my next article.'

I haven't told her about what Caroline has done yet, or the weird things happening with my Thailand build, so I just say, 'I've got some things that I need to work on too. We can open the balcony doors and use the suite's sofa and coffee table as an office, while we listen to the waves crashing on the beach.'

'That sounds perfect. And I'm not surprised you have work to do,' she says with a cheeky grin. 'You've been playing hooky for a whole two days.'

'Mmm,' I murmur, lowering my head so that I can nuzzle the tender side of her throat. 'And they've been the best two days of skiving that I've ever had.'

Best two days *ever*, bar none.

And all because of the woman I'm holding in my arms.

Chapter Six

JASE

On our way past the manager's office, I drop in to have a word, making it clear that we want to have complete privacy during our stay, and make it a point to mention the information that was given to Douglas Hart when he phoned the hotel. When we get to the luxurious suite, Emmy calls Ty to let him know that she's staying with me for a few days, makes another call to her mother, making sure she knows to call Emmy's new mobile instead of her home number, and then we decide to head down to the beach, figuring a walk out in the late afternoon sunshine might help us unwind.

With the iconic white, red-roofed hotel behind us, we walk along the sandy shore, our feet getting wet as the waves crash and roll up against the beach.

'Do you want to talk now?' she asks me, giving my hand a little squeeze.

'I don't really know what to say, Em. I have no fucking clue who Douglas Hart is.'

'No one in your family ever mentioned him?'

I shake my head, thinking about the things Hart had told me. That he'd been working on a nearby estate, the company he'd worked for contracted to carry out an extensive renovation on the historical manor there, and had met my mother at one of the local village fetes.

According to Hart, they'd fallen in love, and were lovers, even after Sarah had learned that she was pregnant. And after my birth, she'd been positive that Hart was the father. But while he'd been desperate for the two of us to return with him to the States once his work in the British countryside was completed, Sarah had refused.

Believing she'd turned him down because he wouldn't be able to give her the same affluent lifestyle Alistair's money provided, Hart had returned to America, determined to build an empire of his own. He was so driven that he'd managed to become a multi-millionaire within four years, but he hadn't contacted Sarah. By that time, he was apparently too bitter over her refusal to leave Alistair. It wasn't until the elderly widow who'd owned the manor he'd once worked on had passed away, that Hart returned to Kent for the funeral. And when he'd seen Sarah again, it'd been impossible for them to stay apart.

Deciding to remain close until he'd finally managed to convince her to take me away from Beckett House and go to America with him, where they could start a new life together, he'd rented a home in one of the nearby villages. But she'd died before he was successful, and her death had nearly destroyed him.

He'd also said that he'd tried to get the local police to investigate the circumstances of her death, but that they wouldn't listen to his concerns. And after all these years, he still refuses to believe that she took her own life. But maybe Hart had just been too self-centered to correctly read her emotional state, or to see what the stress of their affair was doing to her.

As I'd listened to his story, I'd been pissed off that he didn't do a better job at protecting her, even if it were from herself. Surely there had to have been signs that she was suffering from severe depression. And the timing bothers me. Did his coming back into her life push her into a deeper state of melancholy? And if he's telling the truth, and Alistair's *not* my father, did she fear discovery? Is that why she took her own life?

But why do it in my playroom? Was that some kind of sick message to Hart? To Alistair? To *me*?

Fuck, I don't have any answers, and probably never will. Not about her reasons. Her demons. Her choices.

What I *do* know is that Hart claims he was madly in love with my mother, and that he'd wanted to be a father to me, until he'd lost her. After that, he said he hadn't been fit to be a parent, drowning in the bottom of a bottle until he nearly lost the company he'd worked so hard to build.

'I was . . . broken, for a long time, after Sarah's death,' he'd said, sitting on the chair that Emmy grabbed for him from her little dining set, while she and I sat on the sofa. 'And by the time I'd managed to sober up, I figured you were better off where you were. I was a recovering alcoholic, and Alistair had remarried. I thought you'd have a more stable life there. One of not only wealth, but privilege.'

'Shit. You think money and privilege make for a loving childhood?' I'd growled, unable to keep the fury out of my voice.

He'd sighed, looking as if he were aging ten years right before my eyes. 'To be honest, Jase, and it kills me to say this, but I kept my distance because I couldn't stand the thought of seeing her in you. Hell, it took everything I have just to come here today, so that I could finally tell you the truth.'

I'd had to laugh, seeing as how it was either that or hit the bastard. And then I told him to get out, and he'd gone without an argument.

'I've been thinking about what Hart said there at the end,' I say to Emmy, and I can feel the gentle touch of her gaze against my rigid profile as I stare out over the coastline. 'About how he couldn't stand the thought of seeing her in me, and it made me remember.'

Softly, she asks, 'Remember what?'

'The eerie way I'd sometimes catch my mother staring at me. I remember feeling as if she weren't really seeing *me*, but someone else, and then this incredible wave of sadness would come over her. I've always thought it was her depression, and that I somehow caused her distress. But what if . . . Fuck, what if she'd been seeing *Hart* in me? The man she supposedly loved, but for whatever reason, had refused to leave Alistair for.'

'I'm so sorry, Jase.'

I squeeze her hand and we both look up ahead as we hear music begin to play. There's some sort of gourmet food festival being set up right on the beach, and with The White Stripes' 'Seven Nation Army' carrying on the breeze, I link our fingers together and head that way, seeing a sign for what they claim is the world's best margarita.

'Come on,' I say to Emmy, deciding it's time to lighten the mood. 'I think I see a drink with my girl's name on it.'

EMMY

We've been back up in the room for an hour or so now, the delicious, over-sized margarita I'd had at the mini gourmet food festival making me too mellow to work. Instead, I've lounged on the comfortable sectional sofa that sits before the open balcony doors, content to simply play on my new phone, while surreptitiously watching Jase as he rapidly types on his laptop.

Last week, when I'd first seen Jase Beckett on that stuffy Tube car in London, he'd just been this beautiful fantasy that had stolen my breath. But now he's . . . God, he's so much *more*. That gorgeous exterior of his is such a small, insignificant part of who he is. Back then, I'd had no idea about his generosity and his sharp intellect. His clever wit and his dirty sense of humor. Had no idea that he could look at me in a way that makes me feel ridiculously happy. Whole. *Alive*. He's making me a better person just by being close to me, and I know that if I have any brains at all, I'll never leave him again. That I'll stick by him, through the good and the bad that life brings, sharing the ups and the downs with him.

And I have a feeling that with Jase by my side, the good will always outweigh the rest.

Still, this is the real world, and the reality is that there will be times when things are hard. There always are. Pain doesn't touch only the poor and the needy. Pain is a brush that has the ability to paint everyone equally. Sure, some might get missed by its heavier strokes. But no one is safe from it, no matter how much money they might have to throw at the world.

His phone starts to ring from its place on the sofa beside him, and when he glances down at it he says, 'Damn, it's Martin.'

He moves to his feet as he answers the call, then walks into the bedroom. From this distance, his voice is too muffled for me to make out what he's saying, but I can tell from his tense tone that it isn't good news.

'Is everything okay?' I ask when he comes back into the sitting room, his jaw so rigid it looks as if it's been carved from granite.

'You mean other than the fact that I've just learned Cameron is trying to weasel his way into a takeover of my build in Thailand?'

'Holy shit!' I say as I move to the edge of the cushions, outraged on his behalf.

He scrapes a hand back through his hair and sighs. 'Sorry. I know I sound like a dick, but I'm fucking furious.'

I bite my lip, hating to see him upset. And then I take a deep breath, and force myself to say, 'Do you need to go back? Because if you did, I would hate it, but I'd understand.'

He gives me such a fierce, intense look, I swear I can feel its warmth pulsing against my skin. 'I'm not leaving, Emmy. Martin is handling what needs to be handled there, and I can use a phone here just as easily as I can in London. I've already set up a few video conferences that will take place in the morning.'

'Well, would it help if I went back to my apartment?'

'Fuck, no,' he says, shaking his head. 'I'd just follow you back there, and we've got more privacy here.'

'You're sure?' I ask.

He walks over and leans down, forcing me to lean back as he braces his hands against the top of the sofa, caging me in, and there's a determined glint in his deep blue eyes as he says, 'I don't want to sound too possessive, sweetheart, but like hell am I letting you leave me.'

'I'm not talking about leaving *you*,' I say. 'I'm just letting you know that I understand if you need some space.'

'I flew over five and a half thousand miles to be here with you, Em. The last thing I want is space.'

'Okay,' I whisper. 'Then I'll stay.'

His gaze gets heavy, as if my words have soothed him, and he gives me a wicked little smile. 'You know, there's a tub in the bathroom the size of a small swimming pool. Would you like to soak for a bit while I finish up my calls?' He lowers his head, brushing his lips across my ear as he adds, 'It might help with any *aches* you're feeling.'

I give a soft snicker, pushing against his shoulders until he lifts up enough that I can look him in the eye. 'You say it all caring like, but I see right through you, Mr Beckett.'

A husky laugh falls from those lips that are capable of giving me so much pleasure. 'And just what do you see, Miss Reed?'

'That you *love* making my tender bits sore.'

His smile becomes a devilish grin. 'You've caught me, Em. It's one of my all-time favorite activities. One I feel I should devote the rest of my life to, seeing as how I'm so good at it and all.'

I'm laughing by the time he leans down and kisses the hell out of me. His tongue strokes across mine like the sweetest sin, and I can feel the way he's savoring me. Enjoying me. 'Bath,' he groans, nipping my lower lip, 'and then I'm going to pull you out of the hot water and lick every inch of your pink little body from head to toe.'

'Do I get to lick you back?'

'Christ,' he laughs, giving me another quick, hard kiss. 'You'd better run, or I'm going to be fucking you in about two seconds flat, and then your bath will have to wait till tomorrow.'

I quickly scoot out from between him and the sofa, a smile on my lips as I grab my bag and hurry into the bathroom.

Within minutes, I have the tub full of tropical-scented bubbles, and as I lean my head back against its sloped edge, the jets swirling the water around my body in a warm, soothing massage, my thoughts are swirling too. I can't stop thinking about how Jase is so determined to stay here with me, instead of running off to save his deal, the way my father has always done, and I'm ashamed that I ever tried to compare the two men.

Yeah, Jase had hurt me with his stupid offer while we were in Kent – but before that, he'd been nothing but wonderful. And since showing up at my apartment yesterday morning, which feels like a lifetime ago, he's made it clear that his focus is *me* and building a relationship with me. One that certainly won't be easy, given that we live in two different countries. But I have no doubt now that it will be entirely worth it. Whatever it takes – and I still haven't figured things out that far ahead yet – but whatever it is, that's what we'll do. And if we work together, I truly believe we'll be able to make this work.

I also believe that when you want a man badly enough, you make the time for him, no matter how busy or determined you are to succeed. And that was okay, when he was willing to do the same. I mean, the guy was willing to travel halfway around the world for me. How much more serious and willing could he get?

His calls must take longer than he'd planned, because I end up finishing with my soak before he ever comes in to collect me. Feeling clean and relaxed, I wrap myself in one of the hotel's fluffy white robes and head back into the sitting room to look for Jase. He's still on the phone, standing before the open balcony doors, the churning ocean glinting in the moonlight, and there's a delicious smell filling the entire suite. As I look around, taking in the delivery bags by the door, and the sumptuous-looking feast that's been laid out on the coffee table, I realize that he's ordered dinner for us.

I haven't made a sound, but as if he can sense my presence, he looks over his shoulder, his dark eyes smoldering with hunger when they take in my scrubbed face, damp hair, and robe-clad body. It's hardly a seductive ensemble, but something about it must appeal to him, because he quickly ends the call, looking like he'd rather eat me than the meal. There's no way I'm letting this lovely spread go to waste though, so I tell him to sit. I hand him his plate, then settle down beside him and grab my own, a low moan on my lips when I take the first bite of my mouthwatering seafood risotto.

We talk about easy, simple things as we eat, debating what movie we should go and see this weekend, and if we want to try to catch a Padres game, since their new stadium isn't far from here. But as we set our empty plates aside, and settle back on the cushions to enjoy the breathtaking view of the ocean through the balcony doors, I clear my throat a little, and finally ask him the question that's been burning on the tip of my tongue since I woke up that morning. 'Have you been tested? You know, since you were last with someone?'

He turns his head so quickly I'm surprised he doesn't get whiplash, and gives me a deep, searching look as he says, 'I was tested two months ago. And I haven't been with anyone since but you.'

I wet my lips with the tip of my tongue. 'The same for me. Well, it was last year, but I haven't been with anyone since then except you.'

He sets the soda he's been drinking down on the coffee table, then turns to face me. 'What are you trying to say, Em?'

'Well,' I murmur, reaching up and tucking a wayward strand of hair behind my ear, 'I'm on the pill.'

'Yeah?'

'Yeah.' My heart is pounding, but my voice is strong. 'So if you want to do away with the condoms, I'm okay with that.'

His chest expands as he pulls in a deep breath, and he rubs his palm over his mouth as he exhales in an audible rush. 'I've never had sex without one.'

'Me neither.'

He looks at me like he's already inside me, fucking my

brains out. And then he moves to his feet, pulls his shirt over his head, and starts undoing his button fly as he says three low, gruff words that make me melt.

'Open your robe.'

JASE

My shorts and boxers hit the floor at the same time, and I kick them away as I take my cock in my fist, squeezing to hold back the cum that's already boiling in my heavy balls. The idea of fucking Emmy in the raw . . . It's breaking me. Wrecking me. I'm nothing but sharp, visceral hunger, and I have no doubt that my control is already in shreds.

But I want this to be good for her. I want it to be the best she's ever had, ruining her for every other man but me, and so I suck in another deep breath and squeeze my fist even tighter, determined to do this right, and not fall on her like a ravening beast.

'Now lie down and spread your legs, Em. Knees up and thighs as wide as they'll go.'

I haven't even touched her yet, but she's already panting as she follows my gritty command. Her beautiful cunt is shiny and pink, the plump folds still swollen from all the times I fucked her yesterday. I should get my mouth down there and lick her juicy little clit until she comes for me, softening her up. But as addicted as I am to her exquisite taste, the lure of feeling her slick, cushiony sheath on my bare dick is just too strong.

I come down on the sofa with her, bracing myself on one arm with my hand planted by her shoulder, my other hand still holding tight to my cock. The pressure of my fist is making the veins bulge thicker beneath the dark skin, and I swear the heat and weight of her greedy gaze is making me even bigger. My heart pounds and my pulse thunders with anticipation, and I pray to God this isn't going to be over too soon as I notch the wet head against her tiny, tender opening, and start working my way inside, one broad inch at a time. It feels so good that my eyes are burning, my throat tight, the sounds ripping up from my chest so guttural that I sound like an animal.

In this moment, I'm nothing but primitive lust and blistering craving. She molds around me, so incredibly tight and hot and wet, her cunt sucking on me like she wants to pull the cum right out of me. Like she's desperate for it. Like she *needs* it, and fuck but I need to give it to her.

But first, I'm going to ride my beautiful girl until she comes so hard I can feel it down in my bones. Down in my goddamn soul.

'You ready?' I grunt, breathless, staring so deep into her luminous brown eyes that I'm falling into them.

'So ready,' she moans, her soft hands curling over my shoulders as she pulses her hips against me, and that's *it*. I'm *gone*.

I take her hard and fast and violent, our sweat-slick bodies pounding together as I fuck her so rough and deep I'm amazed I'm not slamming into her heart. I curl my hand around the back of her thigh and push it higher, hammering into her snug, wet clasp, and I can't believe how different this feels without a condom. It's like a thousand new nerve-endings in my cock have just come to life, and I know it's more than just the fact that I'm bare-backing for the first time. It's that I'm doing it with *Emmy*. That it's *her* sweet, tight cunt that's suddenly coming on me, squeezing me, drenching me, *milking me*, and I grind my teeth together so hard it's a miracle I don't crack a tooth as my orgasm erupts from me with explosive force. I'm heaving and shouting, my entire body shuddering as I blast her with hot, heavy streams again and again, as if my sole purpose in this world is to fill her up. To pack her so full of me, she can't ever get me out.

At some point, I collapse on top of her, completely spent, and I'm pretty sure she has to shove my torso a bit to the side so she can breathe. My dick stays thick inside her, but then it's in heaven, so that's really no surprise. But I scrounge what energy I can to move my lips, and ask, 'You okay, baby?'

'I'm wonderful,' she breathes. Then she gives a little puff of laughter, and turns her head to smile at me. 'I'm also sticky.'

I manage to cup the side of her flushed, beautiful face in my hand, and say, 'What you are is fucking perfect.' Then I lean over and claim her soft, pink lips with a kiss that quickly shifts from gentle to blistering, and I'm wondering how swiftly I can carry her into the bedroom, needing to be able to twist and turn her curvy body into whatever position I want for round two, when I hear my phone start to ring. I ignore it, letting the call go to voicemail. But whoever it is just calls right back, and with a frustrated curse, I carefully pull out and sit up, kneeling between her spread thighs, and I have no doubt that my expression is dark and raw with lust as I take her in. I can see my cum slipping out of her, glistening against her pink, swollen flesh, and I take a moment to simply soak in the breathtaking sight, committing it to memory, before I move to my feet and grab the bloody phone.

'What?' I snap, after seeing that it's my father's number.

'Jase, this is Caroline. I realize you're off playing with your little tramp in America, but I thought you might want to know that your father's been admitted to the hospital.'

I bite back the words, 'He's not my father.' They catch me by surprise, because until this moment, I haven't fully admitted to myself that I believe Hart's story. But, hell, it's not like I don't look *exactly* like the guy.

Unable to deal with that particular mind-fuck at the moment, I ask her what happened.

'We don't really know,' she says airily. 'Something to do with his liver and blood levels.'

I give a short, wry laugh. 'You mean he drank so much that he nearly killed himself.'

'There's no reason to be snide,' she snaps.

I briefly consider telling her that I know about the calls she's made to the county councilors in London, but decide not to show my hand. Instead, I simply say, 'If you need to relay any information in the future, go through Martin.'

'I'm not calling your stupid assistant!' she shouts. 'Do you have any—'

I disconnect the call, tossing the phone aside, and the thought passes through my head that this might be Caroline's doing. That she's so desperate to get me back in England, she could have damn well poured the gin down Alistair's throat herself, once he'd drunk himself into a stupor, as he often does. It's a twisted theory, but then this is Caroline, so who the fuck knows what she's capable of.

'What happened?' Emmy asks, coming over and wrapping her arms around my waist, and I settle my hands on her naked back as I tell her.

'Maybe I should be more concerned,' I mutter, 'but I'd be faking it. Alistair made his damn bed, and now he's got to lie in it. And I meant what I told them on Sunday. I'm done with their shit.'

'I've said it before and I'll say it again. I don't blame you, Jase. And they don't deserve you.'

'Yeah, well,' I husk, brushing a quick kiss across her lips, 'do you know who does? You. And right now, you're going to get me.'

She blinks at the sudden change in the conversation, but why in the hell would I want to keep talking about Alistair and Caroline when I have this warm, wonderful woman in my arms?

I pick her up, carrying her into the bedroom, and come down over her on the sprawling king-sized bed. I don't waste any time, gripping my cock and notching the head against her, then carefully work my way back inside, going as slow as I can, loving how her tight cunt always makes me work for it.

I reach down and grip the back of her knee, pulling her leg up over my hip, and I love how wide her eyes get when I go even deeper. I'm good at reading women, especially when it comes to sex – but I've never been so in-tune with a woman that I felt like I was in her head. But that's how it is with Emmy. I've thought it before, but I honestly feel like she was made for me. Or hell, maybe I was made for *her*.

Maybe everything about me was put together in a way that I could be what this incredible woman needs.

So that I could be the man who gives her whatever she wants and craves and longs for.

And maybe, just maybe, one day be the man that she loves.

Chapter Seven

Thursday evening

EMMY

One week ago today, I found the gorgeous Jase Beckett parked on the curb outside my apartment. And while it was the last thing in the world that I'd expected, there's no denying that this past week has been the absolute best of my life.

We've done some more sightseeing, taking in the world-famous zoo and spending a day soaking up the sun in La Jolla. But we've also just taken a lot of chill time, sunbathing by the hotel's pool and walking on the beach. And we've worked as well, sitting on the sofa in his suite with the balcony doors open, the sea-scented breeze filling the room as we click away on our laptops, me doing research for the *Luxe* articles and Jase handling his various business dealings that span the globe.

And while Alistair is back at home from the hospital, refusing the rehabilitation center the doctors recommended for him, Cameron is continuing to cause trouble. There's a logical part of me that knows Jase needs to get back to London to deal with the issue in person, and yet I'm terrified of talking to him about it, because I know what it will mean.

That I have to make a choice.

That I have to decide.

But even though I'm not ready for that yet, I've gone all in with Jase. Our physical connection is only growing hotter and more intense, each searing sexual encounter somehow deepening our emotional connection. We fuck hard and raw and aggressively, but with a passion unlike anything I've ever known or even dreamed of. I know every inch of his rock-hard, god-like body, and I crave it with every part of me. Every breath. Every cell.

And the way he is with me, sometimes tender, sometimes not – it's like he's in my head, sensing what I need to get off before I even know it myself. And when he goes all dark and dominant, ordering me to get on my hands and knees for him, I remember the day that we first met, and how I'd sensed his desire to order me around.

That crap might not fly outside of the bedroom, but I'd be lying through my teeth if I said it didn't make me hot as hell when it comes to our so-good-it's-insane sex life.

We've spent the week here at the Del, and he's had me in every corner of the suite. On every surface. Against every wall. In fact, I've thought a few times that it's a good thing the suite doesn't have any connecting walls with another room, or I'm pretty sure we would have already gotten a call from management.

Then again, the hotel management seem thrilled to have Jase here, so they probably wouldn't say a word. But despite how desperate they are to bend over backward for him, I love that he doesn't treat the staff like they're here to serve him. He's friendly, appreciative, and I have a feeling that most of the women working here are already half in love with him. Maybe a few of the men, too.

One night, when there was a rare summer storm raging out

over the Pacific, Jase even took me out on the balcony – and when I say took, I mean fucked me to the point that I was screaming from the force of my orgasms, and he'd had to cover my mouth with his warm palm as he kept pumping into my body, making me come again . . . and again.

And then there's the shower, which is one of my favorites.

Without a doubt, I'm becoming addicted to showering with Jase, and . . . Well, it kind of worries me. Mostly because I'm becoming addicted to every single thing about him – the way he laughs, the sound of his voice, the things he says – and I can't help but stress about how long this little bubble we're living in is going to last. He says he's staying, but for how long? It's like we're living a fairytale, and sooner or later, we're going to have to step out of the pages and face reality.

He calls himself my boyfriend, but what does that really mean? Eventually he'll have to go back and deal with the empire he's built. Does he expect me to go with him? Do I *want* to? Or is he thinking we'll do the whole long distance thing? And if *that's* his plan, then how on earth will it work? Because I don't think I could stand to be apart from him for any significant length of time, and I sure as hell hope he feels the same.

It's all enough to make my head pound when I think about it, but I'm not going to worry about it tonight. My new motto is *Life is short and our moments of happiness are fleeting. So don't waste them. Enjoy them!* And that's exactly what I intend to do.

While we were walking along the beach yesterday, Jase told me that he wanted to get to know Tyler better, since it's obvious that Ty and I are close and he's like my family. So we called Ty and made plans for the three of us to go out together tonight. Ty suggested one of our favorite hangouts in the Gaslamp Quarter, and I thought it was a great idea. The place is decorated like an old-fashioned pub, and it has great food, delicious drinks, and an awesome karaoke stage that we've made fools of ourselves on more than once over the years.

As I finish the last touches on my make-up, Jase comes into the bathroom to tell me we need to leave soon, though I think he really just wanted an excuse to come in and see what I'm wearing. I've chosen the pretty, floral swing dress that I wore during our weekend together in Kent, since Jase packed up all the beautiful clothes and shoes that he'd bought for me and brought them with him.

When he sees what I've chosen to wear, a sin-drenched smile kicks up the corner of his mouth. He comes up behind me and places his hands on my hips as he meets my gaze in the mirror, so tall he's towering over me, and says, 'You got your *Star Wars* knickers on under there, Em?'

'Why?' I ask, smirking at him. 'You looking to join the rebellion?'

He runs his big hands up and down my sides as he laughs, and I can tell *exactly* where his mind has gone. 'I can't wait to get you back here tonight and out of this dress.' His voice is a low, sexy rumble that fits perfectly with the smoldering heat in his sky-blue eyes. 'I never got to work my way up underneath it last time, because you ran off into the shower.'

'I kind of had to, Jase. I was freezing my butt off after your ex-girlfriend dumped her Pimm's down my back.'

We share a laugh at the memory, and I know we're both planning a better ending for him, me, and the infamous dress this time around.

We head out and make good time into the city, and though things are a bit stiff between him and Tyler when we all meet up, the tension doesn't last long once their mutual love of rugby is discovered. As they get fired up talking about teams and players, I just sit back and watch, wishing I hadn't left my phone back at the Del so that I could record them, because they're hilarious. If I weren't so in love with Jase, I'd think he and Tyler were the perfect couple, Jase so dark and Ty so blond, and more mouthwatering muscles between the two of them than any two men could ever deserve.

I'm reaching for my drink when I suddenly freeze, my hand still in midair as shock pulses through my body like an explosion. Holy . . . *shit*. Did I really just think that? Did I honestly just say, in my head, that I'm in love with Jase?

I . . . I love him?

I lower my shaking hand and take a deep breath, the guys completely oblivious for the moment to the emotional bomb that's just landed on me, and as I slowly exhale, I realize that it's true. I'm panicking, but *God*, of course it's true. I'm crazy about the guy. Completely gone for him. I fucking love Jase Beckett! And not in the brotherly, familial way that I love Ty.

No, this is the real deal. The 'lay my body down on a sword for him' kind of love. 'Pack up my life and follow him across the world' kind of love. The 'stand in front of our friends one day and join my life with his' kind of love, and I wonder what I look like right now. If my panic is showing on my face, making me look like a deer that's been caught in a set of headlights.

Only . . . maybe it's not panic at all.

Maybe I'm just excited.

And maybe, just maybe, I'll somehow find the courage to tell him how I feel.

JASE

I never thought I would be sitting in a bar in the Gaslamp Quarter in downtown San Diego, watching my stunning girlfriend sing a drunken rendition of the Spice Girls' 'Wannabe' with her best friend, the two of them using British accents that are some of the worst I've ever heard. But I am, and I can't remember a time when I've ever laughed so hard and often, or felt so at home, even though this isn't my home at all.

Then again, this is Emmy's home, so maybe it is. Maybe it has been since I first stepped off the plane last week, and I just needed to open my eyes to see it and accept it.

She belts out a particularly loud, off-key note, and my head goes back as I laugh, thinking she's a riot. A beautiful, currently sloppy, fascinating riot, and the woman I damn well plan to spend the rest of my life with.

Every day.

Every night.

I've known her for such a short time, but it doesn't matter. She's become the very pulse point of my existence, and I'm no longer trying to fight it.

All that's left is for me to man up and tell her how I feel. That I've fallen completely head-over-heels in love with her.

This is new territory for me, because I've never been in love before, so I've never needed to say the words. But I need to say them now, because they're the most real truth in my world. Every other thing in my life might be turning to chaos, but it doesn't matter, because the only thing that I actually need is this one precious little American blonde who can slay me with a smile. Seduce me with a look. And if I can manage to make her love me back, I'll be the luckiest man in the world.

After the song ends, they relinquish the microphone to the next group, and I have to smile when I notice how they're leaning on each other for support as they make their way back to the table. I've never seen Emmy so tipsy, and it's fucking adorable.

We order a fresh round of soft drinks for everyone, since

they've decided to call it quits on the booze, and as we wait for our drinks, Tyler says that I should let him teach me how to surf.

'No way!' Emmy practically shouts in the guy's face, before I can even respond. She turns her head, giving me an imploring look as she says, 'There are sharks in the Pacific. Big, scary-ass, man-eating sharks, Jase, and I happen to like all your body parts right where they are, thank you very much.'

'You saying you only want me for my body, sweetheart?' I tease her, wrapping my arm around her waist and pulling her closer, until she's plastered up against me on our side of the booth.

'Naw,' she whispers, giving me a slightly crooked, endearing grin. 'I'd keep you no matter what.'

Her quiet words hit me in the chest with the force of a punch, nearly knocking the air from my lungs. 'Yeah?' I husk, wondering how much shit Tyler will give me if I lower my head and kiss the hell out of her, like I'm dying to do.

'Yeah,' she murmurs, cupping the side of my face with one of her soft hands. 'You're nice to look at, Mr Beckett, but I wouldn't be here right now, having spent the week that we've just spent together, if that's what I was interested in. It's who you are on the inside that makes me all swoony.'

My chest burns with emotion, so I just say fuck it and do what I want. What I *have* to, which is claiming that sweet mouth of hers in a long, wet, this-woman-is-*mine* kind of kiss, because this girl . . . She's just made me feel like a king.

When we finally break apart for air, Tyler laughingly proclaims that it's time for the lovebirds to get a room. We pay the bill, and he orders an Uber, since the Ferrari only has two seats.

After Ty and I shake hands, and Emmy gives him a tight hug, we head out. It's late, and we're one of the only cars on the road as we make our way towards the sweeping Coronado Bridge, the lights of the city sparkling around us. Emmy is sitting in the passenger seat with her head back, eyes closed and a beautiful smile on her pink lips, more relaxed than I've ever seen her. And even though she's been drinking, I sense that this is more than just the alcohol. Something's different, that guard of hers almost nonexistent now, and I can't help but wonder what's caused the change. Was it one specific moment, or all the little ones that we've shared since we first met two weeks ago? Two weeks that feel like so much more, and suddenly I know that I've made my decision.

Emmy might not have family here in San Diego, but she and Tyler, they're closer than any family I've ever known. And it's clear that she loves this city like it's her own. So since I can't take her away from it, I'm just going to have to ask her if she'll let me move in with her while I search for the perfect beach house for us to live in together. Or hell, maybe she'll just decide to stay out at the Del with me until we find our dream home.

But first, I need to tell her that I've fallen in love with her. And I'm going to do that just as soon as we get back to the Del. Well, as soon as I've stripped off her sexy dress and buried myself in her mouthwatering cunt, because I want to be inside her when I do it. To have that connection with her, so that she can *feel* as well as hear the words.

We're hitting all the green lights as we head down a road that's taking us through an area that seems to be little more than warehouses, and I'm wondering if I've taken a wrong turn somewhere, when it happens. One second I'm reaching over to take Emmy's hand in mine, and in the next a truck slams into the side of the Ferrari, sending us into a spin until we hit a divider in the middle of the road and flip up into the air, rolling twice before coming to a jarring stop upside down, the air bag pinning me to my seat.

I must black out for a few seconds, because when I blink my eyes open, I hear sirens in the distance. I'm thinking that some-one, maybe the driver of the truck, has already called the emergency services, when I hear a man say, 'We need to take care of this and get out of here. Someone must have heard what's happened and called the cops.'

'Put the fucking gun away,' another man growls, and I man-age to turn my head enough to see their legs just outside my crumpled door. 'The Brit paid us to make his death look like an accident, not a murder!'

What the . . . ? What Brit? An accident? Murder?

Fuck! I turn my head toward Emmy, terrified of what I'm going to find. The truck hit my side, thankfully, but because of the violence of the crash, the entire car is crunched around us. She's unconscious, hanging against the seatbelt that's holding her in place, her air bag deployed as well, but I don't see any major injuries. I'm muttering prayers and promises under my breath that she's okay as I hear heavy footsteps retreating, and hope like hell that the bastards who are responsible have decided to run. I would've loved the chance to beat the shits to within an inch of their lives, and force some information out of them, but right now my only focus is on Emmy and getting her out of this sodding car.

Because I smell fuel, and I'm not going to wait for the para-medics to get here to move her in case this thing is about to go up in flames.

With a lot of cursing and groaning, I manage to climb out through the driver-side window, feeling like I've gone twenty rounds with a heavyweight boxer. I'm pretty sure I'm leaking blood from somewhere on my head because I have to wipe my face a few times before I can see anything, but I don't give a fuck. All I care about is getting to Emmy, and I ignore the various aches in my body as I limp my way around the front of the car.

'Emmy, baby, come on,' I murmur over and over, as I work to get her free of her seatbelt. Finally, after what feels like forever, I'm sitting on the curb at the side of the road, rocking her unconscious body in my arms as the sirens grow closer. I know I probably shouldn't have moved her, but for all I know the car is going to catch fire at any moment, and I wasn't leaving her inside.

When the paramedics arrive, it takes everything I've got to force my arms to loosen their hold as they pull her away from me, then lay her on a trolley. I'm scared shitless, and they're surrounding her, making it impossible to see what they're doing to her. Eventually, they load her into the back of an ambulance, and a cop drives me behind them. He asks me questions about the accident, but I don't tell him what I overheard. There's no way to prove it, and the police are already searching for the truck, since the driver is at fault for a hit-and-run.

They take Emmy to the UCSD hospital in Hillcrest, and wheel her immediately into surgery, though no one will tell me what for. I spend the next thirty minutes worrying myself sick, while a group of nurses and a doctor determinedly look me over despite my assertions that I'm fine and they need to leave me the hell alone.

It's Emmy who's in trouble.

She nearly died because of me. Because some fuckwit tried to kill me tonight.

And I have no idea who. I mean, yeah, my family is a pain in the arse, but why in the hell would they try to off me? They have nothing to gain from it.

So, then, someone I work with? Someone I've pissed off enough during a deal that they would want this? Would be willing to pay to make it happen?

Fuck, my head is pounding from what I'm told is a concussion, as well as the stitches they've put in over my left eye, and I can't seem to focus enough to think of anyone.

Finally, a surgeon comes out to talk to me, and all I can do is stare at the blood on her scrubs. Christ, was Emmy bleeding? It'd been difficult to see her clearly in the moonlight, and once the emergency services arrived on the scene, the flashing lights had been blinding.

But this woman's clothes are spattered with blood. The same blood, I realize as I look down, that's all over my hands. Soaking my shirt and my jeans. Suddenly I feel like I'm drowning in it. Like it's burning my skin. I'm breathing hard, and it's like I'm listening to the surgeon speak through a tunnel as she tells me that a shard of metal had punctured Emmy's abdomen. The good news is that no organs were damaged, but she lost so much blood that they've had to give her a transfusion.

Somehow, I manage to get my voice to work, and I ask if I did anything wrong. If there's something I should have done differently, but she tells me no. That most of the bleeding was internal, and I could have caused her more damage if I'd tried to dislodge the shard or applied pressure to it.

I ask when I can see her, and she tells me that they're still working on her. That she just wanted to find me to let me know that Emmy's out of the danger zone.

I think I manage to thank her, but I'm not positive, her words echoing through my head like a booming death knell as they mix with the ones that I heard before.

Danger. Accident. Murder.

As I stand there in the middle of the quiet hallway, I know I should call Tyler, her mum, *someone*. But I'm numb. I'm shutting down.

Because I know what I have to do. It's the only way, at this point, that I can think of to keep her safe. And that's all that matters. Right now, making sure that none of this shit touches Emmy is the *only* thing I can afford to focus on. I can't let anything else sway my decision, or I'll make the wrong one out of selfishness and she could end up paying the ultimate price for it.

Exactly two weeks ago, I met the woman of my dreams.

And today I nearly got her killed.

When she wakes, I know she's going to hate this place. That what happened to her as a child is going to make her panicked and uncomfortable.

But I have no doubt that she's going to hate me even more.

Because I'll already be gone.

The
Confession

Chapter One

Thursday morning

EMMY

It's been exactly three weeks since Jase Beckett left me on my own in the hospital in San Diego.

When I'd managed to blink my eyes open in the recovery room after my surgery, the first thing I saw was my best friend's tired, concerned face. Tyler Landon's the emergency contact on all my insurance information, and so the hospital had called to notify him that I was there while I was still on the operating table.

'Where's Jase? Is he okay?' I'd croaked from my dry throat, as fragmented memories of jarring, bone-crunching rollovers in the Ferrari made me wince. I knew we'd been in an accident, but that was all, my mind fuzzy from the drugs they were pumping into my system.

'He's good,' Ty had murmured, giving me a worried smile as he carefully brushed my hair back from my face with one of his big hands. I'd exhaled a heartfelt sigh of relief that Jase was all right, until Tyler muttered under his breath, *'For now.'*

'What do you mean "for now"?'

'Shh,' he'd whispered. 'Don't worry, honey. Everything's going to be just fine.'

I slipped back under before I could get him to explain, but in my heart, I'd known there was something bad he was keeping from me. Something he didn't want me to know. When I was finally able to keep my eyes open for more than a few seconds at a time the following afternoon, I'd learned what it was.

Jase 'the bastard from hell' Beckett, as Tyler put it, had done a runner. Ty knew because Jase had left word at the hospital that he was leaving town, after paying not only for the treatment he'd been given, but also making arrangements to cover all my medical costs. And then he'd bailed before Tyler could even get there.

My things from the suite at the Hotel Del out on Coronado had been boxed up and delivered to the hospital that same day, just after Tyler broke the news to me, and there'd been an envelope inside with a handwritten note from Jase.

A goddamn, motherfucking note.

All it'd said was: *I know Tyler will look after you. I'm sorry I can't do this. I thought I could, but it's too much. Be careful, and take care.*

I mean, seriously? What in the ever-loving hell was *that* load of bullshit? And he hadn't even signed it, like he couldn't be bothered or had simply been in too much of a freaking hurry to go.

So, yeah. To say I'd been in a rough emotional state would be putting it lightly. I was so shocked and angry and heartbroken, my usual uneasiness around doctors hadn't even made an appearance during my stay in the hospital, all those other violent emotions stomping it down. I'd cried more that first week than I have in my entire life – and all I could keep thinking was *Thank God I didn't tell him I love him.*

Those nine little words had played on a continual loop of pain in my head, and I hated to admit it, but the truth is that what Jase did to me was a thousand times more painful than having a shard of Ferrari removed from my right side.

Jase's wound had been straight to my heart, and I had no idea how to fix it.

But even worse than the anguish was not knowing what had gone wrong. If he'd been playing me the entire time, in some twisted emotional game of manipulation. Or if the accident had somehow given him cold feet, like he cared about me so little he couldn't be bothered to hang around if I was going to be a burden.

Neither was going to give me any warm fuzzies, and they both made it clear he was a self-centered dick who couldn't be trusted. So I'd crawled into bed when they let me go home, and had started the painful task of rebuilding my emotional walls, one heavy brick at a time.

And Tyler, like always, was my anchor. He basically moved in with me for the first week I was home, playing nursemaid when I'd had to hobble around everywhere because of the pain in my side. But once I was given the all-clear from my doctor, I gave Ty a hug, kissed him on his bearded cheek, and told him he'd done his part and could get back to his own bed. I knew his back had to be killing him after crunching up on my tiny sofa for seven straight days – and that was after sleeping in my hospital room every night I was there, so I wouldn't be alone. He'd headed home, but still came by every day to check on me and bring me groceries, as well as dinner each night. I think he was afraid that if he didn't feed me, I wouldn't bother to eat at all. Especially after Lola sent me the first blog link to a photo of Jase out on a date in London.

It seemed that the man I'd so stupidly fallen in love with

hadn't wasted any time before getting back to his old ways once his feet hit British soil. I'd only been home from the hospital two days when she sent the first link, along with a scathing note about what a sleazy jackass he is. When I'd opened the link and saw the paparazzi-snapped pic of Jase coming out of a fancy London restaurant with a beautiful Italian heiress, I barely had enough time to reach the bathroom before I threw up. Tyler had held my hair back for me, terrified I was going to bust my stitches – though once the tears hit, I think he preferred the puking.

It was like a dam had been broken, and once I started crying, I couldn't stop. I cried for an entire twenty-four hours, and it was only because he knew that I needed him there to take care of me that Tyler hadn't gotten on a plane, flown to London, and beaten the hell out of Jase.

Then, five days after that first blog link, there'd been another one. That time, Jase had been caught on camera with a tall, skinny British model at a black-tie charity event. And even though I managed to keep my food down after I saw it, I'd felt another piece of me die inside.

Jesus, was he touching these women? Kissing them? Fucking them?

The tormenting questions kept me up at night, Jase's behavior so bizarre I simply couldn't wrap my head around it. And it's not the only thing that's been odd, because Tyler swears that there's been a security team watching my apartment since the day he brought me home. Four times now, he's spotted a dark sedan parked across the street from my building. The blacked-out windows on the car have made it impossible to see who is inside, but it actually followed us to one of my doctor's appointments. When Tyler walked over to bang on the driver's window, ready to demand an explanation, the car had sped away – only to be back on my street that night, when I'd peeked around the edge of my bedroom curtains.

And then, three days ago, shit got really weird, when Lola sent through yet another celebrity blog link. Only this one hadn't been accompanied by the previous scathing diatribe about what a 'dickless tosser' she thought Jase was. Instead, it'd simply said: *Look at the bastard's arm. What the HELL does this mean?*

I'd gritted my teeth and looked at the link.

And then my damn heart had stopped.

In the photo, he was wearing a casual white polo shirt, and his right inner forearm was clearly visible as he used it to block the paparazzi's lights. So visible that I could clearly see the new tattoo he'd gotten since leaving San Diego. A distinctive, intricate design of swirling stars and moons that's *identical* to the ink on my right hip.

We never talked about that specific tattoo, but he'd often paid special attention to it with his lips and tongue when he went down on me. Which had been *a lot.* As in every day. Plus, we'd taken a bunch of photos when we were at the beach on Coronado in our bathing suits, so there was a good chance he caught a clear shot of the tattoo on his phone, which he could have shown the artist who had done the work.

When I'd first seen the photo of him on the blog site, I couldn't believe he was walking around with *my* design tattooed on his freaking arm while the bitch who'd poured her Pimm's down my back clung to his other side as they walked out of a VIP box at a rugby match. God, I was going to give him so much shit for that. But as painful as it was to see him out on the town with yet *another* woman, and this one a freaking ex-girlfriend, I was relieved that Lola had sent me the link to the photograph.

I was relieved because it meant that there was a chance I hadn't been a complete and total fool. That there was a sliver of hope the emotions I'd read on Jase Beckett's beautiful face every single time he looked at me had been real and honest and true.

But if that were right, then it also meant that something was *wrong*. That Jase was deliberately trying to shove me away from him – which meant there was a strong chance I was just going to end up getting what was left of my heart shattered if I went after him, only to have him tell me to get lost.

So, I had a choice to make. I could either stay in San Diego and play it safe, doing what I could to glue my pieces back together yet again, and spend God knows how long licking my wounds. Or I could take what was left in my savings account, get my ass on an airplane, and go after the only man I've ever fallen helplessly, uncontrollably, and crazily in love with. I could find him, and then demand a fucking explanation.

The old Emmy would have taken that safe route, and crawled back under the armored shield she'd been slowly rebuilding, adding a shitload of reinforcements to it in the process.

But in a shocking discovery, I realized that the new Emmy has outgrown her shield. Yeah, she still gets scared of putting herself out there and taking those crazy, only-fools-do-things-like-this-for-love chances – but she's badass when it comes to going after what she wants in a way that old Emmy never was.

So now I'm here, in Edinburgh, Scotland, because this is where Jase has apparently been hiding out since he came back. That is, when he hasn't been escorting his dates all over London.

I could have been saved a lot of hassle and flown directly here, if he'd ever bothered to take my calls. I'd started trying to reach the handsome jerk after discovering that damn tattoo, but he never answered, and I wasn't going to talk about it on his voicemail. So I got on a plane and went to London first, since that's where I'd thought he would be. Only, when I got to his office, there'd been no Jase. But good ol' Martin, Jase's friend and longtime assistant, had been only too happy to tell me where I could find his boss.

I have no idea what Jase is doing in Edinburgh, but I'm about to find out. I haven't even taken the time to get dolled up, too eager to just get this over and done with, so I can know, once and for all, what comes next. I'm dressed casual, in a denim jacket, long black skirt, white top, and wide brown leather belt that sits low on my hips and is just loose enough not to bother the small puncture wound that's still healing on my side. But Jase has never given a shit about how I dress. He's always been much more interested in what's *underneath* my clothes, and I swear I feel another little tear in my heart as I wonder if that still holds true. Or if he'll take one look at me and laugh, like he's wondering what he ever saw in me.

'No, he's not like that,' I mutter under my breath, knowing I just need to grow a pair and knock on the door. Jesus, he's probably watching me right now through the peephole, thinking I'm acting like a scared little rabbit.

For some reason, Jase has security covering the building, so I know he knows I'm here. I'd had to give my friggin' name and show my passport down at the front desk, and they only let me up because Martin called (thanks to a text I'd sent him when my Uber dropped me off out front) and told them not to give me any problems. The doorman had looked pretty pissy though, so I'm guessing he's already called Jase to let him know that there's a tired, disheveled-looking American woman getting ready to knock on his door.

I catch the sound of someone moving around inside the flat, so I finally lift my hand and land a hell of a knock against the cream-colored wood. One I immediately regret, since my knuckles are stinging like a bitch. But the pain takes the focus off how hard and fast my heart is pounding as the door suddenly swings open, and I find myself standing face-to-face with Jase.

Oh . . . Oh, God. For a second, I can't even speak. I'm too blinded by the reality of him. By the scent and sight and sheer animal magnetism that has drawn me to this breathtaking man from the first time I ever set eyes on him in a stuffy London Tube car.

Then I blink, and as he comes into sharper focus, I realize how . . . *different* he looks. He's still drop-dead gorgeous, with his thick ink-black hair, dark blue eyes, and that tall, powerful body that could give even Michelangelo's David a run for its money. Still looks like something that I need to hold and lick and kiss for the rest of my freaking life. But he's different, too, with a haggard edge that I've never seen on him before. Not even when he chased me all the way to San Diego a month ago. It looks like he's not sleeping or eating, and there's a new scar just above his left eyebrow, which I'm guessing is from the accident. Concern tightens my chest, while the anger that's been simmering inside me ever since I finally realized he'd bailed catches light like a spark with oxygen.

It's time to do what I came here to do, I think, reaching into the outside pocket on the purse that's slung over my shoulder and grabbing the two pieces of paper that I'd stored there. I pull them out, clutch one in each hand, and then lift my head at the same time I lift my arms, holding the papers up for him to see as I look him right in those beautiful blue eyes and demand, 'So which one is it, Jase? Which one is *real*? And which one is a fucking *lie*?'

Chapter Two

JASE

As my stunned gaze moves from the pathetic, handwritten break-up note that I'd sent with Emmy's things from the Hotel Del, over to the photo that'd been taken of me and Chloe a few days ago, my stomach knots with dread.

Shit! I knew I shouldn't have got the tattoo. But the constant ache I have for Emmy Reed has been eating me raw inside, and I'd just wanted something that made me feel . . . Christ, I'd just wanted to feel *connected* to her, in whatever way I could. So I'd dropped into one of the tattoo parlors in London when I was down there last week, pulled up a beautiful photo of Emmy on the beach in her bikini, and showed the artist what I wanted. I could see Emmy choosing the unique design because of its beauty, and despite the problem it's caused in bringing her here, I love that I have this link with her that can never be undone. Not by the shithead screwing with my life, or by my own stupidity.

My eyes burn as I look away from the note and the photo and devour the sight of her, soaking in every detail like a blind man who's finally been gifted with sight. I've watched Tyler's

Facebook page like a stalker, desperate for any information on how she was doing after the surgery, and am grateful as hell that the guy felt the need to keep Emmy's friends updated. She's a bit paler and has dropped a few pounds, but still shines like a drop of sunshine. Still glitters like a diamond. I'm going to shake my head with embarrassment later for thinking up these cheesy similes, but right now, there's just no help for it. Her beauty is captivating, and I'm drinking it in like this might well be the last sip I ever get.

And the way her skirt and top are wrapped around her mouthwatering body is making it so damn hard to keep my distance, when all I really want is to be buried so deep inside her she can feel me in every part of her.

I've been in shock since the call came in that she was on her way up, unable to believe she's here. When the private security team I've been paying to watch over her in San Diego called to say that she'd gone to the airport with a suitcase, I assumed she was flying back to Georgia to visit her parents. Well, her mother at least. After what went down four weeks ago with her old man, I doubt she's interested in seeing him. But she obviously got on a plane to the UK instead, though that still doesn't explain what she's doing *here*, in Scotland.

I've been hiding out up here in this flat for the simple reason that very few people know my company owns it – and I never even got around to telling Emmy about it. Hell, I've only stayed here twice before, partly because I don't often need to come to Edinburgh, and also because my cousin Oliver owns a flat in the same building, and I try to avoid that little shit as much as possible. I've never even mentioned to him that I own this place. To be honest, the only reason I bought it is because Martin has family in Edinburgh, and I wanted him to have a place to stay when he's here visiting them.

But it occurs to me now that maybe my trusted employee would've simply preferred to stay with his relatives. It's just that given how awful *mine* are, I always assumed he'd rather have his own space.

'Jase!' Emmy snaps, holding the note and photograph up higher, practically shoving them in my face. 'Answer the damn question!'

'You should still be resting,' I bite out, finally finding my voice. Then I quickly follow up with a gritty, 'How the hell did you even find me?'

Her golden brows lift, and I hate the tears that are glistening in her cinnamon-colored eyes, the ring of black around the outer edge as unique as it is stunning. 'Really?' she asks with a harsh laugh, tossing the photograph and the note on the floor between us. '*That's* what you're going with?'

I have the strangest sense of déjà vu, but realize that it's the way she's looking at me that feels so familiar, and not the words themselves, since her expression reminds me of that first argument we had in San Diego, when I'd shown up at her apartment. God, that seems like a lifetime ago. And so much has changed since then, taking a direction I could have never predicted. Not in a million bloody years.

The silence between us is getting painfully heavy, and I know I need to say something, so I grit my teeth and force out a guttural, 'You shouldn't have come, Em. This isn't a good time for me.'

'Yeah?' she asks, marching past me as she barges in. 'You got one of your new fuck bunnies in the bedroom waiting to get serviced?'

I work my jaw a few times as I shut the door behind her, and even though I know I shouldn't, I hear myself snarl, 'You really believe that? You really think I would climb into bed with another woman after what happened between us in San Diego?'

Anger rises in her so quickly I can almost feel its heat charring my skin. 'Exactly which "happening" are you referring to? The one where I gave you every part of me? Or the one where you ran like a fucking coward?'

The smile that curls my mouth is as bitter as it gets. 'Not *every* part, Em.'

Her own lips twitch with a sad smirk, and I realize she probably thinks I'm talking about her round little arse. But I'm not. I'm talking about her *heart*. About the part of her I want most, but can't have, because I love her too much to pull her into whatever shit this is that's started raining down on my life.

It sounds dramatic, but hell. If you can't turn into a belligerent dickhead when someone's trying to kill you, when can you?

Her hurt, glistening gaze is still locked in hard and tight on mine, and I know she's searching for the truth in my eyes as she swipes her tongue over her plump bottom lip, then quietly says, 'Tell me it's been an act, Jase. Tell me you didn't sleep with those other women.'

In this moment, I know I have a choice to make. I can give her the truth, and hold on tight to everything I've ever wanted, ever craved, without even knowing it was possible. That it was out there in the world, waiting for me to find it. To find *her*. Or . . . I can lie and tell her that I've nailed every one of them. That I've had a dozen different women since I flew home, and she'll run out of here so fast my head spins, jump on a plane, and go home. Go back to where I know she'll be safe – or at least a hell of a lot safer than she'll be here with me.

And if I do it, I know that will be it. That I'll never see her precious, beautiful face again.

Truth or lie? *Fuck!* This is such a miserable choice. Only . . .

Hell, there's really no choice at all. Not if I want to do what's truly right for her.

'What?' I force out in a low, mocking drawl, giving her my best impression of an arrogant, self-centered arsehole. 'You really think me feeding you a bunch of pretty little lies is going to make you feel any better, Emmy?'

She jerks back a step like my words have just slapped her across the face, and I fucking die a bit inside. I scrub my hand over my mouth, like I can wipe those shitty words away, and something in my chest crunches. I feel like my heart's being squeezed by a massive, spike-covered fist, and I swallow hard, trying to keep it together and not throw myself at her sandal-covered feet, the way I'm dying to do.

She goes pale, losing all that angry flush of color, and tears track down her cheeks like rainwater against a window. So many tears, I doubt she can even see through them, and my own eyes start to burn even hotter. Burn until I feel like my entire head is about to catch fire.

Without a single word, she suddenly turns and lurches for the door, but I'm there before I even realize what I'm doing, slamming the damn thing shut so hard it makes a booming thud that no doubt just startled every other person on this floor. My hand is big and dark against the pale cream of the wood, and I hear myself make this thick, raw sound at the back of my throat. It's an animal sound, wounded and angry and full of frustration, and I *know* there's not a force in heaven or hell that could get me to move my hand and let her go.

Christ, I tried. But I can't do it. I can't watch her walk away, because I know what it will mean. Know that there won't be any second chances once I've found my way through all this crap, no matter how desperately I beg.

I need to be strong, but this girl ... Shit, this girl is my weakness – my bloody kryptonite and Achilles' heel all rolled into one – and I can't do it. It'd be easier to reach up under my ribs and rip out my beating heart.

'*Move*,' she whispers, her spine stacking up with rage as she grips the doorknob tighter.

'No,' I growl from so deep in my chest, the words are almost coming from my gut. 'No way in hell, baby.'

'Damn it, Jase!' She smacks the door with her free hand, and her entire body starts to tremble. 'Stop playing your stupid games and just let me go!'

'I *can't*.'

'You have to!' she shouts, her voice cracking with pain as she shakes her head so hard her honey-gold curls whip against me. 'Because I can't be here. I don't want to be anywhere near you!'

'No, don't say that,' I scrape out, shuddering, feeling wrecked in a way that even the horrific car crash hadn't accomplished. I'm ravaged and torn and ripped open, all but bleeding out on the floor in the same way she'd nearly bled out on me that night. 'You don't mean that!'

She draws in a deep, shaky breath, and I can sense her gathering her emotions around her like a cloak – or like the armor she hid behind when we first met. In a voice that's suddenly gone cold, she says, 'Get your fucking hand off the door, Jase.'

It's painfully obvious that she's *done* – done with me and this whole fucked-up situation – and panic crawls up my throat so fast that I nearly choke on it. 'It wasn't an accident,' I say in a graveled rush, gasping for breath, my chest so tight I feel like concrete's been poured into my lungs.

The second the words leave my mouth, I flinch and think *Shit!* All my delusions of playing the heroic detective when I flew home, and then swooping back in to win the woman of my dreams, are being reduced to nothing more than a pile of ash and bone. But there's no going back now. All I can do is promise myself that if she decides to stay, I'll do whatever it takes to keep her safe. That I'll protect her with everything I have, to my dying breath.

'You have two seconds to explain yourself,' she snaps in a voice that's clogged with tears, 'and then I start screaming loud enough to bring your neighbors running over here.'

'It wasn't an accident,' I say again, dropping my forehead to the top of her head, her warm, sensual scent filling my lungs each time I gasp for air. 'That night, after we were hit, I . . . I heard them talking. The bastards who were driving the truck. Someone paid them to kill me and make it look like an accident. They just weren't very good at it, because I walked away. But *you* didn't.'

For a moment, she just stands there, the only sound that of her ragged breaths keeping time with my own. And then she spins around and shouts in my face, 'You stupid asshole!'

I blink, and she lifts her hands, shoving against my chest so hard that it knocks me back a step, and I'm amazed she doesn't slap me, because I can see how badly she wants to. How desperately she wants to strike out and share the pain that's burning so violently in her eyes it makes me feel like she *has* hit me. Like she's beating the hell out of me.

'Oh, God, Jase, I could kill you myself,' she sobs, glassy tears spilling past her lashes. 'You actually did it, didn't you? Broke my heart and pulled all this crap with those women because you're trying to *protect* me!' She's screaming now, and her hands are in her hair, pushing it back from her face as she completely loses it. 'You've even had a security team watching me, haven't you? While you staged those stupid photo ops with those women to make everyone think we're no longer seeing each other!'

'It's the only fucking choice I had. I have no idea who's behind the threat. Still don't.'

'And you thought *that* was the answer?' she snarls, kicking the photo of me and Chloe that's lying on the floor.

'It's the *only* answer!' I roar, so much tension pulling across my shoulders I feel like they might snap. 'You're right, I had to make whoever's behind this bullshit believe that we're no longer together. I couldn't risk them coming after you to hurt me!'

They'd already hurt her once because of me, and I wasn't going to let that happen again. I'd had security with me on the three dates I'd deliberately had since coming home, but I knew those women would be safe. I didn't travel with them, the only time I spent with them while we were surrounded by others. There was nothing to say they were significant enough to me to make it worth this dickhead's effort. But a girlfriend? I could all too easily see some sick fuck deciding that was the best place to strike, if their intention is to hurt me, as well as kill me. And since I really don't have a clue what's going on, I couldn't take that chance.

Emmy's head drops forward as she locks her fingers behind her neck and just stares at the floor, her panting breaths still harsh. I lose count of how long she stands there like that, letting my words soak into her brain, while I keep soaking in the sight and scent of *her*, unable to get enough. Knowing damn well that I'll always want more.

Finally, after what feels like forever, she pulls in another sharp breath and slowly lifts her head, her shattered gaze melting into mine. 'How about . . . How about trusting me to be smart enough, and strong enough, to stand by your side? Did that never occur to you? That I could be those things?'

The words are soft and hoarse, but they lash at me like a whip. I shove my hand into my hair so hard I nearly rip it out.

'This isn't about fucking intelligence or strength, Emmy. I can't lose you. I *won't*.'

Her nostrils flare, and she fists her hands at her sides, looking as if she's preparing to go into battle. 'Damn you, Jase! I'm not a child in need of your protection,' she seethes, the look on her tear-streaked face cutting right to the heart of me. 'I'm a grown woman. A partner.'

'You're—'

'The woman who loves you,' she cries. 'Do you understand that? I *love* you! And it's my goddamn right to stand by your side and help you, in whatever way I can!'

She . . . what? What the . . . ? Did she . . . ?

My jaw hangs open as I blink down at her in shock, and I know I probably look like I've just been smacked in the face with a two-by-four, but I can't believe that she's said it first. That she's said it *at all*.

And until this moment, I hadn't realized just how terrified I'd been that my heart was the only one on the line here. I mean, I knew she cared about me, and had harbored the hope that she would come to love me one day. But there'd still been that little voice in my head, that little kernel of fear, whispering that she wasn't on quite the same page as I was. That no matter how much time I gave her, that damn guard of hers would always rise between us, holding her back.

But now she's made the grand gesture, chasing after me. Not only that, she's willing to face the danger with me.

And she's spilled first blood. Her *own*. Opened her heart up and offered it to me in her soft hands, and shit just got real.

I'm on her before I even know I'm moving, my hands fisted in her hair, my mouth at her ear. 'I love you, Emmy. Love you so fucking much,' I gasp, finally able to say the words that have been bottled up inside me for so long. But they come easily now, slipping from my tongue like breaths, and once I start, I can't stop. 'Love you,' I say again, over and over, as I strip her clothes off with unsteady hands, throwing them to the floor, until every inch of her creamy skin is bared to my burning, possessive gaze.

Picking her up, I carry her into the bedroom and lay her down on the bed. I tear my own jeans and T-shirt off so fast I hear seams rip, and then I'm crawling on top of her, my thick, vein-ridged cock so hard and dark and long it looks brutal, and neither of us give a damn that the curtains are drawn wide on the windows, the sunshine pouring in on our naked bodies. There are some buildings close by that are tall enough someone could probably see in, but we don't even care, both of us too focused on touching and tasting as much skin as we can, our bodies coming together like it's what we'd been born for.

I suck and lap at her beautiful breasts, tonguing her pink little nipples until they're so sensitive every pull of my mouth makes her writhe and gasp, while her hands stroke over every inch of my fever-hot skin she can reach. But as much as I love her lush, heavy breasts, it's been three long, miserable weeks since I've had the mouthwatering taste of my woman's juicy cunt on my lips, and I can't wait a second more. I rear back, forcing her thighs out wide with my hands, and shove my entire face against her, the scent of her so warm and sweet it makes me growl. Then I tilt my head a little, open my mouth over that drenched, narrow slit that leads straight to heaven, and push my tongue inside her like I *own* her. Like she's *mine*, because she is. She so fucking is.

I go wild on her then, no practiced technique or experience. I'm just raw, animal hunger, sucking on her sensitive clit until I feel her hands pulling at my hair so she can tug me closer . . . *closer.* I lick my way back to that sweet little hole, and start fucking it with my tongue, getting her so slick and slippery that she's melting all over me, drenching my face, and I love it. Can't get enough of it. She comes for me with a sharp cry that echoes off the walls, flooding my mouth with her juices, the way her tight sheath pulses around my tongue driving me mad, and I nearly shoot my load right then and there. But I reach down and squeeze my cock so hard that the pain pushes it back, just long enough for me to rise up over her and notch the wet, engorged head of my dick against her quivering slit.

I'm ready to drive inside and pound the ever-loving hell out of her – but I freeze at the last second, remembering what's happened. Staggered by my near loss of control, I try to be careful as I push my way inside, one thick, blistering inch at a time, all too aware that she had surgery just three weeks ago. 'Are you sure this is okay?' I ask, my deep voice rough and low as I search her glistening, pleasure-dark gaze. 'Are you sure I won't hurt you?'

'Stop worrying,' she whispers, her pink lips curved in a womanly smile, her hands stroking down the rigid muscles in my back, tugging me closer. 'I'm fine – and I'll be a hell of a lot better once you're fucking me.'

I growl low in my throat, loving it when she's greedy. When she tells me exactly what she wants and needs. And once we get started, there's no stopping. Any control I'd hoped to claw on to is shredded, and we go at it like we've been apart for years instead of weeks. Like our entire existence depends on how hard I can give it to her, and how deep she can take me, my hips working my heavy cock in and out of her plush, tight cunt like a piston, until I'm taking her so rough and fast that the bed is slamming against the wall like a hammer. I brace myself on a straight arm and slide my right hand between us, rubbing my thumb over her swollen clit until she's digging her heels into my arse, her nails in my shoulders. Then I slide my fingers lower, past the tender place where my big, wet dick is spreading and penetrating her, until I reach her tight little arsehole. I rub it with the tip of my thumb, and though she tenses up a bit, she doesn't say no, so I start applying a bit more pressure.

'Just my thumb right now,' I tell her, loving how easily I can read everything I'm making her feel on her beautiful, expressive face. 'But one day soon, Em, I'm squeezing my cock in here. Every hard, thick inch of it.'

'*Oh, God,*' she moans, and her pussy clenches around me, somehow clasping me even tighter.

I keep going, no longer able to control the filthy words coming out of my mouth as I share with her all the things I intend to do to her, *with her*, and I have a feeling she's as bright red from the dirty-talk as she is from the aggressive way that we're fucking. But she loves it, her little teeth sinking into my shoulder as she claws at me, drawing me closer, and this time . . . Yeah, this time we both know that we're never letting go again. We've both run, and we've both chased, and now we're going to stick together through whatever the hell life throws at us.

We crash into climax at the same time, coming in a scalding, blinding rush. I take her mouth in a deep, wet, eating kiss, unable to believe how insanely good it feels to blast my hot cum inside her without anything between us, and I just keep going, feeling like I might never stop.

'I've got more to give you,' I growl against her soft lips. 'Your little cunt's so greedy, Em, it's pulling it right out of me. It's making me give you every goddamn drop.'

'Missed you,' she whispers back, cupping my face in her hands. 'Missed you so much.'

Her words undo me, and I press my forehead to hers as my breath hisses through my clenched teeth. I grind against the moist cushion of her sex as my cock gives a final, mind-shattering pulse, her inner muscles clasping me so tightly that there's a bite of pain with the pleasure that I *love*.

'Damn,' I groan, after I've carefully pulled out and finally collapse at her side, my left hand looking huge as I lay it over her navel. 'No matter how hard or deep I take you, it's never enough. I'd stay inside you twenty-four seven if I could, and never leave. I think you were made for me, Em. Or I was made for you. Either way, we belong together.'

She turns her head towards me and gives me a smile. One that's soft and sweet and so incredibly sexy.

'I love you,' I say in a harsh rumble, reaching up and cupping the side of her face with my hand as I lean in closer. 'I'm so sorry I didn't say it before, when we were in San Diego. I wanted to, I just didn't know how. But I fucking love you, baby. So much.'

She lifts her hand, setting it gently on top of mine as she searches my fierce, burning gaze and asks, 'Do you still want me?'

'Want you?' I mutter with a gritty laugh, stroking my thumb against the corner of her kiss-swollen mouth. 'Jesus, Em. I've died a little more every minute of every day that's gone by since I walked out of that hospital and left you there. I couldn't survive another one. I want you so much I can't breathe. Can't sleep. Can't eat. I want you forever. For *always*.' The lump of emotion sticking in my throat is so thick that I have to swallow against it, my voice little more than a graveled rasp as I say, 'You're so bloody brave, Em. I'm in awe of you. Of the guts that it took for you to get on a plane and come here to face me. You're a fucking miracle.'

'You told me to hold on to you,' she tells me softly. 'You made me promise.'

God, I did, didn't I? That first day in San Diego, after I'd fucked her beautiful brains out on her tiny sofa.

'Well, now it's my turn,' I murmur, sliding my hand down,

over her slender neck and her delicate collarbone, then lower, until I'm curling my long fingers around one of her perfect breasts, my thumb making her gasp as it strokes over her sensitive nipple.

'Yeah?' she whispers, her eyes dilating with desire as she wets her lips with the very tip of her tongue.

'Yeah.' I keep my hungry gaze locked tight with hers, and solemnly say, 'I promise I won't screw up like this ever again.'

Her eyes start to gleam. 'You'd better not.'

'And I promise to always be honest with you, and to not hide things from you.'

This time, there's a wry little twitch at the very edge of her mouth. 'Smart man.'

'And I promise,' I husk, sliding my hand from her breast to the curve of her waist, 'from the absolute bottom of my soul, that I will love you till the day I die.'

She doesn't say anything to that one.

No, the gorgeous girl just leans over and kisses me instead. And in the tender, exquisite touch of her lips, I taste not only our future, but the promise of a life more beautiful than anything I'd ever thought I could have. Had ever even dared to hope for.

I just have to find a way to keep us alive, so that we can have it.

No matter what it takes, I have to make it so that my badass little American and I can have it all.

Because I'm keeping this incredible woman in my life.

Even if it's the last damn thing that I do.

Chapter Three

Thursday afternoon

JASE

As I kiss my way across Emmy's soft belly, I hear the grandfather clock out in the sitting room strike one o'clock. We haven't left the bed since we fell into it hours ago, except for when I had to run and collect her suitcase when she suddenly remembered she'd left it sitting outside the door in the hallway. We're both starving, but instead of struggling out to the kitchen, we've stayed right here, wrapped around each other, making up for lost time. For the twenty-one long, eviscerating days it's been since we last saw each other.

I've spent the last half hour or so simply reacquainting myself with her lovely curves and warm, silky skin – kissing every inch of her sumptuous body, front and back – while paying special attention to the lingering scrapes and bruises from the accident.

And then, finally, I kiss my way over to the scar on her right side, my jaw tightening as I study the jagged little puncture wound. It's still shiny and pink, and will take a long while to fully heal, and my eyes burn as I notice how close it is to the tattoo that flows across her hip.

The tattoo that's identical to mine.

I lower my head again, pressing gentle, lingering kisses to the beautiful, intricate design, knowing only too well how lucky I am to be so close to it again. It's an honor I'd feared might be lost to me forever, but now she's *here*, in my bed, and despite all the shit that's happening in my life, I feel a sense of peace that's been missing since I walked away from her.

'The scar's pretty odd-looking, isn't it?' she says. 'Maybe I should just tell people I was shot. That sounds a lot more badass than being stabbed by a car.'

'Like hell you will,' I mutter, lifting my heavy-lidded gaze up to hers as she sprawls back on the pillows, looking like a sultry nymph who's been sent here for me to pleasure and please. 'There won't be anything to tell, because you're not getting naked for any other bastard but me.'

She rolls her eyes and laughs, like I've made a joke. 'I do wear swimsuits, remember?'

'Don't remind me. I still get tense every time I think about the heads you turned at the pool and the beach.'

She shivers, and I know damn well that she's remembering what would come *after*. The way I'd toss her over my shoulder the second the door to the suite at the Del was shut behind us, carry her into the bedroom, throw her down on the bed whether we were dry or sopping wet from the pool, and come down over her. The way I'd rip her little swimsuits off, line up with her tiny slit, and drive deep, that alpha streak in me (the one she's always giving me shit about) compelling me to stake my claim with a hard, mind-blowing fuck that always meant multiple orgasms for her, and me exploding so violently I knew she could feel the thick, heated pulses of my cum as I spurted inside her, filling her up.

I'm sucking in deep breaths as the carnal, provocative memories roll over me, telling myself I need to let her rest and find some bloody control, when she brushes her hand through my hair and quietly says, 'Jase, we need to talk now. You know, about what's happened.'

'Yeah, okay,' I agree, though it's not what I want. What I *want* is to just keep lying here with her before the open windows, tasting every inch of her creamy skin with my tongue and lips. But this needs to be done, and so I move on to an elbow beside her, and say, 'First, though, I need to tell you that I feel like a fucking failure, Em. The best way to protect you right now is to be apart from you.'

'That's not true,' she argues with a frown. 'Either we're a team, or we're nothing. I get that your heart was in the right place, Jase – but your head wasn't. Because if I'd walked away from here today, I don't care what you might've said to me when you finally came back to San Diego. I wouldn't have listened, because I'd have known that you didn't trust me with the truth. That you didn't treat me like an adult and give me the choice to decide what my future would be.' She turns on to her side to face me, and her voice is firm with conviction as she says, 'We're either equals in this relationship, or there isn't one.'

A scowl tightens its way between my brows. 'It has nothing to do with not trusting you or respecting you. Christ, Em, I'm just trying to protect you. Because it'll kill me if anything happens to you. I nearly lost my damn mind the night of the accident.'

She gives me a knowing, womanly smile. 'And I'm afraid that's just one of those pesky little side effects of being in love.

The worries and the fears. But life is full of good times and shit times, and how we face them is what will make us strong. I don't need you to stand in front of me; I just need to have you beside me.'

'Jesus,' I say with a heavy sigh, 'I hear you. I do.'

'But?'

I shake my head as I snort. 'Don't shove me again, okay? It's just that things would be a hell of a lot simpler if I hadn't fallen for such a smart, independent, courageous little American.'

'They wouldn't be simpler,' she says in a wry drawl, 'because they'd never *be* in the first place. No way would you fall in love with someone who let you walk all over them. You'd be bored out of your mind within five minutes.'

My chest shakes with a husky laugh. 'Then I guess it's a good thing the only woman I'm ever going to love is *you*.'

'Damn straight,' she mutters, leaning over and pressing those soft lips to mine. I try to slip my tongue in, needing the taste of her, but she's already pulling back, and I can tell by the look on her beautiful face that shit's about to get serious. 'Now, tell me what you've found out. Do you have any idea who's behind the accident?'

I shake my head again as I blow out a frustrated breath. 'I'm sure you already know that the police in San Diego weren't able to track down anything about the men in the truck. It'd been stolen that night, and they didn't leave any DNA in it. But I've been in contact with a friend from school who works at Scotland Yard, and he's looking into both Cameron and Caroline for me, as well as a few CEOs whose businesses aren't doing as well as mine and might be holding a grudge.'

Her golden brows lift with surprise. 'I know you said Cameron was causing trouble for you with your build that's taking place in Thailand next year, and Caroline's . . . Well, she's a raging bitch. But what would they have to gain from having you killed?'

'That's what I can't figure out. I mean, it's a hell of a risk to take just because neither of them likes me. Still, I passed their names on to Danny because they're the two people in this world who cause me the most grief. But so far the only thing he's been able to uncover is some weird shit about Caroline's background.'

'Weird how?'

'There's not a lot to go on yet, but it looks like she might have been living under a fake identity since her teens.'

Emmy's eyes go wide. 'Are you serious?'

'Yep. But that still doesn't give her motive to have me killed.'

'Hmm. So then what about any jealous exes? Any bunny boilers in your choirboy past?' she asks with a smirk, knowing damn well that I had a bit of a reputation as a ladies' man before falling head-over-heels for her.

'No bunny boilers,' I murmur, thinking this is one of the *last* things I want to be talking to her about.

'What about jealous boyfriends or husbands?' she asks, tapping her finger against her lips. 'Someone who took exception to you turning their woman's head?'

'Come on, Em,' I say with a scowl, hoping that's not how she really sees me. 'You know me better than that. I might not have been a saint, but I've never screwed around with a woman who was in a relationship. I wasn't *that* much of a dickhead.'

'Well, maybe one of your women didn't tell you the truth about her single status.'

'I didn't have "women",' I growl, getting exasperated. 'It's not like there was a bloody harem following me around. And I was never big on one-night-stands, so it's not like my hook-ups were with strangers. So no, it's not going to be some jealous boyfriend or husband who's got it in for me.'

'Yeah, I guess that really wouldn't make sense anyway,' she says, sitting up and wrapping her arms around her knees as she stares out the window, still working it all through her head. 'I mean, why not just try to have you killed here? Why wait until you were traveling? Unless they just liked the idea of it happening so far away to lessen suspicions.'

'All I know is that none of it makes any fucking sense,' I mutter, sitting up beside her and shoving my hands back through my hair.

Her own golden curls slide over her shoulder as she turns her head toward me. 'Maybe the assholes who wrecked us thought we were someone else. Maybe they didn't mean to come after you at all.'

'But the part about "the Brit" hiring them?' I say, rubbing my palm over my tense jaw. 'That's too much of a coincidence.'

Concern darkens her gaze. 'Then whoever wants to hurt you, they want it bad. Badly enough to try and set it up in another country, which had to have been a hassle. Not that *all* murder-for-hire isn't without its problems, I'm sure.'

'I know,' I sigh, resting my arms over my bent, spread knees. 'Shit, I know.'

'So what's happened since you came back?' she asks.

'Nothing.'

'Seriously?'

'Not a damn thing,' I mutter with a fresh wave of frustration as I curl my hands into fists. 'Even the crazy Becketts are behaving themselves.'

'Huh.'

'I know,' I say again, this time with a growl, my temper getting the better of me. 'I just want this prick to come out of the shadows and fucking face me head-on.'

'Speaking of facing things head-on, have you thought any more about Douglas Hart?'

'Damn, babe,' I rumble with another gritty laugh. 'You're not pulling any punches today, are you?'

'Just answer the question,' she says with a small smile, 'and stop stalling.'

'Yeah, I've thought about him,' I tell her, forcing my hands to relax as I pull in a deep breath, then slowly let it out. 'I've also had one of my IT guys look into the historical building records to verify his story, and we know that he was there, in Kent, during the time that he claims, working on the Grafton family's estate.'

'What about asking Harrison about him? Just because you don't ever remember meeting Hart doesn't mean that your grandfather didn't. They might have even known each other.'

'I know, and you're right. I should talk to him about it. I just . . .'

'You've had a lot on your plate,' she says with a soft smile that tells me she understands. 'But this is important, Jase.'

My chest lifts with another heavy sigh. 'I know.'

She's quiet for a moment, lost in her thoughts as she reaches over and takes hold of the hand that's closest to her, then tugs it down between us, so that our joined hands are resting on the bed. Then she looks at me again and asks, 'When Harrison came to talk to you at Beckett House the night I left, did he say anything about your mom?'

'No. Why?'

'I just keep wondering why, if she was so unhappy, she chose to stay with Alistair. It doesn't make any sense. I mean, I know I didn't know her, but I'm just not buying into Hart's belief that she stayed because of the money.'

'Yeah, I've already asked myself that question about a thousand times.'

'You know, when I was researching Harrison for the *Luxe* article, all the references I ever found about his wife's and daughter's deaths said that they were both killed in tragic accidents. I never saw any mention of suicide.'

'Accidents,' I mutter, thinking it's amazing what money can buy, if you're determined to hide the truth. 'That's one way of putting it, I suppose.' I take another deep breath, and exhale in an audible rush, my throat burning as I say, 'I'm sure Alistair's money had a lot to do with it. He wouldn't have wanted the Beckett name sullied by something he found so embarrassing.'

'He found your mom's death embarrassing?' she asks, sounding horrified. I give a tight nod, and she whispers, 'Jase, that's . . . God, I don't even have words for what that is. I'm so sorry.'

'Me, too, baby.' I let go of her hand to wrap my arm around her shoulders and tug her close, pressing a kiss to the top of her golden head, my heart pounding so hard it hurts. Then I gently grip her hair and tug her head back until she's looking up at me, and brush a soft kiss across her lips as I ask, 'So am I forgiven?'

She closes her eyes for a moment, then blinks them open and locks her steady gaze with mine. 'Did you kiss them?'

I know she's talking about the three women I was photographed with while she was still in San Diego, and I can't help but laugh, then hurry to explain when she stiffens against me. 'No, sweetheart. I didn't kiss them. And I'm not laughing at you, I swear. It's just that, if you'd been there like I was, Em, you'd *know* how awful those three evenings were.'

'Aw, your dates were shit?' she drawls drily, before rolling her eyes at me. 'What the hell, Jase? Do you really think that's going to make me feel bad for you?'

'No, fuck,' I curse, knowing I'm mucking this up. 'It's just that, if you'd been there, then you'd have never even had to ask me that question. Because you'd know there's no way in hell I was letting my mouth get anywhere close to those women. They were three of the absolute worst nights of my life.'

She bites her lip as she laughs, thinking it's funny, which I guess I deserve. Hell, I *know* I deserve it. I start kissing her smiling lips as I fall back against the bed, pulling her down with me so that she's on top, and it only takes me a second to get the heavy head of my cock lodged back inside her. She gasps as I grip her hips and pull her down over my rigid shaft like a tight, wet glove, her hands braced against my chest as she blinks down at me. I plant my feet against the bed and push up, until I'm buried to the root and her warm, slick cunt is hugging every inch of me – then wrap my arms around her and roll us to our sides. 'Now rest,' I say with a soft growl, pressing another kiss to the top of her head as I pull her leg up over my hip.

'What? I can't rest like this,' she laughs against my chest, shaking in my arms, and even that small movement sets off a chain reaction in my dick, the damn thing getting even bigger inside her. She gasps again, wriggling to try to get comfortable, and groans, 'God, Jase. I swear you're not human.'

I smile as I grip her hair and tug her head back again, so that I can see her flushed, beautiful face, feeling so satisfied and hungry that I don't even know how to explain it. 'You need to get used to it, because I can't not be in you, Em. I've been so bloody scared that once I sorted this nightmare out, that no matter how hard I begged, you might never take me back. And now you're here, and you love me, and I *have* to be inside you. I can't not be fucking you, baby.'

She moans my name, and just as I start to take her plump, sweet mouth again, my phone rings. I want to ignore it, given that my girl is finally back in my arms, where she belongs, and my dick's inside *her*, where *it* belongs – but with everything that's happening in my life right now, I can't risk missing something critical. Not when her safety is on the line now as well. And sure enough, when I pull out of her lush clasp and roll over to look at the screen, I see that it's the security company's number shining back at me.

'Shit,' I grumble under my breath, reaching for the phone. 'This is Beckett. What's happened?'

'Sir, we have a Mr Harrison here. He says he's your grandfather, and his identification verifies his name.'

'Uh, yeah, okay,' I mutter, wondering what the hell is going on as I throw my legs over the side of the bed and move to my feet. 'Send him up.'

'Who's here?' Emmy asks, clutching the sheet to her chest as she sits up in the bed.

I grab my jeans and start pulling them on. 'J.J., if you can believe it.'

'You're kidding,' she splutters, quickly climbing out of the bed and running into the sitting room, where her clothes are strewn all over the floor.

'Nope,' I drawl, following after her as I pull on my T-shirt. 'It's like you conjured Beelzebub himself just by mentioning his name earlier.'

She slides me a laughing look. 'Let's see what he wants before you call him that to his face, yeah?'

A few minutes later, we're looking as presentable as two people who have been fucking all day possibly can, and Emmy's shoved the note and photograph she was holding in her hands when she got here back in her bag. When there's a knock on the door, I open it, and my grandfather doesn't even bother with a greeting as he prowls inside with a long, frustrated stride. He's dressed in his usual jeans and T-shirt, but with a dark leather jacket thrown over the top, given that it's a bit chilly here in Edinburgh. Before I can ask him what he's doing here, or how he even knew where to find me, he slides a brief glance over at Emmy, and then the room, taking in its pale cream walls, dark wood floor and overstuffed cream sofas, before quickly looking back at me and lifting a folded newspaper in front of him. With a shake of his hand, he asks, 'Have you seen the paper today?'

'No,' I say, getting a bad feeling in my gut. 'Why?'

'Do yourself a favor and don't look,' he growls, jerking his chin at Emmy. 'It's not something you want your girl having to see.'

'Jesus,' I snap. 'Just spit it out!'

He crosses his arms over his chest, still clutching the newspaper. 'One of the gossip rags in London is running a story on you today, complete with photos of you and Chloe Ellis. Claims you're planning a secret wedding for the two of you.'

A sharp laugh bursts past my lips as I shake my head. 'Why the fuck would I do that?'

With a scowl knitting between his bushy brows, my grandfather mutters seven words that make me see blood-red. 'Because they're saying you've knocked her up.'

Chapter Four

JASE

Emmy makes a strangled noise at my side, and a vein starts to pop in my temple, my fury so raw I can feel it scraping against my skin. 'It's a fucking lie,' I snarl, snatching the paper away from J.J. as he mutters, 'Page four.'

I find the article and am breathing hard by the time I've finished scanning it. Christ, there are even photos of me and Chloe from when we briefly dated, the two of us kissing on a beach and at a picnic, along with the one from earlier in the week, when we were at the rugby match. Though my lips are nowhere near her in that last one.

My pulse is roaring in my ears, but I can still hear J.J.'s raspy voice as he says, 'I might live like a recluse, but I still know important people in London. The kind of important people who can get information.'

I cut him a narrow look from under my brows. 'If you've got something else to say, then say it.'

'According to my source, Caroline's behind the story. She paid the bloody newspaper to print it. Gave them the photos of you and this Chloe girl late last night, and they did a last-minute rush to get it in.'

'Bitch!' Emmy and I both say at the same time, and I crush the paper in my hands, wishing there were a fire I could burn it in.

Rubbing his scruffy jaw, my grandfather pins me with a piercing look that's as curious as it is belligerent. 'Anna's been keeping me apprised of what the gossips are saying, and if half of it is true, I'm going to hazard a guess and say that you have reason to believe that car crash you and Emmy had in San Diego wasn't an accident. That there was a nefarious purpose behind it, so you broke the girl's heart and hightailed it home, where you staged those embarrassing look-at-the-rich-playboy-playing-the-field photo ops, trying to convince the world that you no longer give a damn about her.'

'Wow,' Emmy murmurs with a soft note of awe. 'He's smarter than I am, that's for sure.'

'I'm starting to think he might be a fucking genius,' I murmur back. Then I look at my grandfather, and tell him what I heard the night of the crash.

'So you know what this means, right?' he demands. 'Nothing happens from the time you fly home, and then Emmy shows up yesterday, visiting your office in London, and suddenly Caroline is on the attack again and we're dealing with *that* shit,' he growls, jabbing a finger at the crumpled paper I'm clutching in my fist.

'I get it,' I mutter, wondering when *he* decided to become a part of this.

'Get what?' Emmy asks, her brow furrowed as she looks up at me.

'It's not anyone that I pissed off in the business world or has anything to do with someone I dated,' I growl. 'Cam backed off once I came back. And Caro backed off with the councilors.'

'What councilors?' she asks with confusion.

'Shit. I didn't tell you about that.'

She reaches over and grabs my free hand, giving it a comforting squeeze, her unconditional support meaning the world to me. 'Tell me now,' she says.

'When I flew to San Diego to be with you, Caroline called the county councilors in London who are involved in my plans to build those homeless shelters for teens that we talked about that first weekend we met. She told them that I'd left the country for reasons that "gave my family concern", basically making me sound like I'd gone off the deep end.'

'So that definitely makes her a bitch, which we already knew,' Emmy says, looking like she'd enjoy nothing more than kicking Caroline's bony arse. 'But what does this have to do with whoever's trying to kill you? What am I missing?'

'It's fucking Caroline! Or maybe her and Cam working together, though I'd bet money that Caro is the driving force. For whatever reason, she clearly has an issue with you and me being together.'

'Why would she want to kill you for dating *me*? It doesn't make any sense.'

'Who the hell knows, Em? Maybe she's just bat-shit crazy, and there isn't a rational reason. Maybe she's just a fucking mental bitch.' Sliding my gaze back over to J.J., I ask, 'How did you find me here, anyway?'

'I visited Martin this morning, the same as Emmy did yesterday. When I told him why I needed to find you, and that I meant to help, he gave me this address.'

I have to laugh as I shake my head, thinking it'll be a bloody miracle if Martin's got any work done recently, what with everyone traipsing in and out of his office, looking for me. And when I'm back in London, he and I are going to have a long talk about how he failed to give me a heads-up that Emmy and Harrison were coming here to see me. Though I know damn well he didn't say anything because he knew I might bail, and the guy has been gunning for me to reconcile with Emmy ever since I returned from San Diego in a foul fucking mood. Because while he might be a trusted employee, Martin has first and foremost always been a friend.

Huh. Maybe Emmy's right and he really is like an Alfred. And, damn it, if he's Alfred, then I want to be Batman.

'What are you thinking about now?' she whispers, giving me a funny look. But instead of answering, I just laugh and shake my head again, since it'll be a cold day in hell before I admit to *that* embarrassing thought. God, she'd never let me live it down.

'So, do you have a spare bedroom for me to stay in?' Harrison asks, drawing my attention back to him, and I realize for the first time that he'd set a suitcase down by the door when he'd first stormed in.

I feel my brows arch with surprise. 'You're staying?'

He shoots me a cocky smirk that I swear I must have inherited from him. 'I've been wanting to see that uppity bitch get what she deserves for years. You think I'm just going to scurry back home now and let you have all the fun?'

'Emmy almost fucking *died* in San Diego,' I snap. 'Nothing about this is *fun*.'

'Shit,' he mutters, sliding her an apologetic look. 'I'm sorry, honey. I didn't mean it like that.'

I want to tell him to go to hell, but Emmy gives my hand another squeeze, and so I bite my tongue instead, while she murmurs, 'It's all right, Harrison. I understand what you're saying.'

He gives her a grateful nod, then brings his dark gaze back

to me, and there's a deeper note of emotion in his rough voice as he says, 'I want to help. God knows I've never been there for you before, Jase, but please. Let me be here now.'

Another squeeze from Emmy's hand, and I know there's no sense in fighting it. 'Come on,' I murmur, pulling her with me as I head for the hallway. 'I'll show you to your room.'

* * *

After J.J. gets settled in the spare bedroom, and Emmy grabs a shower, we order in a late lunch/early dinner from one of the local restaurants. And though the food is delicious, none of us seems to have much of an appetite. We're too focused on trying to figure out what our next move should be, and whom we can trust to help us.

Us. Jesus, I've gone from being on my own, to having the love of the most incredible woman I've ever known and the chance of building a solid relationship with my grandfather, and I have no idea how it happened.

No. As I look over at Emmy, watching the gorgeous smile that curves her lips as J.J. makes another one of his bawdy observations on the world, I know *exactly* how it's happened. It's her. My beautiful life-changer.

I've already called the security firm and told them I want a few extra guards on the building. With Emmy here, I'm not willing to take any chances. After Caroline's play with the Chloe article, there's no telling what *her* next move will be, or who she'll get to try to carry it out.

But right now, there's another question that's burning on my tongue, and so I look at my grandfather and finally force it out. 'So, uh, Emmy and I had a visitor when I was in San Diego. An American man named Douglas Hart. Do you know him?'

'No. Should I?'

'He worked on the Grafton estate the year before I was born as part of a special renovation team that was restoring the manor house. When he saw a photo of me and Emmy in the paper last month, he managed to track us down at her apartment, because he wanted to tell me that he knew my mother.'

J.J. sets his fork down, wipes his mouth with his napkin, and then leans back in his chair, giving me a look that says I have his complete attention.

I give a little cough to clear my throat, and then just put it out there. 'He claims they were lovers, and that they were crazy about each other. According to Hart, *he's* my father.'

J.J.'s eyes close for a moment, and then he exhales with a heavy sigh as he opens them and reaches for his glass of wine. 'Is there more?' he rasps.

I fill him in on the rest of Hart's story, and then push my plate aside, resting my crossed arms on the table as I hold my grandfather's dark gaze and say, 'We've never talked about it, but I need to ask you now. Why do you think Sarah killed herself?'

He winces, as if just hearing the words causes him physical pain. 'Christ, Jase. I wish I knew.'

'The . . . The way that she did it,' I scrape out, feeling a cold sweat break out over my brow, just before Emmy reaches over and places her feminine hand against my back, the instant comfort her touch gives me making it possible to go on. 'I just don't understand why she would have wanted me to find her like that. I mean, how could a mother do that to her child?'

'I don't know,' he says, sounding shattered. 'But she loved you more than anything, Jase. She just must not have been herself at the end.'

'Did you ever suspect that Alistair wasn't my father?'

He starts to look away, but I pin him with my stare, silently demanding an answer.

His shoulders drop with a look of defeat, and he slowly shakes his head. 'I'm ashamed to say that I didn't. I feel . . . I feel like I *should have* seen it, but we all know what a blind, stubborn fool I've been. I think I see everything, when like your girl there already told me, I see it only through my own lens of pain. I was blind to Sarah's, because it wasn't mine. But I can tell you that she never loved Alistair.'

'If she didn't love him, then why marry him?'

'Because I failed her,' he mutters, before taking another heavy swallow of his wine. 'Janine wanted the marriage, and it hurts to admit it, but I didn't care enough to cross her on it. Sarah was Janine's world, and she wanted to keep her close. Thought we would be able to ensure that Alistair treated her right.' A scowl curls his upper lip as he says, 'But that pathetic lush was a nightmare from the beginning.'

'Hart's never believed it was a suicide,' I tell him, watching the surprise flicker through his eyes. 'What about you?'

'I'd give anything for that to be true,' he murmurs, 'but Sarah was never the same after Janine killed herself.'

'Still, I think Hart probably knew her better than anyone, so it's worth considering. He tried to get the local police to listen to him, but they wouldn't. I suspect because they're all in Alistair's pocket. But I have a friend who's a detective at Scotland Yard, and once he's finished helping me look into Caroline and Cameron, I plan to ask him to pull Sarah's records from the coroner's office and review them for any signs of tampering or falsification.'

'Jesus,' Harrison sighs, looking like he's just aged ten years.

Emmy strokes her hand up my back, rubbing at the tense muscles across my shoulders, and I slide her a grateful smile. Whatever we find, I know she's going to be the rock that gets me through and keeps me sane.

Across the table, Harrison takes another heavy sip of his wine, then sets the glass down, his attention focused on the way he's twirling the stem with his fingers. 'It might not be what you want to hear, Jase, but I'm happy that bastard isn't your father.'

'Yeah, me too. I just wish I knew the real story.'

He lifts his bleak gaze to mine, and quietly says, 'So do I.'

He moves to his feet then, going out on the balcony to smoke his beloved cigarettes, and I help Emmy clear the table, then put on a pot of decaf. When J.J. comes back inside, we gather on the sofas in the sitting room with our steaming mugs of coffee, and settle into some easier conversation.

As Harrison listens with genuine interest to Emmy telling him her ideas for possible articles she can write for *Luxe*, the premier art magazine that is publishing her first piece – one on Harrison himself – I can't help thinking about the fact that the only reason he's even here is because of *her*. Because she had the strength and determination to stand up to him and tell him he was wrong about me. No one, in my entire life, has ever championed me the way that Emmy does, or been so completely on my side, and I fucking love that about her. But the truth is that I worship every single part of her. Her courage and her kindness. Her clever mind and her laugh and her smile. Hell, I even love the way she calls me on my shit and is never afraid to stand up to me. I'm fucking *gone* for her. Forever. And if I can manage to get my ring on her finger one day, it'll be the most important, significant accomplishment of my entire life.

I know she's still upset about the Chloe article. With Harrison here, we haven't had a chance to discuss it, and I'm not looking forward to the conversation. But I'll tell her whatever she wants to know, because I've learned my lesson.

I just wish my mother and Hart had been able to reach

a point where they were honest with one another as well, because there's something about their history that doesn't sit right with me.

And I hate that I might never know what it is.

EMMY

I'm lying in bed with my back to him, the room still lit with a soft, golden glow from the lamp on his bedside table, when Jase's deep voice reaches out to me, making me shiver with awareness at the same time I'm tensing with dread. 'Are we going to talk about it?'

A brittle laugh falls from my lips before I can choke it back. 'Sure. What do you want to confess?'

'Honestly, Em, there's nothing *to* confess. I've always been careful, and I have *never* been with anyone without using latex. Ever, except for you. And things ended between Chloe and me last October. If she is pregnant, there's no way in hell that it's mine.'

'Okay.'

'Okay?' he repeats, as if he can't believe what he's heard.

'Yeah, okay,' I tell him, rolling over to face him. To stare into his dark, beautiful eyes, his masculine scent filling my head as I pull in a deep breath.

For the past three weeks, I've missed Jase Beckett to the point it'd been a physical pain. A hollow, churning ache that I carried with me every second of the day, not even my dreams giving me a moment's peace. No, that's when I would relive every breathtaking moment that I'd spent in his arms. Every exquisite touch and taste. Every husky, provocative word that fell roughly from his lips.

And now I'm here, lying beside him, and I'm not going to waste this precious gift on Caroline's bizarre hatred. The more

I think about it, the more I think maybe she *is* having some kind of mental breakdown. But sane or not, I'm not letting the bitch get between me and the man I love.

Pressing my hand against the center of Jase's chest, right over the heavy pounding of his heart, I give him a little smile as I say, 'Caroline only has the power we give her, Jase. And I'm not going to let her lies pick and nip at us, until we bicker more than we laugh and make love. You can't change your past any more than I can change mine, and we shouldn't have to. The only thing that matters is where we go from here.'

Those brilliant blue eyes of his start to gleam, the sin-drenched smile on his lips so freaking sexy it makes me melt for him. 'Damn, Emmy. Have I ever mentioned how fucking awesome you are?'

With a playful smirk, I say, 'It might have come up earlier today.'

He slips his warm hand up under the hem of my tank top, stroking my skin with the callused pad of his thumb. 'Well, I'm gonna say it again. Or I could use Tyler's colorful vernacular and tell you that you're the fucking bomb.'

'Wow, look at the Brit boy trying out surfer speak,' I laugh. 'Ty's gonna love it when you do that in front of him.'

Jase's grin slides into a pained grimace. 'Speaking of Tyler, exactly how much does the guy hate me now?'

I don't quite manage to stifle my wince, given how concerned Tyler had sounded when I spoke to him on the phone earlier. 'Well, if we're talking about a scale that goes from one to ten, then you're probably still at about a twenty-five.'

'Yay me,' he says drily, and despite how he's trying to make light of it, I can tell that he's bummed. He and Tyler had finally started to connect the night of the accident, only to have it all go to shit.

'He's wary,' I say, stroking my fingertips over his rugged jaw, 'but only because he loves me and doesn't want to see me get hurt again.'

'You mean for a third time,' he mutters with another frown. 'Fuck, I'm surprised he didn't come with you so he could kick my arse.'

'Oh, he wanted to,' I admit with a wry smile. 'But I told him this was something I had to do on my own. And he'll come around. I have no doubt that the two of you will be best buds one day.'

And it's true. I just don't know if that will be because we're living there, or if it will happen when Tyler's visiting with us in London. Jase and I never did get around to the big 'where are we going to live' discussion. And while I know what my heart is telling me is the right choice at this point in our lives, I'm too worn out to hash it out with him tonight.

'By the way,' he murmurs, stroking his hand lower, over the curve of my hip, 'in the spirit of full disclosure, there's something else you should know.'

'Oh, God. What?' I gasp, deciding to tease him, even though I'm a bit nervous about what he's going to tell me. 'Do you have a secret love child with Madonna? One of the royals? Or is it Angelina?'

He snorts under his breath. 'Funny, but no. There are absolutely no little Jase Becketts, or whatever the hell my last name should be, running around in the world.'

I wince a bit for him when he says the part about his name, and ask, 'Then what did you want to tell me?'

'When you went to call Tyler before the food got here, I told Harrison that *Luxe* loved your article and he asked to read it. So I pulled it up on my phone for him, since I still have the file that you emailed me.'

'You didn't!'

He gives me a smug smile. 'Oh, but I did.'

'Ohmygod,' I groan, covering my eyes with my hand, as if that'll help me deal. 'What did he say? I can't believe he didn't tell me when I was gabbing on about my ideas for my next article.'

'What do you think he said?' he asks, pulling my hand away from my face and pressing a smiling kiss to my palm.

'Um, probably something about me being a nosy American who should mind her own damn business.'

His chest shakes with one of his deep, deliciously sexy laughs. 'That would've been pretty funny,' he drawls, earning him a smack on the shoulder from my palm, 'but no, baby. He thought it was brilliant.'

I blink at him, certain I must have heard him wrong. 'Seriously?'

His dark eyes gleam with pride, and I feel my chest go warm with emotion as he tells me, 'Of course he did. And I've already told you the same thing. You think I was just buttering you up with compliments so you'd let me in your pants?'

'Well,' I laugh, all breathless with excitement, 'my pants *are* a pretty awesome place to be.'

'You don't have to tell me that,' he says with a playful growl. 'Though I prefer you in no pants at all.'

He strips my jammies off, deliberately tickling me in the process, and I'm still laughing when he knees my legs apart and starts to push inside me. But then the size and the heat of his beautiful cock make my breath catch, and I have to bite my lower lip to keep from crying out – before I look up into his smoldering eyes, and say, 'I had no idea, when I first met you, that you would be so perfect for me, Mr Beckett.'

'Miss Reed,' he murmurs, forcing that last hard, thick inch into me, 'I didn't even know what perfect was until I met you.'

The exchange makes me smile, because it's so similar to ones we've had in the past. But then my smile is stolen by a low moan as Jase reaches down and hooks his hand behind my knee, lifting my leg higher, and his next thrust takes him so deep that I have to bite my freaking lip again.

'You okay?' he asks, watching me as he carefully pulls back, searching my face for any signs that the wound in my side is causing me pain.

'You ask me that again,' I warn, stroking my hands down the powerful muscles in his sleek back, 'and I'm going to bite you. Hard.'

He laughs as he leans down and rubs his nose against mine. 'Promises, promises, baby.'

I pinch his bottom, making him jerk inside me. 'Less talking, Mr Beckett. More fucking.'

'Whatever my woman wants,' he growls, nipping my bottom lip, 'she gets.'

And then he gives it to me. God, does he ever.

I'm so freaking happy to have this time with him, to have *him* again – when God only knows what tomorrow's going to bring – that tears blur my vision. But I quickly blink them away, needing his handsome face in sharp focus as he takes me closer and closer to the edge. He braces himself over me, using his muscular thighs and sculpted abs to drive himself into me with deep, hammering thrusts, like he's trying to forge a connection that will last even after he's filled me up, and when I start to come for him the pleasure's so intense it feels like I'm shattering into a million different pieces, everything dark and raw and blissful as I get carried away under the thrashing waves. But he comes down over me, his strong arms holding me together, and I love how every muscle in his magnificent body tenses as he finds his own release. Love how the guttural sound that he breathes into my ear, as he pumps into me, makes the pulses in my body go on and on and on.

When our hearts have slowed and we're finally able to catch our breath, he pulls out as carefully as he always does, then kneels there between my thighs, pushing them a bit wider as he stares down at my still softly pulsing pussy.

'I think you're gorgeous, sweetheart, no matter what you're dressed in, or how you've done your hair, or whether you're wearing make-up or no make-up. But this is my all-time favorite right here,' he says in a low voice, trailing the blunt tip of his index finger over my pink, drenched vulva as his heavy-lidded gaze slides over me. 'When you're soft and relaxed, legs open and nipples tight, lips puffy from how hard and deep I've kissed you, and this pink little part of you is so swollen and drenched with my cum. When you're so full of me that it's spilling out of you. God, I fucking love that.'

'I love it too,' I breathe. 'It makes me feel close to you.'

'Speaking of being close,' he murmurs, setting one of his big hands on my belly and giving it a gentle squeeze, 'I can't wait to put a kid in here.'

I blink up at him, thinking I must have heard him wrong. 'What?'

'Don't you want children?' he asks, staring down at me with a sexy, devastating smile, as if he knows damn well just how far he's thrown me.

'Um, sure. I mean, I've never really thought about it.' Because I never thought I'd find someone who I wanted to share my life with.

'Well, think about it now,' he says in a husky rumble, coming back down over me and rubbing his thumb over my bottom lip, his dark eyes molten and serious. 'Because I want to build a family with you, Em. I'm not talking right away, since I want us to have time where it's just the two of us. But I'm making plans in my head.'

'Baby plans?' I ask, arching one of my eyebrows at him.

'Marriage plans. Baby plans. I want it *all* with you, Emmy.'

My heart is beating so hard and fast that I feel like it might burst, and I have to swallow twice before I manage to say, 'It seems to me that there are some, um, crucial questions that need to be asked before you start running away with things, Mr Beckett.'

He smirks like the cocky beast that he is, already knowing what my answer will be when he eventually asks *that* question. The one that will lead to us becoming man and wife.

'Don't worry about my planning skills, Miss Reed. I promise I've got it covered.'

I smile as I curl my hand around the back of his neck, pulling him down for another blistering kiss, since I've got plans of my own for us.

And they're some of the best I've ever had.

Chapter Five

JASE

When I first open my eyes, I have no idea what's woken me up. Rolling over, I look at the illuminated clock on the bedside table and see that it reads two-thirty a.m. I start to roll back towards Emmy, thinking we can take advantage of the moment with some middle of the night fucking – since we still have three weeks of lost time together to make up for – when I hear it again. Another faint creak of sound, like someone carefully stepping on a floorboard, and I swear it came from the sitting room.

Shit! There's always a chance that it's J.J. and he's stumbling around in the dark for a middle of the night snack, but the tension in my gut tells me this is different, and that someone has broken into the flat. I reach over to gently wake Emmy, putting my fingers to her lips to quiet her when she starts to ask what's wrong. There's just enough moonlight coming in through the window for her to see me shake my head, and her eyes go wide with fear when she takes in the expression on my face. I point at the bed, silently telling her to stay right here, then sound-lessly slide back the duvet and move to my feet. I snag the jeans

I'd taken off earlier, sliding them on, and then grab one of the thick metal candlesticks that sit on either end of the chest. It's not much of a weapon if I end up facing down a loaded gun, but it's all that's available, and I feel like a tool for not thinking to at least keep a knife or a bat with me.

As I creep into the hallway, my heart is pounding like a bloody drum, but it's not from fear. No, I'm too damn furious to be worried about what I'm about to face.

And I'm calling myself every name in the book for not packing Emmy's beautiful little arse up and sending her back to San Diego until this shit is over. I caved because I'd missed her, and I needed her, but if anything happens to her because of me I'll never survive it. It'll fucking destroy me.

When I reach the end of the hallway, I peek around the wall of the sitting room and spot a tall, well-built guy dressed all in black moving around the edge of the room, and he's gripping a long, serrated knife in his right hand. He's shaking with nerves, which means it's unlikely that he's a professional killer. No, this is someone giving it a shot for the first time, and I try to place him, thinking there's something about him that seems familiar. And then he walks past the window, the moonlight washing across his face, and I know why that is.

He's my fucking cousin!

Cameron Beckett has somehow broken into the flat in the middle of the night, armed with a deadly weapon, and I have a strong feeling he's not here for a friendly family discussion.

How the hell did the bastard get past security? They're meant to be watching all entrances to the building, as well as monitoring any suspicious behavior, and I'm paying them a bloody fortune for it. But something has seriously gone wrong with their system, and I tighten my grip on the candlestick, trying to decide when and how I should strike.

He comes around the back of the nearest sofa, where Emmy's jacket is lying over the cushions, and I grit my teeth as he runs the back of his knuckles over the denim like he's stroking her skin. It makes my blood go cold, and I must not choke back my growl as well as I'd thought because he suddenly gives a low laugh and says, 'I know you're there, Jase.'

Since my cover is blown, I step further into the room, wanting to give myself some space to move around in case he comes at me. He counters my move, until he's standing with his back to the hallway, and it takes every ounce of self-control I possess not to flinch when I spot Emmy peeking around the edge of the hallway wall, Harrison's worried face just above hers. *Christ!* They're like something out of some madcap comedy, both sharp eyed and plotting a way to attack, and while I feel the need to keep an eye on them, because God only knows what they're about to do, I'm facing down a prick with a knife, so I can't. Plus, I don't want to clue Cameron into the fact that they're lurking in the hallway. If he's been watching the building, then he knows they're in the flat with me. But I'd rather him think they're hiding in the bedrooms, than about to sneak up behind him.

And then, as if she's just heard the words in my head, Emmy starts tiptoeing into the room, wearing nothing but the tiny set of pajama shorts and top that I'd stripped off her earlier, her golden hair all curly and wild, Harrison just behind her with the other candlestick in his hand, wearing plaid pajamas, ready to offer his assistance. She's so impossibly gorgeous, but clearly stark barking mad, because she's got the wrought-iron lamp from my bedside table clutched in her hands.

Jesus, the three of us are like the bloody fucking light brigade, all armed with lamps and candlesticks, and my girl is fearless as she comes right up behind Cameron.

'I'm almost sorry it's had to come to this, because I'll miss finding ways to screw with your life,' he growls, taking a step towards me, and Emmy lifts the lamp up high, then knocks him over the head with it. The thing is too heavy for her to put much power behind the blow, but she manages to daze him enough that he staggers to his right, giving me the opportunity to move in and grip the wrist of Cameron's knife-holding arm with one hand, while I drop the candlestick and curl my other hand into a hard fist, smashing it across his face. Blood spurts from his nose and his grip on the knife loosens, the long blade falling to the floor as I hit him again, and then a third time. After that, I let go of his wrist, and he slumps to the floor in an unconscious heap.

Looking at my grandfather, I say, 'I think I saw some twine in one of the drawers in the kitchen. Bring it in here and help me tie him up.' As I reach down to get the knife, I ask Emmy to bring in one of the chairs from the dining room, and have to lock my jaw to keep from shouting at her for taking such a foolish chance with her safety. I know she'll just shout back that we're a team, so she wasn't going to let me face the danger on my own, and right now it's an argument that we don't have time for.

Less than a minute later, Harrison and I have Cameron sitting in the chair in the middle of the living room with his hands secured behind his back, as well as attached to the chair. We also attach each ankle to a chair leg, making it impossible for him to stand. Emmy comes in with my phone, as well as the tube of Deep Heat from the medicine cabinet that I'd asked her for, and as I take the cap off and wave the tube under Cameron's nose, the strong-smelling ointment brings him to with a gasp.

He instantly struggles against his restraints, straining and knifing against them, then turns a seething glare up at me as I stand in front of him, Harrison to my right and Emmy to my left. 'What the fuck?' he roars, so enraged that spittle sprays from his lips, the blood from his nose running all the way down to his chin.

'So you're the one,' I mutter, my hands flexing as I fight the urge to start pounding him in the face again.

'The one what?' he snarls.

I cross my arms over my chest, surprised by how calm I sound as I say, 'The one who's been trying to kill me.'

'Fuck you, Jase.' He turns his head, trying to wipe his nose with his shoulder, and gives a quiet laugh. 'Shit, I'm sure there are *lots* of people in this world who would like to see you dead.'

'Maybe so, Cam. Maybe so. But they didn't just get caught breaking into the flat I'm staying in with a fucking knife. Did they?'

'This was just a prank,' he sneers, glaring up at me again. 'No one will believe you.'

'Aw, Cam,' I say with a sad sigh, shaking my head at him. 'You're not thinking too clearly right now, are you, buddy? Because J.J. and Emmy here are both credible witnesses. And I've hidden cameras all over this room that the security team doesn't even know about.'

He pales at the lie about the cameras, and I decide to let him stew on that for a moment while I try the security team on my phone, but there's no answer. And when I call down to the front desk, and the night doorman explains that the four guards told him they were no longer needed just before midnight, I don't even have to ask my cousin how he got past them.

'So you paid the guards off,' I murmur, giving Emmy a pointed look as I hand her the phone, then slide my gaze back over to Cam. 'Clever. Did you also bribe the management for a key?'

'*I* didn't pay anyone,' he snarls, getting a weird look in his brown eyes. 'And you're so fucking stupid. I mean, Jesus, did it never occur to you that you're staying in the same exact building Oliver's flat is in? This is where his little pregnant tramp works. He's always bragging about how she's given him keys to all the luxury flats, and they meet in them to fuck when the residents are away. And seeing as how you and your precious Martin are hardly ever here, I'm betting this was one of their favorites.' A gritty laugh spills from his lips as he says, 'Yeah, I'm betting they've screwed on just about every surface in this place.'

Well, hell. I shove the shit news about Grace aside, since the last thing I want to do is have to get a pregnant nineteen-year-old girl fired, and focus on the first thing this tosser said. 'If you didn't pay the guards off, then who did? And how did you even know I was here?'

'What?' he scoffs, puffing up his chest. 'You think you're the only smart one in the family? We've had a bug planted in Martin's office here since you went running after your American bitch. We've known every move you were making, and you never even had a clue.'

I'm wondering if he even realizes he's slipped into saying 'we' instead of 'I', when he adds, 'Caroline had to blow one of the security guards at your building before he'd give us access to Martin's office, since the fool wouldn't do it for just the money. But she felt it was worth it.'

Fucking Caroline, I think, not at all surprised, given the suspicions we already had. And I have no doubt that she's the mastermind behind all this shit. I just don't understand why Cameron is so willing to be her little lapdog. 'What happened to you, Cam? Why are you slumming around for Caro, doing her dirty work? You're a smart guy. Is she really that good in the sack that you'd throw your life away for her?'

He flinches, and there's a panicked look starting to spill over his mottled face, gleaming wildly in his eyes. He didn't mean to let her name slip, and now that it has, he's shitting himself.

Rubbing one hand across my jaw, I keep my tone deliberately mellow as I say, 'I've known something wasn't right between the two of you for a long time. I just didn't care enough to look into it. I mean, Alistair has his younger mistresses all over London, and I get that you're in on that too. So are you spying on him for Caroline? Is *that* why you hang out with him so often?'

'No,' he mutters. 'I understand Alistair.'

'Well, what's not to understand?' I laugh. 'Booze and women, that's his driving force.'

He shoots me a smarmy, blood-drenched smile. 'Maybe it's mine too.'

I cock my head and let another low laugh fall from my lips. 'And yet here you are, doing Caro's dirty work for her. It doesn't make a lot of sense, Cam, because even if you're that hot to keep nailing her, it's not like it'll last. Shit, all you need to do is look in a mirror to know that you're getting way too old for her tastes.'

He flinches again – then quickly shakes it off and snarls, 'You don't know what the hell you're talking about, Jase.'

'Yeah?' I ask with a lift of my brows, sensing that I'm getting close to pushing the bastard over the edge, so he'll start spilling his guts. And since the phone that's being held casually in Emmy's hand has been recording every word of this conversation since I ended the call with the doorman, we'll have proof of his confession. 'Then I'm guessing you don't know about all her shiny nineteen- and twenty-year-olds in London, do you? The ones she pays to fuck her, sometimes two and three at a time?'

'You don't know anything!' he shouts, straining violently

against the ties again, a vein popping in his temple and the cords of sinew in his neck so pronounced it looks like he's about to have a seizure. 'And you sure as shit don't know Caroline! She'll never be done with me. I was *her* boy!' he roars, before making this godawful whimpering sound and then bursting into tears. Head down and voice cracking, he whispers, 'Only . . . only hers. All hers. Shiny and new. Shiny and new. Shiny and new.'

What. The. Fuck?

I hear Emmy gasp, but can't turn my head to look at her. I'm too in shock, feeling like something slimy has just been thrown in my face, and I break out in a cold sweat, hyperaware of the single drop that starts to slide down the back of my neck.

'Jase,' my grandfather murmurs, his voice sounding like it came from far away, and I shake my head for him to be quiet, my gut churning. Cameron's either losing it, or putting on one hell of an act, and a huge part of me just wants him to shut up so I don't have to hear what's coming. But there's another part that knows if it's true, then I *have* to hear it, so I'll know exactly what that psychotic bitch is truly capable of, and can take her sorry arse down.

I work my jaw a few times, then say, 'You think she's going to visit you in prison, Cam? That you'll mean anything to her at all once you're gone?'

His head jerks up, and there's nothing but raw hatred and fear in his eyes as he shouts, 'She loves me!'

I take a step closer to him. 'No, she's setting you up.'

'You don't understand! She didn't leave me any choice!'

'Have you been in on this with her from the beginning?' I demand, lowering my hands to my sides. 'Did you hire the shit-heads who tried to kill me in San Diego?'

'I don't know anything about San Diego,' he mutters, sweat

and blood flying as he shakes his head. 'You were in a car crash, that's all.'

'Bullshit,' I growl. 'Was it *you*? Or is Caroline the one who contracted those men to kill me and make it look like an accident?'

He grinds his jaw and refuses to answer, looking away from me.

'You either answer the question or I'm calling the cops, Cam. And you don't want that. So tell me the truth. Was it Caroline? Or was it you?'

'Fuck you!' he snarls.

'Is she blackmailing you?' I ask, sensing that he's about to break. 'What dirt does she have on you that's worth trying to commit murder for? Worth spending the rest of your damn life behind bars for?'

'It's none of your fucking business!'

'Emmy, baby, hand me the phone.'

'No!' he shouts up at me, his face so red it's making his eyes look unwardly. 'I . . . Don't! Please. Don't call them.'

'Sorry, Cam. I can't help you if you won't talk.'

'She'll tell everyone!' he bellows, and I'm surprised we haven't had neighbors knocking on the door by now. Hell, from the way he's struggling, I'm surprised he hasn't broken the bloody chair. 'All of it,' he scrapes out, his chest heaving. 'She'll show them the photos. Sell them to all the papers. And then they'll all laugh at me. Every one of those cocksucking bastards will laugh, like I'm some kind of joke.'

'What photos?'

He shudders at my question, and it's like a chill has just spread through the room. The look in his eyes is like staring into the face of fear itself, and I hear Emmy make a low noise, as if she's trying to hold back a sob. J.J. moves behind me and puts his arm around her shoulders, the three of us horrified by what we're watching unfold.

Cam starts rocking back and forth. 'She'll tell Mummy lies about me,' he forces through his clenched teeth, the tendons in his throat looking ready to snap. Then he sucks in a sharp breath and whimpers again, his chin to his chest as he whispers, 'And Mummy will be *mad . . . mad . . . mad.*'

'What the hell did she do to you?' I croak, crossing my arms back over my chest and rubbing my palm over my mouth.

He doesn't lift his head as he whispers, 'Caro says I can't tell, or she'll do things to them too.'

My head jerks back like I've just been clipped on the chin. 'Do things to whom?'

'Jase and Olly. She said *I* have to be the man of the family, because Alistair's just a worthless shit. That I have to be her little man, and make her feel good, or they'll be next.'

Oh, fuck no. No goddamn fucking way.

I don't know if I whisper the words out loud, or if they're only in my head. But Cam's words are burning in my ears like acid, and I have to suck down a deep breath to keep from puking on the floor.

He's sobbing now, and as I turn my head to look back at Emmy, I see that her eyes are glistening with tears too. They're tracking down her cheeks like tiny rivers, and even J.J. looks wrecked.

Looking back at Cam, I heave in another deep breath, and know what I have to do.

I haven't taken more than two steps when my grandfather's rough voice cuts over Cameron's crying, making me pause. 'Jase, be careful.'

I give him a sharp nod, and then keep going, until I'm kneeling down in front of my cousin's vibrating body. 'Cam, if you're still listening, I want you to know something. She's not going to get away with it, so stop worrying about whatever she's threatened you with. I won't let her hurt you anymore. Not ever again, okay? Whatever it takes, I'm going to take her down.'

His head wobbles up, and the man sitting there in the chair doesn't even look like someone I know. It's like Cam's not even in there, hiding behind those tear-wrecked eyes. Instead, this is a man who's finally broken free of a terrible secret that's been weighing him down for decades – one that's twisted and warped his entire life – and as he tries to blink the tears from his eyes, he says, 'Don't. Don't tell . . . Olly.'

I jerk my chin back, feeling like I've just been landed another blow.

'Don't . . . Please, don't call Olly. I don't want him to know. About any of it.'

'I won't. I won't call him.'

'Okay,' he breathes, slumping against the back of the chair, tears still streaking from the corners of his eyes as he squeezes them shut. 'She always said that you hated me. That you told her you hated me and wanted me to die.'

I have to swallow twice against the lump in my throat before I can say, 'She lied, Cam. She fucking lied to you.'

'Yeah,' he sighs, finally passing out from exhaustion, and I fall back on my arse, hanging my head in my hands, and promise myself that whatever it takes, I'm going to find a way to make Caroline Beckett pay.

Chapter Six

Friday morning

EMMY

After a simple breakfast of toast and coffee, we leave the flat not long after Jase's longtime friend Callan Hathaway arrives, and head to London.

With Harrison's help, Jase had managed to get Cameron cleaned up after his breakdown, and then he let the guy stretch out on one sofa, while he kept watch over him the entire night from the other one, reassuring Cam that he was safe whenever his cousin would wake in a panic, before slipping back into an uneasy slumber. I know, because I stayed up with Jase, too worried about him to crawl back into bed and sleep. But I hadn't wanted to make Cameron any more upset than he already was, so I stayed in the dining room and fiddled around on my laptop, making so many cups of coffee for me and Jase that I eventually lost count of how many we'd had.

The two cousins didn't talk much during the night, but I do know that Cameron was able to tell Jase that he has no idea why Caroline is so fixated on keeping the two of us from being together, to the point that she's willing to have Jase killed to keep it from happening. He said she rants about it constantly, claiming I'm going to destroy her entire life.

It doesn't make any freaking sense. But by tomorrow night, Jase is hoping to finally have some answers. And then we'll let justice do its thing, and get on with building our new life together, while she spends the rest of her miserable life behind bars. It's better than what the evil woman deserves, but at least she'll be someplace where she can no longer cause so much damage.

Callan knocked on the door just after nine, and Jase took him into the kitchen to give him a more in-depth briefing on what had happened, while Harrison stayed with Cameron, who was still sleeping on the sofa, and I finished getting ready.

The three of us – me, Jase, and his grandfather – had a brief discussion last night, after Cameron had fallen asleep, and Harrison and I both agreed with Jase that it would be wrong at this point to press charges. Jase has an incredible heart, and despite all the shitty things that Cameron has done to him over the years, all he cares about now is getting help for his cousin. So after our talk, he started quietly making calls, and even though it was the middle of the night, he was able to get results. I think it has to do a bit with his money, but mostly with the fact that he's so respected by those who know him. And in Callan's case, the fact that they've been friends for so long, and have always had each other's backs.

Callan was the first call that Jase had made, and it turned out that his friend, who owns his own private security firm and is a highly trained bodyguard, was in Paris, having just finished up with a conference there. All Jase had to do was tell him that he needed his help, because there was no one else he could trust, and Callan said he'd be on a plane first thing in the morning.

The second call had been to a doctor that Jase knew through some mutual friends, and he was able to secure a place for Cameron at one of the most renowned mental health facilities in Europe. This afternoon, Callan will personally escort Cameron there, via a private jet, and then head back home to New York. And since Harrison collected Cam's bag, which thankfully contained his passport, from Oliver's flat, there won't be any issues with him traveling out of the country.

Then Jase had called Martin, alerting him to the fact that his office was bugged, and instructing him to contact the head of security at the building about the guard who had given Cameron and Caroline illegal access in exchange for money and sexual favors.

His last call had been to the owner of the private security agency whose guards were *meant* to have been protecting us last night. Jase informed the owner of the breach, as well as the fact that he'll be reporting them for misconduct to the appropriate regulatory commissions. The owner was outraged about what had happened and deeply apologetic, claiming he would launch a full internal investigation. He also offered to send new guards for free, but Jase refused. He'd already made arrangements with Callan's company, Hathaway Security, though the new security team won't arrive until tomorrow morning, since they're flying over from the States. The fact that they're based outside the UK is the only reason Jase hadn't gone with them originally, but he said he wouldn't make the same mistake again.

Before we go, Callan shows Jase how to set up the wire he's brought for him to wear, which has Harrison and me sharing dark looks of concern, and then Jase takes a moment to say goodbye to Cameron. While the cousins are talking, Callan gives me a big hug, whispering, 'I told you so, Emmy,' in my ear before he lets me go, and I can't help but smile, remembering what he'd said to me the night I'd run away from Jase at Beckett House. I lean up to kiss him on the cheek just as Jase walks back over to join us, and Callan gives a husky laugh when he catches the possessive way Jase tugs me back into his side, while I simply roll my eyes.

We have a driver who's taking the three of us to the airport, and after he raises the privacy screen, Jase finally shares the plan he's apparently already talked over with Callan, and while it worries us, his grandfather and I both agree that we can't think of a better way to get the results that are needed. Those results being a clear confession from Caroline not only about what she's done to Cameron, but also her unsuccessful attempt to have Jase killed in San Diego, and then again last night.

Jase's phone rings while we're still talking, but it's Martin, so he needs to take the call. While he's on the phone, I turn my attention to the window, soaking in as much of this beautiful city as I can, hoping to be able to come back soon and do some sightseeing.

We fly on a private jet down to London, and Jase has another driver waiting for us at the airport. The man takes us straight to Jase's building, and as we climb out of the Mercedes SUV in the private underground parking garage, I feel like an idiot, because I'd honestly had no idea that he lives in the freaking Shard!

God, this is one of the most prestigious, iconic buildings in London, and my boyfriend lives in one of its largest residential flats. I'm so shocked that I start to feel a little light headed, and it's not from lack of sleep or the elevator ride that we're taking up to the sixty-fifth floor. I'm just . . . I'm overwhelmed, and I can tell by the way that Jase is watching me that he deliberately never mentioned the fact that he lives here. But I'm not that same girl anymore – the one with barbed-wire walls surrounding her heart and a cynical view of wealthy men – and I take his hand in mine and give it a light squeeze to let him know I'm not going to freak out, which brings the first smile to his lips that I've seen all day.

When we get inside the flat, leaving our luggage in the entryway, Jase tells Harrison and me where everything is, then says he has some more phone calls to make. And while I know there probably *are* dozens of calls that need his attention, given the hugely successful company he's been having to run from out of town for weeks now, as well as everything that's happening with his cousin, I suspect he just wants to be alone for a bit. He's been on edge ever since Cameron's heartrending confession, and I know his emotions are at a breaking point, so I give him a soft kiss and tell him to come back when he can.

Setting my purse down on one of the dark end tables, I look around at the beautiful leather sofas and chairs, my feet sinking into one of the plush rugs that are spread out over the ebony hardwood floors, and then soak in the sight of the towering outer wall of glass. It's a simply stunning space, and yet, despite looking like it cost a fortune, the atmosphere is warm and inviting, with lots of lush potted plants and rustic metal candlesticks and bowls. The cool air smells of cedar and sandalwood, and I just want to curl up on one of the deep sofas, pull a cashmere throw over me, and sleep for an entire week. But with Jase going off on his own, I'm not about to bail on Harrison.

I have no idea when Jase is coming back to join us, so I go into the high-ceilinged kitchen and open the stainless-steel refrigerator, relieved to see that someone who obviously works for Jase has completely stocked it with fresh food. I make Harrison and me some antipasti, and cover a plate for Jase, then store it in the fridge.

It's so surreal to think that a month ago, I was researching his grandfather for my article, desperate for any kernel of information I could find, and now I'm *here*, sitting at the marble-topped breakfast bar in Jase's kitchen, while J.J. Harrison, the world-famous artist, and I talk about books and films as we share a meal together. When we're done, we take our glasses of the delicious Cabernet Sauvignon that we've opened and go to stand at the glass wall, taking in the breathtaking view of London as it spreads out below us like a sea of lights. And when I find the courage to ask him how he's handling the things that Jase had told him last night, before all the frightening, then gut-wrenching drama unfolded with Cameron, he starts to open up to me as he talks about the women that he's lost in his lifetime.

'I have so much guilt weighing me down,' he rasps, 'it's a wonder I can walk. Guilt for failing Gianna and my Sarah. Even Janine. And now, knowing what kind of woman I let Jase live with for all those years after Sarah's death, I . . . Christ, I failed him too.'

'I know he doesn't want you feeling that way,' I tell him. 'And he definitely doesn't blame you. So there's no sense in dwelling on the past, no matter how painful it is. For you and Jase, the most important thing is that you have each other now, and where you go from here.'

'Maybe you're right, Emmy. I just hope I'm able to do right by him.'

With a gentle smile, I say, 'The fact that you *want* to tells me you will. You're certainly not the kind of man to change his course once he sets his mind on something.'

He gives a wry, quiet laugh and returns my smile. And though it's only early evening, I know he didn't get much more sleep last night than me and Jase, so I'm not surprised when he says, 'I hate to leave you, but I'm about dead on my feet. Will you think it terribly rude of me if I head on to bed now?'

'Not at all,' I say, carrying our wine glasses into the kitchen. 'I actually think I'll do the same.'

'Tomorrow's going to be a long day,' he murmurs, sounding worried. 'Make sure Jase sleeps.'

'I'll do my best.'

He smirks at my words and I feel my face go pink, thinking Harrison's dirty sense of humor is definitely something his grandson inherited. And the more time I spend with Harrison, the more I notice other little similarities as well, from mannerisms to things they'll say and the way they say them.

Now that they're finally building a relationship, I hope the two remarkable, headstrong men will continue to grow closer, because I truly believe they need each other. Harrison is the only real family Jase has left in the world, and I believe Jase will eventually be able to lure his grandfather out of the dark, lonely world he's made for himself, and back into the light.

I turn off all the lights and head down the opposite hallway from the one Harrison walked down, since the guest suites and master suite are on different sides of the flat. I'm listening for Jase's voice, thinking he's probably still on the phone – but it's the sound of Metallica's 'Enter Sandman' that draws me to a door located on my right. I give a light knock, but doubt he can hear it over the music, so I open the door and peek inside.

I'm surprised to see that the room's not his study or bedroom, but a gym. Though it's not like any home gym I've ever seen. This one is all gleaming equipment, from the state-of-the-art treadmill and rowing machine, to various weight and resistance ones, along with every kind of free weight you can imagine. The wall with the door is covered in weight racks, the two side walls are completely mirrored, and the back one is nothing but glass, the floor the same gleaming ebony hardwood as the rest of the flat.

I have a feeling Jase has been in here since he left me with Harrison, trying to work out his anger and frustration by pushing his big, muscular body to its physical limits. He's dressed only in a pair of black gym shorts, his tanned skin gleaming with sweat as he bench-presses what must be an ungodly amount of weight. I stay where I am, not wanting to distract him. But as soon as he finishes his reps and reaches back, racking the bar, I walk in and shut the door behind me. He instantly sits up as he looks over at me, and there's an expression on his handsome face that I swear I've never seen before. It's this strange, provocative mix of love and need and raw, visceral craving that goes straight to my head.

Straight to my heart.

I can feel my own answering need like a living, breathing thing inside my body, just as fierce and feral as his. It's pacing its cage, demanding to be fed, and as his piercing gaze searches mine, I know he can see it. Can see the hunger that's building inside me, all but burning me alive.

Without a word, Jase reaches down with his battered right hand – his knuckles still swollen and bruised from where he hit Cameron last night – and he picks up the remote that's on the floor. He uses it to lower the volume of the music, instead of turning it off, and as Bullet For My Valentine's 'Waking the Demon' begins to play, Jase moves to his feet in a breathtaking shift of muscle and sinew, and starts walking toward me.

His tall, sweat-slick body is hard and ripped, the look in his dark, heavy-lidded eyes telling me that he's going to use the hell out of me tonight, because I'm the *only* thing that can ease him. And I'm okay with that. I'm so okay with it that I start pulling my clothes off for him before he even reaches me, because this sexy, alpha beast of a man is hurting, and he's *mine*, and I love him. I love him so much I don't even know how to tell him.

So I'm going to show him instead.

'I don't want to talk,' he says, his deep voice so raw and low it makes me shiver. 'Not right now. We'll talk later.'

'But are you okay?' I ask, gazing up at him with concern as he stops a foot away from me. I'm standing in nothing more than a small, lacy black pair of panties, all my clothes strewn around me on the floor, as if I disrobed in a windstorm. But the air in the gym is calm and still, and I know that the storm is inside me, raging in my veins.

'I will be,' he husks, taking that final step that brings his body flush against mine, the heat of him making me gasp. 'I just need to be inside you, Em. As fucking deep inside as I can get.'

He picks me up then, with his hands on my ass, and I wrap my arms around his shoulders, my legs around his waist, and press my trembling lips to his as I nip at his bottom lip, and whisper, 'Take whatever you want from me, Jase. Whatever you need.'

He growls in response, tilting his head as he takes my mouth with a scorching, blistering kiss that has me clinging to him as he carries me across the room, to the bench he was just using that sits parallel to one of the mirrored walls. Setting me on my feet, he says, 'Straddle the bench, with your bare arse to me, Emmy.'

My heart hammers with excitement as I follow the rough command, slipping off my panties and then straddling the black leather bench so that I'm facing the weights, instead of away from them. I turn my head to watch Jase, and as he starts to unwind the black Velcro wrist supports he's wearing, he tells me to reach forward and hold on to the metal bar that extends about five inches on either side of the bench at its head. I do as he says, and his long legs straddle my back as he leans down and uses one of the wrist supports to secure my left hand to the bar, binding me to the bench.

I'm breathing hard and fast, like I'm running a race, but the music's drowning out the sound. I can feel the huge, diamond-hard length of his cock pressing against my back as he leans over to my other side, securing my right wrist, and if I'd ever had any questions about whether bondage would turn me on or off, they've been answered. Because this is one of the hottest damn things I could have ever imagined, and I know it's because of the man that I'm doing it with. Because I trust him, and am willing to go down whatever intense, sexual path Jase wants to take me on, feeling as if he's binding me with so much more than fucking Velcro.

He's binding me with his *need*. With his pain and his passion and his hope for what we're building together, and I love him so goddamn much that it hurts.

And I want him so desperately I'm literally dripping down the insides of my thighs, my pussy already puffy and drenched, and he hasn't even touched it yet.

I start panting harder as he settles on to the bench behind me, my hips rolling as I grind my clit against the warm leather, my nipples so tight I swear I can feel my pulse in them. My wide gaze is glued to the mirror, and I watch as Jase pulls the elastic band of his shorts down over that broad, mouthwatering penis that is all *mine, mine, mine*. I make a low, throaty sound of appreciation when it springs up against his ridged abs, so big and hard that I have no doubt I'm going to have trouble walking tomorrow. But it'll be so freaking worth it.

He wasn't lying about needing to be inside me, because I only get about five seconds to stare at his beautiful cock, and then he's burying it in my cunt. I'm soaked in my juices, but tight, and he's careful to avoid my scar as he grips my hips in a firm hold and starts working his way in with thick, grinding lunges, the way his muscles ripple and flex under his skin so impossibly sexy that I can't stop watching. Then his hands slide lower, over my ass, and I make a hoarse sound of shock when he uses his thumbs to pull my cheeks apart. I look over my shoulder, watching his molten, heavy-lidded gaze turn volcanic blue as he soaks in the sight of his dick thrusting in and out of me, and I know it must be one hell of an explicit view. He's seeing *every* part of me, but I'm not shy or embarrassed, because his body is mine and mine is his. There are no boundaries or borders between us, and I'll gladly let him have whatever view he wants of me, because God knows there are so many that I want of him.

I never realized I could be so dirty, but loving this wickedly sexy alpha has unleashed my inner wild woman, and now I crave every part of him. I want him to fuck my oiled breasts and then come straight down my throat as I open my mouth for him. Want to watch him jack that big, textured penis in his strong fist until he comes all over my bare pussy while I finger myself for his greedy, blistering gaze. Want to sixty-nine with him until we both pass out from exhaustion still knotted around each other, completely drained and quivering with aftershocks. I want it *all*, because it's Jase and I love him and I want to do everything I can to give him pleasure and rock his world. I want to give it to him so good and hot that he's always satisfied, because I know he's always going to do the same for me.

We're the perfect team, and I *know* that I am a lucky, lucky woman.

The song has shifted to Alice in Chains' 'Would?', the heavy beat pulsing through my veins, and I cry out as Jase curls one of his powerful arms around my waist, our legs still straddling the bench as he stands, lifting my lower body until my feet are no longer even touching the floor. He's so strong he handles my weight with ease, my hands still bound to the bar, and I'm so completely in his control that it's mind-blowing.

He throws back his dark head and roars as he starts to take me even faster, his massive cock spreading me apart as he drives in hard and deep, going all the way to the root, and I'm gasping for breath, already on the verge of coming. He's pulling me into each hammering thrust, serving my pussy up to his pounding cock, and I let my head hang down, my hair falling over the bench as I give him my complete and total surrender.

It may be rough as fuck and hotter than hell, but there's more emotion burning between us than could ever be explained. I feel like we're merging and melting together. Our pleasure and pain. Our hopes and needs. Our dreams and hungers. He's the perfect answer to every question my heart has ever had, and I want nothing more than to take him into every part of me and keep him there forever. For always.

'Every part of you,' he growls, making me wonder if I just moaned those words out loud, as he grips one side of my bottom and pushes his thumb deep into my ass, the sudden invasion making me cry out. 'I want it all, Emmy. I'm *taking* it all. Tonight, baby. Right now. I'm going to fuck this tight little arse so hard that you scream.'

Oh . . . *Oh, God.* Just thinking about it has me dripping, and he knows it. Can feel just how excited I am as my pussy gets even wetter for him, his dark shaft gleaming with my juices. 'Yes,' I moan, so full of him I can barely breathe. 'Whatever you want. Whatever you need.'

He makes a harsh, guttural sound deep in his chest that tells me he's close, just as I start coming apart for him, my inner muscles pulsing around his thrusting shaft as a violent burst of pleasure scores its way down my nerve-endings, my body hungry for the feel of him blasting inside me, filling me up. But he pulls out at the last second, and I toss my hair out of my eyes as I turn my head and watch in the mirror as he fists his dark, wet cock and starts jerking it in rough, rapid strokes. His head goes back, chest heaving, every muscle in his arm flexing and coiling as he works his dick faster and harder. And then his head drops forward, and he makes a savage sound at the back of his throat as he presses the bulging head right against the puckered ring of muscle between my ass cheeks.

I gasp his name, and his eyes meet mine in the mirror at the exact moment he starts to come, his hot seed covering the tiny hole and dripping over my skin, sliding down to my pussy, and then pooling on the bench below us, as he just keeps coming . . . and coming.

It's the dirtiest thing I've ever seen. The dirtiest thing I've ever experienced.

And then it just gets filthier, and a thousand times more intimate. He's still rock-hard, the heavy weight of his cock resting against my butt cheek, as he uses two big fingers to start pushing his hot ejaculate inside me, working it inside that tight ring, and I know what's coming. He's already told me exactly what he wants, and though I'm nervous as hell, the truth is that I want it too. Because it's Jase, it's us, and there are no walls between us. No barriers.

He replaces his fingers with the broad, wet head of his dick, and I give a hoarse, shocked cry as he starts to push inside, penetrating me, so many new sensations bombarding my system I can't even make sense of them all. He's careful, but determined, working his heavy cock into my ass one thick, blistering inch at a time, and I know he's going to give me every one of them. That he's going to bury himself to the root, and the awareness makes me shiver and moan. Or maybe that's just from how strange and savagely intimate it feels to have him burying himself in such a forbidden place. I've never, in my entire life, thought I would let a man fuck me in the ass. But with Jase . . . God, there's nothing, no part of me, that I wouldn't offer up to him. And as he pulls back a few inches, then gives me a gentle thrust, I realize that this . . . Yeah, this feels good.

Then he does it again, thrusting a little harder, and I decide that good isn't the right word – because this feels *breathtaking*.

'More,' I groan, the way he stiffens, then shudders, telling me that I've surprised him.

'You want more, sweetheart? You've got it,' he growls, pushing all the way in, until I can feel him pressed up tight against my ass, his heavy balls swinging against the slick lips of my cunt. I hear him mutter a gritty curse, just before he starts working that huge cock in and out of me, and I moan and pant for breath, squeezing the bar under my hands so tightly it'll be a miracle if it isn't dented.

'Harder,' I demand, wriggling my ass for him. 'God, Jase, fuck me harder!'

He snarls as he tightens the arm around my waist and reaches down with the other, fisting his hand in my hair and tugging my head back, my body jerking with each of the hard, relentless thrusts he's hammering into me.

'It's so good,' I gasp, knowing that when I come it's going to be intense, and I'd give anything at that moment to be able to rub my clit. 'Feels so good.'

'You're killing me, baby. Fucking killing me.'

And then he keeps talking to me in that deliciously rough, lust-thick voice, telling me how beautiful I look. How tight and hot and incredible I feel to him, and I can't get enough of it. I'm coming more undone with each husky, guttural word that falls from his lips, and when he reaches around my front and shoves three big, long fingers inside my pussy, I come so hard I start screaming. Screaming so sharp and loud that in some distant part of my mind, I'm hoping that J.J. has the TV in his room on full volume, because if not, breakfast tomorrow morning is going to be seriously awkward.

I'm crying out 'I love you,' over and over, and Jase is growling it back as he finds his own violent release, sweat flying from our bodies as we cement the meaning of the words with the hungers of our flesh.

Then I feel him lean over me and rest his forehead against my upper back, his powerful body shuddering as he empties the last of his orgasm into me, and he groans two quiet words that make me so very glad I sought him out tonight. 'Thank you.'

'Jase.'

'Thank you,' he groans again, lowering us back down to the bench as he wraps both arms around me and presses a tender kiss to my shoulder. 'Thank you for believing in me. For coming after me. For standing beside me and not giving up on me.' His warm lips find my ear, and I swear I can hear the pure, raw emotion in his deep voice as he says, 'But most of all, beautiful girl, thank you for loving me.'

Chapter Seven

JASE

There's a door that connects the gym to the master bedroom, and after I turn off the music and free her wrists, I lift Emmy into my arms and carry her pleasure-limp body straight into the marbled, waterfall shower.

I can't believe what she's just given me, and how insanely good it was.

I'd hoped I wouldn't still be so thick and hard after blowing my load on her, but that's not how it'd worked. If anything, I'd been even bigger, her pink little arsehole stretched so tight around me that each pulsing thrust of my cock had to have come with a bite of pain. But I'd watched her closely, carefully, and she'd never once tried to pull away from me. No, she'd just kept wriggling her little arse for more, the sounds spilling from her lips some of the sexiest that she's ever made.

And the way she'd felt . . . *Christ*, I need to stop thinking about it, because it's just making my dick hard again, and my poor girl needs some bloody rest.

Her gift of herself tonight, and the absolute trust that she's shown she has in me, has quieted the demons in my head, and I cling to her, feeling her love in the soft brush of her lips against my chest, my throat, my mouth. This girl has transformed me, and now I don't know how *not* to tell her how much I love her. Need her. Want her forever. So I just keep saying it, while she gives herself completely over to my care once again, letting me do as I will. I force my constant craving for her pleasure back, wrapping it in chains, and take my time washing her hair, before running the soapy sponge over her creamy, silky skin.

She's so fucking perfect, and what's amazing is that she doesn't even know it. There's not a vain bone in Emmy's body, and it's just one of the endless number of things that I love about her.

She sways against me, exhausted, and I quickly wash my own body, then stand us both under the warm water, rinsing the soap away, before turning the shower off. I grab two large towels and wrap one around my waist, then run the other over Emmy, drying the glistening droplets from her golden skin, and grab another one to wring the water out of her hair.

'Love you,' she murmurs sleepily, when I lift her into my arms and carry her to my bed, and I'm fucking ecstatic that she's finally going to be sleeping right where she belongs. 'Love you so much, Jase.'

'Mmm,' I hum, like I'm savoring something tasty.

There's a small smile on her lips as she blinks up at me. 'What?'

'Every time you tell me you love me,' I say, reaching down to tug the duvet back, then laying her down on the smooth gray sheets, 'I'm going to think about taking your sweet little arse tonight.'

'Oh, God,' she groans with a soft, beautiful laugh, covering her pink face with her hands.

I quickly dry off, toss the towel over the back of a chair, and then climb in beside her. 'Don't be shy now,' I murmur, grinning as I pull her hands away from her blushing cheeks and rub my lips over hers. 'Not with me, sweetheart.'

She kisses me back, snuggling up against me as I stroke my hand down her side and over the curve of her hip. Then she pulls her head back a little, and there's a warm, vibrant look in her eyes as she lifts her hand to my face, her fingertips brushing across the scar from the accident as she says, 'I feel so incredibly lucky, Jase. Lucky that you're still here with me, when I could have so easily lost you the night of the crash. And if you hadn't woken up last night when you did, it all could have gone so differently.'

I give her waist a gentle squeeze. 'I know, baby.'

She sighs as she places her hand against my chest, directly over my heart, and there's a little frown tugging between her brows as she asks, 'What are you going to do about Grace?'

'Hell, I don't know,' I mutter. 'I don't want to get her fired, but she's committing a serious felony by giving Oliver the keys to those people's homes.'

'She is,' she agrees. 'It's such a shit situation.'

'Last night,' I scrape out, my gut instantly knotting with grief and guilt as I think about what happened. 'I always knew Caroline was crazy, but . . . God, Em, I had no idea she was evil. How did I not see it? I mean, I lived with her. I should have known. And maybe if I'd opened my damn eyes, I wouldn't have failed Cam as badly as I did.'

'Don't. Don't do that,' she says, her soft voice vibrating with emotion. 'You don't get to take the blame for this, because you have no part of it. You were just a child, Jase.'

'But she's fucking warped him,' I growl, hating that I've brought this to our bed, but needing to be able to talk it out with her, now that the words are finally coming.

Concern darkens her eyes, and she presses her hand a little harder against my chest as she says, 'And she'll pay for it. We'll make sure of it.'

'Damn straight we will.'

She flinches at the conviction she hears in my low voice, and I can sense the worry and fear moving through her as she clutches my arm and says, 'Are you sure we can't just call the police and have them take her in? Because you're right, she *is* evil, and it scares the ever-loving hell out of me to think of you facing off against her.'

'If there were any other way, I'd do it. But you know how manipulative she is, Em. I can't risk her putting this all on Cameron. And we still don't know how she hired those bastards in San Diego who wrecked us, or what she's planning next.'

'I just don't want anything to happen to you,' she says in a rush, and it kills me when I see the tears gathering in her eyes, glistening on her lashes.

'It won't,' I tell her, pushing my hand into her damp hair and curving it around the back of her head. 'But I *have* to do this, Em. I won't be able to live with myself if I don't.'

'I know,' she breathes, just as the first tear slips away, sliding into her hair. 'I just . . . I'm worried that more pain is waiting for you in that house. So please, just promise me that you'll be careful. Because it'll destroy me if I lose you.'

Feeling like she's just punched me right in the heart, I lean forward and press a tender kiss to her forehead. 'Always, sweetheart. I promise.'

'And there's something else I've been wanting to tell you,' she murmurs.

'What is it, baby?'

She turns her head, brushing her own soft kiss across the

ink on my inner forearm. 'I've been—' she starts to say, but is cut off by a jarring knock against the bedroom door.

We both tense at the sound, then bolt upright, and I'm already moving to my feet when my grandfather's deep voice carries through the door. 'Jase, get out here! We've got a problem!'

I grab a pair of jeans and tug them on, then glance back to make sure that Emmy's covered up, and see her standing on the other side of the bed, wearing the duvet like a toga, and I'd laugh if I wasn't so worried. 'What's happened?' I ask, yanking the door open to find my grandfather standing in the hallway, dressed in the same dark jeans and T-shirt he'd been wearing earlier.

'Anna just phoned me,' he mutters, and since the only Anna I know is his housekeeper, that's who I assume he's talking about. 'She's friends with Evelyn, one of the maids at Beckett House, and the woman just called her. Said that Caroline is packing up nearly everything she owns and throwing it into the back of Alistair's Discovery.'

'Son of a bitch,' I growl, already turning and heading towards my chest of drawers. 'She's planning to make a run for it.'

'I'll be waiting for you at the door,' Harrison says before he turns to walk back down the hall, giving us privacy, and I'm grateful that he's here. Not only because it means I won't have to do this alone, but if not for Anna, Caroline might have slipped away right under our noses.

Emmy, though, still hasn't realized that the plan has changed.

'Why is he waiting at the door?' she asks. 'I don't understand. You can't possibly be thinking to go there *now*.'

Sitting down on the side of the bed to pull on my socks, I say, 'I don't have any choice, Em. I've got to get her confession tonight.'

'But Callan's security team isn't here yet!' she shouts, coming around the foot of the bed looking like she's seriously pissed off. But I know it's because she's worried about me, and I hate like hell that I'm having to put her through this.

'I know,' I say, moving to my feet and pulling on the Henley that I grabbed from the drawer. 'We're just going to have to go in on our own.'

'Fuck that!' she growls, glaring up at me as I walk over and take her flushed face in my hands.

'I love you,' I tell her, leaning down and pressing a hard, swift kiss to her lips. 'But I don't have time to argue with you right now. J.J. and I need to be on the road.'

'Well, you're not leaving me here,' she mutters, dropping the duvet and stomping over to her suitcase, which I'd brought in for her earlier.

'Emmy,' I groan, thinking she's going to be the fucking death of me, even as I can't take my greedy gaze off her gorgeous arse.

'Don't *Emmy* me,' she snaps, grabbing a clean pair of jeans and a dark sweater from her case. 'I'm going with you.'

I try to talk her into staying at the flat, but the stubborn woman refuses to listen to reason. She dresses quickly, then stomps out of the room ahead of me, and I'm so frustrated I almost forget to grab the wire that Callan gave me.

J.J. has no doubt heard her shouting at me, but he's smart enough not to mention it when we meet up with him at the door. As we take the lift down to the parking garage, I tell Emmy that the only way she's coming is if she promises to stay in the damn car when we reach Beckett House, and though she argues, she finally relents when J.J. tells her that her presence would likely only incite Caroline to more extreme behavior. It's the perfect argument, since Emmy's already worried about my safety, and I make a mental note to thank the old guy when we're alone.

It's late and there's hardly any traffic on the motorway, so we make good time to Kent. Especially seeing as how I push just about every speeding law there is, thankfully avoiding the police, since I don't have time for a ticket. We're all silent, clearly lost in our heads, and I can't help thinking that if I'd just had Cameron call Caroline last night, making up some story about how he hadn't been able to break into the flat because we'd changed the locks or some shit, then she wouldn't be panicking right now, obviously worried that he got caught and has snitched her out. But after his breakdown, I hadn't been able to stomach the idea of him having to talk to her, and even though this might all go to shit because of it, I realize that I still stand by my decision. Cameron's been through enough, and if I end up having to hire a legion of investigators to chase her evil arse around the world, then I will. There won't be any safe place for her to hide, and eventually she'll be brought back to pay for what she's done.

And I imagine that between the abuse and blackmail charges, along with attempting to pay for my murder, she'll be going away for a long, long time.

I cut the lights halfway down the massive drive to Beckett House and pull off into the trees to avoid detection, figuring Harrison and I can walk the rest of the way. And seeing as how Emmy's going to be waiting in the car, I don't want it anywhere near the house.

I take a moment to attach the wire, hoping like hell that when I play a snippet of Cameron's confession for Caroline from my phone, her temper and hatred of me will take over and do the rest, leading her straight into her own confession. And if it works, I'll take the recording directly to Danny, and let Scotland Yard deal with her, instead of trusting the local police department.

When I've got the wire in place, I climb out of the car, slip the slender recording device into my pocket, and open the rear driver's side door, since Emmy's sitting in the backseat, still quietly fuming. I reach in, grab her behind the neck, and tug her towards me, giving her a hard, fast kiss, and it might sound corny as hell, but I swear this woman gives me strength.

'Jase, this wasn't the plan,' she says in a voice that's thick with worry when I pull away. 'You're meant to be going in with Callan's team for backup.'

'When Cameron didn't contact her last night, it must have tipped her off. I can't risk her making a run for it and never finding her, Em. That's bullshit.'

She wets her lips, and I can see her pulse pounding at the base of her throat as she says, 'Then let me come with you. I won't even go inside if you don't want me to. I just . . . I need to be close enough to know that you're okay.'

'Fuck no,' I growl. 'That's not happening.'

I make her promise again to stay put, lean in to give her a deep, *I-love-the-hell-out-of-you* kiss, and then step back and shut the door. J.J. meets me around the back of the car, and we're both quiet as we make our way up to the house, until I clear my throat a little, and murmur, 'I'm glad you're here with me.'

He gives me a grandfatherly pat on the back, and I swear I choke up a bit as he says, 'Me too, Jase. Me too.'

When we reach the house, we see Alistair's Discovery parked near the front steps, the back open and already packed with bags and cases. The front door is ajar, so we slip inside, and it's easy to locate Caroline and Alistair from the way they're screaming at each other. There's no sign of any of the household staff, so I'm guessing they've all retreated into the east wing, as they often do when these two have one of their raging, bloodthirsty arguments.

As J.J. and I make our way across the foyer, heading for the music room, I swear it feels like a lifetime ago since I was here, instead of a mere five weeks.

But those five weeks . . . Hell, they've certainly packed a punch. I'd found the girl of my dreams, only to lose her, then get her back, then nearly get her killed and lose her again.

And then she came back to me, and told me she loved me, and after Cameron's confession, I'm about to put an end to this whole fucking nightmare once and for all.

Then I'm taking my girl and riding off into the proverbial sunset. Into a future that's going to be filled with love and warmth, without a single ounce of the cold, cruel bitterness that practically bleeds from these walls.

I share a meaningful look with J.J. as we reach the door to the music room, then twist the handle to open it, and I step inside to find Caroline standing in the center of the room with her back to me, while Alistair leans drunkenly against the side of the gleaming grand piano.

Since he's the only one who's facing the doorway, it's Alistair who sees me first, his bloodshot eyes going wide with surprise. 'Jase! I had no idea you were coming down this week.'

Just as the last syllable leaves Alistair's lips, J.J. steps into the room beside me, his hands casually pushed in his pockets, and Alistair's face instantly stiffens with fear, which I love. J.J. Harrison might be getting up there in years, but he still has the bearing of a man you do *not* want to fuck with. And while Alistair might be a pathetic drunk, he's smart enough to know that my grandfather and I as a united front can't mean anything but trouble for him.

I have no idea what Caroline and Alistair have been arguing

about, or what story she's fed him about why she's packed his Discovery with her bags, but it doesn't matter. She hasn't moved since Alistair said my name, and I can feel the rage pouring off her as she continues to just stand there in the middle the room, her spine ramrod straight, dressed in a sequined dress of all things, with her platinum-blond hair in a refined twist, as if she's getting ready for a night out on the town, instead of making a run for her freedom.

Deciding to goad her, I say, 'Hello, Caroline. Did we catch you at a bad time?'

'What are you doing here, Jase?' She crosses her arms over her chest as she slowly turns to face us, and I'm amazed to see how much older she looks than the last time I saw her, the strain of trying to have me killed clearly taking its toll. 'I thought you were done with this place.'

'I was.' I take my phone out of my pocket, keeping my hard gaze locked tight with hers as I say, 'But J.J. and I are here for some answers.'

She gives a dramatic sigh, as if I'm wasting her time. 'And what, exactly, are your questions?'

I let a husky laugh fall from my lips as I reach up and rub the scar over my eyebrow, just to mess with her, knowing the angrier I get her, the more likely she is to give us what we want. 'Come on, Caro. I think you already know at least one of them.'

Her nostrils flare as she sucks in a sharp breath. 'I'm not a mind reader, Jase. I have no idea what you're going on about.'

'Yeah?' I start turning my phone over in my hand as I take a step closer to her. 'Then why don't we start with how you went about hiring the fuckers who tried to kill me in San Diego three weeks ago?'

She pales for a moment, then flushes a vivid shade of red as her eyes dart to where J.J. stands just behind me, then down to the phone in my hand, her lips compressed into a hard, tight line. 'I . . . I don't have a clue what you're talking about.'

'Honestly,' Alistair slurs, giving me a look of flustered outrage. 'Caroline has her faults, Jase. But she's not a monster. She's a bloody Beckett!'

'You sure that's not the same thing?' I drawl, and I hear J.J. snuffle a quiet snort.

Alistair narrows his eyes, and I decide it's time to go in for the kill, just wanting this over and done with. 'Your wife's been screwing Cameron behind your back for years,' I tell him, and I hear Caroline gasp. But it's Alistair I'm watching, carefully studying his reaction, needing to know if he knows. If he's aware of just how sick she is.

It seems to take a moment for my words to sink in, and then he laughs so hard he falls drunkenly against the side of the piano again, sending out a discordant note from the keys. 'Come on, Jase. Tell me something I *don't* know.'

Softly, I say, 'Did you know it's been happening since he was twelve?'

His laughter dies so abruptly, it's like I've reached into his throat and crushed his vocal cords.

'Cameron broke into the flat I was staying in last night with the intent of killing me for her with a fucking knife. It was her second attempt, and he did it because Caroline's blackmailing him with photos that she took of him when he was a teenager. He said she's got some elaborate story cooked up about him being a rent boy that will ruin his credibility in London, while keeping her own name clean. He broke down after we caught him and he told us everything.' I lift my phone up, and I can feel the seething hatred of Caroline's glare burning against the side of my face as I press my thumb against the phone, letting him hear just a few seconds of Cameron's confession, before stopping it, unwilling to share any more in front of the bitch than I have to.

'It's all recorded on here,' I tell him, lowering the phone back to my side. 'He's fucking broken, Alistair, and it's because of *her*. Because she started abusing him when he was only a boy, threatening to come after me and Oliver next if he didn't do whatever she wanted.'

Alistair's bloodshot eyes nearly bulge out of his skull, and his top lip curls with disgust as he finally looks back over at his wife. 'Jesus, Caroline.'

'Don't you dare look at me like that,' she sneers, giving him a viperous stare. 'I won't take that shit from *you*.'

'Did you do it?' he growls, turning red in the face as he smacks his hand down hard on the piano in a fit of rage. 'Did you honestly hire someone to make an attempt on Jase's life, and blackmail Cameron to try a second time, just because of Emmy Reed? Just so you can protect your stupid fucking secret that no one would have ever discovered in the first place? *Christ*, woman, it's not Jase's fault that you're a goddamn desert bumpkin!'

As Emmy would say, *What the what?*

Alistair slides a calculating look my way, then shakes his head as he snorts. 'She's lost her bloody mind, son. When you brought the American here, Caroline became obsessed with the fear that you would somehow learn the truth about her, just because the girl lives in California. It was preposterous and completely irrational!'

'What truth?' I ask, while keeping a cautious eye on Caroline, since I don't trust her. Especially when she's standing there looking ready to strangle Alistair with her bare hands, her chest heaving as she pants for breath.

'Caro's mother was nothing but a fucking maid to people

like us,' Alistair says with a smarmy twist of his lips, as if he's starting to enjoy himself. 'She had dreams of becoming a famous actress in Los Angeles, so she ran off to America, only to end up falling in love with a two-bit conman. He took her back to his shitty little hometown in the California desert, put a baby in her belly, and then buggered off. And that's where Caroline lived until she turned seventeen and came to England, determined to live the life of the people in the stories her mother had raised her on. Stories of the British upper-class, and the stupid cunt thought she could actually fit in.' He shoots her a derisive look, then belches behind his fist. 'Thought all she had to do was put on a fake accent, invent a new background for herself, and scrub up. But everyone who looks at her knows the truth. That she's nothing but the little whore I started screwing before she was even legal. She's prime mistress material, but has no place being the lady of Beckett House.'

Literally vibrating with rage, Caroline gives a bitter, maniacal laugh, and I feel J.J. place his hand on my shoulder, silently warning me to be on guard. But right now, we're not the ones she's looking to destroy. 'Well, if we're going to start spilling secrets, Alistair, why don't you tell them about the night that Sarah died?'

'Don't even *think* of going there,' he hisses, giving her a sharp look of warning. '*You*, more than anyone, know how easily accidents can happen. I'd hate for you to fall down the stairs and break your pretty little neck, Caroline.'

'What about that night?' I ask, and am surprised by how calm I sound as I slip my phone back into my pocket.

My question snags her attention, and for a moment I think she's going to refuse to answer me, just out of spite. But then she slides a disgusted look back at Alistair, and I realize that their mutual loathing of each other is going to be their downfall, each of them so desperate to draw blood from the other with their verbal barbs that their house of cards is tumbling.

Holding Alistair's hostile glare, her lips curl with a cold smile. 'This drunken idiot isn't your real father, Jasper.'

'I already know that,' I mutter, needing her to get the fuck on with it.

'What? Who told you?' Alistair demands, clearly wanting an explanation. But I'm barely even listening to him, because Caroline's smirking at me now, and I have no doubt that something bad is coming. And while I know it's wrong, because I would never put her in this kind of dangerous situation, I can't help wishing that I had Emmy here with me. Because she's my fucking rock. The thing that makes me strong.

And I need her more than ever when Caroline says, 'Did you know that Sarah was pregnant with your little sister the night Alistair killed her, then staged her body to make it look like a suicide?'

I start forward, but Harrison grips my arm, holding me back, and Caroline just keeps on going.

'Mr Big Shot here is basically shooting blanks,' she boasts with a gleeful laugh, ignoring the way Alistair's all but starting to foam at the mouth. 'He knew the child growing in your mother's belly wasn't his, but was willing to claim you as his own to save face, because people were already gossiping about how he hadn't managed to knock up his pretty wife. But your mother wasn't so keen to stick it out with him. She wanted to run off with the man she loved, and take you with her. So Alistair did what he does best. He threatened and weaseled and played dirty. He told her that if she ran, he wouldn't hurt her, but would do whatever it took to see *you*, her baby boy, dead. Even if it meant draining the family coffers.'

'So she stayed,' I scrape out, feeling like I'm staring at her down a tunnel, my pulse roaring in my ears so loudly it's like a bloody jet engine. Roaring and roaring and roaring.

Or maybe that's me.

But it must not be, because I can hear Caroline as she laughs again, saying, 'Of course she stayed. Until Hart came back, and your mother couldn't stay out of his bed. When she got knocked up a second time, and told Alistair that Hart had the means to protect you and your unborn sister, so she intended to divorce his pathetic arse, he lost it.' She turns her head towards Alistair again, and there's a revolting look of excitement on her face as she hammers the final nail in his coffin. 'I'd been fucking him before she came barging in to their room, and I watched from the balcony windows as he put his hands around her pale throat and squeezed the life right out of her.'

'She helped me!' Alistair screams, shaking and spluttering as he points an unsteady finger at Caroline. 'It was *her* idea to hang Sarah in the playroom. She said it would give the story credibility. That everyone would be so horrified, they wouldn't question anything that seemed out of place. And then she threatened to tell everyone what I'd done if I didn't marry her!'

I hear J.J. make a low, chilling sound of grief beside me, but can't even turn my head to check on him. No, I'm too locked in on Alistair's paunchy face and frightened eyes, the rage that's building inside me unlike anything I've ever known.

Jesus. All these years, I'd thought he was this faithless, pitiful drunk. But he was a fucking killer!

I'm moving before I even realize it, and I literally pick Alistair up and throw him against the wall. With a blood-thirsty snarl on my lips, I stalk over to where he's landed and pick him up again, holding him with one hand fisted in the front of his shirt, while I start slamming my fist into his face with the other. There's a crunch, and I know I've broken his nose, but I just keep going, the most angry, godawful sounds spilling past my lips as I think about the lives that were destroyed because of this worthless piece of shit.

'Stay back!' I hear Harrison shout, and I look up, thinking he's telling me to stop, only to see Emmy running straight into the room.

Her worried gaze darts between the players in this sickening family drama, then comes quickly back to me as she says, 'I heard the crash. Are you okay? What's happened?'

This time, I do let out a deafening roar, so fucking furious that she didn't keep her promise to stay in the car that I'm seeing red. But before I can shout for her to get the hell out of here, Caroline screams, 'You bitch! This is all your fault!'

Everything happens in slow motion then. I let Alistair drop to the floor, every hair on my body standing on end as I watch Caroline's features distort with madness as she lurches for the small table that stands just off to her left, ripping open its top drawer.

Then she pulls out a gleaming black revolver.

I'm roaring again, running, but it's like I'm moving through quicksand, and I'm on the far side of the room from her, knowing damn well I'm not going to reach her in time as she lifts the gun and aims it straight at Emmy's chest. My muscles scream as I push them for more speed, but she's going to pull the trigger any second now, so I shout Caroline's name as I take a flying leap, praying she'll turn the gun on me. The gun fires just as I slam into her, and I turn my head as we crash on to the floor, terrified I'm about to see Emmy's chest torn open by the bullet, when my grandfather throws himself in front of her like a bloody action hero in a movie.

I watch in horror as J.J.'s shoulder jerks back from the bullet, the force of the impact sending him careering into Emmy, who's trying to hold him as they fall to the floor. My ears are ringing from the shot, but I can hear Caroline's sobbing, and as I look down, ready to fight her for the gun, I see that she's already dropped it because the bone in her forearm has nearly been snapped in two. I grab the gun, quickly flicking the safety as I scramble to my feet, and tuck it into the back of my jeans as I hurry over to Harrison and Emmy.

The sound of the gunshot finally brings the staff running in, and I shout for Angus to watch Caroline while I drop down on my knees beside my grandfather.

'Call 999!' I growl, tossing Emmy my phone before grabbing the light cardigan that's lying over the arm of a nearby chair. I quickly wad it up and use it to apply pressure to J.J.'s bleeding shoulder, making him hiss with pain.

Emmy talks to the emergency services, then helps me get J.J. comfortable, grabbing a pillow off one of the sofas and gently tucking it beneath his head. He's conscious, but in pain, and I just keep talking to him, telling him he's going to be just fine, while a shattered-looking Emmy holds his hand and Angus barks orders at the staff, taking charge of the room.

When the paramedics finally arrive, I move back, giving them room to work, and then take the recording device from my pocket, making sure it didn't get damaged when I hit the floor. Or rather, Caroline hit the floor, and I landed on top of her. But the device is fine, and I slip it back into my pocket as they wheel the trolley they've put Harrison on out the door, Emmy right beside him, still holding his hand.

'I've always despised you, because you remind me of your bitch mother,' Caroline sneers, and I turn my head to look back at her. Spittle falls from the corner of her snarling lips as she struggles to sit upright, cradling her broken arm to her chest, while Angus stands over her, still ensuring she doesn't try for another weapon. 'Even when you were a little boy,' she yells, wanting to be heard over all the commotion as a second medical team hurries into the room to deal with her and Alistair, along with four policemen, 'you were so like her.'

'I'll consider that one of the best compliments I've ever had,' I tell her, and I could swear there's a warm breeze that blows across my forehead at that moment, as if my mother's spirit has just reached down and placed a kiss there. It's a fanciful thought, but it still brings a brief smile to my lips.

Then I turn my back on her, hand the gun over to one of the policemen, and head outside to join Emmy in the back of Harrison's ambulance.

As we speed away into the night, I take a final look at Beckett House through the rear window, knowing that I'll never set foot in it again.

And neither will the killers who murdered my mother.

EMMY

As Harrison is wheeled into the operating theater at the local hospital, Jase turns to look at me, and I realize that despite the harrowing things we've been through this week, I've never truly seen him angry.

Until now.

I have a feeling it's about more than the horrible confessions he heard tonight and the fact that his grandfather's been shot. It's about *me*, and the fact that I broke my promise to him and nearly got myself killed.

I want to talk to him and tell him I'm sorry, but before I can even get started, he's got a doctor and two nurses looking me over and checking my vitals, even though I'm perfectly fine, thanks to his and Harrison's bravery. But I know he's also worried about how aggressively he fucked me earlier tonight, and I swear to God that if he says anything to the cute female doctor about what we did, I'm going to punch him right in his beautiful nose.

I make it through the check-up with flying colors, and head back into the waiting room for family members of those in the surgical theaters. I find Jase sitting in one of the spindly plastic chairs, looking breathtakingly gorgeous, with his tousled ink-black hair and dark scruff on his rugged jaw.

'Are we going to talk about it?' I ask as I slip into the chair beside him, giving him back the same words that he said to me after we'd learned about the Chloe article.

Instead of answering, he just tightens his jaw, tilts his back against the wall, and shuts his eyes.

'Fine, sulk,' I say with a huff. 'But you've got to talk to me sooner or later.'

His jaw gets so tight that a muscle starts to pulse at the side, but he still doesn't relent. So I sigh and pull my phone out, using the time to text Tyler and fill him in on what's happened. Once I'm done relaying a brief version of events, and assuring Tyler that I'm fine, he tells me about this awesome new guy he met out on the waves. They're having their first date tonight, and I wish him luck, making him promise to text me first thing tomorrow to let me know how it went. I'm hoping this guy knows how lucky he is to be dating my best friend, and that he treats him right. Because if anyone deserves a beautiful happily-ever-after, it's Ty.

Intent on getting on with my own, I turn to Jase and say, 'I'm sorry I scared you. And, yeah, I know I broke my promise by getting out of the car and sneaking up to the house. But I only did it because I was worried about you and wanted to make sure you were okay.'

His nostrils flare as he sucks in a deep breath, but he still doesn't open his eyes to look at me. I bite my lip as I settle back in my chair, ready to kick him for being so stubborn, even though I know I really *did* scare the hell out of him. That he thought he was going to have to watch me die right before his eyes.

It's weird, but that part hasn't really sunk in yet. I mean, I must have told Harrison a hundred times on the way to the hospital how grateful I am to him for taking that bullet – but I don't think I've fully processed the fact that I would be dead if he hadn't. Caroline had put a bead right on my heart, and there's no way I'd have survived it.

Huh. It might be childish, but after everything that bitch has done, and all the people she's hurt, I really hope they've put her in the grossest jail cell they have, with a clogged-up toilet and stains on the cot.

Eventually they come through to tell us that Harrison's doing well and has been put in a private room, and that we can go in to see him. He's sleeping when we walk in, so we quietly make our way over to the two chairs in front of the window and sit down. I'm hoping that maybe Jase will finally talk to me now, but he just crosses his arms over his chest and leans his head against the back of the chair, closing his eyes again.

'Jase, don't ignore me,' I murmur, running my gaze over every part of his tired, handsome face. 'Please.'

He sucks in another deep breath, then slowly lets it out, his voice little more than a graveled rasp as he says, 'I'm not ignoring you, Emmy. I'm so aware of you, it's like I'm plugged into you.'

'Then why aren't you looking at me?'

'Because if I do, I'm going to grab you, pull you over my lap as I pull down your jeans, and turn your gorgeous arse red for not doing as you were told.'

Even though he can't see it, I arch an eyebrow at him. 'Is that supposed to scare me? Because I gotta be honest, it's just turning me on.'

'I'm awake, you know,' Harrison drawls groggily from the bed, and I gasp with embarrassment, while Jase just gives a husky laugh as he finally opens his eyes.

Moving to his feet, he walks over to his grandfather's bedside and asks, 'How're you feeling?'

'Like I've been shot,' Harrison says drily.

'I don't know if you heard me in the ambulance, but thank you,' I tell him, giving his hand a soft squeeze. 'You saved my life tonight.'

The corner of his mouth twitches with a smile. 'You can repay me by modeling for me sometime.'

'Like hell,' Jase mutters, and this time the laugh that's slipping from his lips is a wry one. 'You must be delusional from the morphine if you think *that's* ever happening.'

'I meant with clothes on,' Harrison huffs, trying to look affronted.

But Jase just snorts under his breath, not buying it for a minute. 'Sure you did, old man.'

The nurse comes in then, checking Harrison's vitals, and by the time she's done, he's starting to doze back off. Jase and I want to stay with him a bit longer, before finding a local hotel for the night, so we settle back in the two chairs by the window. But my butt hasn't been on the pleather cushion two seconds when Jase sprawls back in his chair and crooks his finger at me, then pats his lap, telling me exactly what he wants without uttering a single word.

Since his lap is one of my favorite places in the world to be, I quickly move to my feet and curl up against his broad chest, the knot in my belly finally unclenching as he wraps his strong arms around me, holding me close. He presses a kiss to the top of my head, and then I tilt it back, gazing up at him as he settles back to get as comfortable as he can, and we murmur in quiet voices about everything that's happened.

He fills me in on the part with Alistair and Caroline that I'd missed, though I'd caught most of it. Then he tells me that we'll have to go into the police station in the morning to make our statements. When I mention Hart's suspicions that the local PD have been in Alistair's pocket for years, he says that he's already asked his friend from Scotland Yard to be there, and that Danny's the one he'll be handing the recording from the wire he was wearing over to. I tell him he's a genius, which earns me a slow, sweet kiss that melts me down, my arms going around his neck as I kiss him back, trying to show him just how much I love him. How important he is to me. And how sorry I am for everything that's happened.

'By the way, babe,' he says, pulling his head back and giving me a soft look of curiosity. 'What were you going to tell me earlier tonight, before the old guy pretending to sleep in the bed over there interrupted us?'

'Hey! This old guy could still kick your arse,' Harrison huffs, and I can tell by the humor shining in Jase's blue eyes that he's enjoying giving his grandfather a hard time.

I take a quick breath for courage, and then answer his question. 'I was just going to say that I've decided to move to London, so that I can be with you.'

His eyes widen with surprise, and then he gives another quiet, sexy rumble of laughter. 'Sweetheart,' he murmurs, brushing his thumb against the side of my face, 'I've already decided to move to San Diego to be with *you*.'

I smile, loving that he'd be willing to give up his entire life here to do that for me. For *us*. But I can't let him. Not with everything that's happened. 'Jase,' I say softly. 'You've only just started to work things out with that old guy in the bed over there. And there's going to be a lot of ugly legal things coming up that we'll all have to be a part of. And on top of all that, it'll be so much easier for me to write here, than it would be for you to move your entire company to the States. So my way just makes more sense.'

He glances over at Harrison's hospital bed, and I can tell that he gets what I'm saying. 'You're amazing, Emmy. I know how much you love it there, and I'm blown away that you would leave it all for me.'

Pressing a hand over the heavy pounding of his heart, I say, 'I'm sure we'll get back and visit a ton. And I know Ty will love coming over here to see us. And, believe it or not, Mr Beckett, getting to wake up to your handsome face every day is so worth moving halfway around the world for.'

'Damn it,' he groans, fisting his hand in the back of my hair as he tugs my face closer to his. 'You can't say things like that when we're in a hospital room and I can't fuck you.'

'Would it help if I pretend to be asleep again?' Harrison drawls, and I have to bite my lip to keep from laughing out loud.

Jase glares over at the bed, then brings his molten gaze back to mine, and with one of those wicked little smiles that I love so much, he says, 'And I *know* that moving here and being near that crotchety old bastard over there won't be easy.'

'Hey!' Harrison grumbles. 'I saved your arse tonight. Well, Emmy's arse, which is a hell of a lot prettier than yours. A little kindness wouldn't hurt.'

Jase shakes his head as he snorts, then gives me the most tender, possessive, beautiful look that I've ever seen as he says, 'But I love you, Em. I love you so damn much that I'll make dealing with all his crap worth it. I will worship you with every part of me, every single day of my life.'

'You don't have to do anything, Jase. Just be mine,' I whisper, holding his beloved face in my hands. 'Just be with me.'

'Always,' he whispers back, just as his lips find mine. 'Until the fucking end of time.'

Epilogue

EMMY

I walk into the flat at the Shard and call out for Jase, but he doesn't hear me because he's got The Red Hot Chili Peppers' 'Can't Stop' blasting from his gym. He may be my sexy, rich-as-fuck suit, but his taste in music is a perfect fit for the rugged, alpha-as-hell sex god who takes me to bed each night – a little edgy, sometimes dark, and always deliciously wild. I had a Pilates class this morning with Lola, and am completely beat, but scrounge up enough energy to smile as I picture my beautiful man pumping iron, all those mouthwatering muscles of his flexing under his sweat-slick skin. *Yum*.

I look around for Harrison, but imagine he's back in his studio, working and smoking a cigarette while he burns a candle to try to cover the smell. Jase had one of the flat's five guest bedrooms emptied out, and brought up everything Harrison would need for his work from Elm Manor, so that his grandfather didn't go stir crazy while recuperating with us. And to be honest, I'll be surprised if Jase ever lets Harrison go back to living like a recluse down in Kent. Even Anna has come up to stay with us, and I've enjoyed getting to know her, and learning her secret ways of dealing with the old man himself. And, hey, I like having Harrison around, so I'm happy they're here.

I slip off my shoes and pull the band out of my hair, shaking it out, then head into the kitchen to grab a cold bottle of water, thinking over everything that's happened since the night Jase confronted Caroline and Alistair, and Harrison ended up getting shot to save my life. It was a traumatic time, and I know Jase is still trying to process everything that we learned on that devastating day. We've had long discussions about Cameron and his mom, and he talks with Harrison too. He also called Douglas Hart and told him about what we'd learned, as well as Alistair and Caroline's upcoming trial, and the ongoing investigation into the local police and medical examiner who Alistair had paid off.

It's killing Hart that for all these years he'd thought Sarah wouldn't leave Alistair because of the money, when really she'd only been trying to protect Jase. But I think Hart has taken the news about the baby girl she was carrying the hardest, and Jase and I are both worried about how he's going to cope.

Alistair and Caroline caused so many people so much pain, and I'll personally be happy if they spend the rest of their miserable lives rotting in a cell. It's better than what they deserve, because nothing will ever bring Sarah back, or right all the wrongs that were done to Cameron. But at least there will be justice.

Hart has made it clear that he wants to come over for the trial, and Jase has asked him to stay with us. It will be a brutal time for both men, as well as for Harrison, but I'm hoping it will be a good bonding opportunity for them as well. And Jase has done everything he can to keep Cameron's name out of the media, determined to protect his cousin, after the horrific sacrifice Cam was forced to make as a little boy to protect Jase and Oliver.

And Oliver . . . God, that's *another* shocking story that we're still trying to wrap our heads around. None of us are quite able to believe what happened to him while he and Lottie were in Italy a few weeks ago, just after Harrison was shot. And Jase has investigators searching for Lottie, who hasn't been seen since boarding a flight to the States.

But as with all things, there've been lows, as well as highs, and one of the peaks has been my *Luxe* editor's decision to buy all five of the article proposals I finally sent to them last week, which we celebrated with a fancy dinner and a far too expensive bottle of champagne that I shared with Harrison and Anna. And then, later that night, Jase and I had our own private celebration, and let's just say that there's a certain provocative number that's now my favorite. Honestly, I came so hard, so many times, I had to soak in the tub the next morning before I could walk. But it was so totally worth it. Especially when my sexy beast of a boyfriend joined me, washing my hair and rubbing my back for me, as well as the sore muscles in my legs, the way he cares for me making it clear that I'm the single most important thing in his world, just like he is in mine.

Seriously, life is surreal. And with Jase Beckett by my side, so sublime.

And, yes, he's decided to keep the Beckett name. I think some of the reasons are emotional ones, since it was Sarah's name when she died. But I also think it's because he was Mr Beckett when I met him, and he says he can't imagine me calling him anything else. So Beckett it is.

I've settled in well in London, and while I miss Tyler, he's already planning to spend a few weeks with us at the end of the summer. I'm looking forward to introducing him to Harrison and Anna, as well as to the friends that I have here in the city, and I know he's going to get along great with everyone, because that's just the kind of guy Tyler is.

And last night, Jase finally met my friends Lola and Ben. We all went to dinner together at this awesome restaurant that Jase had picked out, and though there were a few awkward moments, like when Lola felt the crazy need to apologize for all the awful things she'd called Jase behind his back, the night turned out to be a blast. Plus, Jase and I finally got the chance to slow dance to a song from beginning to end, without a single interruption. It was to Coldplay's 'Yellow', and Lola snapped a few photos of us which turned out great. There's this one, though, where Jase is giving me one of his sin-drenched smiles as I gaze up into his gorgeous face, that I'm definitely getting framed for my desk. He looked so freaking handsome in his sharp black suit, and I wore the new dress that he'd bought for me. It's a sexy, backless lacy one that clings to my curves, leaving little to the imagination, and I'd thought he was going to throw me over his shoulder and carry me to bed the instant he saw me in it.

He'd managed to hold off on the ravishment until we got home, and by then we were both so desperate that the dress barely survived the way he tore it from my body. But I wasn't much kinder to his designer suit, so I couldn't complain. Not that I would, when what came after was the kind of bone-melting, breathtaking night that most women only get to read about in the kind of deliciously steamy romances that are packed on to my e-reader.

Amazingly, given how many times we went at it last night, I'm already desperate for him again, and I shake my head a bit as I smile, knowing damn well that I'm a lucky girl. Not only because he loves me, but because his desire for me is something that I never have to question, and knowing it feels so freaking good it's insane.

As I head down the hallway that leads back to the master bedroom, I pass by the home office on my left that we both share, and am excited about setting up my bookshelves when they arrive next week. Jase paid a company to pack up everything in my apartment that I wanted to bring over now (under Tyler's supervision) and it's already on its way, most of the furniture going into storage until I decide what I want to do with it.

When I step into the gym a moment later, I expect to find Jase working out, and it's clear from the sweat glistening on his tanned skin that that's exactly what he was doing. But something has obviously grabbed his attention, because he's got his laptop propped up on top of a cabinet that holds different belts and other lifting equipment, and as I come up beside him, I see that he's got his email open and is looking at photos of a beautiful beach house.

'Ooh, whose is that?' I ask, thinking it probably belongs to a friend of his, and that they've sent the photos over to show off their fabulous new home.

But Jase floors me when he looks over at me with a sexy grin, and says, 'Ours.'

I blink up at him, certain that I've just heard him wrong. 'What the what?'

He picks me up, setting me down on the cabinet beside his computer, then steps between my legs and places his big hands on my waist. They stroke up my sides, his thumbs brushing the heavy undersides of my breasts as he says, 'I love that you want to live here so we can be close to Harrison, Em. But we need to be close to Tyler too. And I fell in love with San Diego just as deeply as you love it. So I bought us this beach house. It's in La Jolla, and there's a cottage for Harrison round the back that has plenty of space for a studio. If he wants, he can spend the summers and holidays with us there, because that's where we're going to be.'

'You bought us a San Diego house?' I say in a breathless rush, unable to believe what I'm hearing.

He cups the side of my face in his hand, and gives me a gentle, loving look. 'I did. But if you don't like it, we can get something else. We can buy whatever you want.'

'No, I . . . I love it.' I curl my hands around his strong forearm, the intricate design of his tattoo pressed against my skin as I say, 'I'm just shocked. But I love it, Jase. I completely love it.'

He laughs as he cocks his head, his blue eyes shining and warm. 'You haven't even seen it yet, sweetheart.'

'It doesn't matter, because *you* picked it out for us. So I know it'll be awesome.'

His expression instantly tightens with emotion, and his gaze turns molten, telling me exactly how much he likes what I've just said. 'Jesus, baby. Your faith in me is a little scary sometimes.'

'Scary?' I ask with a laugh, and he smiles at me in a way that makes me want to kiss him so badly I can taste it.

'Maybe that's not the right word,' he murmurs, rubbing the corner of my mouth with his thumb. 'I just . . . I don't want to ever disappoint you, Emmy. I want to give you whatever you want, and every single thing that you need.'

'Jase, you *are* everything I want and need. You're what I *love*. So stop worrying and just relax. Just enjoy.'

'You *are* my joy,' he says with a soft growl, pushing his hand into my curls as he presses a kiss to the center of my forehead. 'You're the thing that I hold close, because you feel so damn good. You're the best fucking feeling in the world.'

I sniff a little as I smile, my chest melting as I remember

saying almost those exact same words to him in San Diego, when he'd asked me about my sketches.

'I have another confession to make,' he husks, only this time the rough words are spoken against my lips as he brushes a kiss across them.

'What's that?'

Instead of answering the question, he just gives me a wicked smile, and I have a feeling my gorgeous alpha is about to show me, rather than tell.

And as he lifts me in his powerful arms, holding me against his broad chest, I'm smiling too. With my lips, my eyes, and my deliriously happy heart.

When I left San Diego to come after Jase Beckett, I'd had no idea we were about to be hit with more confessions than we could have ever possibly been prepared for. Beautiful ones. Horrific ones. Ones that can change the future, and ones that have simply changed the way we view the past.

And through it all, Jase and I have learned valuable lessons. I'll continue to work on my writing career, and he'll continue to build incredible buildings around the world, because we're the kind of people who need challenges to thrive and succeed. But our careers won't be the driving force of our lives.

That will be our love.

And the family we make together.

We've talked it over, and decided to take a few years where it's just the two of us. But then . . . God, then Jase wants a small battalion, and I can't help but look forward to it, because I know he'll be a wonderful father. The best. And our kids will have the coolest Uncle Tyler in the world, and we'll make Martin an honorary uncle too.

And they'll have their great-grandfather. The world-renowned artist who is about to turn the art world on its head with the show he's planning. One where sculpture is the medium, and love is the theme. He says that my and Jase's story has inspired him, but really I think he's just ready to move on from the past and let go of as much of the self-hatred and mountains of regret as he can. His new work is still evocative and edgy, but without the bitterness that's colored his life for so long, and I have a strong feeling it'll be a huge success.

Of course, there's a part of me that can't help but wonder what Gianna will think of it. That wonders if she's been following Harrison's career all these years, and if so, what this new change will mean for her as well.

As Jase carries me into our bedroom and lays me down on our bed, I take a quick peek up at the painting of her that hangs on the wall above our headboard, and marvel at how far we've come since that first day at Beckett House all those weeks ago. When he comes down over me, I lock my watery gaze with his heavy, smoldering one, and love how perfect this feels. The way that we can be here together, in this moment, without a single guard or wall or shield between us.

There's just love and need and the wild, passionate hunger that binds us together.

And a bright, beautiful hope for what's to come.

Read on for an extract from
TAKE ME UNDER
the first novel in the Dangerous Tides series . . .

Prologue

Three years earlier . . .

'I thought you didn't screw around with married women.'

Ben Hudson rested his back against the patio wall of the crowded restaurant and scowled at his younger brother. 'Mind your own damn business,' he muttered, irritated that Michael had noticed the stares he kept directing through the mass of people. As a homicide detective in Miami, Ben had worked hard at learning how to hide his reactions. But at the moment his training wasn't enough to cover the fact that he'd spotted a woman he'd like to fuck. Hard and rough and repeatedly, if his cock had anything to say about it. Which it didn't, considering the lady had a husband and was off-limits.

'And I don't screw around with them,' he tacked on more for his benefit than Michael's, thinking the verbal reminder couldn't hurt. He knew damn well what kind of shit could be stirred up when spouses strayed from their commitments, and he wanted no part of that kind of life.

Michael propped one shoulder against the wall and gave a quiet laugh. 'Uh-huh. Your lips are saying one thing, Ben. But your eyes already have her stripped and spread.'

Choking back a dry curse, he tilted his bottle up to his lips, enjoying the icy burn as the beer slid down his throat. He tried to take his eyes off the woman in question, but it wasn't happening.

'Just because I like the look of her doesn't mean I'm planning to do anything about it.' He kept his voice low, mindful of the fact they were surrounded by listening ears. 'You know me better than that.'

'Yeah, I do.' Michael's pale green eyes, a shade lighter than Ben's, zeroed in on the brunette. 'But I also know that a woman like *that* is probably worth breaking a rule or two for.'

Ben gritted his teeth, hating that Michael had noticed the same things he had. At first glance, she was just another pretty face at a party that was currently packed with plenty of pretty faces. It was his cousin Gary's thirtieth birthday, and friends and family of both Gary and his wife, Connie, had been invited to the celebration that was taking place at McClain's Beach House. McClain's was one of Moss Beach, Florida's most popular restaurants, with a prime location right on the waterfront. The floor was usually dusted with sand, but it only added to the restaurant's laid-back, kick-up-your-feet atmosphere, and the food was always excellent, which meant the place was always busy.

Tonight was no exception. People kept moving around the covered patio area, obscuring his view of the woman who stood out from all the others like a shiny new penny. But he couldn't put his finger on what it was exactly that set her apart. He just knew that he couldn't take his fucking eyes off her. When a guy he recognized as Gary's old college roommate turned to the blonde beside him, it cleared the way between Ben and the woman again. Only this time she looked a little to her left and stared right back at him. Big, dark eyes blinked, locked with his, and held. The look couldn't have lasted for more than a few seconds before she quickly looked away again, but it was enough to make his dick go hard and his skin go hot. Fuckin' A.

'Oh, shit.' Michael choked back a laugh. 'You should see your face, man. If you sport wood in front of Gran, I swear I'll never let you live it down.'

Since there was no use denying how close he was to doing just that, Ben decided to find out how much Michael knew about the mystery woman. He hadn't made it to Gary and Connie's wedding earlier that year, since he'd been wrapping up a case at the time, but Michael had been there. Odds were good that his brother might have met the woman at the wedding. 'You know her name?' he asked, taking a fresh beer from one of the waiters who strolled by.

'Reese Leighton, though she was a Monroe before she married the Yankee lawyer who has his arm wrapped around her waist. She's one of Connie's older sisters, but I think only a year separates them.'

Huh. He wouldn't have guessed the two women were related. Connie was tall and blonde and stacked, and this woman . . . wasn't. Not that he gave a shit.

Reese. An unusual name, but it fit her. She was an unusual woman. Beautiful, but not in a classical way. Long, dark hair that looked thick and soft fell over feminine shoulders bared by a stylish black sundress, contrasting sharply with skin that was creamy and pale. She was probably only around five-five, slimmer than his usual taste, but curvy enough that she didn't look like a toothpick. Instead, she looked warm and soft and like something that should be under him. He couldn't tell exactly what color her eyes were from that distance, only that they were dark, her gaze sharp with intelligence when she'd held his stare. Her mouth could only be described as lush, with a full lower lip that begged for the nip of his teeth, and he could see that there was a spattering of freckles sweeping across her cheeks and the petite bridge of her nose.

It was the damn freckles that got him.

It wasn't that they made her look too young for a guy his age. He wasn't into robbing the cradle like a lot of the men he knew who'd hit their thirties. There was just something about that sprinkling of freckles that looked so damn sexy on her. Ben wanted to touch his mouth to them, one by one, and work his way down from there, over her breasts and her stomach, until he'd buried his face between her legs and learned if her pussy was even half as delicious as she looked. If it was, it might be hours before he came up for air.

And he really needed to get his brain onto a new train of thought before he did something stupid, like make an ass of himself in front of his family and friends. Reminding himself that he did *not* hit on married women, he glanced at Michael. 'What else do you know?' he asked, the words gritty with lust. He'd have blamed his reaction on a lack of sex, only he'd been sleeping with one of the traffic cops back home on a casual basis for a few months now. And he'd never been the type of guy not to get sex when he wanted it. That wasn't bragging, just a simple fact. He was tall and stayed in shape, and women had always seemed to like his dark hair and green eyes. But he thought it was more of an attitude thing. When he wanted something, he went after it. He didn't let shit stand in his way.

But this was the first time Ben could remember really wanting a woman who he knew he couldn't have. He didn't care for the feeling; but he also couldn't stop his gaze from sliding right back to her.

HEADLINE
ETERNAL

FIND YOUR HEART'S DESIRE...

VISIT OUR WEBSITE: www.headlineeternal.com
FIND US ON FACEBOOK: facebook.com/eternalromance
CONNECT WITH US ON TWITTER: @eternal_books
FOLLOW US ON INSTAGRAM: @headlineeternal
EMAIL US: eternalromance@headline.co.uk